全新!NEW GEPT

全民英檢

初級 聽力&閱讀 題庫解析

新制修訂版

LTTC語言中心委員會、郭文興──著

全書 MP3 一次下載

9789864541522.zip

「iOS 系統請升級至 iOS 13 後再行下載,
此為大型檔案,建議使用 WIFI 連線下載,以免佔用流量,
並確認連線狀況,以利下載順暢。」

CONTENTS

目錄

NEW GEPT 全新全民英檢初級
聽力&閱讀題庫解析 [新制修訂版]

全民英語能力分級檢定測驗的問與答

　　財團法人語言訓練中心（LTTC）自 2000 年全民英檢（General English Proficiency Test, GEPT）推出至今，持續進行該測驗可信度及有效度的研究，以期使測驗品質最佳化。

　　因此，自 2021 年一月起，GEPT 調整部分初級、中級及中高級的聽讀測驗題數與題型內容，並提供成績回饋服務。另一方面，此次調整主要目的是要反映 108 年國民教育新課綱以「素養」及「學習導向評量（Learning Oriented Assessment）」為中心的教育理念，希望可以透過適當的測驗內容與成績回饋，有效促進國人的英語溝通能力。而調整後的題型與內容將更貼近日常生活，且更能符合各階段英文學習的歷程。透過適當的測驗內容與回饋，使學生更有效率地學習與應用。

Q 2021 年起，初級測驗的聽力與閱讀（初試）在題數與題型上有何不同？

初級的聽力測驗維持不變，而閱讀測驗部分調整如下：

調整前	調整後
■ 第一部分 詞彙與結構 15 題	■ 第一部分 詞彙 10 題
■ 第二部分 段落填空 10 題	■ 第二部分 段落填空 8 題
■ 第一部分 閱讀理解 10 題	■ 第一部分 閱讀理解 12 題
共 35 題	共 30 題

調整重點：

1. 第一部分「詞彙和結構」，改為「詞彙」。

2. 第二部分「段落填空」增加選項為句子或子句類型。

3. 第三部分「閱讀理解」增加多文本、圖片類型。

◑ 考生可申請單項合格證書

另外，證書核發也有新制，除了現在已經有的「聽讀證書」與「聽讀說寫證書」外，也可以申請口說或寫作的單項合格證書，方便考生證明自己的英語強項，更有利升學、求職。

◑ 本項測驗在目的及性質方面有何特色？

整體而言，有四項特色：

（1）本測驗的對象包含在校學生及一般社會人士，測驗目的在評量一般英語能力（general English proficiency），命題不侷限於特定領域或教材；

（2）整套系統共分五級--初級（Elementary）、中級（Intermediate）、中高級(High-Intermediate)、高級（Advanced）、優級（Superior）一根據各階段英語學習者的特質及需求，分別設計題型及命題內

容，考生可依能力選擇適當等級報考；

（3）各級測驗均重視聽、說、讀、寫四種能力的評量；

（4）本測驗係「標準參照測驗」（criterion-referenced test），每級訂有明確的能力指標，考生只要通過所報考級數即可取得該級的合格證書。

Q 本測驗既包含聽、說、讀、寫四項，各項測驗方式為何？

聽力及閱讀測驗採選擇題方式，口說及寫作測驗則採非選擇題方式，每級依能力指標設計題型。以中級為例，聽力部分含 35 題，作答時間約 30 分鐘；閱讀部分含 35 題，作答時間 45 分鐘；寫作部分含中翻英、引導寫作，作答時間 40 分鐘；口說測驗採錄音方式進行，作答時間約 15 分鐘。

Q 何謂 GEPT 聽診室 — 個人化成績服務？

「GEPT 聽診室」成績服務，提供考生個人化強弱項診斷回饋和實用的學習建議，更好的是，考生在收到成績單的一個月內即可自行上網免費閱覽下載，非常便利。其中的內容包括：

1. 能力指標的達成率—以圖示呈現您（考生）當次考試的能力表現
2. 強弱項解析與說明—以例題說明各項能力指標的具體意義。
3. 學習指引—下一階段的學習方法與策略建議。
4. 字彙與句型—統計考生該次考試表現中，統整尚未掌握的關鍵字彙與句型。

Q 英檢初級的聽力需要達到什麼程度及其運用範圍為何？

初級考生須具備基礎英文能力，並能理解與使用淺易的日常用語，其參考單字範圍以「教育部基礎 1200-2000 字」為主，而聽力測驗考生必須聽出這 1200 字以內，並能聽懂母語人士語速慢且清晰的對話，並大致掌握談話主題。透過視覺輔助，理解人、事、時、地、物的簡單描述，例如簡單的問路與方向指示。考生應能大致聽懂日常生活相關的對話，例如簡短的公共場所廣播、體育賽事、天氣狀況播報、電話留言等。

Q 英檢初級的閱讀需要達到什麼程度及其運用範圍為何？

閱讀測驗考生必須可以認出並理解 2000 單字以內，與個人生活、家庭、朋友及學校生活相關的基本詞彙與用語。並能看懂與日常生活相關的淺易英文、閱讀標示／公告／廣告／個人書信／簡訊／文字對話訊息／故事／說明文／簡單菜單（menu）／行程表／時刻表／賀卡…等。

考生應能掌握短文主旨與部分細節、釐清上下文關係與短文結構，並整合與歸納兩篇文本的多項訊息。

Q 英檢初級初試的通過標準為何？

級數	測驗項目	通過標準
初級	聽力測驗 閱讀測驗	兩項測驗成績總和達 160 分，且其中任何一項成績不得低於 72 分。

Q 這項測驗各級命題方向為何？考生應如何準備？

全民英檢在設計各級的命題方向時，均曾參考目前各級英語教育之課程大綱，同時也廣泛搜集相關教材進行內容分析，以求命題內容能符合國內各級英語教育的需求。同時，為了這項測驗的內容能反應本土的生活經驗與特色，因此命題內容力求生活化，並包含流行話題及時事。

由於這項測驗並未針對特定領域或教材命題，考生應無需特別準備。但因各級測驗均包含聽、說、讀、寫四部分，而目前國內英語教育仍偏重讀與寫，因此考生必須平日加強聽、說訓練，同時多接觸英語媒體（如報章雜誌、廣播、電視、電影等），以求在測驗時有較好的表現。

Q 通過「全民英檢」合格標準者是否取得合格證書？又合格證書有何用途或效力？

是的，通過「全民英檢」合格標準者將頒給證書。以目前初步的規畫，全民英檢測驗之合格證明書能成為民眾求學或就業的重要依據，同時各級學校也可利用本測驗做為學習成果檢定及教學改進的參考。

Q 國中、高中學生若無國民身分證，如何報考？

國中生未請領身分證者，可使用印有相片之健保 IC 卡替代；高中生以上中華民國國民請使用國民身份證正面。外籍人士需備有效期限內之台灣居留證影本。

Q 初試與複試一定在同一考區嗎？

本中心原則上儘量安排在同一地區，但初試、複試借用的考區不盡相同，故複試的考場一律由本中心安排。

Q 請問合格證書的有效期限只有兩年嗎？

合格證書並無有效期限，而是成績紀錄保存兩年，意即兩年內的成績單，如因故遺失，可申請補發。成績單申請費用 100 元，證書 300 元，申請表格備索。

Q 複試是否在一天內結束？

不一定，視考生人數而定，確定的時間以複試准考証所載之測驗時間為準。

Q 報考全民英檢是否有年齡、學歷的限制？

除國小生外。本測驗適合台灣地區之英語學習者報考。

Q 合格之標準為何？

初試兩項測驗成績總和達 160 分，且其中任一項成績不低於 72 分者，複試成績除初級寫作為 70 分，其餘級數的寫作、口說測驗都 80 分以上才算通過，可獲核發合格證書。

Q 初試通過，複試未通過，下一次是否還需要再考一次初試？

初試通過者，可於二年內單獨報考複試未通過項目。

★關於「全民英語能力分級檢定測驗」之內容及相關問題請洽：

財團法人語言訓練測驗中心

中心地址：106台北市辛亥路二段170號 (台灣大學校總區內)

郵政信箱：台北郵政第 23-41號信箱

電話：(02)2362-6385~7

傳真：(02)2367-1944

辦公日：週一至週五(週六、日及政府機構放假日不上班)

辦公時間：上午八點至十二點、下午一點至五點

全民英檢初級

第一回 初試 聽力測驗

TEST01.mp3

本測驗分四個部分，全部都是單選題，共 30 題，作答時間約 20 分鐘。作答說明為中文，印在試題冊上並經由光碟放音機播出。

第一部分　看圖辨義

　　共 5 題（為第 1 題至第 5 題）。每題請聽光碟放音機播出題目和三個英語句子之後，選出與所看到的圖畫最相符的答案。每題只播出**一遍**。

例題：（看）

（聽）　Look at the picture.
　　　　Which is the cheapest?
　　　　A.　The computer.
　　　　B.　The telephone.
　　　　C.　The TV set.

正確答案為 B，請在答案紙上塗黑作答。

聽力測驗第一部分試題自本頁開始

A:　Question 1

B:　Question 2

C:　Question 3

$25,000，20%OFF

D:　Question 4

THSR Train Timetable

Number ＼ Destination	Taipei	Taichung	Zuoying
007	08:00	09:00	10:00
012	08:00	-	09:30
028	08:30	09:30	10:30

共 10 題（為第 6 題至第 15 題）。每題請聽光碟放音機播出的英語句子，再從試題冊上三個回答中，選出一個最適合的答案。每題只播出<u>一遍</u>。

例：　（聽）　Do you speak English?
　　　（看）　A.　No, I speak English quite well.
　　　　　　　B.　Yes, a little.
　　　　　　　C.　No, it's a useful language.

正確答案為 B，請在答案紙上塗黑作答。

6.　A.　I don't have a shorter one.
　　B.　Just give me another minute.
　　C.　There is nothing to do here.

7.　A.　May I ask a question?
　　B.　Isn't it on the left?
　　C.　Can you read it out for us?

8.　A.　This seat is already taken.
　　B.　I will pay by credit card.
　　C.　A salad and a chicken pie, please.

9.　A.　Let's do some outdoor activities.
　　B.　You have to wave your hand.
　　C.　It's going to rain.

10.　A.　Same here. It's too crowded.
　　　B.　I'm not sure. Maybe he will call me tonight.
　　　C.　You're right. I have one, too.

11.　A.　I will wear a special costume.
　　　B.　I will invite all my friends.
　　　C.　I don't think so.

12.　A.　I didn't pass, either.
　　　B.　I got a good grade, too.
　　　C.　I guess you have to fill it up.

13.　A.　Mom, I have to wake up early tomorrow.
　　　B.　Mom, I promise I will be back in ten minutes.
　　　C.　Mom, it's too late.

14. A. It must be expensive.
     B. You shouldn't miss it.
     C. I can't believe he scored it
         from that distance.

15. A. Let's take the stairs.
     B. Let's take yours.
     C. Third floor, please.

共 10 題（為第 16 題至第 25 題）。每題請聽光碟放音機播出一段對話和一個相關的問題後，再從試題冊上三個選項中，選出一個最適合的答案。每段對話和問題只播出**一遍**。

例： （聽） (Woman)　Could I sit here?

　　　　　(Man)　　I'm sorry, but this seat is occupied.

　　　　Question: Where do you think the dialogue takes place?

　　（看）　A.　In an office
　　　　　　B.　In a taxi
　　　　　　C.　In a restaurant.

正確答案為 C，請在答案紙上塗黑作答。

16. A. He's asking the woman
some questions.
    B. He's doing his homework.
    C. He's watching TV.

17. A. Science.
    B. Mathematics.
    C. History.

18. A. In a public library.
    B. In a department store.
    C. In a national park.

19. A. She is fired.
    B. She is lazy.
    C. She is ill.

20. A. To help another person
carry something.
    B. To ask another person about
his culture.
    C. To give another person
some money.

21. A. They are worried.
    B. They are excited.
    C. They are thirsty.

22. A. She wants to learn how to paint.
    B. She wants the man to paint her house.
    C. She wants the man to teach her.

23. A. Five thirty.
    B. Six o'clock sharp.
    C. Half past six.

24. A. She is not feeling well.
    B. She has to work in England.
    C. She is not used to driving on the left side.

25. A. Principals.
    B. Teachers.
    C. Parents.

第四部分　短文聽解

　　共 5 題（為第 26 題至第 30 題）。每題有三個圖片選項。請聽光碟放音機播出的題目，並選出一個最適當的圖片。每題只播出**一遍**。

例：（看）

A.　　　　　　　B.　　　　　　　C.

（聽）
Listen to the following short talk. What might Judy buy?

　　Judy is making a cake for her boyfriend. She checked her refrigerator and found that she had run out of sugar. But she still has lots of flour.

正確答案為 C，請在答案紙上塗黑作答。

Question 26

A.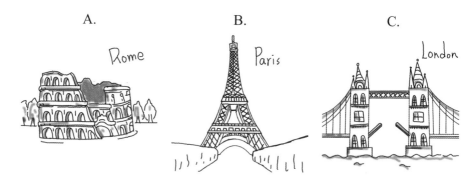

B.

C.

Question 27

A.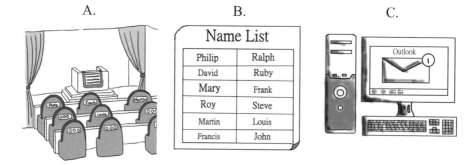

B.

C.

Question 28

A.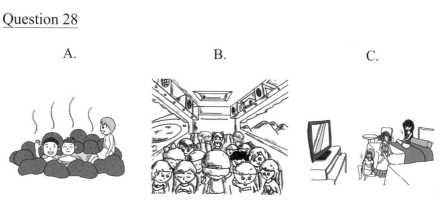

B.

C.

Question 29

A.

B.

C.

Question 30

A.

B.

C.

第一回 初試 閱讀測驗

本測驗分三部分，全部都是單選題，共 30 題，作答時間 35 分鐘。

第一部分：詞彙

共 10 題，每個題目裡有一個空格。請從四個選項中選出一個<u>最適合</u>題意的字或詞作答。

1. Everyone _____ mistakes in life. It's OK as long as we learn from our mistakes.
   - A. takes
   - B. does
   - C. uses
   - D. makes

2. Learning a new language may not cost a lot of money, but it _____ a lot of time.
   - A. has
   - B. takes
   - C. spends
   - D. pays

3. Your body temperature is 39.8°C. You are running a high _____.
   - A cancer
   - B. fever
   - C. danger
   - D. heater

4. Stop making fun of the new student. Just _____ him alone.
   - A. leave
   - B. hold
   - C. take
   - D. show

5. May I _____ some money from you? I promise to return it next week.
   - A. lend
   - B. borrow
   - C. rent
   - D. buy

6. Joe: What's the matter with you? Jane: I came _____ the flu.
   A. down with
   B. up with
   C. away with
   D. in with

7. What would you like for _____? I am getting myself some ice cream.
   A. degree
   B. desert
   C. dessert
   D. department

8. He didn't learn to play the piano _____ he was thirty years old.
   A. however
   B. so
   C. until
   D. from

9. My younger sister is _____ of the dark. She always sleeps with the lights on.
   A. afraid
   B. fond
   C. proud
   D. jealous

10. I can't stand my neighbors. They are really hard to _____.
    A. look out for
    B. get along with
    C. pass down from
    D. run out of

共 8 題，包括二個段落，每個段落各含四個空格。每格均有四個選項，請依照文意選出最適合的答案。

Questions 11-14

Many people confused reading ___(11)___ studying. It is especially true in Taiwan. To both parents and students alike, studying is often about memorization because students ___(12)___ to memorize the correct answers to a list of questions. Studying is seen as ___(13)___ deal with tests and exams. Reading, on the other hand, is about finding out topics students are interested in. Serious readers are curious readers at the same time. Though we live in the information age, knowledge is not just about what we know but what we do with what we know. Since so much information is already provided on the Internet, we need to know ___(14)___ and not a little about everything.

11. A. by
    B. from
    C. with
    D. for

12. A. expected
    B. have expected
    C. are expecting
    D. are expected

13. A. a way to
    B. the way of
    C. in a way
    D. by the way

14. A. who our readers are
    B. a lot about something
    C. how to choose our books
    D. reading and studying are both important

Questions 15-18

Steve Jobs was a great man of vision. He saw what the future held for us in a way no one else could have done. _____(15)_____, he often joked that his customers did not know what they need or want until he showed it to them. This was true of the iPod, the iPhone and the iPad. _____(16)_____ I admire about Steve Jobs is that he was not interested in _____(17)_____ money. His lifelong passion was to change the way people live with his products. _____(18)_____, making it more convenient and creative. He was so successful that at one point in time, his company had more cash than the U.S. government. Today, when we look at an iPhone or iPad, we are looking at the genius of a great man who dared to do the impossible and realized his dreams.

15. A. In fact
    B. At times
    C. In short
    D. In conclusion

16. A. One thing
    B. Some things
    C. Anything
    D. Nothing

17. A. make
    B. to make
    C. making
    D. having to make

18. A. He wanted to change our lifestyle
    B. He was interested in making money
    C. He dreamed of being a rich man
    D. He was thinking of building a house

第三部分：閱讀理解

共 12 題，包括 4 個題組，每個題組含 1 至 2 篇短文，與數個相關的四選一的選擇題。請由試題冊上的選項中選出最適合的答案。

Questions 19-21

SALES RECEIPT

Order# 526841250
Order Date: June 27th , 2020
Name: Jimmy Lin

QUANTITY	ITEM	UNIT PRICE	TOTAL
1	Table	$6,000	$6,000
4	Chair	$3,500	$14,000
2	Couch	$40,000	$80,000
		Subtotal	$100,000
		VIP Discount (-10%)	-$10,000
		Shipping Fee	$2,000
		Total	$92,000

From:	jimmylin@gmail.com
To:	susanlu@nyfoutlet.com
CC:	
Subject:	Something wrong with my order

Dear Sir,

My name is Jimmy Lin and I made an order for some items of your merchandise. I placed it on June 27th, 2020. But I'm afraid there's something wrong with the order. Actually, I only ordered two chairs instead of four. I will send back the extra chairs, and also please mail me a correct sales receipt. Thank you so much.

Jimmy Lin

19. What kind of items did Jimmy Lin buy?
    A. Home furniture.
    B. Gardening tools.
    C. Office supplies.
    D. Electronic devices.

20. How much is the price deduction on this receipt?
    A. $100,000.
    B. $10,000.
    C. $2,000.
    D. $92,000.

21. What's the purpose of this letter?
    A. To place more orders.
    B. To compare different prices.
    C. To report a mistake on the receipt.
    D. To explain how to make an order.

Used Books For Sale

Check out our website for latest additions.

Most books are 50% off of their regular prices

Free shipping for purchases worth 500 NT dollars and above.

You can also sell us the novels you have finished reading

(Must be in good condition with no missing pages).

---

22. What is true about the poster?
    A. You can find the newest and latest novels on the website.
    B. You can probably get a lower price for the books.
    C. They will buy your old novels if only one or two pages are torn.
    D. They collect magazines and old textbooks, too.

23. Do you have to pay the shipping cost?
    A. Yes, if you spend less than five hundred dollars.
    B. Yes, if you spend more than five hundred dollars.
    C. No, if you buy more than five books.
    D. No, if your books are in good condition.

24. Who is possibly interested in this poster?
    A. Someone who needs to buy furniture.
    B. Someone who loves reading novels.
    C. Someone who got lost.
    D. Someone who has a pet dog.

Green Dot Museum
The museum that tells you so much more about the Earth.

Entry Fees: NT$200
Students: Half price
Groups of twenty persons and above: 20% off
BB Bank Credit Card holders: 10% off

Free Admission
Children under 7 years old
Elderly folks above 65
Persons with disability

Open from 10 AM to 9 PM
Note: Museum is closed on the first and third Monday of every month.

---

25. What is the purpose of this announcement?
    A. To encourage customers to visit a special exhibition.
    B. To ask customers to turn off their cellphones.
    C. To invite guests to an opening of a museum.
    D. To advertise online ordering and delivery services.

26. Mr. and Mrs. Chen are taking their two-year-old daughter to the museum. How much do they need to pay in total if they have a BB Bank credit card?
    A. NT$200.
    B. NT$320.
    C. NT$360.
    D. NT$440.

27. What is NOT true about the museum?
    A. It offers a 50% discount to students.
    B. It offers a lot of information about Earth.
    C. It is run by a bank.
    D. It is closed twice a month.

Mei-ling has been fond of reading. Since young, her mom read
her bedtime stories. Her favorite story is *The Little Mermaid*. She
likes this story because she is touched by the little mermaid's great
love. The little mermaid could not be together with the prince she
(5)   loved but she was still happy for him. There is something else
special about it. All the other fairy tales have a happy ending, except
The Little Mermaid. From this tale, Mei-ling knows that life is not
always fair. Even as a child, she knew that not **every cloud has a
silver lining**.

Her dad is a heavy drinker. He refused to go to work and hit her
(10)   mom whenever he got drunk. To protect Mei-ling, her mom made a
difficult decision and left her dad. It wasn't easy for them. They had
to rent a tiny room and money was and is still a problem. However,
her mom allows her to any book she is interested in. Her mom
believes that reading is a good habit. Besides novels, Mei-ling also
likes to read about famous people. She is amazed by their success
(15)   and she learned a lot from them. In fact, she hopes to be a writer in
the future so she can write touching stories that will help to change
people's lives.

28. Mei-ling likes the story of *The Little Mermaid* because _____.
    A. It is about a little girl who lost her parents.
    B. It is closer to what happens in real life.
    C. It has a wonderful ending.
    D. It talks about fairies and angels.

29. What might **every cloud has a silver lining** mean?
    A. Bad things may happen but everything will get better.
    B. Clouds are beautiful and interesting to watch.
    C. People can know when a heavy rain is coming.
    D. Money is not the most important thing.

30. What is true about Mei-ling's mother?
    A. She is rich but she hates to spend money.
    B. She is poor but generous with Mei-ling.
    C. She drinks a lot and hits her daughter.
    D. She hopes to be a writer one day.

第一回

初試 聽力測驗 解析

第一部分 / 看圖辨義

Q1

For question one, please look at picture A.

What subject are the students learning?
這些學生在學習什麼科目？

A. History.
B. Physics.
C. Biology.

A. 歷史
B. 物理
C. 生物

詳解　　　　　　　　　　　　　　　　　　　　　　　答案：B

　　在圖片題中，黑板上有一些數學符號。就算看不太懂，也知道這些符號跟算式有關。選項中沒有數學，所以合理的答案是物理，因為物理也需要用到一些公式。圖中 $E=MC^2$ 為質能等價理論，是愛因斯坦狹義相對論最重要的推論。

單字片語| **physics** [`fɪzɪks] 物理 / **physical education** 體育 (PE) / **chemistry** [`kɛmɪstrɪ] 化學 / **biology** [baɪ`ɑlədʒɪ] 生物 / **geography** [`dʒɪˋɑgrəfɪ] 地理

Q2

For question two, please look at picture B.

What is true about the picture?
關於這張圖，何者正確？

A. The fork is between the knife and the spoon.
B. The knife is next to the fork.
C. The spoon is in the middle.

A. 叉子在刀子和湯匙之間。
B. 刀子在叉子旁邊。
C. 湯匙在中間。

詳解　

　　先注意圖中此 3 件物品的位置（湯匙在中間，刀子在左，叉子在右）與其英文名稱，聽懂關鍵字 knife（刀子）、fork（叉子）、spoon（湯匙）、between（在…之間）、next to （在…旁邊），還有 middle（在中間），這題就應該不難。

|單字片語| **fork** [fɔrk] 叉子 / **knife** [naɪf] 刀子 / **spoon** [spun] 湯匙 / **between** [bɪˋtwin] 在…之間 / **next to** 在…旁邊 / **in the middle** 在…中間

Q3

For question three, please look at picture C.

How much do you have to pay for the laptop?
這台筆記型電腦需要付多少錢？

A. $25,000
B. $20,000
C. $15,000

詳解　

　　從圖片中可知此商品是一台筆記型電腦，原價格是 25,000 元，旁邊又標註有 20% off 的折扣，20% off 表示原價再打八折（原價再拿掉 20%）的意思，因此 25,000×0.8 = 20,000。

<補充說明>

　　在台灣習慣用 notebook computer 的表達，簡稱筆電。相較於 desktop computer（桌上型電腦），laptop 的原意是讓使用者放在 lap（大腿）的 top（上）。早期的智慧型手機被稱為 palmtop（掌上型電腦），顧名思義就是放在 palm（手掌）的 top（上）使用。

Q4

For question four, please look at picture D.

THSR Train Timetable 台灣高鐵火車時刻表

Number \ Destination	Taipei	Taichung	Zuoying
007	08:00	09:00	10:00
012	08:00	-	09:30
028	08:30	09:30	10:30

Which train should Mr. Smith take from Taipei if he wants to arrive at Zuoying station in Kaoshiung as soon as possible?

若想要盡快抵達高雄左營站，Smith 先生應該從臺北坐哪一班車？

A. Train number 007.
B. Train number 012.
C. Train number 028.

A. 007 號列車。
B. 012 號列車。
C. 028 號列車。

詳解　　　　　　　　　　　　　　　　　　　　答案：B

　　從表格的 Train Timetable 和 Destination 可知是火車時刻表。主要是問最快到 Zuoying 的車，007 號在十點抵達 Zuoying，012 號在九點半就能抵達，所以 Smith 先生應該選擇 012 號列車。

Q5

For question five, please look at picture E.

What will the woman probably say to the man?

這位女士應該會對男士說什麼？

A. Could you give me a hand?
B. How are you doing today?
C. Isn't that your box?

A. 你可以幫我一個忙嗎？
B. 你今天過得如何？
C. 那不是你的盒子嗎？

詳解　　　　　　　　　　　　　　　　　　　　答案：A

　　從圖可知女士的東西掉了，手上又拿了幾本書。題目問女士此時可能會對男士說的話，她應該會請男士幫她的忙撿起掉落的東西。

補充說明

　　幫某人一個忙（give someone a hand），給某人熱烈的掌聲（give someone a big hand），向某人伸出援手（lend someone a helping hand）。

Q6

What's taking you so long in there?

你在裡面這麼久做什麼呢？

A. I don't have a shorter one.	A. 我沒有比較短的。
B. Just give me another minute.	B. 再給我一分鐘就好。
C. There is nothing to do here.	C. 這裡沒事情做。

詳解

　　主要是問在裡面這麼久的原因。一人問為什麼這麼久，另一人最適當的回答應是快好了或者還需要多久時間，Just give me another minute.（再給我一分鐘就好）表示快好了，是正確答案。

〈補充說明〉

　　just a second 表示「快好了」「再一下下」的意思，並非如字面上只需要 one second（一秒）而已。

|單字片語| **take** [tek] 花費（時間）/ **minute** [ˈmɪnɪt] 分鐘

Q7

Is everyone clear about the report you have to write?

每個人對於自己要寫的報告都清楚嗎？

A. May I ask a question?	A. 我可以問一個問題嗎？
B. Isn't it on the left?	B. 不是在左邊嗎？
C. Can you read it out for us?	C. 你可以為我們唸出來嗎？

詳解

　　選項都是疑問句。從題目中的 clear about、report、write 等可判斷，說話者應該是老師或主管，聽者應是學生或職員，主要是問大家是否清楚，依常理判斷，學生或職員會回「清楚」或者表達出疑問，因此選項 A.提到「我可以問一個問題嗎？」是正確答案，表示還有疑問。選項 B. 故意利用 left（左邊）讓考生誤以為題目的 write 是 right（右邊）。選項 C.明顯文不對題。

|單字片語| **clear** [klɪr] 清楚 / **report** [rɪˈport] 報告 / **write** [raɪt] 寫 / **on the left** 在左邊 / **everyone** [ˈɛvrɪˌwʌn] 每個人

第 1 回

第 2 回

第 3 回

第 4 回

第 5 回

第 6 回

Q8

May I take your order now, sir?
先生，我可以為您點餐嗎？

A. This seat is already taken.
B. I will pay by credit card.
C. A salad and a chicken pie, please.

A. 這個位子已經有人坐了。
B. 我將用信用卡付費。
C. 麻煩一個沙拉和一個雞肉派。

詳解　　　　　　　　　　　　　　　　　　　答案：C

　　選項的敘述看起來都是在餐廳裡會用到的表達。題目是問可否開始為聽者點餐，order 可當名詞，表示「點餐」，take one's order 表示為某人點餐，是經常在餐廳聽到的慣用語，說話者為服務生，因此直接回答某餐點名稱或回答還沒決定要點餐，都會是正確答案，答案為 C。

補充說明

　　order 也有「訂購」的意思，在網路上訂購東西通常會用 order。preorder 是「預購」的意思，在這裡 pre 是之前的意思，例如 prepare 是在事前做好準備。

單字片語 **take one's order** 為某人點餐 / **sir** [sɚ] 先生 / **seat** [sit] 座位 / **credit card** 信用卡 / **salad** [ˈsæləd] 沙拉 / **chicken** [ˈtʃɪkɪn] 雞肉 / **pie** [paɪ] 派

Q9

It looks like we are going to have fine weather today.
看起來我們今天會有很好的天氣。

A. Let's do some outdoor activities.
B. You have to wave your hand.
C. It's going to rain.

A. 我們來做一些戶外活動吧。
B. 你得揮動你的手。
C. 要下雨了。

詳解　　　　　　　　　　　　　　　　　　　答案：A

　　題目提到天氣不錯，選項中最合理的回覆是去外頭做一些戶外活動。

單字片語 **weather** [ˈwɛðɚ] 天氣 / **outdoor activity** 戶外活動 / **wave** [wev] 揮動 / **look like** 看起來像

Q10

I hate to take the bus during rush hour.
我討厭在尖峰時段搭公車。

A. Same here. It's too crowded.
B. I'm not sure. Maybe he will call me tonight.
C. You're right. I have one, too.

A. 我也是。太擁擠了。
B. 我不確定。也許他今晚會打電話給我。
C. 你說的沒錯。我也有一個。

詳解

從題目的 hate to take the bus 和 rush hour 可知，說話者討厭在尖峰時段搭公車，最合理的回應是贊同說話者或反對說話者，A.提到 Same here 表示自己也認同，並說明理由，是正確答案。

補充說明

交通繁忙的「尖峰時段」除了用 rush hour 表示，也可用 peak hour，而「非尖峰時段」則是 off-peak hour。rush 可當動詞用，意思是趕時間和催促某人，例如 stop rushing me（不要再催我）。

┃單字片語┃ **hate** [het] 討厭 / **during** [ˋdjʊrɪŋ] 在⋯期間 / **rush hour** 尖峰時段 / **Same here.** 我也是 / **crowded** [ˋkraʊdɪd] 擁擠的 / **sure** [ʃʊr] 確定的

Q11

Will you prepare the food for the party?
你會為派對準備食物嗎？

A. I will wear a special costume.
B. I will invite all my friends.
C. I don't think so.

A. 我會穿一套特別的服裝。
B. 我會邀請所有的朋友。
C. 我不認為我要。

詳解

從 Will you~ prepare~ food 可知在問對方是否會準備食物，最適合的回應是表達會準備或不會準備。選項 A.和 B.雖然都用 I will 開頭，但後面提到的動作都與問句無關。選項 C.的 I don't think so.表示自己不會準備，是正確答案。

┃單字片語┃ **prepare** [prɪˋpɛr] 準備 / **party** [ˋpɑrtɪ] 派對 / **costume** [ˋkɑstjum] 服裝 / **invite** [ɪnˋvaɪt] 邀請

Q12

I failed my math test again.
我的數學測驗又不及格了。

A. I didn't pass, either.
B. I got a good grade, too.
C. I guess you have to fill it up.

A. 我也沒通過。
B. 我也得到了好成績。
C. 我想你需要把它裝滿。

詳解

聽到 failed 和 test 可知，說話者把測驗考糟了，最適合的回應是提到自己

也是一樣的狀況，或者是給予鼓勵相關的表達。選項 A. 提到 didn't pass, either 表示自己也沒有通過，是正確答案。either 用在句尾表示「也不」。放在句中時通常會搭配 or，用 either A or B 表示「A 或 B」。

例句

I don't have a car, and she doesn't, either. 我沒有車子，她也沒有（車子）。
You can buy either a new car or an old one. 你可以買新車或二手車。

|單字片語| **fail** [fel] 不及格 / **math** [mæθ] 數學 / **pass** [pæs] 通過 / **either** [`iðə] 也（不）/ **grade** [gred] 成績 / **guess** [gɛs] 想 / **fill up** 裝滿

Q13

Isn't it too late for you to be going out?
這個時候出去不會太晚了嗎？

A. Mom, I have to wake up early tomorrow.
B. Mom, I promise I will be back in ten minutes.
C. Mom, it's too late.

A. 媽，我明天得早起。
B. 媽，我答應你我十分鐘後回來。
C. 媽，太晚了。

詳解

從選項中稱呼對方為 Mom 可知，題目說話者是一位母親。題目問句提到現在出門的時間有點晚，比較適合的回覆是「我答應你我十分鐘內就回來」，因此 B.是正確答案。

|單字片語| **late for** 對於…晚到 / **go out** 出去 / **wake up** 起床 / **early** [`ɝlɪ] 早 / **promise** [`prɑmɪs] 答應，承諾

Q14

What a wonderful goal!
好精彩的進球！

A. It must be expensive.
B. You shouldn't miss it.
C. I can't believe he scored it from that distance.

A. 一定很貴。
B. 你不應該錯過這個。
C. 我無法相信他從那個距離得分。

詳解

聽到 What a~ 可知是一個感嘆句。goal 是目標的意思，也是足球比賽中進球的意思，用在足球和曲棍球這類有 goalkeeper（守門員）的運動中。說話者因

第 1 回
第 2 回
第 3 回
第 4 回
第 5 回
第 6 回

看到進球的精彩畫面而表達出興奮，聽者最適合的回覆是表達與進球畫面的相關內容，因此 C.是正確答案。

score 當名詞時有分數和比分的意思，例如比數為 77 比 82，可以用 The score is 77 to 82.。score 當動詞時是得分的意思，適用於多數球類比賽。

例句

He scored the winning goal. 他踢進了致勝的一球。（足球）
He scored another three-pointer. 他又投進了一記三分球。（籃球）

|單字片語| **goal** [gol] 目標，球門 / **miss** [mɪs] 錯過 / **score** [skor] 得分 / **distance** [ˋdɪstəns] 距離

Q15

Come on. Not again! Both elevators are out of order. I live on the top floor.
天啊，不會又來了吧？兩台電梯都壞了。我住在頂樓。

A. Let's take the stairs.　　　　　A. 我們爬樓梯吧。
B. Let's take yours.　　　　　　　B. 我們用你的吧。
C. Third floor, please.　　　　　　C. 三樓，麻煩你。

詳解　　　　　　　　　　　　　　　　　　　　　　　

從題目的 elevators 和 out of order 可知電梯故障，選項中最適合的回覆是 A.。

out of order 用於電子或電器產品表示故障之意。要說某個東西無法運作，我們也可以用 ~ is not working.。至於車子拋錨，則會說 The car broke down.。

|單字片語| **elevator** [ˋɛləˌvetɚ] 電梯 / **out of order** 故障 / **stairs** [stɛrz] 樓梯

第三部分 / 簡短對話

Q16

Woman: Have you done your homework yet?
你做完你的功課了嗎？

Man: Just a few more questions to go. 還有幾題就完成了。

Woman: Good. Finish it before you watch TV.
很好。在看電視之前要先把功課做完。

Q: What is the man probably doing?
這位男士可能在做什麼？

A. He's asking the woman some questions.

B. He's doing his homework.

C. He's watching TV.

A. 他在問女士一些問題。

B. 他在做他的功課。

C. 他在看電視。

詳解

答案：B

從一開始可知女士正在問男士是否做完功課，所以選項 A 是錯的。男士說 Just a few more questions（還有幾題），可以得知他尚未完成他的功課，而女士用祈使句提到 Finish it before you watch TV.，可推測男士現在正在做功課，因此答案為 B。女士說做完功課才能看電視，所以選項 C 是錯的。

補充說明

Have you done your homework yet? 的時態為【現在完成式】，動詞是 have + p.p. 的結構，中文的意思表示「已經…了」。如果已經做完功課，可以用【現在完成式】回答 Yes, I have.。還沒做完，可以回答 No, I haven't.。不過，對於用【現在完成式】的問句，不一定要用【現在完成式】回答，也可以說 No, I am still doing it.，強調動作正在進行中。

|單字片語| finish [ˋfɪnɪʃ] 完成，結束 / probably [ˋprɑbəblɪ] 可能，大概

Q17

Man: The earth is round and it goes around the sun.
地球是圓的，它繞著太陽轉。

Woman: It takes about 365 days, right?
需要花大約 365 天的時間，對吧？

Man: Correct. Now, let's take a look at the other planets.
沒錯。現在，我們來看看其他星球。

41

Q: What lesson is the woman having?

這位女士正在上什麼課？

A. Science.

B. Mathematics.

C. History.

A. 自然科學

B. 數學

C. 歷史

詳解　　　　　　　　　　　　　　　　　　　　　　　　答案：A

從選項可推測，題目是問與學科相關的問題。從 earth（地球）、sun（太陽）、planet（星球）這些關鍵字可推測，這是一堂自然科學課。

補充說明

一年有 365 又 4 分之 1 天，每四年會多出一天，也就是會出現在 2 月 29 日。有 2 月 29 日的這一年被稱作閏年，英文是 leap year。

|單字片語| **earth** [ɝθ] 地球 / **round** [raʊnd] 圓的 / **go around** 繞著…轉 / **planet** [ˋplænɪt] 星球 / **take a look at** 看看…

Q18

Woman:　Next, please. That will be nine thousand dollars in total.

　　　　麻煩下一位。總共是九千元。

Man:　　Can I pay by credit card?　可以用信用卡付款嗎？

Woman:　Of course you can.　當然可以。

Q: Where might the man and woman be?

這位男士和女士可能在哪裡？

A. In a public library.

B. In a department store.

C. In a national park.

A. 在公共圖書館。

B. 在百貨公司。

C. 在國家公園。

詳解　　　　　　　　　　　　　　　　　　　　　　　　答案：B

從選項都是 in~ 的表達與題目 Where ~ man and woman 可知，主要是問對話的男女所在的位置。從對話中金額（~dollars in total）和信用卡（credit card）這兩個關鍵字，可判斷說話者在進行結帳，選項中最為合理的場所為百貨公司。圖書館不太可能進行書籍的販售，而且圖書館也沒有刷卡的服務。

|單字片語| **in total** 總共 / **pay by** 用…付款

Q19

Man: Mary caught a cold last night. She's too weak to walk.
瑪莉昨晚感冒了。她太虛弱了以至於無法走路。

Woman: Does that mean she is not coming to work today?
那表示她今天不會來上班嗎？

Man: We'll just have to do without her. 沒有她我們還是只能照常做。

Q: What has happened to Mary?
瑪莉發生什麼事了？

A. She is fired.   A. 她被開除了。
B. She is lazy.   B. 她很懶惰。
C. She is ill.   C. 她生病了。

詳解   答案：C

看到選項 She ~ 與聽到題目 What ~ happened to Mary 可知，主要是問 Mary 所發生的事情。一開始提到 Mary 感冒（caught a cold），表示她生病了（ill），所以正確答案是 C.。

補充說明

...do without... 是外國人常用的表達方式，表示「在沒有…的情況下也必須…」。例如：The air-conditioning is down. We will have to do without it.（空調壞了。沒有空調我們也必須忍耐。）當要對某個人說「我沒有你不行」，英文要說 I cannot do without you.。

|單字片語| **too ... to** 太…而不能… / **weak** [wik] 虛弱 / **mean** [min] 表示，意指 / **happen** [ˋhæpən] 發生

Q20

Woman: Remember to give the man a tip for carrying our luggage.
記得給幫我們拿行李的那位男士小費。

Man: Why should I? I paid for the hotel room already.
為什麼我要這麼做？我已經付飯店房間的錢了。

Woman: That's part of their culture.
這是他們的文化之一。

Q: What did the woman ask the man to do?
這位女士要求男士做什麼？

A. To help another person carry something. 幫另一個人搬東西。
B. To ask another person about his culture. 問另一個人關於他的文化。
C. To give another person some money. 給另一個人一些錢。

詳解

　　看到選項 To 動詞的表達（為了去做～）與聽到題目 What ~ woman ask ~ man ~do 可知，主要是問女士請男士做的事情。女士一開始對男士說 give ~ a tip，表示請他給某人小費，也就是給一些錢的意思，所以正確答案是 C.。在某些國家，給小費是一種文化（culture），本題考的是理解對話內容，不能因聽到對話中的 culture 就選擇有 culture 這個單字的選項。

＜補充說明＞

　　如果要給餐廳服務生或計程車司機小費時，可以用 keep the change 來表達，字面意思是「不用找了」。不過在歐美國家，許多地區的小費計算方式是總金額的 10%~15%，所以在給小費時務必先算好。

|單字片語| **tip** [tɪp] 小費 / **carry** [ˋkærɪ] 拿，攜帶 / **luggage** [ˋlʌgɪdʒ] 行李 / **culture** [ˋkʌltʃə] 文化

Q21

Man: Gosh. It hasn't rained for months.
天啊。已經好幾個月沒下雨了。

Woman: According to the latest news report, the water supply is running dangerously low.
根據最新的新聞報導，水量的供應低得相當危險。

Man: Let's hope for the best.　我們只能希望情況會好轉。

Q: What is true about the speakers?
關於說話者，以下何者正確？

A. They are worried.　　　　　　　A. 他們很擔心。
B. They are excited.　　　　　　　B. 他們很興奮。
C. They are thirsty.　　　　　　　C. 他們口渴。

詳解

　　從選項與題目可知，主要是問說話者的心情。一開始提到 hasn't rained for months，又說 water supply ~ dangerously low，表示水位低到危險的程度，由此可知說話者很擔心現狀。

＜補充說明＞

　　我們有時候可以從語氣來了解說話者的感受，從以上對話可判斷他們沒有感到興奮。

|單字片語| **gosh** [gɑʃ] （表示驚奇等）啊；糟了；天啊 / **according to** 根據 / **latest** [ˋletɪst] 最新的 / **supply** [səˋplaɪ] 供應 / **dangerously** [ˋdendʒərəslɪ] 危險地 / **low** [lo] 低 / **hope** [hop] 希望

Q22

Woman: I didn't know you are such a good painter.
　　　　我之前不知道你是如此了得的畫家。

Man: 　 It's a new hobby. I am still taking lessons.
　　　　這是新嗜好。我還在上課學習中。

Woman: Maybe I should join you. 　也許我應該跟你一起去上課。

Q: What does the woman most likely mean?
這位女士想表達的意思最有可能是什麼？

A. She wants to learn how to paint. 　　A. 她想要學習如何畫畫。
B. She wants the man to paint her house. B. 她想要這位男士油漆她的家。
C. She wants the man to teach her. 　　 C. 她想要這位男士教她。

詳解　　　　　　　　　　　　　　　　　　　　　　　　答案：A

　　從對話一開始可知男士是畫家，而且男士有在上課學習畫畫，女士最後說
~ join you，表示加入男士的行列，也就是去學畫畫，但並沒有提到要男士教她
畫畫，因此正確答案是 A.。paint 可表示「畫畫」、「油漆」，painter 可以是
「油漆工人」或「畫家」，但對話中並沒有 B.和 C.的意思。

〈補充說明〉

　　draw 和 paint 都是畫畫，差別在於 paint 是用筆刷等工具繪畫、彩繪的意
思，而 draw 是指素描、描出線條的意思。painting 可表示油畫和水墨畫，而
drawing 表示素描。順便一提，painter 是畫家的意思，而 drawer 則意指製圖的
人或物，也有抽屜的意思，因為 draw 有抽取的意思。幸運籤的英文是 lucky
draw。

Q23

Man: 　 It's five thirty now and I will be at your place in half an hour.
　　　　現在五點半。半個小時後我會到你那。

Woman: What? So soon? I need at least another hour to get ready.
　　　　什麼？這麼快？我還需要至少一個小時的時間準備。

Man: 　 It's all right. I can play with your pet.
　　　　沒關係。我可以跟你的寵物玩。

第1回
第2回
第3回
第4回
第5回
第6回

Q: When will the man probably arrive at the woman's house? 男士可能會在什麼時候到女士的家？

A. Five thirty.
B. Six o'clock sharp.
C. Half past six.

A. 五點三十分。
B. 六點整。
C. 六點半。

詳解

　　從選項和題目可知，是問男士到女士家的時間。從對話一開始可知，現在時間是 5:30，男士提到半小時後（in half an hour）會到女士家，5:30 加 30 分鐘就是 6:00，所以答案是 B。

補充說明

　　表達一小時除了可用 one hour，也常用 an hour，此時冠詞用 an，因為 hour 的 h 不發音。半小時可以說 half an hour，也可以說 a half hour。請注意，用 one and a half hours「一個半小時」，hour 的字尾要改成複數形，要加上 s，我們可以看作是 (one and a half) hours，因為是 1+½ 超過 1，所以 hour 是複數。

Q24

Woman: I'm not used to driving on the left side of the road. Here in England, the driver's seat is on the right.
　　　　我不習慣在道路的左側開車。在英國這裡，駕駛座在右邊。

Man: 　　In that case, let me do the driving. Your job is to enjoy the scenery. 　這樣的話，讓我來開吧。你負責欣賞風景就好。

Woman: That's really kind of you. 　你人真好。

Q: Why doesn't the woman want to drive?
　　為什麼這位女士不想要開車？

A. She is not feeling well.
B. She has to work in England.
C. She is not used to driving on the left side.

A. 她人不舒服。
B. 她必須在英國工作。
C. 她不習慣開在道路的左側。

詳解

　　從選項和題目可知是問女士不想開車的原因。女士一開始說她不習慣（not used to）開在道路的左側，因此正確答案是 C。從 Here in England 可知她人在英國， 有概念的人應該知道，在英國，汽車的駕駛座在右邊，會在道路分隔線的左側行駛。

第 1 回

第 2 回

第 3 回

第 4 回

第 5 回

第 6 回

〈補充說明〉

　　英國，日本、澳洲、香港、新加坡和馬來西亞等國家，其駕駛座都在右邊，和台灣（在左邊）相反。

|單字片語| **be used to + v-ing** 習慣於… / **England** [ˋɪŋglənd] 英國 / **in that case** 這樣的話 / **scenery** [ˋsinərɪ] 風景 / **kind** [kaɪnd] （人）很好的，體貼的

Q25

Man:　　Some students are spending too much time on their cell phones. I don't get it. Why do their parents allow them to do that?

　　　　有些學生花太多時間在手機上。我不明白，為什麼他們的父母會容許他們這麼做？

Woman:　I hate to remind the kids in my class to put away their cellphones before I begin my lesson.

　　　　我討厭在開始上課前總要提醒班上的孩子把手機收起來。

Man:　　I have the same problem with my class. We should let the principal know the problem.

　　　　我的班也有同樣的問題。我們應該要讓校長知道這個問題。

Q: What are the speakers?
　說話者是做什麼的？

A. Principals　　　　　　　　A. 校長
B. Teachers　　　　　　　　B. 老師
C. Parents　　　　　　　　　C. 家長

〈詳解〉

　　從選項可知是問身分。對話內容中提到 students（學生）、my class（我的班級）、before I begin my lesson（從在我上課之前），以及提到學生使用手機過長的問題，可以知道說話者的職業為教師。

|單字片語| **spend time + v-ing** 花時間做… / **cellphone** [ˋsɛlfon] 手機 / **allow** [əˋlaʊ] 容許 / **remind** [rɪˋmaɪnd] 提醒 / **put away** 把…收好

Q26

For question number 26, please look at the three pictures.

Please listen to the following short talk. 請聽以下的簡短談話。

Which country does the speaker plan to visit next year?
說話者明年打算去哪一個國家？

Look at this photo. I took it when I was in Rome last year. I had dinner with an Italian friend of mine and it ended at almost midnight. I hope to visit Europe again next year. Both England and France are good choices, but I think I will choose London because I have already been to Paris once.

看這張照片。這是我去年在羅馬拍的。我跟我的一位義大利籍朋友吃晚餐，結果幾乎到半夜才結束。明年我希望再去歐洲。英國和法國都是很好的選擇，但我覺得我會選擇倫敦，因為巴黎我已經去過一次了。

詳解

答案：C

從圖片可推測是問與「哪一個國家」相關的問題。題目問的是說話者明年（next year）要去的國家。一開始提到去年去了羅馬，也就是去過義大利。短文最後提到 I hope to visit Europe again next year. 可知明年會去歐洲，接著又說 I think I will choose London because I have already been to Paris once. 從 choose London 可知，說話者明年會去英國，所以 C 是正確答案。

補充說明

義大利的著名地標有比薩斜塔 Tower of Pisa，倫敦有俗稱倫敦眼的摩天輪 London Eye / The Wheel，德國有勃蘭登堡門 Brandenburg Gate，而美國則有自由女神像 Statue of Liberty。

第1回

第2回

第3回

第4回

第5回

第6回

Q27

For question number 27, please look at the three pictures.

Please listen to the following telephone message. 請聽以下的電話留言。

What does Michael have to prepare?
Michael 必須準備什麼？

Hi there, Michael. This is Phoebe. I am calling to remind you that you need to plan the seating arrangement in the school hall. Make sure the guests of honor are seated in the front row. I am preparing the name list now. I will give it to you as soon as possible. Remember to check your email later.

嘿，Michael。我是 Phoebe。我打電話來是要提醒你，你需要規畫一下學校禮堂的座位安排。一定要讓榮譽嘉賓坐在第一排。我現在在準備名單。我會儘早給你。等一下記得去收一下你的電子信箱。

A.

B.

Name List	
Philip	Ralph
David	Ruby
Mary	Frank
Roy	Steve
Martin	Louis
Francis	John

C.

詳解   答案：A

從圖片與聽到的題目 What ~ Michael ~ prepare 可知，主要是問 Michael 要準備的東西。從一開始提到的 Hi ~, Michael. This is Phoebe. 可知，說話者是 Phoebe，聽者是 Michael。接下來提到 you need to plan the seating arrangement in the school hall，表示告知 Michael 要規畫學校禮堂的座位安排，因此圖片中有座位、有名單的 A 是正確答案。名單是由 Phoebe 準備的。

|單字片語| **plan** [plæn] 計畫 / **seating** [`sitɪŋ] 座位 / **arrangement** [ə`rendʒmənt] 安排 / **hall** [hɔl] 禮堂 / **make sure** 一定，務必要 / **guest of honor** 榮譽嘉賓 / **be seated** 坐 / **row** [ro] （一）排 / **as soon as possible** 儘早

For question number 28, please look at the three pictures.

Please listen to the following announcement.　請聽以下的廣播。

Where might you hear this announcement?
你可能會在什麼地方聽到這個廣播？

　　May I have your attention, please? If you look out to the right, you will see the mountains that are famous for its hot springs. In fact, we will be staying at a hotel there tonight. On your left is a fresh water lake. Though there are swans in the water, you can see people swimming in it. Our next stop is the national museum and our bus will arrive in about ten minutes.

　　請注意。如果你從右邊看出去,你會看到以溫泉著名的高山。事實上,我們今晚將會住在那裡的飯店。在你的左邊是一個淡水湖。雖然水裡有天鵝,但你可以看到人們在游泳。我們的下一站是國家博物館,我們的巴士會在大約十分鐘後抵達。

A.

B.

C.

詳解　　　　　　　　　　　　　　　　　　　　　　　　　**答案：B**

　　從圖片可推測是與地點相關的題目。從題目Where ~ hear ~ announcement可知,主要是問這段短文進行的地點。說話者一開始在介紹周遭的景色,關鍵是在 Our next stop is the national museum ~ our bus will arrive ~,表示目前正前往國家博物館途中,從 our bus 也可推斷說話者正在此巴士上進行這段談話,因此正確答案是遊覽車車內有許多乘客的 B。

|單字片語| **announcement** [əˋnaʊnsmənt] 廣播 / **attention** [əˋtɛnʃən] 注意 / **famous** [ˋfeməs] 著名的 / **hot spring** 溫泉 / **swan** [swɑn] 天鵝 / **museum** [mjuˋzɪəm] 博物館 / **view** [vju] 景色

第 1 回
第 2 回
第 3 回
第 4 回
第 5 回
第 6 回

For question number 29, please look at the three pictures.

Please listen to the following news broadcast. 請聽以下的新聞廣播。

When will the typhoon leave Taiwan?
颱風會在什麼時候離開台灣？

As you can see on the screen, typhoon Phoenix is picking up speed and heading toward Taiwan. At this speed, heavy rains are to be expected as early as Monday. It is likely to land somewhere around Ilan on Tuesday night. On Wednesday, it will probably be on its way north toward Japan.

正如您在螢幕上所看到的，鳳凰颱風正在加速朝台灣而來。以這個速度，最快星期一預估會有超大豪雨。颱風可能在星期二晚上在宜蘭附近登陸。到了星期三，颱風可能會往北朝日本前進。

A.

May
Monday
23

B.

May
Tuesday
24

C.

May
Wednesday
25

詳解

答案：C

從圖片可推測是與日期相關的題目。從題目 When ~ typhoon ~ leave 可知，主要是問颱風離開的時間。聽到 typhoon ~ heading toward Taiwan ~ land somewhere around Ilan on Tuesday night 可知，颱風在星期二晚上登陸 Ilan（宜蘭），接著又說 On Wednesday ~ toward Japan，表示到了星期三颱風會朝日本前進，所以真正離開台灣的時間是星期三，正確答案為 C。

|單字片語| **screen** [skrin] 螢幕 / **typhoon** [taɪˋfun] 颱風 / **speed** [spid] 速度 / **head toward** 朝⋯前往 / **heavy rain** 豪雨 / **be expected** 預估 / **it is likely to** 有可能⋯ / **land** [lænd] 登陸

For question number 30, please look at the three pictures.

Please listen to the following short talk.　請聽以下的簡短談話。

What might the man do for a living?
這位男士很有可能以什麼為生？

　　Good. Now that you have made up your mind to wear it short, would you like it a little shorter at the back? Summer's coming and it's going to be hot. That's what many of my customers wanted. I think I will also dye some of it brown to make you look younger. This way, please. I will have to wash it before we get started.

　　好的。既然你已下定決心要剪短髮，你後面的頭髮想要再短一點嗎？夏天要到了，要開始熱了，所以我很多的客人都會想再剪短一點。我想我會幫你染棕色，讓你看起來年輕一點。請往這邊走。開始剪之前，我要先幫你洗頭。

A.	B.	C.

詳解　　　　　　　　　　　　　　　　　　　　答案：A

　　從圖片可推測是與職業相關的題目。聽到題目 What ~ man do 可知，題目主要是問說話者的職業。從 a little shorter（再短一點）、dye some of it brown（染成棕色）、wash it（清洗）可推斷，理髮師是比較會進行這些剪髮、染髮動作的人，牙醫與游泳教練比較不會做這些事情。

|單字片語| **now that** 既然 / **make up one's mind** 下定決心 / **customer** [ˈkʌstəmə] 顧客 / **dye** [daɪ] 染色 / **brown** [braʊn] 棕色

第 1 回
第 2 回
第 3 回
第 4 回
第 5 回
第 6 回

第一回

初試 閱讀測驗 解析

第一部分 / 詞彙

Q1

Everyone _____ mistakes in life. It's OK as long as we learn from our mistakes.

每個人都會犯錯。只要我們從錯誤中學習，犯錯是可以接受的。

A. takes 需要

B. does 做

C. uses 使用

D. makes 做，製造

詳解

答案：D

　　這題考的是慣用語，雖然 make 和 do 的中文意思都有「做」的意思，但是「犯錯」要用 make mistakes 表達，而非 do mistakes。順便一提，everyone、someone、anyone 和 no one，都要視為第三人稱單數，動詞字尾要加上 s 或者是改成第三人稱單數的形態。例如 Everyone has a smartphone. 的 has，以及 He makes cakes.中的 makes。

補充說明

　　do something 中的 do 是指做某事情，make something 中的 make 則是指製造東西。發生緊急狀況時，人們會說 Please do something.，意思是指請採取行動來解決問題。

Q2

Learning a new language may not cost a lot of money, but it _____ a lot of time.

學習語言或許不需要花很多錢，但需要很多時間。

A. has 有

B. takes 需要

C. spends 花（時間）

D. pays 付錢

詳解

答案：B

　　英文的文法有時候很像數學公式，請熟悉以下的「文法公式」。請注意，spend 前面的主詞是人，take 前面的主詞是虛主詞或動名詞。這題考的是如下表的句型五：It + takes + （人）+ 時間 + to V 事情。

句型一	人 + spend + 金錢 + on + 物品 He spent $5000 on this watch. 他花了 5000 元在這支手錶上。
句型二	人 + pay + 金錢 + for + 物品 He paid $5000 for this watch. 他付了 5000 元為了買這支手錶。
句型三	物品/It + costs + 人 + 金錢 + (to V) This watch cost him $5000. 這支手錶花了他 5000 元
句型四	人 + spend + 時間 + V-ing + 事情 He spent two hours cleaning the house. 他花了兩小時打掃房子。
句型五	It + takes +（人）+ 時間 + to V 事情 It took him two hours to clean the house. 花了他兩小時的時間打掃房子。

Your body temperature is 39.8°C. You are running a high _____.

你的體溫是 39.8 度。你在發高燒。

A. cancer 癌症　　　　　　　　B. fever 發燒
C. danger 危險　　　　　　　　D. heater 熱水器

詳解　　　　　　　　　　　　　　　　　　　　　　答案：B

　　從空格前面的敘述 body temperature~ 39.8°C 可推斷，主要是在講發高燒，要表達「你發燒」，英文是 You have a fever.，而「你發高燒」則是 You are running a high fever.。

補充說明

　　以下來了解各症狀的英文表達：
感冒 a cold ／ 咳嗽 a cough ／頭痛 a headache ／牙痛 a toothache ／喉嚨痛 a sore throat ／流感 the flu

Stop making fun of the new student. Just _____ him alone.

別再作弄新同學了。就讓他自己一個人在那，別去吵他。

A. leave 留下；離開　　　　　　B. hold 握住；舉辦
C. take 拿；搭乘　　　　　　　　D. show 給…看

54

詳解

空格前面用祈使句 Stop...student，表示不要對此學生做某事，而從選項中的動詞也可知，空格所在的句子也是祈使句，him 代替前面的 student，根據語意，最適合的答案是 leave him alone，正確答案是 A.。

<補充說明>

leave 有兩個意思，這兩個意思在中文字面上不同，有「留下」和「離開」的意思，務必從上下文來判斷到底是什麼意思。

例句一：You shouldn't leave your wallet in the car. 你不該把錢包留在車上。
例句二：You shouldn't leave home without your wallet. 你不應該沒帶錢包就離開家裡。

在「leave 某人 alone」的句型中，leave 是把某人留在某地方的意思，leave him alone 表示讓他自己一個人在那裡，不要打擾他。而當我們對人說 just leave me alone，意思是讓我一個人靜一靜。

Q5

May I _____ some money from you? I promise to return it next week.

我可以向你借一些錢嗎？我答應你下週就還給你。

A. lend 借（給…）　　　　　　B. borrow （向…）借
C. rent 租；租金　　　　　　　D. buy 購買

詳解

從選項可知空格要填的是動詞，受詞部分是 some money from you（向你…一些錢），而且後面還提到 return it（還給…），表示空格要填入的是 borrow。「向別人借東西」用 borrow，「借給別人」用 lend。borrow 的介系詞用 from，以表示「從」某人那邊借過來，lend 的介系詞用 to，以表示借「給」某人。

Q6

Joe: What's the matter with you?
Jane: I came _____ the flu.

Joe: 你怎麼了？ Jane: 我得到流感了。

A. down with　　　　　　　B. up with
C. away with　　　　　　　D. in with

詳解

空格後面是 flu，是疾病症狀，空格前面是 came，動詞片語 come down with 表示「得了／患了流感或感冒」，所以 A.是正確答案。come up with 是「想出點子或辦法」的意思。

Q7

What would you like for _____? I am getting myself some ice cream.

你想要什麼甜點？我自己要去拿些冰淇淋。

A. degree 文憑 　　　　　　B. desert 沙漠
C. dessert 甜點 　　　　　　D. department 部門

詳解

從句子最後的 ice cream 可知，說這句話的人要去拿冰淇淋，所以問句中的空格應填入與 ice cream 相關的 dessert（甜點）。

│單字片語│ **dessert** [dɪˋzɝt] 甜點 / **desert** [ˋdɛzət] 沙漠

Q8

He didn't learn to play the piano _____ he was thirty years old.

他之前都沒有學過鋼琴，直到他三十歲才學。

A. however 然而 　　　　　　B. so 所以
C. until 直到 　　　　　　D. from 從

詳解

空格前後都是子句，所以空格要填入連接詞。雖然 so 是連接詞，但語意不符。until 表示「直到…」的意思，放在句中時，前一子句會搭配否定句，後一子句是肯定句，可理解為「…沒有…直到…才」，是本題的正確答案。

Q9

My younger sister is _____ of the dark. She always sleeps with the lights on.

我妹妹怕黑。她總是開著燈睡覺。

A. afraid 害怕的 　　　　　　B. fond 喜歡的
C. proud 驕傲的 　　　　　　D. jealous 嫉妒的

詳解

　　空格後面是 dark，後面又提到 sleeps...with the lights on，從「黑暗」以及「開燈睡覺」可知，is afraid of the dark 是正確答案。

補充說明

　　afraid 除了可表示「害怕」，也有「擔心」跟「恐怕」的意思。為了表示禮貌，向別人提出要求或拒絕別人時經常用 I am afraid...，以表達「恐怕…」「恐怕無法…」的語意。

I'm afraid that you will have to wait for another ten minutes. 恐怕你要再等十分鐘。
I'm afraid that I can't go to your party. 我怕我不能去你的派對。

Q10

I can't stand my neighbors. They are really hard to _____.

我受不了我的鄰居。他們真的很難相處。

A. look out for 尋找　　　　　　B. get along with 相處
C. pass down from 從…傳下來　　D. run out of 用完

詳解

　　根據語意，從前面的 can't stand ~（無法忍受）可知，最適合的表達是 hard to get along with（很難相處）。get along well with 表示相處得很好。

|單字片語| **stand** [stænd] 忍受 / **neighbor** [ˋnebɚ] 鄰居 / **hard** [hɑrd] 難的

Questions 16-20

Many people confused reading (11) with studying. It is especially true in Taiwan. To both parents and students alike, studying is often about memorization because students (12) are expected to memorize the correct answers to a list of questions. Studying is seen as (13) a way to deal with tests and exams. Reading, on the other hand, is about finding out topics students are interested in. Serious readers are curious readers at the same time. Though we live in the information age, knowledge is not just about what we know but what we do with what we know. Since so much information is already provided on the Internet, we need to know (14) a lot about something and not a little about everything.

很多人把閱讀和研讀混為一談。在台灣尤其是如此。對許多家長和學生來說，研讀常跟死背有關，因為學生被期望死背一連串問題的正確答案。研讀被視為一種應付測驗和考試的方法。在另一方面，閱讀是關於找出學生有興趣的話題。認真的讀者同時也是好奇的讀者。雖然我們活在資訊年代，但知識不僅僅是我們所知道的，而是我們如何運用我們知道的知識。因為很多資訊都已經提供在網路上，我們必須對某件事知道很多，而不是對所有的事情都只懂一點點而已。

Q11

A. by 藉由…
B. from 從…
C. with 和…
D. for 為了…

詳解

答案：C

這題考的是介系詞，看到 confuse，後面的介系詞要用 with，confuse...with 表示「把…和…搞混」。同樣的用法還有：compare...with...（拿…和…做比較），mix...with...（把…和…混合在一起）。

補充說明

with 除了「和」的意思之外，還可表示「有…」跟「用…」的意思。
I want coffee with milk. 我要有加鮮奶的咖啡。
Most smartphones come with cameras. 大部分智慧型手機都有照相機。
We saw a house with a large garden. 我們看到一棟有個大花園的房子。
He likes girls with long hair. 她喜歡有長頭髮的女生。
She writes with her left hand. 她用她的左手寫字。
The teacher hit the boy with a ruler. 老師用尺打那個男孩。

Q12

A. expected	B. have expected
C. are expecting	D. are expected

詳解

　　從空格所在的句子可知，此句時態為現在式，所以空格中的動詞用現在的時態。are expecting 表示懷孕的意思，不符合句意。are expected 表示被預期的意思，主詞是 students，students are expected to 做某件事，表示老師期待學生做某件事的意思，所以用被動語態的 are expected 是正確答案。

Q13

A. a way to …的一種方法	B. the way of …的方法
C in a way 在某種意義上	D. by the way 順帶一提

詳解

答案：A

　　空格前面是 is seen as（被視為），後面是原形動詞 deal with（處理…），選項中都是用 way 表達的不同片語。the way of 後面要接 -ing，所以 B 不正確。in a way 是「某種意義上」的意思，by the way 是「順帶一提」的意思，具有副詞的功能，但都不符合此句意。be seen as a way to deal with 表示被視為一種應付…的方法，是正確答案。

Q14

A. who our readers are

B. a lot about something

C. how to choose our books

D. reading and studying are both important

詳解

答案：B

　　空格前面提到「很多資訊提供在網路上」，後面提到「而不是所有的事情只懂一點點而已」，從「很多資訊」可知，我們「針對某些事情」需要知道「很多」，故答案選 B.，這樣才能跟後面否定的語意做連結。

第 1 回　第 2 回　第 3 回　第 4 回　第 5 回　第 6 回

Steve Jobs was a great man of vision. He saw what the future held for us in a way no one else could have done. (15) In fact, he often joked that his customers did not know what they need or want until he showed it to them. This was true of the iPod, the iPhone and the iPad. (16) One thing I admire about Steve Jobs is that he was not interested in (17) making money. His lifelong passion was to change the way people live with his products. (18) He wanted to change our lifestyle, making it more convenient and creative. He was so successful that at one point in time, his company had more cash than the U.S. government. Today, when we look at an iPhone or iPad, we are looking at the genius of a great man who dared to do the impossible and realized his dreams.

賈伯斯是個有遠景的人。他用一種沒有人辦到的方式，看到了我們的未來有什麼。事實上，他經常開玩笑說，顧客並不知道他們需要的或想要的是什麼，直到他把東西拿出來給他們看。iPod、iPhone 和 iPad 的確是如此。我欣賞賈伯斯的一點是他對賺錢本身沒有興趣。他終身的熱情是用他的產品改變人們生活的方式。他想要改變我們的生活方式，讓我們的生活更方便也更有創意。他是如此地成功以至於在某段時期，他的公司所擁有的現金比美國政府還要多。今天，當我們看到 iPhone 或 iPad 時，我們看到的是這位勇於挑戰不可能和實現夢想的偉人的天賦。

Q15

A. In fact 事實上　　　　　　B. At times 有時候
C. In short 簡言之　　　　　　D. In conclusion 總之

詳解

　答案：A

空格前面提到賈伯斯看到我們的未來有什麼 (He saw what the future held for us)，空格後面補充了實際的案例，因此用 In fact（事實上）來強調提到的案例。

例句

Eating fruits and vegetables is good for health. In fact, many diseases can be prevented if we eat less meat. 吃蔬菜和水果有益健康。事實上，如果我們少吃肉，很多疾病可以避免。

Q16

A. One thing 某件事；一點
B. Some things 一些東西
C. Anything 任何事
D. Nothing 沒有

> **詳解**　　　　　　　　　　　　　　　　　　　　　　　　　　　答案：A

　　從空格後面來看，此句的主要動詞是 is，所以從「空格到 Jobs」是主詞，而空格要填入的是 I admire 的受詞，選項中符合語意的是 A。One thing I admire about... is~是「我欣賞…的一點／一件事是～」的意思。除了 admire，我們還可以替換成 like（喜歡）、learn（學到），來表達不同的意思。

Q17

A. make
B. to make
C. making
D. having to make

> **詳解**　　　　　　　　　　　　　　　　　　　　　　　　　　　答案：C

　　空格前面是介系詞，而介系詞接名詞或動名詞 -ing，即 be interested in N/V-ing，因此正確答案是 C。相同的情況有 be excited about N/V-ing, be bored with N/V-ing。

Q18

A. He wanted to change our lifestyle
　　他想要改變我們的生活方式
B. He was interested in making money
　　他對賺錢感興趣
C. He dreamed of being a rich man
　　他夢想成為有錢人
D. He was thinking of building a house
　　他考慮蓋一棟房子

> **詳解**　　　　　　　　　　　　　　　　　　　　　　　　　　　答案：A

　　空格前面提到「用他的產品改變人們的生活方式」，後面提到「讓某某事物更方便與更有創意」，可知空格的地方應該要是填入跟「改變生活方式」有關的內容，後面再接續改變哪一方面，故答案選 A.。

第 1 回
第 2 回
第 3 回
第 4 回
第 5 回
第 6 回

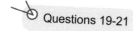

Questions 19-21

SALES RECEIPT

Order# 526841250
Order Date: June 27th , 2020
Name: Jimmy Lin

QUANTITY	ITEM	UNIT PRICE	TOTAL
1	Table	$6,000	$6,000
4	Chair	$3,500	$14,000
2	Couch	$40,000	$80,000
		Subtotal	$100,000
		VIP Discount (-10%)	-$10,000
		Shipping Fee	$2,000
		Total	$92,000

第 1 回
第 2 回
第 3 回
第 4 回
第 5 回
第 6 回

收據

訂單編號# 526841250
訂購日期：2020年6月27日
姓名：Jimmy Lin

數量	品項	單價	總計
一	桌子	6 千元	6 千元
四	椅子	3 千 5 百元	1 萬 4 千元
二	沙發	4 萬元	8 萬元
	小計		10 萬元
	貴賓折扣 (-10%)		減 1 萬元
	運費		2 千元
	總金額		9 萬 2 千元

From:	jimmylin@gmail.com
To:	susanlu@nyfoutlet.com
CC:	
Subject:	Something wrong with my order

Dear Sir,

My name is Jimmy Lin and I made an order for some items of your merchandise. I placed it on June 27th, 2020. But I'm afraid there's something wrong with the order. Actually, I only ordered two chairs instead of four. I will send back the extra chairs, and also please mail me a correct sales receipt. Thank you so much.

Jimmy Lin

寄件者：	jimmylin@gmail.com
收件者：	susanlu@nyfoutlet.com
副本：	
主旨：	訂單有誤

親愛的先生您好，

我的名字是 Jimmy Lin，我訂購了你們商品中的一些品項。我是在 2020 年 6 月 27 日下訂單的。但恐怕這個訂單出了一些問題。事實上，我只有訂兩張椅子，而非四張。我將會寄回多出來的兩張椅子，也麻煩您再寄給我一張正確的收據給我。非常感謝！

Jimmy Lin

l單字片語l **subtotal** 小計 / **shipping fee** 運費 / **merchandise** 商品 / **instead of** 而不是… / **correct** 正確的 / **sales receipt** 收據

What kind of items did Jimmy Lin buy?

Jimmy Lin 買了什麼品項？

    A. Home furniture.　家具。
    B. Gardening tools.　園藝工具。
    C. Office supplies.　辦公室用品。
    D. Electronic devices.　電子設備。

詳解

    從第一張的收據圖表中 ITEM 的 Table、Chair、Couch 可知，Jimmy Lin 買的東西有桌子、椅子和沙發，也就是家用的一些家具，故答案選 A。

第 1 回
第 2 回
第 3 回
第 4 回
第 5 回
第 6 回

Q20

How much is the price deduction on this receipt?

在這張收據上有多少錢被扣除？

    A. $100,000.　十萬元。

    B. $10,000.　一萬元。

    C. $2,000.　兩千元。

    D. $92,000.　九萬兩千元。

詳解　　　　　　　　　　　　　　　　　　　　　　　答案：B

    在收據上有看到 VIP Discount、-10% 以及 -$10,000，可知帳單減除10%的貴賓折扣，即一萬元，故答案選 B。

Q21

What's the purpose of this letter?

這封信的目的是什麼？

    A. To place more orders.　下更多的訂單。

    B. To compare different prices.　比較不同的價格。

    C. To report a mistake on the receipt.　說明收據上的錯誤。

    D. To explain how to make an order.　解釋如何下訂單。

詳解　　　　　　　　　　　　　　　　　　　　　　　答案：C

    信中提到：Actually, I only ordered two chairs instead of four... and also please mail me a correct sales receipt.，表示寫信者只有訂兩張椅子而非四張，並請對方再寄一張正確的收據，言下之意是要說明訂單收據有誤，故答案選 C。

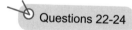
Questions 22-24

Used Books For Sale

Check out our website for latest additions.

Most books are 50% off of their regular prices

Free shipping for purchases worth 500 NT dollars and above.

You can also sell us the novels you have finished reading

(Must be in good condition with no missing pages).

二手書出售

請上我們的網站查看新增品項。
大部分的書籍都是原價再打五折
購滿新台幣 500 元以上免運費。
你也可以把已經看完的小說賣給我們。
（必須是良好狀態，沒有缺頁）

|單字片語| **used** [juzd] 二手的 / **for sale** 待售，出售 / **check out** 查詢 / **website** [`wɛb͵saɪt] 網站 / **free shipping** 免運費 / **worth** [wɝθ] 值…（價值）/ **sell** [sɛl] 賣 / **novel** [`nɑvəl] 小說 / **condition** [kən`dɪʃən] 狀況

Q22

What is true about the poster?

關於這張海報，何者正確？

A. You can find the newest and latest novels on the website.
   你可以在網站上找到最新版的小說。
B. You can probably get a lower price for the books.
   你或許可以用比較低的價格買到書。
C. They will buy your old novels if only one or two pages are torn.
   如果你舊的小說只有一、兩頁破損，他們仍會跟你買。
D. They collect magazines and old textbooks, too.
   他們也收雜誌和舊課本。

詳解

答案：B

　　latest additions 在這裡表示新增的產品，但沒有提到是否有新版小說，所以 A 不正確。從 Most books are 50% off of their regular prices 可知，可以買到比原價更便宜的書，因此 B 是正確答案。海報中提到 You can also sell us the novels... Must be in good condition with no missing pages，表示要賣的書不可以有漏頁的狀況，所以 C 不正確，而 D 並未從海報中提到。

補充說明

　　雖然「二手書」也可以說是 second-hand books，不過英文比較習慣把二手說成「used 用過的」。二手書為 used books，中古車為 used cars，但中古屋卻不能用 used houses，而是 pre-owned house。

Q23

Do you have to pay the shipping cost?

你必須付運費嗎？

 A. Yes, if you spend less than five hundred dollars.
   是的，如果你花費少於五百元。

 B. Yes, if you spend more than five hundred dollars.
   是的，如果你花費超過五百元。

 C. No, if you buy more than five books. 不，如果你買超過五本書。

 D. No, if your books are in good condition. 不，如果你的書狀況良好。

詳解

  關於運費部分，從 Free shipping for purchases worth 500 NT dollars and above.可知，免運費的條件是購滿新台幣 500 元以上，因此 A 是正確答案。

Q24

Who is possibly interested in this poster?

誰最有可能對此廣告有興趣？

 A. Someone who needs to buy furniture. 需要購買家具的人。

 B. Someone who loves reading novels. 喜歡看小說的人。

 C. Someone who got lost. 迷路的人。

 D. Someone who has a pet dog. 有養寵物狗的人。

詳解

  從標題 Used books for sale 可知，會注意到這個內容的人應該是想買書的人，且下面提到書籍折扣、可把自己看過的小說賣給張貼此海報的人，故答案選 B。

Questions 25-27

Green Dot Museum

The museum that tells you so much more about the Earth

Entry Fees: NT$200
Students: Half price
Groups of twenty persons and above: 20% off
BB Bank Credit Card holders: 10% off

Free Admission
Children under 7 years old
Elderly folks above 65
Persons with disability

Open from 10 AM to 9 PM
Note: Museum is closed on the first and third Monday of
every month.

綠點博物館

可以讓你知道更多關於地球的博物館。

入場費用：新台幣兩百元
學生：半價
二十人以上的團體：八折
有 BB 銀行信用卡者：九折

免費入場
7 歲以下的小孩
65 歲以上的年長者
殘障人士

開放時間從早上 10 點到晚上 9 點
注意：博物館在每個月的第 1 和第 3 個星期一閉館。

|單字片語| **entry fee** 入場費 / **group** [grup] 團體 / **credit card holder** 信用卡持有者 /
elderly [ˈɛldəlɪ] 年長的 / **folk** [fok] 人們 / **disability** [dɪsəˈbɪlətɪ] 殘障

What is the purpose of this announcement?
此公告的目的是什麼？

A. To encourage customers to visit a special exhibition.
鼓勵顧客參觀特展。
B. To ask customers to turn off their cellphones.
要求客人關手機。

C. To invite guests to an opening of a museum.
邀請貴賓參加博物館開幕。

D. To advertise online ordering and delivery services.
宣傳線上訂購和運送服務。

詳解

　　從標題 Museum 及小標的 The museum that tells you... the Earth.可知，這是博物館某特展的宣傳，故答案選 A。

Q26

Mr. and Mrs. Chen are taking their two-year-old daughter to the museum. How much do they need to pay in total if they have a BB Bank credit card?
陳先生和陳太太要帶兩歲的女兒去博物館。如果他們持有 BB 銀行的信用卡，他們總共需要付多少錢？

A. NT$200.

B. NT$320.

C. NT$360.

D. NT$440.

詳解

　　文中在 Free Admission 的地方提到 Children under 7 years old，表示 7 歲以下免費入場，所以他們的 two-year-old daughter 是免費入場的。在 Entry Fees（入場費用）提到 NT$200，又提到 BB Bank Credit Card holders: 10% off。所以原本是一個大人 NT$200，兩張的話是 NT$400，持有 BB 銀行的信用卡可享九折，所以 NT$400×0.9 = NT$360，總共需付 NT$360。

Q27

What is NOT true about the museum?
關於這個博物館，何者不正確？

A. It offers a 50% discount to students.　它提供學生五折優惠。

B. It offers a lot of information about the Earth.
它提供很多關於地球的資訊。

C. It is run by a bank.　它是由一家銀行經營的。

D. It is closed twice a month.　它一個月關閉兩次。

從文中的 Students: Half price 可知學生價是五折的半價優惠，所以 A 正確。從副標題的 tells you so much more about the Earth 可知 B 也正確，從 Museum is closed ... first and third Monday of every month.可知一個月有兩天是關閉的，所以 D 也正確。文中並沒有提到博物館的經營者，只提到凡持有 BB 銀行的信用卡可享有 9 折優惠，不表示博物館由 BB 銀行經營，所以 C 不正確，是正確答案。

Questions 28-30

Mei-ling has been fond of reading. Since young, her mom read her bedtime stories. Her favorite story is *The Little Mermaid*. She likes this story because she is touched by the little mermaid's great love. The little mermaid could not be together with the prince she loved but she was still happy for him. There is something else special about it. All the other fairy tales have a happy ending, except *The Little Mermaid*. From this tale, Mei-ling knows that life is not always fair. Even as a child, she knew that not **every cloud has a silver lining**.

Her dad is a heavy drinker. He refused to go to work and hit her mom whenever he got drunk. To protect Mei-ling, her mom made a difficult decision and left her dad. It wasn't easy for them. They had to rent a tiny room and money was and is still a problem. However, her mom allows her to any book she is interested in. Her mom believes that reading is a good habit. Besides novels, Mei-ling also likes to read about famous people. She is amazed by their success and she learned a lot from them. In fact, she hopes to be a writer in the future so she can write touching stories that will help to change people's lives.

美玲喜歡閱讀。從小，她媽媽會在睡前念故事給她聽。她最喜歡的故事是《小美人魚》。她喜歡這個故事是因為她被小美人魚偉大的愛所感動。小美人魚不能跟她所愛的王子在一起，但是她還是為他感到快樂。還有一點很特別。所有的童話故事都有快樂的結局，除了《小美人魚》例外。美玲知道人生不是事事都公平。即使身為小孩，她知道不是每朵烏雲背後都有美好的事。

她的父親是一個酒鬼。他不願意去上班，而且每當他喝醉都會毆打她的媽媽。為了保護美玲，她的媽媽做出困難的抉擇，離開了她的父親。這對他們來說並不容易。她們必須租一間小房間。錢在之前和現在都還是個問題。然而，她的媽媽允許她買任何她感興趣的書籍。她的媽媽相信閱讀是一個好習慣。除了小說以外，美玲也喜歡讀關於名人的故事。她對這些名人的成功感到驚訝，也從他們

身上學到很多。事實上，她希望未來能成為一名作家，這麼一來她就能寫一些感人的故事，來幫助改變人們的生活。

|單字片語| be fond of 喜歡… / bedtime [ˋbɛd͵taɪm] 適於睡前的/ mermaid [ˋmɝ͵med] 美人魚 / touch [tʌtʃ] 使…感動 / prince [prɪns] 王子 / except [ɪkˋsɛpt] 除…例外 / fair [fɛr] 公平的 / cloud [klaʊd] 雲朵 / silver [ˋsɪlvɚ] 銀色的 / heavy drinker 酒鬼 / refuse [rɪˋfjuz] 拒絕 / protect [prəˋtɛkt] 保護 / rent [rɛnt] 租用 / be amazed by 對於…感到驚訝 / learn [lɝn] 學習到

Q28

Mei-ling likes the story of The Little Mermaid because _____.
美玲喜歡《小美人魚》的故事因為…

　　A. It is about a little girl who lost her parents.
　　　　它是關於一個失去父母的女孩的故事。
　　B. It is closer to what happens in real life.
　　　　它比較接近真實生活中發生的事。
　　C. It has a wonderful ending. 它有一個美好的結局。
　　D. It talks about fairies and angels. 它談論到仙女和天使。

詳解

答案：B

　　文中提到 Her favorite story is *The Little Mermaid*...because she is touched by the little mermaid's great love. ，表示美玲喜歡此故事是因為小美人魚的大愛，也就是小美人魚跟王子即使沒辦法在一起，但仍默默地為王子而快樂地活下去，是與其他結局美滿的童話故事不一樣的地方，也讓美玲了解現實生活中不是事事都是公平的，所以可推測美玲喜歡《小美人魚》是因為它比較接近真實生活。

Q29

What might __every cloud has a silver lining__ mean?
「every cloud has a silver lining」這句話可能是什麼意思？

　　A. Bad things may happen but everything will get better.
　　　　壞的事情可能會發生，但一切會好轉。
　　B. Clouds are beautiful and interesting to watch.
　　　　雲朵看起來很美、很有趣。
　　C. People can know when a heavy rain is coming.
　　　　人們會知道何時會有豪大雨。
　　D. Money is not the most important thing. 錢不是最重要的。

　　不知道此句的意思時，可從上下文來推敲、用選項刪去法來答題。上一句提到 Mei-ling knows that life is not always fair. ，表示美玲知道人生中並非事事都公平，接著的 she knew that not every cloud has a silver lining. 應該就是用換句話說的方式來補充上一句，從 not always fair 與 not every cloud has a silver lining. 中 not 後面的內容來推斷，every cloud has a silver lining 應該和 fair 都有正面、好的的意義，因此正確答案是 A。在這裡，雲可理解為烏雲密布，銀色的邊表示美好的事物。表示壞的事情可能會發生，但一切會好轉，類似中文的山窮水盡疑無路、柳暗花明又一村。

What is true about Mei-ling's mother?

關於美玲的媽媽，何者為真？

A. She is rich but she hates to spend money.　她很有錢，但她討厭花錢。
B. She is poor but generous with Mei-ling.　她很窮，但她對美玲很大方。
C. She drinks a lot and hits her daughter.　她常常喝酒，並毆打她女兒。
D. She hopes to be a writer one day.　她希望有一天能當作家。

　　從文中可知，離開父親後，美玲的母親總是缺錢，不過她允許美玲買任何她感興趣的書本，答案為 B。常喝酒並毆打家人的是美玲的爸爸，而希望有一天能當作家的是美玲，而非美玲的媽媽，所以 C, D 都不正確。

全民英檢初級

第二回 初試 聽力測驗

TEST02.mp3

本測驗分四個部分，全部都是單選題，共 30 題，作答時間約 20 分鐘。作答說明為中文，印在試題冊上並經由光碟放音機播出。

第一部分　看圖辨義

　　共 5 題（為第 1 題至第 5 題）。每題請聽光碟放音機播出題目和三個英語句子之後，選出與所看到的圖畫最相符的答案。每題只播出**一遍**。

例題：（看）

（聽）　Look at the picture.
　　　　Which is the cheapest?
　　　　A.　The computer.
　　　　B.　The telephone.
　　　　C.　The TV set.

正確答案為 B，請在答案紙上塗黑作答。

A:　Question 1

B:　Question 2

C: <u>Question 3</u>

D: <u>Question 4</u>

共 10 題（為第 6 題至第 15 題）。每題請聽光碟放音機播出的英語句子，再從試題冊上三個回答中，選出一個最適合的答案。每題只播出**一遍**。

例：　（聽）　Do you speak English?
　　　（看）　A.　No, I speak English quite well.
　　　　　　　B.　Yes, a little.
　　　　　　　C.　No, it's a useful language.

正確答案為 B，請在答案紙上塗黑作答。

6. A. Yes, the closet is delivered.
   B. No, do you have any more dirty clothes?
   C. I have no idea how to use the oven.

7. A. Sure. I will return it to you tomorrow.
   B. I'm afraid not. I lent it to someone else.
   C. No. Let's take a taxi there.

8. A. I have fed them already.
   B. That's why I don't like pets.
   C. Let's hope we will have sun soon.

9. A. It cost me an arm and a leg.
   B. Let's keep our fingers crossed.
   C. You shouldn't judge a book by its cover.

10. A. You don't have to pay cash.
    B. We will invite you for dinner.
    C. That depends on which bank it is.

11. A. So do I.
    B. So have I.
    C. Me, either.

12. A. How could she do that?
    B. When did she have an operation?
    C. Shouldn't she be on time?

13. A. I don't mind waiting for you.
    B. I am sure we are going in the right direction.
    C. I think you look just fine.

14. A. No, I will never go near a
       snake.
    B. No, I am still quite full.
    C. No, I have a pet already.

15. A. Maybe he is just tired.
    B. I'm sure he will find it
       soon.
    C. You should let him go there
       on his own.

第三部分　簡短對話

　　共 10 題（為第 16 題至第 25 題）。每題請聽光碟放音機播出一段對話和一個相關的問題後，再從試題冊上三個選項中，選出一個最適合的答案。每段對話和問題只播出<u>一遍</u>。

例：　(聽)　(Woman)　Could I sit here?
　　　　　　(Man)　　I'm sorry, but this seat is occupied.

　　　　　Question: Where do you think the dialogue takes place?

　　(看)　A.　In an office
　　　　　B.　In a taxi
　　　　　C.　In a restaurant.

正確答案為 C，請在答案紙上塗黑作答。

16. A. Go on a diet.
    B. Be careful with the amount of feed.
    C. Feed the fish at least twice a day.

17. A. She forgot to do the housework.
    B. Her telephone bill will cost her a lot of money.
    C. Emily couldn't fix the washing machine.

18. A. Her son's grades.
    B. Her son's weight.
    C. Her son's safety.

19. A. She has classes today.
    B. She was in a meeting.
    C. She was in a movie theater.

20. A. She thinks the room is too hot.
    B. She thinks the room is too noisy.
    C. She thinks the room is too dirty.

21. A. The woman is talented.
    B. The woman is funny.
    C. The woman is boring.

22. A. Collecting coins and stamps.
    B. Designing clothes and shoes.
    C. Making cakes and bread.

23. A. In a hospital.
    B. In a theater.
    C. In a factory.

24. A. They should teach John English.
    B. They should leave now.
    C. They should wait for John.

25. A. The man enjoys taking tests.
    B. The man agrees with the woman.
    C. The man wants the woman to repeat what she just said.

第四部分　短文聽解

　　共 5 題（為第 26 題至第 30 題）。每題有三個圖片選項。請聽光碟放音機播出的題目，並選出一個最適當的圖片。每題只播出**一遍**。

例：　(看)

A.　　　　　　　　B.　　　　　　　　C.

(聽)
Listen to the following short talk. What might Judy buy?

　　Judy is making a cake for her boyfriend. She checked her refrigerator and found that she had run out of sugar. But she still has lots of flour.

正確答案為 C，請在答案紙上塗黑作答。

Question 26

A.

B.

C.

Question 27

A.

B.

C.

Question 28

A.

B.

C.

Question 29

A.

B.

C.

Question 30

A.

B.

C.

第二回 初試 閱讀測驗

本測驗分三部分，全部都是單選題，共 30 題，作答時間 35 分鐘。

第一部分：詞彙
    共 10 題，每個題目裡有一個空格。請從四個選項中選出一個**最適合**題意的字或詞作答。

1. My grandpa used to fix watches and clocks _____ a living.
   A. for   B. with
   C. as   D. by

2. My daughter told me that her teacher hit her _____ a ruler.
   A. with   B. by
   C. for   D. about

3. There was a _____ accident on the freeway. Many people were badly hurt.
   A. slender   B. strict
   C. serious   D. simple

4. I need to _____ these books to the library. They are due today.
   A. remind   B. repeat
   C. return   D. reply

5. It feels a little _____ in here. I think we'll need a fan.
   A. cool   B. dry
   C. warm   D. messy

6. We found the door open. A thief _____ our house.
   A. broke up   B. broke off
   C. broke down   D. broke into

7. The kids were so excited when they saw a rainbow _____.
   A. appear   B. imagine
   C. fail   D. pass

8. _____ he doesn't make a lot of money, _____ he is happy with
   what he has.
   A. Though ; x   B. Though ; but
   C. Because ; x   D. Because ; so

9. I couldn't _____ my luck. I won the first prize – a 60-inch TV!
   A. decide   B. believe
   C. change   D. promise

10. Betty's husband gave her a diamond ring, and she is showing it _____
    to everyone she sees.
    A. out   B. off
    C. up   D. down

第二部分：段落填空

　　共 8 題，包括二個段落，每個段落各含四個空格。每格均有四個選項，請依照文意選出最適合的答案。

Questions 11-14

　　It seems that from time to time, the public was told that some food is not safe ___(11)___ . Whether it is soy-sauce, tea or vegetables, the food we eat on a ___(12)___ basis contains chemicals that are harmful to the body. The reasons ___(13)___ are usually the same—companies wanted to cut costs and save time, which is another way of saying they wanted to make more money. The government has come up with stricter rules to make sure the food we eat is safe. Individuals or manufacturers that produce poisonous food will be heavily fined and could be sent to jail. Sales of imported foods increased as ___(14)___ . In particular, international supermarket chain-stores like Costco are enjoying good business.

11. A. have eaten
　　B. to eat
　　C. ate
　　D. will eat

12. A. dairy
　　B. diary
　　C. daily
　　D. delay

13. A. given
　　B. which given
　　C. were given
　　D. had been given

14. A. more and more people believe that saving money is a good habit
　　B. more and more people are concerned with strict rules
　　C. more and more people lose faith in local products
　　D. more and more customers are invited to a special exhibition

Questions 15-18

Time is a strange thing. Sometimes it passes so painfully slow and yet sometimes it seems to travel at the ___(15)___ of light. Time passes awfully slow ___(16)___ when the lesson happens to be your least favorite subject. You might ___(17)___ if the clock is out of order. You can almost hear the ticking of the clock, but the minute hand just doesn't move as fast as you wish.

However, time has a way of sneaking past you. You were celebrating the start of the summer vacation, and before you knew it, it was time to go back to school. You couldn't believe the date you saw on the calendar. It has been two months but it felt like two weeks. One thing about time though, it is fair to everyone. ___(18)___, you have exactly twenty-four hours a day.

15. A. dawn
    B. order
    C. speed
    D. weight

16. A. luckily
    B. especially
    C. hardly
    D. carefully

17. A. decide
    B. guide
    C. refuse
    D. wonder

18. A. No matter how rich or poor you are
    B. As time goes by
    C. Because of lack of time
    D. When you are having a good time

第三部分：閱讀理解

共 12 題，包括 4 個題組，每個題組含 1 至 2 篇短文，與數個相關的四選一的選擇題。請由試題冊上的選項中選出最適合的答案。

Questions 19-21 新題型

Weather Report

Friday	
Saturday	
Sunday	
Monday	

Dear Aaron,

We are going to take a hike with some of my neighbors this weekend. Do you want to come? In fact, we're not sure if the weather will be nice. I don't like rainy days or snowy days; therefore, taking a hike on either sunny days or cloudy days is what I hope for. Anyway, I think I will check the weather report later, and decide to go on one or the other. Drop me a line if you are interested in it.

Vivian

19. What activity do they want to do this weekend?
    A. Have a picnic.
    B. Go hiking.
    C. Go sunbathing.
    D. Read some school reports.

20. What day will most likely be chosen for the activity?
    A. Friday.
    B. Saturday.
    C. Sunday.
    D. Monday.

21. What does "drop me a line" mean?
    A. Give someone a rope.
    B. Accidentally bump into someone.
    C. Write some words.
    D. Check more weather information.

Warning: Power Out

Elevators out of order

Please use the stairs.

Repair work will be carried out as soon as possible.

Sorry for any inconvenience caused.

By: King's Mansion Apartment Committee. 01/26/2016

22. Why are the elevators not working?
    A. They are overweight.
    B. They are out of town.
    C. There is no electricity.
    D. There is a new stairway.

23. When will the problem be fixed?
    A. By January 26th, 2016.
    B. Within three days.
    C. At least a week.
    D. We were not told.

24 Who will likely read this announcement?
    A. Residents.
    B. Teachers.
    C. Police officers.
    D. Shoppers.

Questions 25-27

Mom, I arrived at London this morning. Uncle Sam picked me up at the airport. He drove for six hours to reach his house. He explained that home prices around London are sky-high. He said my school is only 10 minutes' walk from his house. I can either go to school on foot or ride a bike there. Edward is my age but he has a driver's license, so he doesn't need his bike anymore. I can borrow his bike. He said my English is a little strange, but he has no problem understanding what I say. He believes that I will change the way I speak after spending three years here. Edward and I share many common interests. He is also a Harry Potter fan and we had a long discussion about the characters and magic powers in the novels. He promised to take me to the Harry Potter Studio next month. By the way, there is no Internet in Uncle Sam's house so I can only send you messages using my cell phone.

Love, Andy.

25. How might Andy go to school?
    A. He might walk there.
    B. He might take a bus there.
    C. He might go there by car.
    D. He might go there by train.

26. Why doesn't Edward need his bicycle anymore?
    A. He goes to school on foot.
    B. He is old enough to drive a car.
    C. His dad bought him a house in London.
    D. His friend lent him another bike.

27. What is NOT true about Andy?
    A. He can speak English.
    B. He is staying with his uncle.
    C. He has a lot to chat about with Edward.
    D. He can surf the Internet now.

Questions 28-30

Don't be surprised that people like to use "furry-children" to describe their pet dog. People are spending a lot more on them. There are more and more pet shops in cities and towns. In addition to pet food and related products, pet shops also provide bathing and other services. A SPA treatment for your medium-sized dog can cost more than a thousand NT dollars, enough to buy you ten meals if you spend a hundred dollars on lunch. Clinics for pets are also on the rise as owners are more worried about their pets' health than before.

Our love for animals raises a curious but serious question. Do pets take the place of children? Are young couples having pets instead of children? Compared to bringing up a child, keeping a pet doesn't cost as much. For one thing, pet owners do not have to worry about their pets' education. If you need to travel abroad, asking your friends to take care of your cute pets for a week shouldn't be a problem. Try asking them to babysit your child for several days. That could be a problem for most people. Even if friends do agree, you might find it hard to part with your child. What's more, raising children means you need a bigger house. With such high home prices, a bigger apartment seems an unlikely dream for many people.

28. What can be said about the pet business?
    A. Pet-owners are more willing to spend money now.
    B. Pet-owners started many pet shops and clinics.
    C. It costs more than to take care of a child.
    D. Pets and people use the same hospitals.

29. People keep pets rather than have children for the following reasons
    EXCEPT _____.
    A. Pets are less expensive to bring up.
    B. Pets do not need to attend school.
    C. Pets can take care of you when you are old and sick.
    D. You do not necessarily need more space to raise pets.

30. What is true about this passage?
    A. All young couples have pets.
    B. People with pets have to buy a bigger house.
    C. People with children can't have pets at home.
    D. Pet owners cared less about their pets' health in the past.

第一部分 / 看圖辨義

Q1

For question one, please look at picture A.

What is the man's occupation?
這位男士的職業是什麼？

A. He's a diplomat.
B. He's a guard.
C. He's a mechanic.

A. 他是一位外交官。
B. 他是一名警衛。
C. 他是一個維修員。

詳解

答案：C

　　從圖中男子手持工具、身穿工作服在修理車子輪胎的狀態可知，男子是維修員，聽到題目 What ~ occupation 可知是問職業，正確答案為 C。

|單字片語| **machine** [mə`ʃin] 機器 / **mechanic** [mə`kænık] 維修員 / **lifeguard** [`laɪf͵gɑrd] 救生員 / **bodyguard** [`bɑdɪ͵gɑrd] 保鏢 / **security guard** 保全人員

Q2

For question two, please look at picture B.

Why was the man's car being towed away?
為什麼這位男士的車子被拖走？

A. He didn't pay the fine.
B. He didn't park it at the right place.

C. He didn't drive it home.

A. 他沒有繳付罰款。
B. 他沒有把車子停在正確的地方。

C. 他沒有把車子開回家。

詳解

答案：B

　　從圖片中可知，車子準備被拖吊，這台車的旁邊有 NO PARKING 的告示，表示這裡不准停車，也就是說，因為違規把車子停放在不該停的位置而被拖吊，聽到題目 Why ~ car ~ towed 可知，主要是問車子被拖走的原因。選項中與 No Parking 相關的是 B 的 didn't park ~ right place，所以答案為 B。

|單字片語| **tow** [to] 拖 / **fine** [faɪn] 罰款 / **park** [pɑrk] 停（車）

Q3

For question three, please look at picture C.

What is the relationship between the man and the woman?

這位男士和女士之間的關係是什麼？

A. Boss and secretary.
B. Clerk and customer.
C. Wife and husband

A. 老闆和祕書。
B. 店員和客人。
C. 先生和太太。

詳解

答案：C

　　從圖片中可看兩個人，請注意此兩人的動作男子穿著西裝，女子穿著白紗，而且男子正為女子戴戒指，可推測此二人是新郎和新娘的關係。聽到題目 What ~ relationship ~ man ~ woman 可知，主要是問男子與女子之間的關係，正確答案是 C。

Q4

For question four, please look at picture D.

What sport are the people in the picture doing?

圖片中的人們在做什麼運動？

A. They are playing tennis.
B. They are playing badminton.
C. They are playing volleyball.

A. 他們在打網球。
B. 他們在打羽球。
C. 他們在打排球。

詳解

答案：B

　　從圖片中人物手拿著羽球拍可知，他們在打羽毛球，聽到題目 What sport ~ doing 可知，主要是問人物在做的運動為何。聽到 badminton 可知正確答案是 B。

|單字片語| **badminton** [ˋbædmɪntən] 羽球 / **volleyball** [ˋvɑlɪˌbɔl] 排球 / **tennis** [ˋtɛnɪs] 網球 / **soccer** [ˋsɑkə] 足球 / **basketball** [ˋbæskɪtˌbɔl] 籃球 / **baseball** [ˋbesˌbɔl] 棒球 / **dodge ball** 躲避球

第 1 回
第 2 回
第 3 回
第 4 回
第 5 回
第 6 回

Q5

For question five, please look at picture E.

What's wrong with the girl?
這位女孩怎麼了？

A. She hurt herself.
B. She was bitten by a dog.
C. She can't find her scissors.

A. 她弄傷了自己。
B. 她被狗咬了。
C. 她找不到她的剪刀。

詳解

答案：A

　　從圖片判斷，小女孩手指受傷、流血，而且地上有一把剪刀，可以知道女孩用剪刀不小心割傷自己，聽到題目 What's wrong ~ girl 可知，主要是問女孩怎麼了。聽到 A 的 hurt herself 可知是正確答案。

|單字片語| **scissors** [ˈsɪzəz] 剪刀 / **bitten** [ˈbɪtən] 咬（bite 的過去分詞）

第 1 回
第 2 回
第 3 回
第 4 回
第 5 回
第 6 回

Q6

Have you done the laundry yet?
你洗完衣服了嗎？

A. Yes, the closet is delivered.
B. No, do you have any more dirty clothes?
C. I have no idea how to use the oven.

A. 是的，衣櫃寄到了。
B. 還沒，你還有髒衣服嗎？
C. 我不知道要如何使用烤箱。

詳解　　　　　　　　　　　　　　　　　　　　　答案：B

　　聽到 Have you done~ the laundry，可知主要是問對方衣服洗完了沒，A 雖然提到 Yes，但後面內容與問句無關。B 先用 No 提到還沒洗完，接著問是否還有髒衣服，表示跟對方確認還有沒有衣服要洗，是正確答案。C 與問句內容無關。

|單字片語| **laundry** [ˋlɔndrɪ] 要洗的衣服，洗好的衣服 / **closet** [ˋklɑzɪt] 衣櫃 / **deliver** [dɪˋlɪvɚ] 寄送 / **dirty** [ˋdɝtɪ] 髒的 / **oven** [ˋʌvən] 烤箱

Q7

May I borrow your bicycle?
我可以跟你借腳踏車嗎？

A. Sure. I will return it to you tomorrow.
B. I'm afraid not. I lent it to someone else.
C. No. Let's take a taxi there.

A. 當然可以。我明天會還給你。
B. 恐怕不行。我把它借給別人了。
C. 不。我們坐計程車過去吧。

詳解　　　　　　　　　　　　　　　　　　　　　答案：B

　　聽到問句 May I borrow~ 提到要跟對方借東西，因為還沒有借到東西，A 卻回答說明天會把東西歸還，明顯文不對題。B 提到已經借給別人，表示無法把腳踏車借出，是正確答案。C 與問句無關。

補充說明

　　要向別人借東西時，英文用 borrow 物 from 人；把東西借給別人時，英文用 lend 物 to 人。

Q8

It has been raining cats and dogs for two days.
已經下了兩天的傾盆大雨。

A. I have fed them already.
B. That's why I don't like pets.
C. Let's hope we will have sun soon.

A. 我已經餵過他們了。
B. 這就是為什麼我不喜歡寵物。
C. 希望晴天快點來。

詳解

　　此為一個直述句，聽到 raining cats and dogs 要知道是下起傾盆大雨的意思，所以要選擇與天氣或攜帶雨具相關的回答。C 提到希望晴天快點來，表示希望不要再下雨，所以 C 是正確答案。

Q9

Do you think we have a chance to win the first prize?
你認為我們有機會贏得第一大獎嗎？

A. It cost me an arm and a leg.
B. Let's keep our fingers crossed.
C. You shouldn't judge a book by its cover.

A. 它花了我很多錢。
B. 希望能夠如願以償。
C. 你不應該以貌取人。

詳解

　　聽到問句 Do you think~ win~ 問對方是否有機會得獎，應選擇有提到祝好運之類的選項。A 的 cost me an arm and a leg 字面上是指花費一隻手和腳，表示代價不斐、花很多錢的意思。B 字面上是指把手指交叉的意思，表示祈求有好運發生的意思，是最適合的答案。C 字面上指不要用一本書的封面判斷這本書，表示不要只看外表，以貌取人。

◁補充說明▷

　　與 You shouldn't judge a book by its cover. 意思相似的是 Never judge a man by his appearance.（不要用一個人的外貌判斷這個人）。

|單字片語| **prize** [praɪz] 獎項 / **arm** [ɑrm] 手臂 / **leg** [lɛg] 腳 / **cross** [krɔs] 使交叉 / **judge** [dʒʌdʒ] / **cover** [ˋkʌvɚ] 封面

Q10

Will I get a discount if I pay by credit card?
如果我用信用卡付費，我會得到折扣嗎？

A. You don't have to pay cash.
B. We will invite you for dinner.
C. That depends on which bank it is.

A. 你不需要付現金。
B. 我們會邀你吃晚餐。
C. 要看是哪一家銀行。

詳解　　　　　　　　　　　　　　　　　　　　　　　　　　　　答案：C

　　聽到 Will ~ get a discount ~ pay by credit card 可知，主要是問對方自己用信用卡是否有優惠，由此可知說話者是消費者，回答者為店員。A、B 的回答與問句無關，C 提到有沒有優惠折扣是要看該信用卡是哪一家銀行的，是正確答案。

補充說明

　　把 discount 拆開來看，-count 有數和計算的意思，dis- 則有否定的意思，所以可以把 discount 理解為不要數，而不要數的部分也就是折扣。所以當提到 20% discount 時，英美人士想要表達的是指原價中的 20%不用數，可省下原價的 20%。而華人的思維則不同，表達折扣時主要是提到究竟應該要付多少錢，所以會直接說打八折，表示要付原價的百分之八十。

Q11

I have a hobby of collecting coins from different countries.
我有收集來自不同國家錢幣的習慣。

A. So do I.
B. So have I.
C. Me, either.

A. 我也是。
B. 我也已經。
C. 我也沒有。

詳解　　　　　　　　　　　　　　　　　　　　　　　　　　　　答案：A

　　從選項可知都是與「我也～」相關的表達，可推測題目是直述句。題目用現在式肯定句提到有一個習慣。題目中的 have 是一個現在式的動詞，當要用倒裝句表達「我也是」時，助動詞要用現在式 do，正確答案是 A。若題目是用現在完成式 have + p.p.表達，回答時助動詞才用 have。C 是否定的表達，與題目有衝突。

|單字片語| **hobby** [ˋhɑbɪ] 嗜好 / **collect** [kəˋlɛkt] 收集 / **country** [ˋkʌntrɪ] 國家

99

Q12

Susan canceled the party at the last minute.
Susan 臨時取消了派對。

A. How could she do that?	A. 她怎麼可以這麼做？
B. When did she have an operation?	B. 她何時動手術的？
C. Shouldn't she be on time?	C. 她不應該準時嗎？

詳解　　　　　　　　　　　　　　　　　　　　　　　　答案：A

　　題目提到 Susan 在最後一分鐘（at the last minute）取消（canceled）派對，應為讓人失望的舉動，正確的選項最有可能是與詢問取消原因相關的內容。A 提到 How could she do that?，表示對於取消的舉動表達疑惑，是正確答案。

|單字片語| **cancel** [ˋkænsl] 取消 / **cancer** [ˋkænsɚ] 癌症 / **Cancer** [ˋkænsɚ] 巨蟹座

Q13

I need to do something about my weight.
關於我的體重，我需要有所行動來改變。

A. I don't mind waiting for you.	A. 我不介意等你。
B. I am sure we are going in the right direction.	B. 我很確定我們的方向是對的。
C. I think you look just fine.	C. 我覺得你看起來很好呀。

詳解　　　　　　　　　　　　　　　　　　　　　　　　答案：C

　　此為一直述句，關鍵字是 do something 和 my weight，表示針對體重想辦法、採取行動來解決體重問題，也就是對自己的體重感到不滿意的意思，選項中 C 提到「你看起來很好，不會太重」，是最適合的回應方式。

|單字片語| **weight** [wet] 重量 / **mind** [maɪnd] 介意

Q14

Would you like to have a snack?
你想要吃點心嗎？

A. No, I will never go near a snake.	A. 不，我絕對不會靠近蛇。
B. No, I am still quite full.	B. 不，我挺飽的。
C. No, I have a pet already.	C. 不，我已經有寵物了。

第 1 回
第 2 回
第 3 回
第 4 回
第 5 回
第 6 回

詳解

答案：B

從選項中都以No開頭的表達，可推測題目會聽到一問句。題目 Would you like~ snack 主要是問是否要吃點心，A 和 C 的內容都利用 snack 與 snake 的發音相似性來誤導考生，是錯誤選項。B 提到不想吃點心，還很飽，是最符合的正確答案。

補充說明

如果覺得 snake 和 snack 聽起來很像，可以用「微笑」來分辨。唸 snake 的時候要微笑，母音是 [e] 的音。唸 snack 不微笑，而是把嘴巴張開，有點下巴掉下來的感覺。

|單字片語| **snack** [snæk] 點心 / **snake** [snek] 蛇 / **full** [fʊl] 飽的

Q15

My son can't seem to focus on his school work.
我兒子似乎無法專注在課業上。

A. Maybe he is just tired.
B. I'm sure he will find it soon.
C. You should let him go there on his own.

A. 或許他只是累了。
B. 我確定他很快就會找到的。
C. 你應該讓他自己到那裡。

詳解

答案：A

此為一直述句，從 My son、can't 和 focus on ~ school work 可知主要提到自己兒子無法專心於課業上。A 提到他可能是累了，可作為無法專心的原因，是正確答案。其他選項都不適合作為不能專心的理由。

補充說明

focus 當名詞時是相機焦距，焦點，重點的意思，focus 當動詞時，表示鎖定焦點、全神貫注、把焦點集中在某件事上的意思。

Q16

Woman: Should I feed these fish twice a day?

這些魚一天要餵兩次嗎？

Man: No, once a day and just a little will do. They will die if they eat too much.

不，一天一次，而且餵一點點就行了。他們吃太多會死的。

Woman: I see. I didn't know that. 原來如此。我之前並不知道。

Q: What does the man suggest the woman do?

這位男士建議這位女士做什麼？

A. Go on a diet.
A. 去節食。

B. Be careful with the amount of feed.
B. 小心餵的量。

C. Feed the fish at least twice a day.
C. 給魚餵食一天至少兩次。

詳解　　　　　　　　　　　　　　　　　　　　　　　　　　答案：B

　　從選項中都是祈使句（去～）的表達可推測，題目是與「去做什麼」相關的問句。題目問男子給女子的建議為何。女子一開始確認給魚餵食的次數，男子提到一天餵一次，且餵一點點即可，也就是建議女子要注意餵食的量，所以B是正確答案。

補充說明

　　feed 當動詞時是餵食的意思，當名詞時則是飼料的意思。

單字片語 **feed** [fid] 餵 / **suggest** [sə`dʒɛst] 建議 / **diet** [`daɪət] 節食，控制飲食 / **amount** [ə`maʊnt] 數量 / **at least** 至少

Q17

Man: You've been on the phone for three hours straight.

你講電話已經連續講三個小時了。

Woman: Just a second, Emily.（接著對男子說）It doesn't cost a single cent.

Emily，你先等一下。這又不需要花費一毛錢。

Man: Well, the laundry is still in the washing machine.

嗯，衣服還在洗衣機裡面。

第 1 回

第 2 回

第 3 回

第 4 回

第 5 回

第 6 回

Q: What is the woman's problem?
這位女士的問題是什麼？

A. She forgot to do the housework.
B. Her telephone bill will cost her a lot of money.
C. Emily couldn't fix the washing machine.

A. 她忘了做家事。
B. 她的電話帳單會花她很多錢。

C. Emily 無法修理洗衣機。

詳解　　　　　　　　　　　　　　　　　　答案：A

　　主要是問女子的問題。男子一開始對女子抱怨說她一直在講電話，接著又說女子的衣服還在洗衣機裡面，言外之意是指女子應該要先去完成家務，不要一直講電話。

|單字片語| **do the laundry** 洗衣服 / **laundromat** 自助洗衣店

Q18

Woman: Always leave the window open when you turn on the water heater.　打開熱水器時，窗戶要一直開著。

Man: But it's cold, mom. Why can't I close the window?
但是媽媽，這樣很冷。為什麼我不能把窗戶關起來？

Woman: Because you could die. Just do what I told you to do.
因為你這樣可能會死掉。照我說的去做就對了。

Q: What is the woman worried about?
女士擔心什麼？

A. Her son's grades.
B. Her son's weight.
C. Her son's safety.

A. 她兒子的成績。
B. 她兒子的體重。
C. 她兒子的安全。

詳解　　　　　　　　　　　　　　　　　　答案：C

　　主要是問女子擔心的事項。從男子的對話內容中可知人物是母子關係。女子一開始要求男子使用熱水器時窗戶要打開，並提到不這樣的話會失去生命，表示在意男子的生命安全，所以正確答案為 C。

|單字片語| **leave... open** 保持開著的狀態 / **turn on** 打開（電器）/ **water heater** 熱水器

Q19

Man: Why didn't you answer my call? I thought you don't have classes today.　你為什麼沒有接我的電話？我以為你今天沒有課。

Woman: I was in a group meeting. I turned my cell phone off.
我在開小組會議。我把手機關機了。

Man: Never mind. We still have enough time to see a movie.
沒關係。我們還有足夠的時間看電影。

Q: **Why didn't the woman answer the man's call?**
為什麼女士沒有接男士的電話？

A. She has classes today.　　　　　A. 她今天有課。
B. She was in a meeting.　　　　　B. 她在開會。
C. She was in a movie theater.　　　C. 她在電影院。

詳解　　　　　　　　　　　　　　　　　　　　　　　　**答案：B**

　　主要是問女子沒接電話的原因。男子提出女子沒接電話的疑惑之後，女子回答因為在開會（in a~ meeting）才把手機關機，因而沒有接電話，所以正確答案是 B。

Q20

Woman: This heat is killing me. It's not even summer yet.
這股熱氣讓我受不了。還沒到夏天呢。

Man: But mom says we are only allowed to use the air-conditioner in the room starting from July.
但是媽媽說我們從七月開始才能使用房間裡的冷氣。

Woman: She won't know if you keep quiet about it.
如果你不說的話，她不會知道。

Q: **What is the woman's problem?**
女士的問題是什麼？

A. She thinks the room is too hot.　　A. 她認為房間太熱了。
B. She thinks the room is too noisy.　B. 她認為房間太吵了。
C. She thinks the room is too dirty.　C. 她認為房間太髒了。

詳解　　　　　　　　　　　　　　　　　　　　　　　　**答案：A**

　　從選項中都是 She thinks~ 的表達可推測，題目是與女子相關的問句。主要

是問女子提到的問題為何。女子一開始提到 heat（熱氣）、not ~ summer yet（還沒到夏天），可知女子覺得天氣很熱，男子則提到現在不能開 air-conditioner（冷氣），女子則要求男子不要把開冷氣的行為說出去，表示堅持要開冷氣的意思，可判斷女子的問題是認為房間太熱了。

第 1 回
第 2 回
第 3 回
第 4 回
第 5 回
第 6 回

Q21

Man:	You really have a gift for drawing.　你在畫畫方面真的很有天分。
Woman:	Are you saying that just to make me happy? 你這麼說是為了讓我開心嗎？
Man:	I'm serious. Look at these cartoons. They are so full of life. 我是說真的。你看這些卡通。他們栩栩如生。

> Q: **What does the man mean?**
> **男士所指的意思是什麼？**
> A. The woman is talented.　　　A. 這位女士很有才華。
> B. The woman is funny.　　　　B. 這位女士很好笑。
> C. The woman is boring.　　　　C. 這位女士很無聊。

詳解　　　　　　　　　　　　　　　　　　　　　　　　答案：A

　　主要是問男子在整個對話中對於女子想表達的意思。男子一開始說女子在畫畫方面有天分（gift for drawing），之後又補充說明女子所畫的卡通栩栩如生，由此可知男子稱讚女子很會畫畫，所以 A 是正確答案。

< 補充說明 >

　　gift 有「禮物」、「天賦」（可理解為上天賜的禮物）的意思，某人在某方面有天賦，我們會說 someone has a gift for...。talent 是「天分」、「才華」的意思，某人有才華可以說 someone is talented。

Q22

Woman:	I didn't know that you can bake so well. 我從來不知道你這麼會烘焙。
Man:	My dream is to have a bakery of my own. 我的夢想是開一間屬於自己的麵包店。
Woman:	I will be your regular customer when you do. 當你開的時候，我會是你的常客。

Q: **What is the man interested in?**
男士對什麼感興趣？

A. Collecting coins and stamps.
B. Designing clothes and shoes.
C. Making cakes and bread.

A. 收集硬幣和郵票。
B. 設計衣服和鞋子。
C. 製作蛋糕和麵包。

詳解　　　　　　　　　　　　　　　　　　　　　　　　　　　　　　　答案：C

　　主要是問男子的興趣。從女子一開始稱讚男子的 bake（烘焙）技巧，以及男子提到要開 bakery（麵包店）可知，男子對製作麵包感興趣，正確答案為 C。

Q23

Man: It's so dark in here.　這裡面好暗。

Woman: Just be quiet and find our seats.　安靜一點，來找座位。

Man: I told you to come in earlier. The show has already started.
　　　我告訴過你要早一點進來。表演已經開始了。

Q: **Where might the man and the woman be?**
這位男士和女士可能在什麼地方？

A. In a hospital.
B. In a theater.
C. In a factory.

A. 在醫院。
B. 在劇院。
C. 在工廠。

詳解　　　　　　　　　　　　　　　　　　　　　　　　　　　　　　　答案：B

　　從選項中都是「In + 地方名詞」可推測，題目是與地點相關的問句。主要是問對話人物的所在地。從 dark in here（這裡面好暗）、find our seats（找座位），以及 show has already started（表演已經開始）可知，說話者在劇院或電影院裡。相信大家可能都有這樣的經驗，因為太晚進到戲院裡，電影已經開始了，戲院裡一片漆黑，只能安靜地找到自己的座位。

Q24

Woman: I don't think John will be here on time.
　　　　我不認為 John 會準時到。

Man: I have the same feeling.　我也有同感。

Woman: Maybe we should leave without him just to teach him a lesson.
　　　　或許我們應該不等他就離開，來給他點教訓。

Q: What does the woman suggest?
女士建議什麼？

A. They should teach John English.	A. 他們應該教 John 英文。
B. They should leave now.	B. 他們應該現在離開。
C. They should wait for John.	C. 他們應該等 John。

詳解　　　　　　　　　　　　　　　　　　　　　　　　　　　　答案：B

　　從選項中都是 They should 的表達可推測，題目是與建議相關的問句。主要是問女子的建議。女子一開始提到 John 不會準時到，之後又說不等 John 直接離開，所以 B 是正確答案。「學到教訓」的英文是 learn a lesson，「教訓別人」的英文是 teach someone a lesson。

Q25

Man:　　How come we have so many tests? I can't stand it anymore.
　　　　為什麼我們有這麼多測驗？我再也受不了了。

Woman:　Coming out with test papers is something teachers enjoy doing.
　　　　出考卷是一件老師喜歡做的事情。

Man:　　You can say that again.　你說的沒錯。

Q: What is true about the conversation?
關於這個對話，何者正確？

A. The man enjoys taking tests.	A. 這位男士喜歡考試。
B. The man agrees with the woman.	B. 這位男士同意女士的說法。
C. The man wants the woman to repeat what she just said.	C. 這位男士要女士重複她剛剛說的話。

詳解　　　　　　　　　　　　　　　　　　　　　　　　　　　　答案：B

　　從 What ~ true ~ conversation 可知，主要是問與對話內容相符的選項。男子一開始抱怨有很多考試（How come ~ many tests?），快要受不了了（can't stand it），可以知道男子不喜歡考試，所以 A 不正確。女子提到老師喜歡出考卷，暗指自己也不喜歡考試。You can say that again 字面上的意思是你可以再說一次，表示非常認同，所以 B 是正確答案。

補充說明

　　關於同意對方的表達，還有 I can't agree more，字面意義為「我無法同意更多了」，表示我非常同意你的意思。也可以用 You're right、You bet 來表達「你說的沒錯」。

Q26

For question number 26, please look at the three pictures.

Please listen to the following short talk.　請聽以下的簡短談話。

What is the man trying to sell?
這位男士在賣什麼？

　　Are you sick and tired of people telling you that you are overweight? Did you try many ways to stay in shape but they just didn't work? Our Step-and-Sweat machine is designed to help you exercise without even realizing it. Just step on it when you watch TV or listen to music. Try it for a month and if it doesn't work, you can have your money back.

　　對於人們一直說你過重，你是否感到厭煩了？你試過很多方法來維持身材但是都沒用嗎？我們的 Step-and-Sweat 踩上去就流汗的機器是特別設計來讓你在不知覺的情況下運動。當你在看電視或聽音樂時，你只需要踩上去。試用一個月，如果沒用的話，你可以全額退費。

A.

B.

C.

詳解

答案：A

　　從 What ~ woman ~ sell 可知，主要是問女子所賣的商品為何。從一開始點出的 overweight（過重的）和 exercise（運動），可以得知應該是賣減肥產品的廣告。從 Step-and-Sweat machine 以及後面接到的 step on it 可知，此產品是用踩的。step 是踩上去的意思、sweat 是流汗的意思，所以該產品長得應該比較像圖 A，而不是跳繩。

第 1 回
第 2 回
第 3 回
第 4 回
第 5 回
第 6 回

〈補充說明〉

　　「發福、體重增加」的英文是 gain weight 和 put on weight。gain 是「得到」的意思，weight 是「重量」的意思，得到重量也就是胖了的意思。put on 有「穿上」的意思，把 put on weight 理解為穿上體重，也就是「變胖」的意思。「減肥」或「變瘦」的英文是 lose weight，lose 是「失去」的意思，失去重量也就等於是變瘦的意思。

|單字片語| **be sick/tired of** 對於…感到厭煩 / **overweight** [ˋovəˌwet] 超重的 / **stay in shape** 維持身材／體態 / **work** [wɜk] 發揮效用 / **step** [stɛp] 踩 / **sweat** [swɛt] 流汗 / **design** [dɪˋzaɪn] 設計

Q27

For question number 27, please look at the three pictures.

Please listen to the following announcement.　請聽以下的公告廣播。

What will the students probably do next?
這些學生接下來會做什麼？

　　Listen up, kids. This is your first outdoor activity, so pay attention to what I am going to say. The bus will take us to the beach. You will pick up plastic bottles, plastic bags and other trash. Now, please line up outside in pairs before you get on the bus.

　　孩子們，聽好。這是你們的第一次戶外教學，所以注意聽我要說的話。公車會帶我們到海邊。你們要撿起塑膠瓶、塑膠袋和其他垃圾。現在，請到外面兩個兩個排好隊，準備等下上公車。

A.

B.

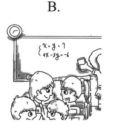

C.

詳解　　　　　　　　　　　　　　　　　　　　　　　　　答案：C

　　從圖片可推測，主要是跟學生相關的題目。聽到 What ~ students ~ do next 可知，主要是問說話者在說這段話之後，學生（也就是聽者）接著會先做的事為何。選項 A 是在海邊撿垃圾，是學生戶外教學時要去做的事，而非接著要做的事。這段話最後提到 Line up outside in pairs now，表示要求學生兩個兩個排好隊，所以學生接下來要做的事是排隊。

|單字片語| **outdoor** [`aʊt͵dor] 戶外的 / **pay attention to** 注意… / **beach** [bitʃ] 海邊 / **plastic** [`plæstɪk] 塑膠的 / **line up** 排隊 / **in pairs** 兩個地，成對地

Q28

For question number 28, please look at the three pictures.

Please listen to the following short talk.　請聽以下的簡短談話。

What did the man do in the morning?
這位男士在早上做了什麼？

　　My boss gave us half a day off and said we can do whatever we like until lunch time. I stayed in the office and I was at my desk this morning. I was surfing the Internet and looked for information for my vacation. My wife and I plan to go diving. That's all I have done this morning.

　　我老闆給了我們半天的假，還說直到午餐前，無論我們想做什麼都可以。我今天早上在辦公室，坐在辦公桌前。我在上網搜尋度假的資訊。我太太和我打算去潛水。這就是我今天早上所做的事。

A.

B.

C.

詳解

答案：B

　　從圖片可推測，主要是跟男士所做的事情相關的題目。聽到 What ~ man ~ do in the morning 可知，主要是問男士早上所做的事情。男子提到 I stayed in the office ~ at my desk this morning ~ surfing the Net，可以知道男士待在辦公室裡上網，所以正確答案為 B。surf 有「瀏覽」和「衝浪」的意思，surf the Net 是「上網」的意思。

|單字片語| **until** [ən`tɪl] 直到 / **lunch time** 午餐時間 / **surf** [sɝf] / **look for** 尋找 / **dive** [daɪv] 潛水

Q29

For question number 29, please look at the three pictures.

Please listen to the following voice message. 　請聽以下的語音留言。

What might David be doing in class tomorrow?
明天 David 可能會在班上做什麼？

　　Hi, David. This is Angela. I have an important message for you from Mr. Andrews, our science teacher. Please bring a plastic bottle and a balloon for tomorrow's science class. By the way, Mr. Andrews said that we can speak Chinese to one another in his class if that helps us understand better. See you tomorrow.

　　嗨，David。我是 Angela。我要告訴你一個來自我們科學課老師 Andrews 先生的重要訊息。明天的科學課請帶一個塑膠瓶和一個氣球。順便一提，Andrews 先生說如果說中文可以幫助我們理解他的課，我們可以用中文跟彼此對話。明天見。

A.

B.

C.

詳解　　　　　　　　　　　　　　　　　　　　　　　　　　　答案：C

　　從圖片可推測，主要是跟課堂相關的題目。聽到 What ~ David ~ doing in class tomorrow 可知，主要是問 David 明天會在班上做的事情，請注意關鍵字 David 和 tomorrow。從 Hi, David. This is Angela.可知，說話者在對 David 講話，並提到 I have an important message for you from ~ our science teacher.，表示要跟 David 傳達來自科學課老師交代的訊息，接著又說 Please bring a plastic bottle and a balloon for tomorrow's class.，言下之意，明天 David 要上科學課，而且要帶塑膠瓶和一個氣球，合理的推斷是 David 會在科學課上做實驗。因此圖片中可以看到氣球、寶特瓶，而且在做實驗的 C 是正確答案。

|單字片語| **message** [ˋmɛsɪdʒ] 訊息 / **science** [ˋsaɪəns] 科學 / **bottle** [ˋbɑtəl] 膠瓶 / **balloon** [bəˋlun] 氣球 / **one another** 互相（指三者以上）

For question number 30, please look at the three pictures.

Please listen to the following news report.　請聽以下的新聞報導。

What might have happened?
可能發生了什麼事？

According to the local people who saw the accident, the building fell down without any warning. At least ten workers were in it. Six bodies have been found so far. Though there was no fire. A few cars were also damaged but nobody was hurt. This is Nick Tsai from CCB news, Kaohsiung.

根據目擊到意外發生的當地人，建築物毫無預警倒塌。至少有十名工人在裡面。目前為止已經找到了六具屍體。現場沒有起火。有幾部車子也遭受損壞，但沒有其他人受傷。這是 CCB，Nick Tsai 來自高雄的報導。

A.

B.

C.

詳解　　　　　　　　　　　　　　　　　　　　　　　　答案：C

　　從圖片可推測，主要是跟意外災害相關的題目。聽到 What ~ happened 可知，主要是問文中所提到的事件。一開始提到 saw the accident，可知有意外發生，接著又說 the building collapsed，表示建築物倒塌。此外，文中提到沒有失火 (there was no fire)，所以選項 A 是錯的。雖然有幾台車子遭受波及，不過這不是交通事故，選項 B 也是錯的。因此正確答案是 C。

補充說明

　　雖然初級英檢單字量為 2500，不過短文聽解這個部分往往還是會出現一些範圍以外的單字，所以在聽音檔前務必要先看圖，聯想出可能會有的關鍵字，並藉由音檔中的上下文來理解。

|單字片語| **local** [ˋlokəl] 當地 / **accident** [ˋæksədənt] 意外 / **building** [ˋbɪldɪŋ] 建築 / **warning** [ˋwɔrnɪŋ] 警告，警報 / **damage** [ˋdæmɪdʒ] 破壞

第二回

初試 閱讀測驗 解析

\第一部分/ **詞彙**

Q1

My grandpa used to fix watches and clocks _____ a living.

我爺爺過去以維修手錶和時鐘為生。

A. for
C. as

B. with
D. by

詳解

答案：A

　　選項都是介系詞，空格後面是 a living，這時要想到慣用語 for a living（以…為生）。英文的 What do you do for a living?，相當於中文的「您是做什麼的？」。

Q2

My daughter told me that her teacher hit her _____ a ruler.

我女兒說她的老師用尺打她。

A. with
C. for

B. by
D. about

詳解

答案：A

　　選項都是介系詞，空格前後分別是 hit her 和名詞 a ruler，可以推斷應該是要表達「用尺打她」，所以介系詞要選含有「用」「有」意義的 with。with 的相反詞是 without，是「沒有」的意思。

〈補充說明〉

　　請看以下 with 和 without 的用法
　　Cut the ham **with** this knife. 用這把刀切火腿。
　　I want coffee **with** milk. 我要有加牛奶的咖啡。
　　I can't live **without** my cell phone. 沒有我的手機我活不下去。

Q3

There was a _____ accident on the freeway. Many people were badly hurt.

高速公路上有一場嚴重的意外。很多人受了重傷。

A. slender 苗條的   B. strict 嚴格的
C. serious 嚴重的；認真的   D. simple 簡單的

詳解   答案：C

　　選項都是形容詞，空格後面是 accident on the freeway，提到交通事故，所以要形容的名詞是車禍，最適合的答案是 serious（嚴重的）。strict（嚴格的）用來描述人的個性或表情，不能形容車禍的嚴重度。另外，在電影中常聽到 serious 的用法，通常是指「認真的」，例如 Are you serious?（你是認真的嗎）。

l單字片語l **freeway** [ˋfrɪˏwe] 高速公路 / **badly** [ˋbædlɪ] 嚴重地

Q4

I need to _____ these books to the library. They are due today.

我需要把這些書拿到圖書館歸還。它們今天到期。

A. remind 提醒   B. repeat 重覆
C. return 歸還   D. reply 回覆

詳解   答案：C

　　空格後面是 these books to the library，又提到 They are due，表示圖書館的書要到期了，所以空格要填入有「歸還」意義的 return。

◁補充說明▷

　　re 是英文常見的字首，表示「重來；再次」的意思，return（歸還）、repeat（重覆）和 reply（回覆）都是 re 開頭。在 mind（注意）前面加上 re，表示再次注意，也就是提醒的意思。其他以 re 開頭的還有 rewrite（重寫）、redo（重做）和 recycle（資源回收再利用）。

Q5

It feels a little _____ in here. I think we'll need a fan.

這裡有點熱。我想我們需要一台電風扇。

A. cool 涼爽的；酷的   B. dry 乾的
C. warm 溫暖的；熱的   D. messy 凌亂的

詳解   答案：C

    選項都是形容詞，從 feels（感覺）以及後面的 need a fan（需要電風扇）可知，主要是要表達這裡有點熱，所以答案是 C。

Q6

We found the door open. A thief _____ our house.
我們發現門是開著的。小偷闖入我們的家。

A. broke up 分手   B. broke off 分開；分離
C. broke down 故障   D. broke into 闖入

詳解   答案：D

    選項都是與 break 相關的動詞片語。從空格前提到 door open（門是開著的）以及 thief（小偷）和 house（房屋）可知，主要是要表達小偷闖入家裡，正確答案是 D。

|單字片語| **thief** [θif] 小偷

Q7

The kids were so excited when they saw a rainbow _____.
當孩子們看到彩虹出現的時候十分興奮。

A. appear 出現   B. imagine 想像
C. fail 失敗   D. pass 通過

詳解   答案：A

    選項都是動詞，從空格前面提到的 they saw a rainbow 可知，主要是要選擇以 rainbow 當主詞的動詞。就語意上來看，彩虹會出現，而不會通過、失敗、想像，所以答案是 A。

|單字片語| **excited** [ɪk`saɪtɪd] 感到興奮的 / **rainbow** [`ren͵bo] 彩虹

Q8

_____ he doesn't make a lot of money, _____ he is happy with what he has.
雖然他沒有賺很多錢，他對於他所擁有的很滿意。

第 1 回
第 2 回
第 3 回
第 4 回
第 5 回
第 6 回

A. Though 雖然；x
B. Though 雖然；but 但是
C. Because 因為；x
D. Because 因為；so 所以

詳解

　　題目是兩個子句，所以空格位置要選出連接詞。英文的邏輯不同於中文，連接詞的定義是把兩個子句「連」在一起，兩個子句用一個連接詞就夠了，而不用兩個連接詞，所以 B 和 D 可以先淘汰。就語意上來看，「雖然 (Though) 沒賺很多錢，但對於所擁有的很滿意」，會比「因為 (Because) 沒賺很多錢，所以對於所擁有的很滿意」來得通順，因此答案是 A。記住英文的口訣：有雖然 (though) 就沒有但是 (but)，有但是 (but) 就沒雖然 (though)。同樣的，有因為 (because) 就沒所以 (so)，有所以 (so) 就沒有因為 (because)。

Q9

I couldn't _____ my luck. I won the first prize – a 60-inch TV!

我不敢相信我的運氣。我贏得頭獎——一台六十吋的電視！

A. decide 決定
B. believe 相信
C. change 改變
D. promise 答應

詳解

　　選項都是動詞，空格後面提到 my luck，又說已贏得頭獎，由此可知主要是要表達不敢相信自己的運氣，所以答案是 B。如果連續發生了許多倒楣事，也可以說 I couldn't believe my luck.。

|單字片語| luck [lʌk] 運氣 / inch [ɪntʃ] 英吋

Q10

Betty's husband gave her a diamond ring, and she is showing it _____ to everyone she sees.

Betty 的丈夫給了她一個鑽戒，而她對所有她遇到的人炫耀。

A. out
B. off
C. up
D. down

詳解

　　選項都是副詞，主要是考動詞片語的運用。空格前面提到 gave her a diamond ring（給了她一個鑽戒），又說 she is showing it，可以得知主要是表達炫耀她的鑽戒，因此答案是 B。

|單字片語| show off 炫耀 / show up 出席 / showdown 攤牌；一次定勝負

第二部分 / 段落填空

Questions 11-14

It seems that from time to time, the public was told that some food is not safe (11) to eat. Whether it is soy-sauce, tea or vegetables, the food we eat on a (12) daily basis contains chemicals that are harmful to the body. The reasons (13) given are usually the same—companies wanted to cut costs and save time, which is another way of saying they wanted to make more money. The government has come up with stricter rules to make sure the food we eat is safe. Individuals or manufacturers that produce poisonous food will be heavily fined and could be sent to jail. Sales of imported foods increased as (14) more and more people lose faith in local products. In particular, international supermarket chain-stores like Costco are enjoying good business.

似乎每隔一段時間，大眾就會被告知某些食品不安全。不管是醬油、茶或蔬菜，我們每天吃的食物含有對身體有害的化學物品。所給的理由通常都一樣，公司想要減少成本和節省時間，換句話說就是，他們想要賺更多的錢。政府已經想出更加嚴格的規定來確保我們所吃的食物是安全的。生產有毒食品的人或製造商將被重重地罰款，而且也可能入獄。進口食品的銷售量增加了，因為越來越多人對本地的產品失去信心。尤其像是好市多這類的國際連鎖超市生意都非常好。

Q11

A. have eaten
C. ate

B. to eat
D. will eat

詳解　　　　　　　　　　　　　　　　　　　　　　　答案：B

選項都是 eat 的各類變化，空格接在形容詞 safe 後面，務必要記住：「主詞 + be safe to + 動詞」原形的慣用法，所以 B 是正確答案。

Q12

A. dairy 乳製品
C. daily 每日的

B. diary 日記
D. delay 耽誤

詳解 答案：C

　　空格所在的句子可看成 the food (we eat on a ~ basis) contains chemicals，括弧中的子句是用來修飾 the food 的形容詞子句，food 是 eat 的受詞，而 on a ~ basis 是一個副詞片語。選項中適合填入 on a ~ basis 的只有 C，以表示「每天」「以每天為基礎」。

|單字片語| **dairy** 乳製品 / **diary** 日記 / **daily** 每日的

〈補充說明〉

　　和 daily 同類的單字還有以下：
weekly 每週的 / monthly 每月的 / yearly 每年的

Q13

A. given   B. which given
C. were given   D. had been given

詳解 答案：A

　　原因 (The reasons) 是被提出來、被給予 (were given) 的，所以要用被動式，但答案不是 C。空格在 The reasons ＿＿＿＿＿ are usually the same 中是形容詞子句的功能，用來修飾 reasons，完整的寫法為：The reasons (which were given) are usually the same.，而關係代名詞 which 和 were 可以省略，只剩下 given。形容詞子句不能只省略關係代名詞，必須要連同 be 動詞一起省略。

The student (who was) chosen to be the leader is usually popular. 被選為班長的學生通常會受到歡迎。
→The student chosen to be the leader is usually popular.

Q14

A. more and more people believe that saving money is a good habit
　　越來越多人相信省錢是個好習慣
B. more and more people are concerned with strict rules
　　越來越多人擔心嚴格的規定
C. more and more people lose faith in local products
　　越來越多人對本地的產品失去信心
D. more and more customers are invited to a special exhibition
　　越來越多顧客受邀參加特展

詳解　答案：C

選項都是用到 more and more 相關的表達，空格前面提到跟食安相關的問題，並指責黑心廠商，接著提到「進口食品的銷售量增加」。從「進口食品的銷售量增加」可推測，正因為越來越多人對國內食品失去信心，才會仰賴進口食品。因此答案是 C。

|單字片語| **more and more** 越來越多的

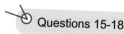 Questions 15-18

Time is a strange thing. Sometimes it passes so painfully slow, and yet sometimes it seems to travel at the (15) speed of light. Time passes awfully slow (16) especially when the lesson happens to be your least favorite subject. You might (17) wonder if the clock is out of order. You can almost hear the ticking of the clock, but the minute hand just doesn't move as fast as you wish.

However, time has a way of sneaking past you. You were celebrating the start of the summer vacation, and before you knew it, it was time to go back to school. You couldn't believe the date you saw on the calendar. It has been two months but it felt like two weeks. One thing about time though, it is fair to everyone. (18) No matter how rich or poor you are, you have exactly twenty-four hours a day.

時間是一種奇怪的東西。有時候它慢到令人抓狂，而有時卻似乎以光速前進。尤其當某堂課剛好是你最不喜歡的科目，時間會過得非常地慢。你可能在懷疑時鐘是不是壞了。你幾乎可以聽到時鐘的滴答聲，但分針卻不依你希望的那樣快速移動。

然而，時間有一種在你身邊悄悄溜走的方法。你正在慶祝暑假的開始，但是在你還不知道之前已經是要開學了。你無法相信你在日曆上看到的日期。已經過了兩個月，但感覺像是兩個星期而已。儘管如此，關於時間，還有一點是時間對每個人都是公平的，無論你貧窮或富裕，你每天都是二十四小時。

Q15

A. dawn 黎明　　　　　　　B. order 秩序；順序
C. speed 速度　　　　　　　D. weight 重量

詳解

空格前面提到 Time ~ passes ~ slow，表示時間過很慢，之後用 and yet 來提示後面的句子是相反的語意。前面提到時間過很慢，後面就會說明時間過很快，所以最適合的答案是 speed（速度）。

<補充說明>

at the speed of light 表示「以光的速度」，with lightning speed 表示「以迅雷不及掩耳的速度」。順便一提，speed 當動詞時是「加速」和「超速」的意思，而 be fined for speeding 是指因為超速而被開罰單。

A. luckily 幸運地　　　　　　B. especially 尤其是
C. hardly 幾乎不　　　　　　D. carefully 小心地

詳解　　　　　　　　　　　　　　　　　　　　　　　答案：B

選項都是副詞，而空格前面提到時間過得很慢，後面則舉例提到在上自己最不喜歡的課的時候，最適合的答案是 especially（尤其是）。請見以下例句：

I seldom eat fruits, especially those that are sour. 我很少吃水果，特別是那些酸的。

Q17

A. decide 決定　　　　　　　B. guide 引導
C. refuse 拒絕　　　　　　　D. wonder 想知道

詳解　　　　　　　　　　　　　　　　　　　　　　　答案：D

選項都是動詞，而空格前面提到「上自己最不喜歡的課的時候，時間過得很慢」，而空格後面提到時鐘故障，因此最適合的動詞是 wonder（想知道）。字典給 wonder 的定義為「想知道」，但翻譯成「不曉得；不知道」是比較接近中文的意思。當我們說我們「不曉得；不知道」，意思就是「很想知道」。

I wonder if you are free tonight. 不曉得你今晚是否有空？
I wonder why she is late. 不曉得她為什麼遲到。

Q18

A. No matter how rich or poor you are
　無論你是貧窮還是富裕

B. As time goes by
   隨著時間的流逝
C. Because of lack of time
   因為缺乏時間
D. When you are having a good time
   當你玩得愉快

詳解

　　文章前面提到時間感的快慢，空格前面則提到時間對每個人都是公平的，空格後面則說每天都是二十四小時，從「每個人都是公平的」可推測，這裡指的每個人是指不論其身分富貴貧賤。因此答案是 A。

補充說明

　　no matter 後面可以加 how、what 等副詞，例如 no matter how + adj.（無論多麼）、no matter what（無論什麼）、no matter where（無論在哪裡）、no matter who（無論是誰）。另外一種用法是 however + adj. + 主詞 + 動詞（無論主詞多麼）、whatever + 主詞 + 動詞（無論主詞做什麼）、wherever + 主詞 + 動詞（無論主詞在哪裡做）、whoever + 主詞 + 動詞（無論誰做）。

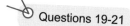

Weather Report **氣象報告**	
Friday 星期五	
Saturday 星期六	
Sunday 星期日	
Monday 星期一	

Dear Aaron,

We are going to take a hike with some of my neighbors this weekend. Do you want to come? In fact, we're not sure if the weather will be nice. I don't like rainy days or snowy days; therefore, taking a hike on either sunny days or cloudy days is what I hope for. Anyway, I think I will check the weather report later, and decide to go on one or the other. Drop me a line if you are interested in it.

Vivian

親愛的 Aaron

　　本週末我們將要跟一些我的鄰居去健行。你想要一起來嗎？事實上，我們並不確定是不是好天氣。我不喜歡雨天或下雪天，因此我希望在有太陽時，或是多雲的時候去健行。不管怎樣，我想我待會兒會先看氣象報告，再決定要在週末的哪一天去。寫信給我，讓我知道你是否有興趣喔。

Vivian

Q19

What activity do they want to do this weekend?
他們本週末想做什麼活動？

A. Have a picnic.　野餐。
B. Go hiking.　去健行。
C. Go sunbathing.　做日光浴。
D. Read some school reports.　讀一些學校報告。

詳解

　　在第二篇文中的第一句提到：We are going to take a hike... this weekend. Do you want to come?，提到本週末邀約對方一起去健行，故答案選 B.。

Q20

What day will most likely be chosen for the activity?
最有可能選哪天進行此活動？

A. Friday.　週五。
B. Saturday.　週六。
C. Sunday.　週日。
D. Monday.　週一。

詳解

　　在第二篇文中的第一句提到：We are going to take a hike... this weekend.，可知是要在週末（週六或週日）去。根據第一篇的圖表所示，週六是下雪、週日是晴天。而根據第二篇文，寫信者不喜歡下雪天（I don't like rainy days or snowy days; therefore, taking a hike on either sunny days or cloudy days is what I hope for.），提到不喜歡雨天或下雪天，希望在有太陽時，或是多雲的時候去。故答案選 C.。

Q21

What does "drop me a line" mean?

「**drop me a line**」是什麼意思？

A. Give someone a rope. 給某人一條繩子。

B. Accidentally bump into someone. 不小心撞到某人。

C. Write some words. 寫一些字句。

D. Check more weather information. 確認天氣資訊。

詳解

答案：C

　　在第二篇文一開始的 Dear Aaron 和最後的 Vivian可知，這是一封書信。書信最後提到 Drop me a line if you are interested in it.，可推測寫信者（即Vivian）要收信者回信，因此 drop me a line 的意思也就是回信或是給某人一些訊息，故答案選 C。

|單字片語| **take a hike** 健行 / **weather report** 氣象報告 / **go sunbathing** 做日光浴 / **drop me a line** 回信或是給某人訊息

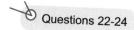

Questions 22-24

Warning: Power Out

Elevators out of order
Please use the stairs.
Repair work will be carried out as soon as possible.
Sorry for any inconvenience caused.
By: King's Mansion Apartment Committee. 01/26/2016

警告：停電

電梯故障
請用樓梯
維修工作將儘早進行
我們為所造成的不便感到抱歉

由：國王豪宅公寓委員會 2016 年 1 月 26 日

|單字片語| **elevator** [ˈɛləˌvetə] 電梯 / **out of order** 故障 / **stairs** [stɛrz] 樓梯 / **repair** [rɪˈpɛr] 維修 / **inconvenience** [ˌɪnkənˈvinjəns] 不便 / **committee** [kəˈmɪtɪ] 委員會

Q22

Why are the elevators not working?

為什麼電梯無法運作？

    A. They are overweight.　他們超重了。
    B. They are out of town.　他們出差。
    C. There is no electricity.　沒有電。
    D. There is a new stairway.　有新的樓梯。

詳解　　　　　　　　　　　　　　　　　　　　　　　答案：C

    從 Why ~ elevators not working 可知，主要是問電梯故障的原因。聽到 What ~ happened 可知，從 power out（停電）跟 Elevators out of order（故障）這兩個關鍵句可得知，電梯是因為沒有電而無法運作。

Q23

When will the problem be fixed?

問題將於何時處理？

    A. By January 26th, 2016.　在 2016 年 1 月 26 日之前。
    B. Within three days.　三天內。
    C. At least a week.　至少一個星期。
    D. We were not told.　我們沒被告知。

詳解　　　　　　　　　　　　　　　　　　　　　　　答案：D

    從 When will ~ problem ~ fixed? 可知，主要是問問題解決的時間。關於時間，這張公告只說 Repair work will be carried out as soon as possible.，表示維修工作將儘快進行，並沒有承諾什麼時候會修好。所以答案是 D。01/26/2016 是指委員會 (By: ~ Committee) 張貼此公告的時間，所以 A 不正確。

Q24

Who will likely read this announcement?

    A. Residents. 居民。　　　　　　B. Teachers. 老師們。
    C. Police officers. 警官。　　　　D. Shoppers. 購物者們。

詳解　　　　　　　　　　　　　　　　　　　　　　　答案：A

    從公告最後的署名 By: Mansion Apartment 中的 Apartment 可推測，這是寫給公寓居民看的公告，故答案選 A。

第 1 回
第 2 回
第 3 回
第 4 回
第 5 回
第 6 回

Mom, I arrived at London this morning. Uncle Sam picked me up at the airport. He drove for six hours to reach his house. He explained that home prices around London are sky-high. He said my school is only 10 minutes' walk from his house. I can either go to school on foot or ride a bike there. Edward is my age but he has a driver's license, so he doesn't need his bike anymore. I can borrow his bike. He said my English is a little strange, but he has no problem understanding what I say. He believes that I will change the way I speak after spending three years here. Edward and I share many common interests. He is also a Harry Potter fan and we had a long discussion about the characters and magic powers in the novels. He promised to take me to the Harry Potter Studio next month. By the way, there is no Internet in Uncle Sam's house so I can only send you messages using my cell phone.

Love, Andy.

媽，我今天早上抵達倫敦了。Sam 叔叔到機場接我。他開了六個小時的車才到他家。他解釋說倫敦附近的房價高得嚇人。他說從他家走路到我學校只需要十分鐘。我可以步行到學校或騎腳踏車去。Edward 跟我一樣大，但他有駕照，所以他不再需要他的腳踏車了，這麼一來我就跟他可以借了。他說我的英文有點奇怪，但他聽得懂我在說什麼。他相信，在這裡度過三年後，我說話的方式會改變。Edward 和我有很多共同興趣。他也是哈利波特迷，我們花很長的時間討論小說中的人物和魔法。他答應下個月帶我去哈利波特影城。順便一提，Sam 叔叔家裡沒有網路，所以我只能用手機傳簡訊給你。

|單字片語| **reach** [ritʃ] 抵達 / **explain** [ɪkˋsplen] 解釋 / **price** [praɪs] 價格 / **sky-high** 非常高的 / **on foot** 步行 / **common** [ˋkɑmən] 共同的

Q25

How might Andy go to school?
Andy 可能會如何去學校？

A. He might walk there.　他可能會走路去。
B. He might take a bus there.　他可能會搭公車去。
C. He might go there by car.　他可能會開車去。
D. He might go there by train.　他可能會搭火車去。

詳解

答案：A

從 How~ Andy~ to school 可知主要是問去學校的方式。從文章最後的署名 Love, Andy.可知，Andy 是寫這封信的人。文中提到 my school is only 10 minutes' walk ~ I can either go to school on foot or ride a bicycle there.，表示 Andy 可以用走的或騎腳踏車去上學，所以答案是 A。

 Q26

Why doesn't Edward need his bicycle anymore?

為什麼 Edward 不再需要他的腳踏車？

A. He goes to school on foot. 他走路去學校。

B. He is old enough to drive a car. 他夠大了可以自己開車去。

C. His dad bought him a house in London. 他的爸爸在倫敦幫他買了房子。

D. His friend lent him another bike. 他的朋友借了他另一台腳踏車。

詳解

答案：B

先找到文中關於 Edward 以及 bike 相關的內容。文中提到 Edward ~ has a driver's license, so he doesn't need his bike anymore.，從這兩子句可知，Edward 已經有駕照 (driver's license)，所以不再需要他的腳踏車，答案是 B。在國外，能考駕照的年齡比台灣低。

 Q27

What is NOT true about Andy?

關於 Andy，何者不正確？

A. He can speak English. 他會說英文。

B. He is staying with his uncle. 他跟他的叔叔一起住。

C. He has a lot to chat about with Edward.
他跟 Edward 有很多可以聊的。

D. He can surf the Internet now. 他現在可以上網。

詳解

答案：D

從文中可知，Andy 住在叔叔家（Uncle Sam），所以 B 正確。從 my English is a little strange but he has no problem understanding what I say 可以知道，Andy 會說英文，所以選項 A 正確。Andy 和 Edward 有很多共通的興趣（many common interests），所以 C 也是正確的，只有 D 是錯的，叔叔家裡沒有網路，所以 Andy 無法上網。

Don't be surprised that people like to use "furry-children" to describe their pet dog. People are spending a lot more on them. There are more and more pet shops in cities and towns. In addition to pet food and related products, pet shops also provide bathing and other services. A SPA treatment for your medium-sized dog can cost more than a thousand NT dollars, enough to buy you ten meals if you spend a hundred dollars on lunch. Clinics for pets are also on the rise as owners are more worried about their pets' health than before.

Our love for animals raises a curious but serious question. Do pets take the place of children? Are young couples having pets instead of children? Compared to bringing up a child, keeping a pet doesn't cost as much. For one thing, pet owners do not have to worry about their pets' education. If you need to travel abroad, asking your friends to take care of your cute pets for a week shouldn't be a problem. Try asking them to babysit your child for several days. That could be a problem for most people. Even if friends do agree, you might find it hard to part with your child. What's more, raising children means you need a bigger house. With such high home prices, a bigger apartment seems an unlikely dream for many people.

看到「毛小孩」這幾個字不要感到驚訝。這是人們用來形容寵物狗的用詞。人們現在花很多錢在他們身上。越來越多寵物店出現在城市和鄉鎮。除了寵物飼料和相關產品，寵物店也提供洗澡和其他美容服務。中型犬的 SPA 療方可能要花超過一千元新台幣，如果你一頓午餐花一百元，那足以買十頓飯。寵物診所的數量也在上升，因為寵物主人比以前更加擔心寵物的健康。

我們對動物的愛引發了一個讓人好奇卻又嚴重的問題。寵物會取代孩子的位置嗎？年輕夫婦飼養寵物而不生小孩嗎？相較於扶養孩子，飼養寵物不需要那麼多錢。還有一點，寵物主人不需要擔心寵物的教育。如果你需要出國旅行，請你的朋友幫你照顧可愛的寵物一個星期應該沒問題。試著要求他們當孩子的保姆幾天，對許多人來說這可能是個問題。就算朋友同意，你可能還是會覺得難以和孩子分開。還有，扶養孩子表示你需要更大的房子。房價高得嚇人，比較大的公寓對很多人來說是個不可能的夢。

┃單字片語┃ **furry** [ˋfɝɪ] 毛皮的/ **describe** [dɪˋskraɪb] 形容，描述 / **medium** [ˋmidɪəm] 中型的 / **clinic** [ˋklɪnɪk] 診所 / **serious** [ˋsɪrɪəs] 嚴重的 / **take the place of** 取代… / **compared to** 相較於 / **bring up** 培育，扶養 / **babysit** [ˋbebɪsɪt] 當…的保姆 / **raise** [rez] 扶養

Q28

What can be said about the pet business?
關於寵物相關的產業提到了什麼？

A. Pet-owners are more willing to spend money now.
   寵物主人現在比較願意花錢。

B. Pet-owners started many pet shops and clinics.
   寵物主人開了很多寵物店和診所。

C. It costs more than to take care of a child.
   照顧寵物比照顧小孩要花更多錢。

D. Pets and people use the same hospitals.
   寵物和人們使用同樣的醫院。

詳解　　　　　　　　　　　　　　　　　　　　　　　　答案：A

　　文章提到人們現在花很多錢在他們（寵物）身上 (People are spending a lot more on them)，這裡的「他們」指的是寵物，所以 A 是正確答案。B 在文中並未提到。而從 Compared to bringing up a child, keeping a pet doesn't cost as much. 可知，養寵物花的錢不比照顧小孩還要多。從 Clinics for pets are also on the rise 可知，有為寵物專門設立的診所，表示寵物和人是去不一樣的醫院。所以 C、D 不正確。

Q29

People keep pets rather than have children for the following reasons EXCEPT _____.
人們養寵物而不生孩子，是因為以下的原因，除了

A. Pets are less expensive to bring up.　把寵物養大比較沒那麼貴。

B. Pets do not need to attend school.　寵物不需要去上學。

C. Pets can take care of you when you are old or sick.
   當你老了或者生病時，寵物可以照顧你。

D. You do not necessarily need more space to raise pets.
   養寵物不一定要有更大的空間。

詳解　　　　　　　　　　　　　　　　　　　　　　　　答案：C

　　主要是問養寵物而不生孩子，何者不是原因。文中提到飼養寵物不需要那麼多錢，而且也不需要擔心寵物的教育，所以 A、B 都是原因。文中也提到 raising children means you need a bigger house，表示把小孩扶養到長大，需要更大的房屋空間，所以 D 也是原因。只有 C 沒有提到，是正確答案。

第 1 回
第 2 回
第 3 回
第 4 回
第 5 回
第 6 回

Q30

What is true about this passage?

關於此文章，以下何者正確？

A. All young couples have pets.　所有年輕的夫妻都有養寵物。

B. People with pets have to buy a bigger house.
有寵物的人需要買更大的房子。

C. People with children can't have pets at home.
有孩子的人不能在家裡養寵物。

D. Pet owners cared less about their pets' health in the past.
有寵物的人在過去比較不關心寵物的健康。

詳解　　　　　　　　　　　　　　　　　　　　　　　　　　　　

　　文中只用疑問句提到 Are young couples having pets instead of children?，但並未提到所有年輕的夫妻都有養寵物，所以 A 不正確。B、C 並未在文中提到，也不正確。從 owners are more worried about their pets' health than before. 可以知道，有養寵物的人比以前更加擔心寵物的健康，表示以前並沒那麼在乎寵物健康的問題，所以 D 是正確答案。

全民英檢初級

第三回 初試 聽力測驗

TEST03.mp3

本測驗分四個部分，全部都是單選題，共 30 題，作答時間約 20 分鐘。作答說明為中文，印在試題冊上並經由光碟放音機播出。

第一部分　看圖辨義

共 5 題（為第 1 題至第 5 題）。每題請聽光碟放音機播出題目和三個英語句子之後，選出與所看到的圖畫最相符的答案。每題只播出**一遍**。

例題：（看）

（聽）Look at the picture.
Which is the cheapest?

A. The computer.
B. The telephone.
C. The TV set.

正確答案為 B，請在答案紙上塗黑作答。

A:　Question 1

B:　Question 2

C: Question 3

D: Question 4

E: Question 5

第二部分　問答

共 10 題（為第 6 題至第 15 題）。每題請聽光碟放音機播出的英語句子，再從試題冊上三個回答中，選出一個最適合的答案。每題只播出**一遍**。

例：　（聽）　Do you speak English?
　　　（看）　A.　No, I speak English quite well.
　　　　　　　B.　Yes, a little.
　　　　　　　C.　No, it's a useful language.

正確答案為 B，請在答案紙上塗黑作答。

6.　A.　Let me do the dishes now.
　　B.　It is going to rain soon.
　　C.　I will help to set the table.

7.　A.　You're welcome.
　　B.　I didn't do it on purpose.
　　C.　I forgive you.

8.　A.　I just took the medicine.
　　B.　It's too sweet for me.
　　C.　That's a good suggestion.

9.　A.　You're right. Someone turned it off.
　　B.　Not really. My birthday is the day after tomorrow.
　　C.　Are you kidding? It's the busiest day of the week.

10.　A.　I'm terribly sorry.
　　B.　I will sign it right now.
　　C.　I can't allow you to do that.

11.　A.　It's parked in the garage, isn't it?
　　B.　It's growing really fast, isn't it?
　　C.　It's in your pocket, isn't it?

12.　A.　We could have won.
　　B.　There was nothing important in it.
　　C.　Let's ask someone for directions.

13.　A.　He's busy writing a novel.
　　B.　He's up to no good.
　　C.　He is my cousin.

14. A. Whatever you say.
    B. No wonder.
    C. Just go straight.

15. A. Please take off your shoes.
    B. That will be NT$240.
    C. Just a minute.

第三部分　簡短對話

　　共 10 題（為第 16 題至第 25 題）。每題請聽光碟放音機播出一段對話和一個相關的問題後，再從試題冊上三個選項中，選出一個最適合的答案。每段對話和問題只播出**一遍**。

例：　(聽)　(Woman)　Could I sit here?
　　　　　　(Man)　　I'm sorry, but this seat is occupied.

　　　　　　Question: Where do you think the dialogue takes place?

　　　(看)　A.　In an office
　　　　　　B.　In a taxi
　　　　　　C.　In a restaurant.

正確答案為 C，請在答案紙上塗黑作答。

16. A.　He can give the woman a ride.
　　B.　He has no idea.
　　C.　He is in a hurry.

17. A.　In a post office.
　　B.　In a supermarket.
　　C.　In a police station.

18. A.　Taking out the trash.
　　B.　Fighting with the truck driver.
　　C.　Playing online games.

19. A.　He is very careful.
　　B.　He is very rich.
　　C.　He is very angry.

20. A.　Take a rest.
　　B.　See a doctor.
　　C.　Take some medicine.

21. A.　Take the dog for a walk.
　　B.　Help to clean the kitchen.
　　C.　Buy some chicken on his way back.

22. A.　Lend her the dictionary.
　　B.　Look up new words with a cell phone.
　　C.　Call his uncle.

23. A.　He is a guide.
　　B.　He is a salesman.
　　C.　He is a lawyer.

24. A. A kind of food.
    B. A baby boy.
    C. An animal.

25. A. She needs to go to the bathroom.
    B. She needs to drink more water.
    C. She needs to buy some glasses.

第四部分　短文聽解

共 5 題（為第 26 題至第 30 題）。每題有三個圖片選項。請聽光碟放音機播出的題目，並選出一個最適當的圖片。每題只播出**一遍**。

例：　（看）

A.　　　　　　　　　　B.　　　　　　　　　　C.

（聽）

Listen to the following short talk. What might Judy buy?

　　Judy is making a cake for her boyfriend. She checked her refrigerator and found that she had run out of sugar. But she still has lots of flour.

正確答案為 C，請在答案紙上塗黑作答。

Question 26

A.

B.

C.

Question 27

A.

B.

C.

Question 28

A.

B.

C.

Question 29

A.

B.

C.

Question 30

A.

B.

C.

第三回 初試 閱讀測驗

本測驗分三部分，全部都是單選題，共 30 題，作答時間 35 分鐘。

第一部分：詞彙
　　共 10 題，每個題目裡有一個空格。請從四個選項中選出一個<u>最適合</u>題意的字或詞作答。

1. Put the plastic bottles into the _____ bin so we can make them into something useful.
   A. cleaning　　　　　　B. recycling
   C. holding　　　　　　 D. washing

2. It didn't _____ to him that yesterday was his wife's birthday.
   A. think　　　　　　　B. realize
   C. happen　　　　　　 D. occur

3. What does the sign over there _____? I can't make it out because some letters are missing.
   A. say　　　　　　　　B. tell
   C. write　　　　　　　 D. learn

4. Excuse me. I am going to the central library. Which stop should I _____?
   A. get up　　　　　　　B. get off
   C. get down　　　　　　D. get away

5. Taking the plane will help us _____ some time though we have to pay more for it.
   A. spend　　　　　　　B. make
   C. use　　　　　　　　D. save

6. The children were playing and shouting _____ doing their homework.
   A. so that
   B. for example
   C. instead of
   D. such as

7. All of us will have to do our _____ if we want to win the next game.
   A. life
   B. part
   C. role
   D. event

8. His mother _____ him go to cram schools after school. He has no time for himself.
   A. wants
   B. asks
   C. suggests
   D. makes

9. Amy: My mom bought me a watch. Emily: _____
   A. What a nice watch!
   B. What is nice a watch!
   C. How a nice watch!
   D. How nice is the watch!

10. On my way home last night, I _____ an old classmate.
    A. ran into
    B. ran out of
    C. ran away
    D. ran after

第二部分：段落填空

共 8 題，包括二個段落，每個段落各含四個空格。每格均有四個選項，請依照文意選出**最適合**的答案。

Questions 11-14

Is taking a nap ____(11)____ ? Why is it that people in Western cultures do not have to take an afternoon nap in order to work better? In Asia, people of different races have the habit of taking a nap after lunch. It ____(12)____ that a short rest after eating is helpful for both body and mind. For ____(13)____ who work outdoors, taking a break during noontime to avoid the terrible heat sounds perfectly reasonable. However, questions are raised when office workers in the comfort of air-conditioning are found sleeping for hours after lunch. As for students, some complained of tiredness on days when they did not take a nap while others mentioned that ____(14)____ . In short, old habits die hard. It will be hard to make people believe that they do not need a nap.

11. A. careful
    B. necessary
    C. actual
    D. greedy

12. A. believes
    B. is believed
    C. was believed
    D. has believed

13. A. they
    B. them
    C. those
    D. that

14. A. they believe that going to bed early is a good habit
    B. the early bird catches the worm
    C. sleeping for hours after lunch is acceptable
    D. they feel more tired after taking a nap

On his way home yesterday, Kevin noticed a brown wallet on a bench in the park. He thought perhaps he should open the wallet and see who it ____(15)____ to. As soon as he picked up the wallet, a man appeared ____(16)____ . "Got you. You are a thief. You stole my wallet. I took a picture of you holding it." Kevin was at a loss for ____(17)____ . Before he could say anything, the man said, "I will forgive you if you pay me a thousand dollars. But if you refuse, I will make a police report." ____(18)____ The guy was a conman, a liar. "Yes, please call the police. In fact, I will do it for you." Kevin said, without showing any fear. The man looked shocked. He grabbed the wallet and ran away.

15. A. returns
    B. belongs
    C. happens
    D. spreads

16. A. all of a sudden
    B. all the suddenly
    C. in a sudden
    D. in suddenly

17. A. events
    B. records
    C. ideas
    D. words

18. A. The man run out of the money.
    B. A guy then contacted the owner of the wallet.
    C. Kevin immediately went back home.
    D. Kevin soon realized what this was all about.

第三部分：閱讀理解

　　共 12 題，包括 4 個題組，每個題組含 1 至 2 篇短文，與數個相關的四選一的選擇題。請由試題冊上的選項中選出最適合的答案。

Questions 19-21

X-Market Recommended items

ITEMS	PRICE
A carton of milk	$ 80
A bunch of bananas	$ 110
A box of cookies	$ 90
A loaf of bread	$ 100

NOTICE

Welcome shoppers:

　　Starting from next Sunday, we will extend our opening hours. We will be open from 7:00 in the morning until eleven at night. Also, for your shopping convenience, we will be open seven days a week. In other words, there will be no day-off on Monday anymore. And please note that only on Sundays, customers who arrive during the first thirty minutes after the doors open will get a 10% discount coupon. It can be used on any items except dairy goods.

19. What is the main idea of this notice?
    A. Hire more employees.
    B. Give information on new goods.
    C. Recommend a new branch of X-Market.
    D. Inform the change of business hours.

20. How much does a customer with a coupon pay if he buys a carton of milk?
    A. $ 100.
    B. $ 80.
    C. $ 90.
    D. $ 72.

21. Which of the following statements is NOT true?
    A. X-Market used to have a day-off on Mondays.
    B. Customers can shop at X-Market on Tuesday and Saturday afternoon.
    C. Two boxes of cookies cost one hundred and eighty dollars.
    D. Shoppers who come at 8:00 in the morning on Sundays can get a coupon.

Questions 22-24

Photography Competition

Attractive cash prizes and discount vouchers to be won!
See your pictures printed on magazines with your name
on them.

(5)

Details:

No limit on types of cameras used
Each participant can send up to three digital photos.
Send your pictures to nicepics4u@yahoo.com.tw.
Each picture must be not more than 25 megabytes.

(10)

Winners will be informed by email.

22. Which is NOT an advantage of taking part in the competition?
    A. Win some money.
    B. See your works on magazines.
    C. Get a new camera.
    D. Show off your talent.

23. What is true about the rules above?
    A. Only certain cameras are allowed.
    B. There is no limit on the number of photos you can send.
    C. The picture you send must be less than 25 megabytes.
    D. You have to sign your name on the back of each photo.

24. How can we take part in the competition?
    A. By making a phone call.
    B. By visiting the store.
    C. By sending an email.
    D. By faxing.

Message For: Mr. Anderson

Time and Date: 12 March, 2016. 3:15 P.M.

Taken by: Derrick

From: Miss Tsai, ACC Company

(5)   Message: My boss has agreed to purchase twenty chairs, two tables and one overhead projector for the conference room. Please make the delivery to our office on the 16th of March. I will be in the office. Someone needs to show me how to connect the projector to a

(10)   laptop computer.

25. What is the purpose of this message?
    A. To place an order.
    B. To give advice on buying a projector.
    C. To ask for a refund.
    D. To make an appointment.

26. Who received the message?
    A. Mr. Anderson
    B. Derrick
    C. Miss Tsai
    D. The boss of ACC Company

27. What does Mr. Anderson have to do on the 16th of March?
    A. Call Miss Tsai back.
    B. Buy a new laptop computer.
    C. Send some things to ACC Company.
    D. Hold a meeting in the conference room.

Dear Dad,

(5)   Mom is driving me crazy. I never expect senior high school to be such a **nightmare**! She makes me go to cram school every day, including the weekends! She makes sure the teachers in every cram school give me extra homework. It's not fair! Come on, Dad. How many hours a day do you work? I go to school at seven in the morning, followed by cram school until 9:30 p.m. That's more than fourteen hours of school a day. What's worse, I stay up until 2:00 a.m. to finish all the homework. Did I tell you about the tests? I have

(10)   at least two or three tests a day. I have no time to rest or relax. The only thing I want to do on the weekend is get a little more sleep. Guess what? Mom had me signed up for three different cram schools on Saturday and another two on Sunday. I used to enjoy music lessons and drawing class but now I hate them.

(15)   You said you would be back by the end of this month. I hope you can keep your word. Please discuss this matter with Mom. She keeps reminding me that I am not an adult so I have to listen to her. I can't stand the stress much longer. Anyway, I wish you success in your business from your factory.

(20)   Yours sincerely,

                                                     Mike.

28. What does a **nightmare** in line 3 probably mean?
    A. Something terrible which happens in a dream or real life.
    B. Something wonderful which happens in a dream or real life.
    C. An animal which only appears at night.
    D. A person who can help you solve your problems.

29. What is true about Mike?
    A. He doesn't have enough homework.
    B. He doesn't talk to his mother at all.
    C. He doesn't like music lessons anymore.
    D. He doesn't want his father to succeed.

30. What does Mike's father do for a living?
    A. He owns a factory.
    B. He owns a cram school.
    C. He is a teacher of a senior high school.
    D. He is a private tutor.

初試 聽力測驗 解析

第一部分 / 看圖辨義

Q1

For question one, please look at picture A.

Why is the woman angry?
為什麼這位女士在生氣？

A. The door is open.
B. The room is warm.
C. The floor is dirty.

A. 門打開了。
B. 房間太熱。
C. 地板髒了。

詳解　　　　　　　　　　　　　　　　　　　　　　答案：C

　　從 Why~ woman~ angry 可知主要是問女士在生氣的原因。從圖片可知，地板上有許多鞋子的腳印，這位女士生氣的原因是人有把地板弄髒了。

Q2

For question two, please look at picture B.

What musical instrument is the girl playing?
這個女孩在彈奏什麼樂器？

A. The violin.
B. The flute.
C. The piano.

A. 提琴。
B. 長笛。
C. 鋼琴。

詳解　　　　　　　　　　　　　　　　　　　　　　答案：B

　　從圖片中的長笛可知，女孩在吹長笛。聽到 musical instrument 和 playing 可知，主要是問圖片中女孩吹奏的樂器為何。聽到 flute 的 B 是正確答案。

||單字片語|| **instrument** [ˈɪnstrəmənt] 樂器，儀器 / **piano** [pɪˈæno] 鋼琴 / **violin** [ˌvaɪəˈlɪn] 小提琴 / **flute** [flut] 笛子 / **guitar** [ɡɪˈtɑr] 吉他 / **trumpet** [ˈtrʌmpɪt] 小號

第 1 回
第 2 回
第 3 回
第 4 回
第 5 回
第 6 回

Q3

For question three, please look at picture C.

What does the woman do?
這位女士是做什麼的？

A. She is talking to someone.
B. She is a reporter.
C. She does not like her job.

A. 她在跟某個人說話。
B. 她是一名記者。
C. 她不喜歡她的工作。

詳解   答案：B

從 What 和 woman do 可知，主要是問女士的職業。圖片是關於颱風天的畫面，女士面對攝影機說話，所以是一名記者。

補充說明

若題目問 What do you do?，其語意是「你是做什麼的？」，也就是問工作。如果題目是用現在進行式來問 What are you doing?，就是「你正在做什麼？」的意思，主要是問進行的動作。

Q4

For question four, please look at picture D.

Where are these people?
這些人在什麼地方？

A. They are in a museum.
B. They are in a restaurant.
C. They are in a forest.

A. 他們在博物館.
B. 他們在餐廳。
C. 他們在森林裡。

詳解   答案：A

從牆壁上的畫作和玻璃展示櫃，可判斷這些人在博物館。聽到 Where~ people 可知，主要是問人物所在位置。聽到選項 A 的 in a museum 是正確答案。

Q5

For question five, please look at picture E.

What is the day after tomorrow?
後天是星期幾？

A. It's Wednesday.　　　　　　A. 星期三。
B. It's Thursday.　　　　　　 B. 星期四。
C. It's Friday.　　　　　　　 C. 星期五。

詳解　　　　　　　　　　　　　　　　　　　　　**答案：C**

　　從圖片中可知今天（today）是十月八號星期三，聽到 What is + the day~，就要知道是在問星期，the day after tomorrow 是「後天」的意思，而 the day before yesterday 是「前天」的意思。今天是是期三可以推算後天是星期五。

|單字片語| **today** [təˋde] 今天 / **yesterday** [ˋjɛstɚde] 昨天 / **tomorrow** [təˋmɔro] 明天 / **the day after tomorrow** 後天 / **the day before yesterday** 前天 / **Monday** [ˋmʌnde] 星期一 / **Tuesday** [ˋtjuzde] 星期二 / **Wednesday** [ˋwɛnzde] 星期三 / **Thursday** [ˋθɝzde] 星期四 / **Friday** [ˋfraɪˌde] 星期五 / **Saturday** [ˋsætɚde] 星期六 / **Sunday** [ˋsʌnde] 星期日

154

Q6

Dinner will be served in five minutes.
晚餐會在五分鐘後上桌。

A. Let me do the dishes now.
B. It is going to rain soon.
C. I will help to set the table.

A. 現在讓我來洗碗吧。
B. 就快下雨了。
C. 我來幫忙排碗筷。

詳解　　　　　　　　　　　　　　　　　　　　　　　　　　　　　**答案：C**

　　題目是一直述句，從 Dinner 和 in five minutes 可知主要是說晚餐要準備好了。通常是吃完晚餐才洗碗（do the dishes），所以選項 A 不合理。因為晚餐快要準備好上桌了，所以應該要幫忙排碗筷才對。

Q7

Look what you have done! My dress is ruined.
看你做了什麼！我的洋裝毀了。

A. You're welcome.
B. I didn't do it on purpose.
C. I forgive you.

A. 不用客氣。
B. 我不是故意的。
C. 我原諒你。

詳解　　　　　　　　　　　　　　　　　　　　　　　　　　　　　**答案：B**

　　聽到 Look what you ~ done 以及 My ~ ruined 可知，此直述句在指責對方，最合理的回應是 B。purpose 是「目的」的意思，on purpose 也就是「故意的」的意思。類似狀況，也可以說是個意外（It was an accident.）。

Q8

You had better take your coat with you.
你最好帶外套。

A. I just took the medicine.
B. It's too sweet for me.
C. That's a good suggestion.

A. 我剛吃了藥。
B. 對我來說太甜了。
C. 那是個好建議。

第1回　第2回　第3回　第4回　第5回　第6回

You had better + V 通常用來向對方提供建議或命令，這裡提到建議對方帶外套，對方最為合理的回應是 C。

|單字片語| **had better** 最好 / **coat** [kot] 外套 / **take the medicine** 吃藥

Q9

May I take a day off tomorrow?
明天我可以請假嗎？

A. You're right. Someone turned it off.
B. Not really. My birthday is the day after tomorrow.
C. Are you kidding? It's the busiest day of the week.

A. 你說的對。有人把它關掉了。
B. 不完全是。我的生日是在後天。
C. 你在開玩笑嗎？明天是本週最忙碌的一天。

詳解

答案：C

take a day off 是「請一天假」的意思，題目是確認自己可否請假。選項中較合理的是 C，從 Are you kidding? It's the busiest day 可知明天最忙，暗示不准請假的意思。表達「請假」，比較正式的說法是 go on leave，「請病假」是 on sick leave。

|單字片語| **take a day off** 請假 / **turn... off** 把（電器）關掉

Q10

Didn't you read the sign? It says no smoking allowed.
你沒看到標誌嗎？它說不准吸菸。

A. I'm terribly sorry.
B. I will sign it right now.
C. I can't allow you to do that.

A. 我很抱歉。
B. 我現在就簽名。
C. 我不允許你這麼做。

詳解

答案：A

聽到 Didn't ~ read ~ sign 以及 no smoking 可知，這裡不准抽菸，也表示聽者現在正在吸菸，合理的回應是道歉，答案為 A。題目中的 sign 是名詞，是「標誌」的意思，而 B 的 sign 是動詞，是「簽名」的意思。在聽力測驗中，利用題目中相同字但不同的意思做陷阱選項，是很典型的出題手法。

第 1 回
第 2 回
第 3 回
第 4 回
第 5 回
第 6 回

Q11

Did you see my car key?
你有看到我的車鑰匙嗎？

A. It's parked in the garage, isn't it?
B. It's growing really fast, isn't it?
C. It's in your pocket, isn't it?

A. 車子停在車庫，不是嗎？
B. 成長真快，不是嗎？
C. 在你的口袋，不是嗎？

詳解   答案：C

聽到 see ~ car key 的疑問句可知，主要是問車鑰匙的所在位置。因為重點是車鑰匙，不是車子，車鑰匙才有可能放在口袋，所以 C 是答案。正確答案也有可能是 No, I didn't see it.（不，我沒看到）。

Q12

It looks like we lost our way.
看起來我們迷路了。

A. We could have won.
B. There was nothing important in it.
C. Let's ask someone for directions.

A. 我們原本可以贏的。
B. 沒有重要的東西在裡面。
C. 我們向別人問路吧。

詳解   答案：C

題目中提到的 way 是「方向」，所以 lost one's way（失去方向）也就是迷路的意思，最適合的回應是去問（ask）別人正確的方向（directions）。

補充說明

way 在生活當中很常表示「方向」「方式」，例如表達「往這邊走」會說 go this way，表達「用這個方式」會說 in this way。

Q13

What is Peter up to these days?
Peter 這些日子都在忙些什麼？

A. He's busy writing a novel.
B. He's up to no good.
C. He is my cousin.

A. 他忙著寫小說。
B. 他不懷好心。
C. 他是我的表哥。

詳解

　　從選項的 He 可推測，題目會提到某一位男子。問句 What's ~ up to 是會話中常用的表達方式，意思是問某人最近在做什麼。所以正確答案是 A。有時候在路上遇到對方會簡略為 What's up。up to no good 表示某人想做不好的事情，「心懷不軌」的意思。

Q14

I don't feel like talking. Just leave me alone.
我不想要講話。讓我一個人靜一靜。

A. Whatever you say.　　　　　　A. 無論你說什麼都行。
B. No wonder.　　　　　　　　　B. 難怪。
C. Just go straight.　　　　　　　C. 直走就對了。

詳解

　　聽到 leave me alone（讓我一個人靜一靜），最為合理的回應是「好吧，你說什麼都好」，所以答案是 A。

〈補充說明〉

　　whatever（無論什麼）在口語中時常會用到，例如 whatever you need（無論你需要什麼），whatever it takes（無論代價是什麼）。

|單字片語| **feel like** 想要

Q15

Could you check if my food is ready?
你可否確認一下我的食物準備好了嗎？

A. Please take off your shoes.　　A. 請脫掉鞋子。
B. That will be NT$240.　　　　　B. 那會是新台幣 240 元。
C. Just a minute.　　　　　　　　C. 請稍等。

詳解

　　聽到 Could you check if 問句，可以知道這句是在拜託某人確認某事，說話者可能是在跟服務生說「我的食物準備好了嗎？」，最合理的回答是「好的，請稍等。」

Q16

Woman: Excuse me. How can I get to the subway station?
抱歉。我要怎麼去地鐵站？

Man: I'm afraid I can't help you. I am not familiar with this place.
恐怕我幫不上忙。我對這個地方不熟悉。

Woman: It's all right. Thanks anyway.
沒關係。還是謝謝你。

Q: What does the man mean?
這位男士的意思是什麼？

A. He can give the woman a ride.
B. He has no idea.
C. He is in a hurry.

A. 他可以載這位女士一程。
B. 他不知道。
C. 他在趕時間。

詳解

答案：B

從選項的 He 可推測，題目會問與男子相關的問題。主要是問男子在對話中所表達的重點。女子一開始問怎麼去地鐵站（How~ to~ station），男士表示他對這個地方不熟悉（not familiar with this place），也就是說他也不知道怎麼去地鐵站。所以答案是 B。

Q17

Man: Here's your stamp. Please provide a return address.
這是你的郵票。請提供回寄的地址。

Woman: Why do I have to? Can't I leave it out?
為什麼需要這麼做？不能讓它空白嗎？

Man: Just in case the person doesn't receive your package.
只是以防萬一對方沒有收到你的包裹。

Q: Where might the woman be right now?
這位女士現在可能在什麼地方？

A. In a post office.
B. In a supermarket.
C. In a police station.

A. 在郵局。
B. 在超市。
C. 在警察局。

詳解

答案：A

從選項中都是「In + 地方名詞」可推測，題目是與地點相關的問句。聽到 Where 和 woman 可知主要是問女士的所在位置。從 stamp（郵票）、address（地址）、package（包裹）這些關鍵字可判斷，女子在郵局。

Q18

Woman: Jack, take out the garbage. The truck is almost here.
　　　　Jack，把垃圾拿出去。垃圾車快到了。

Man:　　Mom, I'm busy fighting and killing monsters.
　　　　媽，我正忙著跟怪獸對抗、殺怪獸。

Woman: You will have to fight me if you don't do it now.
　　　　如果你現在不去，你就是要跟我作對了。

Q: What might the man probably be doing?
　　這位男士應該在做什麼？

A. Taking out the trash.　　　　　A. 把垃圾拿出去丟。
B. Fighting with the truck driver.　B. 在跟卡車司機打架。
C. Playing online games.　　　　　C. 在玩線上遊戲。

詳解

答案：C

從選項中都是「動詞 -ing」可推測，題目會問與「做什麼」相關的問題。聽到 What 和 man ~ doing 可知主要是問男士正在做的事。男士提到 I'm ~ fighting and killing monsters.（正忙著殺怪獸），可推測男士最有可能的是在打電玩遊戲，正確答案為 C。

Q19

Man:　　Shampoo, towel, toothbrush, flashlight. What else did I miss?
　　　　洗髮精、毛巾、牙刷、手電筒。我還少了什麼？

Woman: You went through the checklist twice already.
　　　　你已經看這張清單兩次了。

Man:　　Better to be safe than sorry.　小心一點總比後悔來得好。

Q: What is true about the man?
　　關於這位男士何者正確？

A. He is very careful.　　A. 他很小心。
B. He is very rich.　　　B. 他很有錢。
C. He is very angry.　　C. 他很生氣。

答案：A

　　從選項的 He 可推測，題目會問與男子相關的問題。從對話一開始列出一些物品以及提到 What else did I miss? 可知，男子在確認是否有遺漏什麼，女子也提到 went through ~ twice ，表示已經確認過兩次了，可見這位男士非常謹慎小心。

|單字片語| **shampoo** [ʃæm`pu] 洗髮精/ **towel** [`taʊəl] 毛巾 / **toothbrush** [`tuθ͵brʌʃ] 牙刷 / **flashlight** [`flæʃ͵laɪt] 手電筒 / **miss** [mɪs] 錯過，遺漏 / **go through** 仔細檢查 / **twice** [twɪce] 兩次

Q20

Woman: I have to prepare for the final exams but I have a terrible headache.
我必須準備期末考，但我的頭痛得很厲害。

Man: Why don't you go and take a nap? I am sure you will feel better.　你為什麼不去睡午覺？休息完之後會比較好一點。

Woman: But time is running out. I have only two weeks left.
但是時間不夠了。我只剩下兩個星期。

Q: **What does the man suggest the woman should do?**
這位男士建議女士應該做什麼？

A. Take a rest.
B. See a doctor.
C. Take some medicine.

A. 休息一下。
B. 去看醫生。
C. 吃點藥。

答案：A

　　從選項都是動詞可推測，題目會問與「做什麼」相關的問題。聽到 What ~ man suggest ~ woman 可知，主要在問給女士什麼建議。聽到男士提到 Why don't you ~ take a nap?，可知男士建議女士去睡午覺，意思是要她去休息一下。

|單字片語| **final exam** 期末考 / **headache** [`hɛd͵ek] 頭痛 / **take a nap** 睡午覺 / **run out** 用完

Q21

Man: Honey, I am going to walk the dog. Do you want to come along?　親愛的，我要去遛狗。你要一起去嗎？

Woman: No, I will pass. I need to clean the kitchen.
我還是不要好了。我需要清理廚房。

Man: Leave something for me to do. I will do my part when I come back.　留一點事給我做。我回來後會做我該做的。

Q: What is the man probably going to do now?
這位男士現在可能要做什麼？

A. Take the dog for a walk.
B. Help to clean the kitchen.
C. Buy some chicken on his way back.

A. 帶狗去散步。
B. 幫忙清理廚房。
C. 在回來的路上買一些雞肉。

詳解 　　　　　　　　　　　　　　　　　　　　　　　**答案：A**

　　從選項都是動詞可推測，題目會問與「做什麼」相關的問題。聽到 What ~ man ~ do now 可知，主要是問男士現在要做什麼。男士一開始說要去溜狗，而女士說 I need to clean the kitchen（清理廚房），男士接著說 Leave something for me ~ I will do my part when I come back.，表示男士回來後才會幫忙做家事，所以現在應該會去溜狗。選項 C 故意用 kitchen（廚房）和 chicken（雞肉）的發音相似性來讓考生搞混，是錯誤選項。

Q22

Woman: What? I can't believe you are using such a thick dictionary.
　　　　什麼？我不敢相信你在用這麼厚的字典。

Man: 　 What's wrong with that? This book used to belong to my uncle.
　　　　這有什麼不對嗎？這以前是我叔叔用的。

Woman: Every word you need to look up is on my cell phone.
　　　　Welcome to the twenty-first century.
　　　　你想要查的每一個單字都在我的手機裡。歡迎來到二十一世紀。

Q: What does the woman suggest the man do?
這位女士建議這位男士做什麼？

A. Lend her the dictionary.
B. Look up new words with a cell phone.
C. Call his uncle.

A. 借她字典。
B. 用手機查生字。
C. 打電話給他的叔叔。

詳解 　　　　　　　　　　　　　　　　　　　　　　　**答案：B**

　　從選項都是動詞可推測，題目會問與「做什麼」相關的問題。聽到 What ~ suggest ~ man do 可知，主要是問給男士什麼建議。對話一開始可知，男士在用一般的書籍字典，女士則說 Every word ~ need to look up is in ~ cell phone.，表示用她的手機就可以查單字，不用再拿厚厚的字典，最後一句的「歡迎來到二十一世紀」是指要這位男士多利用新科技，也就是使用手機，因此正確答案是 B。

|單字片語| **thick** [θɪk] 厚的 / **dictionary** [ˋdɪkʃənˌɛrɪ] 字典 / **What's wrong with** ～有什麼不對嗎？ / **look up** 查詢（單字） / **century** [ˋsɛntʃʊrɪ] 世紀

Q23

Man: This wall you see here was built more than two hundred years ago.　你在這裡看到的牆是兩百多年前建造的。

Woman: What do those Chinese words up there mean?
上面那些中文字是什麼意思？

Man: It says this is the south gate. Please follow me.
它説這是南門。請跟我來。

> **Q: What most likely is the man?**
> **這位男士最有可能是做什麼的？**
>
> A. He is a guide.　　　　　　A. 他是一名導遊。
> B. He is a salesman.　　　　　B. 他是一名售貨員。
> C. He is a lawyer.　　　　　　C. 他是一名律師。

詳解　　　　　　　　　　　　　　　　　　　　　答案：A

　　從選項都是「He is + 職業別」可推測，題目會問與男士工作相關的問題。聽到 What ~ is the man 可知，主要是問男士的職業。從有兩百多年歷史的牆、解釋文字的意義，以及對女士説 Please follow me 可知，説話者正在參觀某古蹟，而這位男士應該是一名導遊。

|單字片語| **build** [bɪld] 建造 / **south** [saʊθ] 南方 / **gate** [get] 門

Q24

Woman: Look at my little pet. Isn't it cute?
你看我的小寵物。牠很可愛，對吧？

Man: It's lovely. What does it eat? Hi, little guy. Ouch! It bit me.
牠好可愛。牠吃什麼？嗨，小傢伙。哎呀！牠咬我。

Woman: You have to be gentle with it.　你必須對牠溫柔一點。

Q: What are the speakers talking about?
說話者在談論什麼？

A. A kind of food.
B. A baby boy.
C. An animal.

A. 一種食物。
B. 一個男嬰。
C. 一隻動物。

詳解

答案：C

聽到 What ~ talking about 可知，主要是問對話中討論的內容。從 pet、What does it eat? 可知，對話中提到的是一隻寵物，也就是一種動物。

Q25

Man: Your skin is a little dry. How many glasses of water do you drink a day?　你的皮膚有點乾。你一天喝幾杯水？

Woman: Not many (glasses). I keep going to the bathroom if I drink too much.　不多。如果我喝太多水，我會一直上廁所。

Man: Drinking enough water is very important for your skin.
喝足夠的水對皮膚是很重要的。

Q: What is the woman's problem?
這位女士的問題是什麼？

A. She needs to go to the bathroom.
B. She needs to drink more water.
C. She needs to buy some glasses.

A. 她需要去上廁所。
B. 她需要多喝水。
C. 她需要買一些杯子。

詳解

答案：B

從選項都是 She needs 可推測，題目會問與「女士該做什麼」相關的問題。對話一開始男士對女士說 skin ~ dry（皮膚乾燥），並問到 How many glasses of water ~ drink（一天喝幾杯水），而女士則回答 Not much，由此可知女士皮膚比較乾燥是因為水喝得比較少，也就是需要多喝水的意思。

|單字片語| **skin** [skɪn] 皮膚 / **dry** [draɪ] 乾的

第 1 回
第 2 回
第 3 回
第 4 回
第 5 回
第 6 回

第四部分 短文聽解

Q26

For question number 26, please look at the three pictures.

Please listen to the following announcement. 請聽以下的廣播。

Where might you probably hear this announcement?
你可能會在哪裡聽到這個廣播？

Attention all passengers. This is your Captain speaking. Welcome aboard flight TZ 730. Please put on your safety belt whenever the seat belt sign is on. We will land in Sydney 10 minutes earlier than we are expected. In the meantime, enjoy the refreshments that the flight attendants will bring to you shortly.

各位乘客請注意。我是您的機長。歡迎搭乘 TZ 730 班機。每當安全帶警示燈亮起時，請繫好安全帶。我們將比預期時間早十分鐘抵達雪梨。在此同時，請享用空服人員即將為您帶來的點心和飲料。

A.

B.

C.

詳解

答案：C

從圖片可推測，題目內容與交通工具有關。從 Where ~ this announcement? 可知，題目是問廣播進行的地點。從 Attention all passengers（各位乘客請注意）、captain（機長）和 Welcome aboard flight（歡迎搭乘班機），可判斷這段廣播會在飛機上聽到，所以答案是 C。

|單字片語| **passenger** [ˋpæsəndʒɚ] 乘客 / **captain** [ˋkæptɪn] 機長 / **aboard** [əˋbord] 搭乘 / **safety belt** 安全帶 / **whenever** [hwɛnˋɛvɚ] 每當 / **in the meantime** 同時 / **refreshment** [rɪˋfrɛʃmənt] 點心 / **flight attendant** 空服人員 / **shortly** [ˋʃɔrtlɪ] 立刻，馬上，不久

For question number 27, please look at the three pictures.

Please listen to the following short talk. 請聽以下的簡短談話。

What is NOT needed to make this dish?
做這道菜餚不需要什麼？

Hi, everyone. Thanks for watching *Healthy Food Healthy Life*. I am your host, Judy. Today, I will show you how to make a delicious salad. We will use lots of lettuce and some other vegetables you can see here. We will also need a boiled egg so you won't feel hungry too quickly. Now, the most important part: the salad dressing. Yes, instead of using salad dressings that are ready-made, we are going to make our own salad dressing.

大家好。感謝收看「健康食品、健康生活」的節目。我是各位的主持人 Judy。今天，我要示範如何製作美味的沙拉。我們將使用您在這裡可以看到的許多生菜和其他蔬菜。我們也需要一個水煮蛋，這樣您才不會太快感覺到餓。現在，最重要的部分：醬料。是的，與其使用現成的醬料，我們要製作我們自己的沙拉搭配醬料。

A.   B.   C.

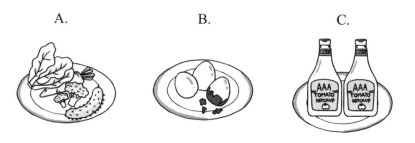

詳解　　　　　　　　　　　　　　　　　　　　　　**答案：C**

　　從圖片可推測，題目內容與食物有關。從 What ~ not needed ~ make ~ dish 可知，這題是問這道菜餚「不需要」什麼。從 how to make a delicious salad 可知，要做的菜餚是沙拉，接著又說 We will use ~ vegetables ~ also need a boiled egg，可知雞蛋和蔬菜是必要的。說話者最後提到會用自製的醬料（instead of using salad dressings ~ ready-made, we are going to make our own salad dressing），沒提到會用到現成的番茄醬（ketchup），C 是答案。

|單字片語| **dish** [dɪʃ] 菜餚 / **lettuce** [ˋlɛtɪs] 生菜，萵苣 / **boiled** [bɔɪld] 水煮的，煮沸的 / **ready-made** 現成的 / **salad dressing** 生菜沙拉用的醬料

第 1 回
第 2 回
第 3 回
第 4 回
第 5 回
第 6 回

Q28

For question number 28, please look at the three pictures.

Please listen to the following short talk.　請聽以下的簡短談話。

What might Lisa be wearing now?
Lisa 現在可能身穿什麼？

　　Lisa, why are you wearing shorts and a T-shirt now? I thought you are going to the graduation party tonight? I know that you hate to wear a dress but come on, the party will be held at a five-star hotel. This evening dress will make you look like a princess.

　　Lisa，你為什麼現在還穿著短褲和 T 恤？我以為你今晚要去畢業派對？我知道你討厭穿洋裝，但是派對將在五星級飯店舉辦。這套晚禮服會讓你看起來像公主一樣。

A.

B.

C.

詳解

答案：A

　　從圖片可推測，題目內容與穿著有關。一開始提到 Lisa，是談話的聽者，接著問「你為什麼現在還穿著短褲和 T 恤？」，表示 Lisa 現在正穿著短褲和 T 恤（shorts and a T-shirt），題目問到 Lisa 現在的穿著，所以答案是 A。晚禮服（evening dress）是晚上去畢業派對才需要穿的。

|單字片語| **shorts** [ʃɔrts] 短褲 / **graduation** [ˌgrædʒʊˋeʃən] 畢業 / **princess** [ˋprɪnsɪs] 公主

For question number 29, please look at the three pictures.

Please listen to the following talk.　請聽以下的簡短談話。

What is the speaker?
說話者是做什麼的？

　　I believe that an operation is the last choice we have. This is the patient's only chance. I understand that it will be hard for the family to see their child without an arm. However, if we wait any longer, the poor kid will lose his life. If they agree to it, I can begin the operation right away.

　　我相信動手術是最後的選擇。這是病人唯一的希望。我明白家屬很難接受看到自己的孩子少一隻手臂。然而，如果我們再等待的話，這可憐的孩子會失去生命。如果他們同意，我會立刻動手術。

A. 　　　B. 　　　C.

詳解　　　　　　　　　　　　　　　　　　　　　　　　　　　答案：A

　　從圖片可推測，題目內容與職業有關。從 What ~ speaker? 可知，主要是問說話者的職業身分。從說話者提到的 operation（手術）和 patient（病患），以及 I can begin the operation（我會開始動手術）可推斷，說話者是醫生。

|單字片語| **operation** [ɑpəˋreʃən] 手術 / **agree** [əˋgri] 同意 / **right away** 立刻 / **patient** [ˋpeʃənt] 病人

Q30

For question number 30, please look at the three pictures.

Please listen to the following short talk.　請聽以下的簡短談話。

What are the people celebrating?
這些人在慶祝什麼？

　　I am sick of dressing up as Santa Claus every year. I think the children are too old to enjoy candy, so I am not going to buy any. We can still decorate the house and the Christmas tree because our neighbors will surely do it. One more thing, let's eat out for a change. I don't mind preparing dinner but I hate to do the dishes.

　　我每年都扮聖誕老人，讓我感到很膩了。我想孩子們也大了，不會再喜歡糖果，所以我不會再買。我們還是可以佈置房子與聖誕樹，因為鄰居們一定會這麼做。還有一件事，我們換個方式，出去外面吃吧。我不介意準備晚餐，但是我討厭洗碗。

A.

B.

C.

詳解　　　　　　　　　　　　　　　　　　　　　　　　　　　**答案：B**

　　從圖片可推測，題目內容可能與節日有關。而且從 What ~ celebrating? 可知，主要是問正在為了什麼而慶祝。一開始提到 Santa Claus（聖誕老人）、Christmas tree（聖誕樹），由此可知，正要為聖誕節而慶祝，所以圖片中有聖誕樹的 B 是答案。

〈詳細補充〉

　　關於西方主要的節日中，在萬聖節（Halloween）時會看到扮鬼的人提南瓜燈，在聖誕節（Christmas）會有聖誕樹和聖誕老人，而在感恩節（Thanksgiving）時會有火雞大餐。

|單字片語| **Santa Claus** 聖誕老人 / **decorate** [ˋdɛkəˌret] 佈置 / **surely** [ˋʃʊrlɪ] 一定 / **one more thing** 還有一件事 / **mind** [maɪnd] 介意 / **prepare** [prɪˋpɛr] 準備 / **eat out** 吃外食，出去吃

初試 閱讀測驗 解析

第一部分 / 詞彙

Q1

Put the plastic bottles into the _____ bin so we can make them into something useful.

把塑膠瓶放入資源回收桶，這樣我們可以把它們製成有用的東西。

A. cleaning 清潔　　　　　　B. recycling 回收
C. holding 握著；裝著　　　　D. washing 清洗

詳解　　　　　　　　　　　　　　　　　　　　答案：B

　　這題考的是慣用語與整個句意的理解。空格前面提到「把塑膠瓶放入」，而後面是 bin（桶子），後面又說 make ~ something useful（變成有用的東西），可以得知答案是 recycling bin。cycle 是循環的意思，而 recycle 則是回收再利用，資源循環的意思。

Q2

It didn't _____ to him that yesterday was his wife's birthday.

他沒想到昨天是他太太的生日。

A. think 認為；思考；想　　　B. realize 發現；領悟到
C. happen 發生　　　　　　　D. occur 想到；發生

詳解　　　　　　　　　　　　　　　　　　　　答案：D

　　這題考的是單字與語意。選項都是動詞，空格後面是 to him（對他）以及「昨天是他太太的生日」。由於最前面的主詞 it 在這裡所指的對象不明確，所以可理解為虛主詞。think 和 realize 要跟對象明確的主詞搭配，如 John、we 等等，所以 A, B 不正確。it + happen + to 人表示「發生在人身上」的意思，與後面內容語意不符，而 it + occur + 人是「想到」的意思，通常跟 suddenly（突然）搭配，形容某人突然想到某件事。用在否定句時，則表示原本應該想到的事情，卻完全沒想到。請見以下例句：

It suddenly occurred to him that he left his wallet at home.
他突然想到他把錢包留在家裡。
It didn't occur to him that he took the wrong lunch box home.
他完全沒想到他拿錯餐盒回家。

Q3

What does the sign over there _____? I can't make it out because some letters are missing.

那裡的標誌在說什麼？我看不出來，因為有些字母不見了。

A. say 說　　　　　　　　　B. tell 告訴
C. write 寫　　　　　　　　D. learn 學會

詳解　　　　　　　　　　　　　　　　　　　　答案：A

　　這題考的是慣用語。選項都是動詞，空格前面的主詞是 the sign（標誌）。我們要表達「此標誌在寫什麼」時，英文要理解為「此標誌在說（say）什麼？」，所以答案是 A。而要表達「看懂」標誌，動詞則是用 read。例如 Can't you read the sign? It says, "No smoking."（你看不懂標誌嗎？上面寫著：請勿吸菸）。同樣的，在英文的邏輯中，我們會說信裡在「說（say）」什麼，而不是「寫（write）」什麼。

│單字片語│ **make out** 了解，辨認 / **letter** [ˈlɛtɚ] 字母 / **missing** 不見的

Q4

Excuse me. I am going to the central library. Which stop should I _____?

抱歉。我要去中央圖書館。我應該在哪一站下車？

A. get up 起來　　　　　　　B. get off 下車
C. get down 下去　　　　　　D. get away 逃走

詳解　　　　　　　　　　　　　　　　　　　　答案：B

　　這題考的是片語的理解。選項都是與 get 相關的片語，空格前面提到「要去圖書館，應該要在哪一站…」，選項中最合理的是「get off 下車」。up 是上，down 是下，off 是離開，away 是離開，但與 get 結合之後，get up 是起床的意思，get down 是下來的意思。get on 是上車，get off 是下車。

第 1 回
第 2 回
第 3 回
第 4 回
第 5 回
第 6 回

Q5

Taking the plane will help us _____ some time though we have to pay more for it.

搭飛機會幫助我們節省一點時間,雖然我們要付更多錢。

A. spend 花費　　　　　　　B. make 製造;使
C. use 使用　　　　　　　　D. save 省;存;救

詳解 答案:D

　　這題考的是動詞與語意的理解。選項都是動詞,空格前後提到 help us ~ some time(幫助~一些時間),又用 though 表達轉折語氣,並提到「雖然要付更多錢」,因此 save 是適合的答案。

詳細補充

　　save 的意思很多,這裡的 save time 是「節省時間」的意思。以下是 save 的其他表達。
Save up for rainy days. 未雨綢繆。
Save me! 救我!
Save the cake for me. 把蛋糕留給我。

Q6

The children were playing and shouting _____ doing their homework.

孩子們正在玩和喊叫,而不是做功課。

A. so that 這樣才能　　　　B. for example 例如
C. instead of 而不是　　　　D. such as 例如

詳解 答案:C

　　這題考的是連接詞。空格前面是一個完整的子句,後面則是一個以動名詞開始的動詞片語。從選項來看,so that 後面要接子句。for example 通常放到句尾,或是放在句中(前後會有逗號),或是句首(後面會有逗號),所以 A、B 在用法上都不正確。空格前面提到孩子在玩和喊叫,後面是做功課,用 such as 在語意上不通順,選項中只有 C 最通順。

詳細補充

　　instead of 是高中很常見的連接詞,若把 instead of 拿到句首,會比較容易理解。就題目這個句子,我們可以把 instead of~ 這部分內容放到句首:
Instead of doing their homework, the children were playing and shouting.
孩子們沒有在做功課,反而是在玩和喊叫。

Q7

All of us will have to do our _____ if we want to win the next game.

如果我們要贏得下一場比賽的話，我們所有人都需要盡自己的本分。

A. life 生命　　　　　　　　B. part 部分；本分
C. role 角色　　　　　　　　D. event 事件

詳解　　　　　　　　　　　　　　　　　　　　　答案：B

　　這題考的是慣用語。選項都是名詞，空格前面是主要動詞 have to do + our，而後面提到「如果要贏得下一場比賽的話」，可知前一子句要表達「盡本分」，慣用的表達是 do one's part，答案是 B。do one's part（盡某人本分）可理解為做自己該做的部分（part）、分內的事。而 role（角色）要搭配動詞 play（扮演）。例如，要表達「扮演重要的角色」時，會說 play an important role。

Q8

His mother _____ him go to cram schools after school. He has no time for himself.

他的媽媽要他放學後都到補習班。他沒有自己的時間。

A. wants 想要　　　　　　　B. asks 請
C. suggests 建議　　　　　　D. makes 使

詳解　　　　　　　　　　　　　　　　　　　　　答案：D

　　這題考的是使役動詞，重點是空格後面的受詞 him 和原形動詞 go。want 和 ask 後面接受詞 + to V。suggest 後面主要是用主詞（he）引導一子句而非受詞 + 動詞原形。只有 make 是後面接受詞 + 動詞原形，所以答案為 D。像是 make 這類使役動詞的，還有 let、have 和 help，後面都接受詞和原形動詞。

使役動詞	意志動詞
His mom **made** him study hard.	His mom **suggested** that he study hard.

Q9

Amy: My mom bought me a watch. Emily: _____

Amy: 我媽買了一支錶給我。　Emily: 真是好看的手錶！

A. What a nice watch!　　　　B. What is nice a watch!
C. How a nice watch!　　　　D. How nice is the watch!

這題考的是驚嘆句的用法。選項中有 what 和 how 引導的驚嘆句,從題目可知 Emily 要針對 Amy 提到的手錶表達讚美。而驚嘆句有兩種,一種用How...!,另一種用 What...!,其組成結構如下表:

How...! 驚嘆句	What...! 驚嘆句
How + 形容詞(+ 主詞 + 動詞)!	What + 不定冠詞 + 形容詞 + 名詞 !
How cute! How cute your dog is!	What a cute dog! What a cute dog it is!

因此 A 的 What + a nice watch!是正確答案。若要改成 How 的話,就會用 How nice! 或是 How nice the/your watch is!。

On my way home last night, I _____ an old classmate.
昨晚在回家的路上,我遇到一位老同學。

A. ran into 遇見;撞到　　　　　B. ran out of 用完
C. ran away 逃走　　　　　　　D. ran after 追逐

詳解

這題考的是動詞片語。選項都是與 run 相關的片語,空格前面提到在回家路上,後面是一位同學,由此可知最合理的動詞是「遇見」,A 是正確答案。動詞片語 run into 和 bump into 的意思與用法一樣,都表示「遇見」「撞到」。

◁補充例句▷

I saw the car bump into the tree. 我看到那台車子撞到樹。
I saw the car run into the tree. 我看到那台車子撞到樹。

第二部分 段落填空

Questions 11-14

Is taking a nap (11) necessary? Why is it that people in Western cultures do not have to take an afternoon nap in order to work better? In Asia, people of different races have the habit of taking a nap after lunch. It (12) is believed that a short rest after eating is helpful for both body and mind. For (13) those who work outdoors, taking a break during noontime to avoid the terrible heat sounds perfectly reasonable. However, questions are raised when office workers in the comfort of air-conditioning are found sleeping for hours after lunch. As for students, some complained of tiredness on days when they did not take a nap while others mentioned that (14) they feel more tired after taking a nap. In short, old habits die hard. It will be hard to make people believe that they do not need a nap.

睡午覺是有必要的嗎？為什麼西方文化的人們不需要睡午覺以獲得更好的工作品質？在亞洲，不同種族的人都有午餐過後睡午覺的習慣。據說，飯後休息一下對身體和腦袋都有幫助。對於那些在戶外工作的人，為了避開難受的熱氣而在午餐時間休息，聽起來完全合理。不過，在冷氣房的辦公室員工，被發現在午餐之後一睡就睡上好幾個小時，卻引起一些質疑。至於學生，有些人抱怨在沒有睡午覺的那天會感到疲倦，而其他的學生卻說睡完午覺之後更累。簡言之，習慣是根深蒂固的。要讓人們相信不需要睡午覺，這是很難的。

Q11

A. careful 小心的
B. necessary 必要的；需要的
C. actual 真實的
D. greedy 貪心的

詳解　　　　　　　　　　　　　　　　　　　　　　　　　　　答案：B

這題考的是形容詞。選項都是形容詞，就語意上來說，B 比較通順，而且從後面的 Why ~ people in Western cultures do not have to take an afternoon nap ~? 中的 do not have to 可判斷，與其相呼應的是 necessary。

|單字片語| necessary [ˋnɛsəˌsɛrɪ] 必要的 / **not necessarily** 非必要 / **necessity** [nəˋsɛsətɪ] 必需品

175

Q12

A. believes   B. is believed
C. was believed   D. has believed

詳解   答案：B

　　這題考的是動詞用法。選項都是與 believe 相關的用法，空格前面是主詞 it，後面是一個 that 引導的子句，可以得知這裡的 it 是虛主詞（代替後面的 that 子句），我們可以把本句看成：(That a short rest after eating is helpful ~) is believed.，括弧裡面的就是真主詞。

it is believed that ~ 同時也是常用的慣用語，可理解成「～被大家相信」，所以要用被動語態，其他的相似用法還有：It is said that...（據說）、It is seen as...（被視為）。

Q13

A. they   B. them
C. those   D. that

詳解   答案：C

　　看到空格後面的關係代名詞 who，可判斷這是關係子句。從關係代名詞 who 可知空格提到的對象是人，所以空格位置應該是 those people，也就是 For those people who work outdoors（對於那些在戶外工作的人），而 people 可以省略，所以答案為 those。

〈補充例句〉

For those of you who like dogs, here is some good news.
對於你們那些愛狗的人來說，這裡有一些好消息。

Q14

A. they believe that going to bed early is a good habit
   他們相信早睡是一個好習慣

B. the early bird catches the worm
   早起的鳥兒有蟲吃

C. sleeping for hours after lunch is acceptable
   午睡幾個小時是可以接受的

D. they feel more tired after taking a nap
   睡完午覺之後更累

詳解

　　空格前面是用 while 連接的兩個句子，透過 while 可推測 while 前後的兩個句子句意是相反的。while 前面提到「有些人抱怨在沒有睡午覺的那天會感到疲倦」，因此可以推測空格的內容與「抱怨沒睡午覺」語意會是相反。從選項可知，與前句相反的是：睡完午覺之後更累，故答案選 D.。

Questions 15-18

　　On his way home yesterday, Kevin noticed a brown wallet on a bench in the park. He thought perhaps he should open the wallet and see who it (15) belongs to. As soon as he picked up the wallet, a man appeared (16) all of a sudden. "Got you. You are a thief. You stole my wallet. I took a picture of you holding it." Kevin was at a loss for (17) words. Before he could say anything, the man said, "I will forgive you if you pay me a thousand dollars. But if you refuse, I will make a police report." (18) Kevin soon realized what this was all about. The guy was a conman, a liar. "Yes, please call the police. In fact, I will do it for you." Kevin said, without showing any fear. The man looked shocked. He grabbed the wallet and ran away.

　　在回家的路上，Kevin 注意到公園的長椅上有一個皮夾。他認為或許他應該打開來看看這個皮夾是屬於誰的。他一撿起皮夾，一個男子突然出現。「抓到你了。你是小偷。你偷了我的錢包。我剛剛拍了一張你拿著皮夾的照片。」Kevin 完全說不出話來。在他還沒能說出什麼之前，該男子對他說：「如果你付我一千元，我就原諒你。但是如果你不這麼做，我就報警。」Kevin 馬上明白這是怎麼一回事。這個傢伙是個騙子。「好吧，請報警。事實上，我挺想幫你報的。」Kevin 毫無恐懼地說。那個男子看起來很震驚。他搶走皮夾並逃走。

Q15

A. returns 歸還；回到　　　　B. belongs 屬於
C. happens 發生　　　　　　D. spreads 蔓延；擴散

詳解

　　這題考的是動詞。空格後面是 to，前面有一子句 he should open the wallet and see 以及用 who 引導的名詞子句 who it ~ to，作為 see 的受詞。這裡的 it 是指前面的 wallet，若還原成 open the wallet and see who **the wallet** ~ to，可知最通順的動詞是 belongs to。

|單字片語| **belong to** 屬於 / **belonging** [bəˋlɔŋɪŋ] 隨身物品 / **a sense of belonging** 歸屬感

Q16

A. all of a sudden
B. all the suddenly
C. in a sudden
D. in suddenly

詳解

這題考的是副詞片語。英文表達「突然間」的正確用法只有兩個 suddenly 和 all of a sudden。所以答案是 A。

Q17

A. events 事件；賽事
B. records 紀錄
C. ideas 點子
D. words 文字；話語

詳解

這題考的是慣用語。選項都是名詞，空格前面是 at a loss for，而從前後文也可判斷 Kevin 這時不知道要說什麼，表達「無話可說」時英文用 at a loss for words。假如沒學過 at a loss for words 此慣用語，可從前後文猜測 Kevin 此時應無話可說，所以要選出與「話語」相關的 words。

補充說明

word 除了有「單字」的意思之外，也表示「話語」，西方也有人言為信的概念。請見以下例句：
He is a man of his word. 他是個說到做到的人。
You can't go back on your word. 你不能食言。

Q18

A. The man run out of the money. 那男子把錢花完了。
B. A guy then contacted the owner of the wallet.
　有一個人接著聯絡了皮夾的主人。
C. Kevin immediately went back home. Kevin 立刻回家。
D. Kevin soon realized what this was all about.
　Kevin 馬上明白這是怎麼一回事。

詳解

空格前面是一位男子針對Kevin撿皮夾的行為所講的話，威脅Kevin付男子錢，不然就會報警。空格後面的內容則提到此男子是個騙子，而且Kevin也完全不害怕，反而是男子嚇得逃跑，可知空格應該是要說Kevin 明白這是一場騙局，故正確答案為D。

Questions 19-21

X-Market Recommended items

ITEMS	PRICE
A carton of milk	$ 80
A bunch of bananas	$ 110
A box of cookies	$ 90
A loaf of bread	$ 100

X 超市推薦商品

品項	價格
一盒牛奶	80 元
一串香蕉	110 元
一盒餅乾	90 元
一條麵包	100 元

第 1 回
第 2 回
第 3 回
第 4 回
第 5 回
第 6 回

NOTICE

Welcome shoppers:

Starting from next Sunday, we will extend our opening hours. We will be open from 7:00 in the morning until eleven at night. Also, for your shopping convenience, we will be open seven days a week. In other words, there will be no day-off on Monday anymore. And please note that only on Sundays, customers who arrive during the first thirty minutes after the doors open will get a 10% discount coupon. It can be used on any items except dairy goods.

公告

歡迎各位購物者：

從下週日起，我們將延長我們的營業時間。我們將從早上 7 點營業到晚上 11 點。同時，為了您購物方便，我們一週營業七天。換句話說，取消了原本每週一的休息日。另外請注意，僅限每週日，凡在本店開門後的前三十分鐘內抵達的顧客，都將獲得打九折的折價券。它可以用於除了乳製品之外的任何品項上。

What is the main idea of this notice?
這份公告的主旨是？

A. Hire more employees. 雇用更多員工。
B. Give information on new goods. 提供新商品的資訊。
C. Recommend a new branch of X-Market. 推薦X超市的新分店。
D. Inform the change of business hours. 告知營業時間的變更。

詳解

在第二篇文的公告中提到 from next Sunday, we will extend our opening hours... open from 7:00 in the morning until eleven at night... will be open seven days a week. ，主要是提到營業時間的更動。故答案選 D。

第 1 回

第 2 回

第 3 回

第 4 回

第 5 回

第 6 回

Q20

How much does a customer with a coupon pay if he buys a carton of milk?

假如一位擁有折價券的顧客要買一盒牛奶，他要付多少錢？

A. $ 100. 100元。
B. $ 80. 80元。
C. $ 90. 90元。
D. $ 72. 72元。

詳解 　　　　　　　　　　　　　　　　　　　　　　　　　　　　答案：B

　　在第二篇文的公告中提到 customers who arrive during the first thirty minutes after the doors open will get a 10% discount coupon... used on any items except dairy goods. ，提到折價券可用在任何品項上，除了乳製品之外，所以題目問到的牛奶並無打折。表格中 A carton of milk 所對應的是 $ 80。故答案選 B.。

Q21

Which of the following statements is NOT true?

下列敘述何者有誤？

A. X-Market used to have a day-off on Mondays.
　 X 超市之前在每週一是休息不營業的。
B. Customers can shop at X-Market on Tuesday and Saturday afternoon.
　 顧客可以在週二與週六下午於 X 超市購物。
C. Two boxes of cookies cost one hundred and eighty dollars.
　 兩盒餅乾要 180 元。
D. Shoppers who come at 8:00 in the morning on Sundays can get a coupon.
　 每週日早上 8 點來的購物者，可以得到一張折價券。

詳解 　　　　　　　　　　　　　　　　　　　　　　　　　　　　答案：D

　　在第二篇文的公告中提到，And please note that only on Sundays, customers who arrive during the first thirty minutes after the doors open will get a 10% discount coupon. ，表示凡在本店開門後的前三十分鐘內抵達的顧客，都可獲得折扣券，由於本文一開始提到 We will be open from 7:00 in the morning，即從早上 7 點開始營業，而開門後三十分鐘內抵達，也就是指早上 7 點半前到，而非 8 點前到，故答案選 D。

|單字片語| opening hour 營業時間 / coupon 折價券 / dairy goods 乳製品

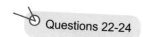

Photography Competition
攝影比賽

Attractive cash prizes and discount vouchers to be won!

See your pictures printed on magazines with your name on them.

贏得吸引人的獎金和折價券！

會在各雜誌上看到你的照片和名字。

Details:

No limit on types of cameras used

Each participant can send up to three digital photos.

Send your pictures to nicepics4u@yahoo.com.tw.

Each picture must be not more than 25 megabytes.

Winners will be informed by email.

細節：

不限所要使用的相機款式。

每位參賽者最多可傳送三張數位相片。

將相片寄至 nicepics4u@yahoo.com.tw

每張照片的大小不能超過 25M。

優勝者將會以電子郵件通知。

|單字片語| **photography** [fə`tɑgrəfɪ] 攝影 / **competition** [.kɑmpə`tɪʃən] 比賽 / **attractive** [ə`træktɪv] 吸引人的 / **voucher** [`vaʊtʃə] 折價券 / **participant** [pɑr`tɪsəpənt] 參賽者 / **digital** [`dɪdʒɪtəl] 數位的 / **be informed** 被通知

第 1 回
第 2 回
第 3 回
第 4 回
第 5 回
第 6 回

Q22

Which is NOT an advantage of taking part in the competition?

哪一個不是參加比賽的好處？

A. Win some money.

贏得獎金

B. See your works on magazines.

看到自己的作品在雜誌上

C. Get a new camera. 得到新的相機

D. Show off your talent. 展現自己的才華

詳解　　　　　　　　　　　　　　　　　　　　　　　　　答案：C

　　從 Which ~ NOT ~ advantage of ~ competition 可知，主要是問何者不是比賽的好處。一開始提到此比賽有機會贏得獎金和折價券，還可以看到自己的名字、自己拍出的相片作品印在雜誌上，這也是展現出自己的才華，所以 A、B、D 都是好處，但並沒有提到可以贏得新的相機。

Q23

What is true about the rules above?

關於以上規則，什麼是屬實的？

A. Only certain cameras are allowed.

只允許使用某些相機。

B. There is no limit on the number of photos you can send.

你可以寄的照片數量無限。

C. The picture you send must be less than 25 megabytes.

所寄的照片必須低於 25M。

D. You have to sign your name on the back of each photo.

你必須在相片背後簽名。

詳解　　　　　　　　　　　　　　　　　　　　　　　　　答案：C

　　從 What ~ true ~ rules 可知，主要是問關於文中提到的規則內容。文中提到不限相機款式（No limit on types of cameras used）、最多可傳送三張數位相片（send up to three digital photos），而且也沒提到要在相片背後簽名，唯獨 C 是正確答案。

Q24

How can we take part in the competition?
我們可以如何參加比賽？

A. By making a phone call. 透過打電話。
B. By visiting the store. 透過前往門市現場。
C. By sending an email. 透過寄電子郵件。
D. By faxing. 透過傳真。

詳解

題目問到參加比賽的辦法，文中提到 Each participant can send up to three digital photos. 及 Send your pictures to nicepics4u@yahoo.com.tw，可知是要透過寄電子郵件來參加比賽，故答案選 C。

Questions 25-27

Message For: Mr. Anderson
Time and Date: 12 March, 2016. 3:15 P.M.
Taken by: Derrick
From: Miss Tsai, ACC Company

訊息給：Anderson 先生
時間和日期：2016 年 3 月 12 日。下午 3 點 15 分。
接收訊息的人：Derrick
訊息來自：ACC 公司的蔡小姐

Message: My boss has agreed to purchase twenty chairs, two tables and one overhead projector for the conference room. Please make the delivery to our office on the 16th of March. I will be in the office. Someone needs to show me how to connect the projector to a laptop computer.

訊息：我老闆同意為會議室購買 20 張椅子，兩張桌子和一個投影機。請在 3 月 16 日把貨送到。我會在辦公室。需要有人教我如何連結投影機到筆電。

|單字片語| **overhead projector** 高射投影機 / **conference room** 會議室 / **delivery** [dɪˋlɪvərɪ] 寄送，投遞 / **connect** [kəˋnɛkt] 連接

Q25

What is the purpose of this message?

此訊息的目的是什麼？

    A. To place an order. 下訂單。

    B. To give advice on buying a projector. 針對購買投影機提供建議。

    C. To ask for a refund. 要求退款。

    D. To make an appointment. 預約。

詳解　　　　　　　　　　　　　　　　　　　　　

    題目問到訊息的目的，文中提到 has agreed to purchase twenty chairs... Please make the delivery to our office，可知寄件者的訊息主要是要跟收件者確定一筆訂單，也就是要下訂商品，故答案選 A。

Q26

Who received the message?

誰接收到此訊息？

    A. Mr. Anderson　Anderson 先生

    B. Derrick　Derrick

    C. Miss Tsai　蔡小姐

    D. The boss of ACC Company　ACC 公司的老闆

詳解　　　　　　　　　　　　　　　　　　　　　

    從 Who received ~ 可知，主要是問訊息接收者。Message For 表示此訊息的對象，Taken by 表示接收訊息的人，而 From 則是發出此訊息的人。因此訊息是由 Derrick 接收的（Taken by Derrick），正確答案是 B。

Q27

What does Mr. Anderson have to do on the 16th of March?

Anderson 先生在三月十六日當天必須做什麼？

    A. Call Miss Tsai back. 回電給蔡小姐。

    B. Buy a new laptop computer. 買一台新的筆記型電腦。

    C. Send some things to ACC Company. 將一些東西送到 ACC 公司。

    D. Hold a meeting in the conference room. 在會議室裡舉行會議。

詳解　　　　　　　　　　　　　　　　　　　　　　　答案：C

　　從 What ~ Anderson ~ do ~ 16 of March 可知，主要是問 3 月 16 日 Anderson 要做的事。已知 Anderson 是此訊息的對象。關於 the 16 of March 此日期，文中提到 Please make the delivery ~ on the 16th of March. I will be in the office.，表示請 Anderson 先生當天把某某東西送到，而發此訊息的人是 ACC 公司的蔡小姐，她當天會在 ACC 公司辦公室，所以是把東西送到 ACC 公司，C 是正確答案。

Questions 28-30

Dear Dad,

　　Mom is driving me crazy. I never expect senior high school to be such a nightmare! She makes me go to cram school every day, including the weekends! She makes sure the teachers in every cram school give me extra homework. It's not fair! Come on, Dad. How many hours a day do you work? I go to school at seven in the morning, followed by cram school until 9:30 p.m. That's more than fourteen hours of school a day. What's worse, I stay up until 2:00 a.m. to finish all the homework. Did I tell you about the tests? I have at least two or three tests a day. I have no time to rest or relax. The only thing I want to do on the weekend is get a little more sleep. Guess what? Mom had me signed up for three different cram schools on Saturday and another two on Sunday. I used to enjoy music lessons and drawing class but now I hate them.

　　You said you would be back by the end of this month. I hope you can keep your word. Please discuss this matter with Mom. She keeps reminding me that I am not an adult so I have to listen to her. I can't stand the stress much longer. Anyway, I wish you success in your business from your factory.

Yours sincerely,
Mike.

親愛的爸爸：

　　媽快把我逼瘋了。我從來沒想到高中是如此一場惡夢。她要我每天都去補習班，包含週末！她確認每間補習班老師給我額外的功課。這不公平！拜託，爸，你一天工作幾個小時？我早上七點去學校，接著到補習班，直到晚上九點半。那超過 14 個小時。更糟的是，我為了要完成所有的功課熬夜到凌晨兩點。我告訴過你關於測驗嗎？我一天至少有 2 到 3 個測驗。我沒有時間休息或放鬆。在週末

我唯一想要做的只是多睡一點。你知道嗎？媽為我在星期六報名了 3 個不同補習班的課程，星期天也有兩個課程。我之前很喜歡音樂和畫畫課，但現在很討厭。

你說你在月底會回來。我希望你遵守承諾。請跟媽媽討論這個問題。她一直提醒我，我還不是大人，所以我必須聽她的話。我快受不了這種壓力了。不管怎樣，我還是希望你在工廠那邊的事業順利。

Mike 敬上

|單字片語| **drive** [draɪv] 迫使 / **nightmare** [`naɪt,mɛr] 惡夢 / **what's worse** 更糟的是 / **sign up for** 報名… / **drawing** [`drɔɪŋ] 畫畫 / **discuss** [dɪ`skʌs] 討論 / **remind** [rɪ`maɪnd] 提醒

Q28

What does a nightmare in line 3 probably mean?

第三行的 nightmare 應該是什麼意思？

    A. Something terrible which happens in a dream or real life.
       一種發生在夢中或真實生活中可怕的事情。

    B. Something wonderful which happens in a dream or real life.
       一種發生在夢中或真實生活中美好的事情。

    C. An animal which only appears at night. 一種只有在晚上才出現的動物。

    D. A person who can help you solve your problems.
       一個可以幫你解決問題的人。

詳解　　　　　　　　　　　　　　　　　　　　　　　

    從信中得知，Mike 快被他媽媽逼瘋（driving me crazy），上了高中後天天要上補習班（go to cram school every day, including the weekends），忙得不可開交，壓力非常大（can't stand the stress much longer），可見 nightmare 是負面的東西。nightmare 的中文意思是「噩夢」或「夢魘」，最接近的解釋為 A。

Q29

What is true about Mike?

關於 Mike，何者正確？

    A. He doesn't have enough homework. 他的功課不夠多。

    B. He doesn't talk to his mother at all. 他都不跟他的媽媽說話。

    C. He doesn't like music lessons anymore. 他不再喜歡音樂課。

    D. He doesn't want his father to succeed. 他不想要他的父親成功。

主要是問選項中關於 Mike 與文章相符的內容。一開始可知 Mike 的功課很多，除了學校還有補習班的功課要寫（teachers in every cram school give me extra homework）。文章中並未提到 Mike 是否不跟他媽媽說話，最後也提到 I wish you success in your business.，表示祝福父親事業上成功，因此 A、B 和 D 都是錯的。從 I used to enjoy music lessons ~ but now I hate them.，表示 Mike 之前喜歡音樂，但現在卻很討厭，所以他不再喜歡音樂課。

Q30

What does Mike's father do for a living?

Mike 的父親是做什麼的？

A. He owns a factory. 他擁有一間工廠。

B. He owns a cram school. 他擁有一家補習班。

C. He is a teacher of a senior high school. 他是一所高中的老師。

D. He is a private tutor. 他是私人家教。

　　從 What ~ Mike's father do for a living 可知，主要是問 Mike 父親的職業。文章中提到 I wish you success in your business from your factory.，you business from your factory 指工廠的事業，可見 Mike 的父親擁有一間工廠。

全民英檢初級

第四回 初試 聽力測驗

TEST04.mp3

本測驗分四個部分，全部都是單選題，共 30 題，作答時間約 20 分鐘。作答說明為中文，印在試題冊上並經由光碟放音機播出。

第一部分　看圖辨義

共 5 題（為第 1 題至第 5 題）。每題請聽光碟放音機播出題目和三個英語句子之後，選出與所看到的圖畫最相符的答案。每題只播出**一遍**。

例題：（看）

（聽）　Look at the picture.
　　　　Which is the cheapest?
　　　　A.　The computer.
　　　　B.　The telephone.
　　　　C.　The TV set.

正確答案為 B，請在答案紙上塗黑作答。

A: <u>Question 1</u>

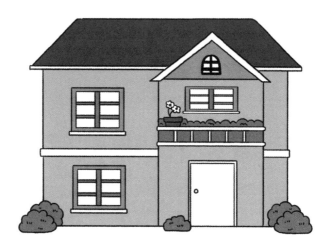

B: <u>Question 2</u>

C: Question 3

D: Question 4

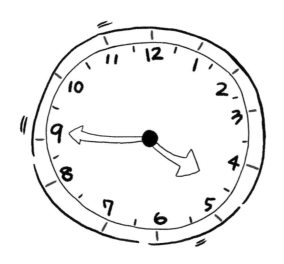

第二部分　問答

共 10 題（為第 6 題至第 15 題）。每題請聽光碟放音機播出的英語句子，再從試題冊上三個回答中，選出一個最適合的答案。每題只播出**一遍**。

例：　（聽）　Do you speak English?
　　　（看）　A.　No, I speak English quite well.
　　　　　　　B.　Yes, a little.
　　　　　　　C.　No, it's a useful language.

正確答案為 B，請在答案紙上塗黑作答。

6. A. Sure. Count me in.
　 B. Sure. It depends.
　 C. Sure. Leave me out.

7. A. I was.
　 B. I can.
　 C. I won't.

8. A. Why did it end so early?
　 B. What are we waiting for?
　 C. It starts today.

9. A. He just can't sit still.
　 B. We should pick him up at the airport.
　 C. I hope he gets well soon.

10. A. To experience different cultures.
　　B. To memorize every word.
　　C. To finish this school year.

11. A. You can hear the noise it makes.
　　B. You should clean it with soap.
　　C. You had better slow down and turn on the headlights.

12. A. Should I wear a tie?
　　B. Where are my jeans?
　　C. Don't you think the scene is beautiful?

13. A. I think something is burning.
　　B. I haven't told them about the fire.
　　C. I can't agree more.

14. A. Thank you. This is just what I want.
    B. I'm sorry. It's all my fault.
    C. Never mind. Don't do it again.

15. A. Let me introduce myself.
    B. You should be proud of yourself.
    C. There was a traffic jam.

第三部分 簡短對話

共 10 題（為第 16 題至第 25 題）。每題請聽光碟放音機播出一段對話和一個相關的問題後，再從試題冊上三個選項中，選出一個最適合的答案。每段對話和問題只播出<u>一遍</u>。

例： (聽) (Woman) Could I sit here?
(Man) I'm sorry, but this seat is occupied.

Question: Where do you think the dialogue takes place?

(看) A. In an office
B. In a taxi
C. In a restaurant.

正確答案為 C，請在答案紙上塗黑作答。

16. A. Computer knowledge.
B. Movie ticket information.
C. Physical exercise.

17. A. To play online games.
B. To take an exam.
C. To wake him up.

18. A. The man should have been honest.
B. The man should be jealous.
C. The man should help her with her schoolwork.

19. A. In the mountains.
B. By the lake.
C. At the beach.

20. A. She is a police officer.
B. She is a principal.
C. She is a secretary.

21. A. The man and the woman are in a cram school.
B. The man's math grade is worse than the woman's.
C. The man and the woman did poorly on a math test.

22. A. There is something wrong with the woman's eyes.
B. Mr. Chen should use a darker color.
C. The light in the room is not working.

23. A. He didn't gain any weight.
    B. He didn't control his diet.
    C. He didn't work out in the gym.

24. A. They will buy her a birthday present.
    B. They will get her some roses.
    C. They will take her to a restaurant for dinner.

25. A. The man wants the woman to return him the money.
    B. The man wants to lend her some money.
    C. The man hasn't returned the woman the money he borrowed.

第四部分　短文聽解

　　共 5 題（為第 26 題至第 30 題）。每題有三個圖片選項。請聽光碟放音機播出的題目，並選出一個最適當的圖片。每題只播出**一遍**。

例：（看）

A.   B.   C.

（聽）

Listen to the following short talk. What might Judy buy?

　　Judy is making a cake for her boyfriend. She checked her refrigerator and found that she had run out of sugar. But she still has lots of flour.

正確答案為 C，請在答案紙上塗黑作答。

Question 26

A.

B.

C.

Question 27

A.

B.

C.

Question 28

A.

B.

C.

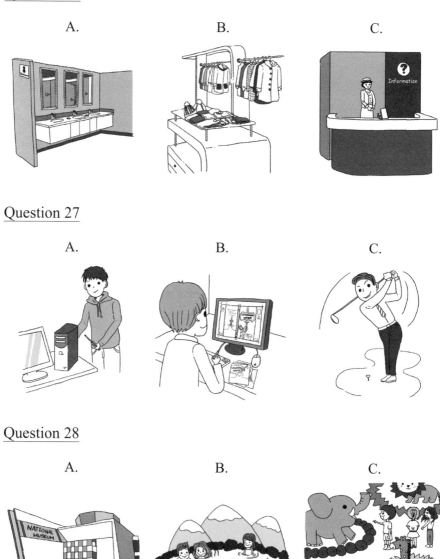

Question 29

A.

B.

C.

Question 30

A.

B.

C.

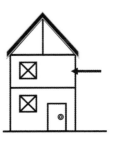

第四回 初級 閱讀測驗

本測驗分三部分，全部都是單選題，共 30 題，作答時間 35 分鐘。

第一部分：詞彙

共 10 題，每個題目裡有一個空格。請從四個選項中選出一個<u>最適合</u>題意的字或詞作答。

1. My parrot copied what I said _____ repeated it word for word.
   A. while   B. because
   C. and   D. if

2. This place is getting _____. A lot of people are waiting to see the fireworks. Let's find some seats before it is too late.
   A. damaged   B. interested
   C. crowded   D. polluted

3. After the terrible accident, those with serious injuries _____ to the nearest hospital at once.
   A. took   B. will take
   C. were taken   D. have taken

4. I would like to _____ you to my birthday party next week.
   A. visit   B. invite
   C. celebrate   D. report

5. The music is too loud. Could you _____ it _____ a little, please?
   A. turn; on   B. turn; off
   C. turn; down   D. turn; up

6. You have been living in Taiwan for many years, _____?
   A. don't you?   B. haven't you
   C. aren't you   D. won't you

7. I left my wallet here but now it is _____. Someone must have taken it.
   A. missing   B. disappearing
   C. running   D. preparing

8. Does the cell phone come _____ an extra battery?
   A. from   B. with
   C. out   D. in

9. _____ who are getting on the train should give way to those who are getting off.
   A. Passage   B. Passer-by
   C. Passionate   D. Passengers

10. He has a fever. He was _____ in the rain last night.
    A. dropped   B. caught
    C. fallen   D. held

第二部分：段落填空

共 8 題，包括二個段落，每個段落各含四個空格。每格均有四個選項，請依照文意選出**最適合**的答案。

Questions 11-14

_____(11)_____ of the hardest things to do is get along with your neighbors. The key to _____(12)_____ friendly neighbors is respect. Learn to respect others before you expect them to listen to you. Greet them whenever you see them, _____(13)_____ those who are elder. Give them a big warm smile. Share with them some gifts during special occasions such as Chinese New Year, Mid-autumn Festival or even Christmas.

It is common to have small disagreements. Understand that these little problems cannot be avoided but keep in mind that they are little problems, _____(14)_____. It is not worth the time and trouble getting angry over who is right and who is wrong.

11. A. One
    B. Some
    C. Any
    D. Both

12. A. have
    B. having
    C. be having
    D. have had

13. A. instead
    B. especially
    C. than
    D. however

14. A. so do not turn them into big problems
    B. but it is important to wear a smile
    C. in other words, it is lucky to have a friendly neighbor
    D. however, to get along well with your neighbors is hard

Questions 15-18

  I have never traveled to any foreign country. One reason is (15)
I do not want to spend so much money on air tickets. Another reason is I
think Taiwan is big and beautiful (16) . There are many parts of
Taiwan I have never set foot on.

  Last month, I visited Xitou in Nantou. It was located in the mountains
and the air was fresh. Despite the hot summer, it was cool and comfortable
in the forest. As a matter of fact, it got a little cold in the early morning as
the (17) dropped below twenty degrees Celsius. I took a lot of
pictures and my friends were amazed. (18) and it was hard to tell the
difference. Therefore, I would encourage you to visit every part of Taiwan
before you decide to travel abroad.

15. A. this
  B. that
  C. which
  D. why

16. A. yet
  B. though
  C. still
  D. enough

17. A. climate
  B. weather
  C. heat
  D. temperature

18. A. We compared these photos
   with those that my friends
   took in Switzerland
  B. My friends encouraged me
   to travel abroad
  C. It is highly recommended
   to visit Taiwan for your first
   travel this year
  D. We soon realized that these
   photos were lost

第三部分：閱讀理解

共 12 題，包括 4 個題組，每個題組含 1 至 2 篇短文，與數個相關的四選一的選擇題。請由試題冊上的選項中選出最適合的答案。

Questions 19-21 新題型

From:	sueroberts@cghadmin.com
To:	jeffreychen11058@gmail.com
CC:	
Subject:	Results of a checkup

Dear Jeffrey Chen,

We have the results of your checkup. Everything seems fine, except your blood sugar. That is a little high. Please make another appointment with Dr. Wu. He will talk with you about the test results and also give you some advice.

Thank you very much.

Sue Roberts
Administration
County General Hospital

County General Hospital Automated Booking Service		
Patient's Name	Doctor	Date/Time
Jeffrey Chen	**Dr. Wu**	**At 9:00 AM** **Wednesday May 5th**

19. Why did Sue Roberts write to Jeffrey Chen?
    A. To tell him about a health problem.
    B. To explain what blood sugar is.
    C. To suggest a treatment on blood sugar.
    D. To introduce a new hospital to him.

20. What will Jeffrey Chen do on Wednesday May 5th?
    A. Reschedule his doctor's appointment.
    B. Get some medical treatment suggestions.
    C Show up at 10:00 PM in County General Hospital.
    D. Meet Sue Roberts for a checkup.

21. Which of the following statements about Dr. Wu is correct?
    A. His blood pressure is too high.
    B. He did a checkup for himself.
    C. He will see his patient on May 5th.
    D. He hasn't worked in County General Hospital in a long time.

Euro dollars at all-time low
Now is the time to visit Europe

Twin package: NT$150,000 per person
Family package (at least four members): NT$135,000 per person.

10 Day Tour to Europe
All packages include air tickets, hotels, meals, transport and entrance fees to museums and amusement parks.

Tips for local guides at 20 Euros a day per person, including children.
Call Horizon Travel at 0800-330-XXX or surf our website below for more information.

www.horizontravel.com/home

---

22. Who is possibly interested in this advertisement?
    A. A traveler who gets lost.
    B. A newlywed couple who is planning a honeymoon travel.
    C. A graduate who is looking for a job.
    D. A mother who has difficulty with sleeping.

23. What is the main reason for traveling to Europe during this time?
    A. It is the peak season.
    B. It is less expensive.
    C. It is free of charge.
    D. It is more convenient.

24. If Mr. and Mrs. Lin with their 2 sons are joining the tour, how much do they have to pay for the tips in total?
    A. 200 Euros
    B. 400 Euros
    C. 800 Euros
    D. 1000 Euros

You are invited to the wedding party of John Woo and Mary Wang

Venue: The Holy Cross Church
Address: 40, Heping West Road, Taipei City.
Date: 28 Feb 2016 (Sunday)

Time:
5:00 ~ 5:30 p.m. (PPT Slideshow)
5:30 ~ 6:00 p.m. (Speech by fathers from both sides)
6:00 ~ 6:30 p.m. (Wedding Ceremony)
6:30 ~ 7:30 p.m. (Dinner)
7:30 ~ 8:00 p.m. (Photo-taking with newly-wed couple)

Please kindly be seated half an hour before the slideshow presentation.
You are welcome to sign on the guest book and view the wedding pictures.
Instead of the traditional wedding dinner, we will have an all-you-can-eat buffet.
Vegetarian food will also be provided.

25. What time are the guests expected to show up?
    A. 4:30 p.m.
    B. 4:45 p.m.
    C. 5:00 p.m.
    D. 5:30 p.m.

26. How many people will be invited to speak?
    A. 1
    B. 2
    C. 4
    D. 8

27. What is NOT true about this invitation?
    A. The wedding will be held in a church.
    B. Vegetarian food is provided for the buffet.
    C. Friends are invited to take pictures with the couples.
    D. Those who arrive early will be seated in the first row.

It is no secret that more people are killed on the road than in the air. Driving around is much more dangerous than traveling on a flight. Take the recent news for example, when a tire burst, sending the passengers in the car over the bridge, six lives were lost. Only a
(5)   woman survived. Family members and hospital staff are still keeping her in the dark. They fear that she will blame herself for her friends' deaths, which might make her injuries worse.

Most traffic accidents can be avoided. There are several important things drivers can do to ensure safety. First, have the car
(10)   checked on a regular basis, especially for cars that are in service for more than 10 years. Have the mechanics check everything inside out, from the engine to the tires. Second, keep a safety distance and avoid switching lanes suddenly. Make sure you check the rear and side mirrors to see if there are cars behind or beside you before you change lanes. Last but not least, keep in mind that the higher the
(15)   speed, the more dangerous it becomes. Do not go beyond the speed limit. Remember, it is always better to be late than never. A little patience makes all the difference.

28. What is true about the only person who survived the car accident?
    A. She doesn't have any injury at all.
    B. She doesn't know the other people in the car.
    C. She doesn't want to believe that the accident happened.
    D. She doesn't know that the other passengers have died.

29. How can accidents be avoided?
    A. Check the car once every ten years.
    B. Follow the car in front closely.
    C. Keep within the speed limit.
    D. Drive faster when you are late.

30. What is the writer trying to say in the last paragraph?
    A. Time is precious.
    B. All doctors are patient.
    C. Being careful and patient makes driving safer.
    D. It's better to stay in a hospital.

初試 聽力測驗 解析

第一部分 / 看圖辨義

Q1

For question one, please look at picture A.

What is true about the house?
關於這個房子，何者正確？

A. It's a two-story building.
B. A man is on the second floor.
C. The windows are broken.

A. 它是個兩層樓的建築物。
B. 二樓有一個人。
C. 窗戶破了。

詳解

答案：A

主要是問與圖對應相符的選項。從圖中可知，房子有兩層樓，窗戶都沒破，而且圖中沒有人，所以答案為 A。

補充說明

在美式英文中，表達「故事」或「樓層」時都是用 story 這一個單字，而英式英文的拼法則是 storey，意指「樓層」，複數為 storeys。

Q2

For question two, please look at picture B.

What can you tell from the weather forecast?
從天氣預報中可以知道什麼？

A. It will be sunny on Tuesday.
B. Wednesday is a good day for a picnic.
C. Good weather can be expected on Thursday.

A. 星期二會是晴天。
B. 星期三是去野餐的好天氣。
C. 星期四可預期是好天氣。

詳解　　　　　　　　　　　　　　　　　　　　　　　答案：C

　　從圖中可知，星期二是陰天。而星期三是雨天，星期四是晴天。主要是問與圖對應相符的選項，關鍵在於星期與天氣。從選項可知星期四會是好天氣，所以答案為 C。

|單字片語| **weather forecast** 天氣預報 / **sunny** [`sʌnɪ] 晴天的 / **expect** [ɪk`spɛkt] 預期，期待

Q3

For question three, please look at picture C.

Why does the man look worried?
為什麼這位男士看起來很擔心？

A. He can't find his wallet.
B. He can't reach his pocket.
C. He can't finish his food.

A. 他找不到他的錢包。
B. 他摸不到他的口袋。
C. 他吃不完他的食物。

詳解　　　　　　　　　　　　　　　　　　　　　　　答案：A

　　從圖中可知，男子在結帳櫃檯，發現忘了帶錢包，從 Why ~ man ~ worried 可知主要是問男士擔心的原因，關鍵在於結帳與找不到錢包。所以答案為 A。

|單字片語| **worried** [`wɝɪd] 感到擔心的 / **wallet** [`wɑlɪt] 錢包 / **pocket** [`pɑkɪt] 口袋 / **reach** [ritʃ] 伸手去拿

Q4

For question four, please look at picture D.

What time does the clock show?
時鐘所顯示的時間是幾點幾分？

A. A quarter past five.
B. Four fifteen.
C. A quarter to five.

A. 五點十五分。
B. 四點十五分。
C. 四點四十五分。

詳解　　　　　　　　　　　　　　　　　　　　　　　答案：C

　　從圖中可知，現在時間是 4 點 45 分。題目是問圖中時鐘所顯示的時間。選項 A, B, C 都提到 A quarter，A quarter 指的是一刻，也就是十五分鐘的意思，這時必須注意後面接續的用法。past 表示過了，to 表示還沒到，A quarter to five 指還沒到五點，也就是還差十五分鐘才會到五點，五點扣掉十五分鐘就等於四點四十五分。

　　表達時間時，最簡單的表達方式就是「數字」+「o'clock」，以表示「～點鐘」，此數字表示小時；或是「數字」+「數字」，以表示「～點～分」，前面數字表示小時，後者表示分鐘。不過，還有另一種比較複雜、需要思考一下的表達，我們就用 five past nine（9 點 5 分）和 five to nine（8 點 55 分）此例子來解說，其結構為「數字」+「to」+「數字」，或是「數字」+「past/after」+「數字」，前面數字表示分鐘，後者表示小時，現在就來理解規則，先舉以下例子：

five past nine（9 點 5 分）
five to nine（8 點 55 分）

規則	說明
1. 前面的數字：分鐘 　　後面的數字：小時	five 指分鐘（5 分鐘），nine 指小時（9 點）
2. 數字中間的 past 表示「加」，to 表示「減」	five past/after nine 中的 past 或 after，是指「過了」的意思，請理解成「9 點過了 5 分鐘」，所以用「加法」來思考。
	five to nine 中的 to，是指「還沒到，還差～就要到」的意思，請理解成「還差 5 分鐘就要 9 點」，所以用「減法」來思考。

　　分鐘的位置，還可以換成像是 a quarter（四分之一）以表示一刻（15 分鐘），或是 a half（二分之一）以表示半小時（30 分鐘）。
　　quarter 是四分之一，100 的 quarter 是 25。一小時有 60 分鐘，60 分鐘的四分之一為 15 分鐘。

Q5

For question five, please look at picture E.

Where is the woman?

這位女士在什麼地方？

A. She is in a garden.
B. She is in a garage.
C. She is in a gym.

A. 她在花園。
B. 她在車庫。
C. 她在健身房。

詳解

　　從圖中可知這位女士在澆花，從 Where ～ woman 可知主要是問女士的位置所在。最合理的答案是在花園裡。

|單字片語| **garden** [`gɑrdn] 花園 / **garbage** [`gɑrbɪdʒ] 垃圾 / **garage** [gə`rɑʒ] 車庫

第 1 回
第 2 回
第 3 回
第 4 回
第 5 回
第 6 回

Q6

Would you like to join our group meeting?
你想要參加我們的小組會議嗎？

A. Sure. Count me in.
B. Sure. It depends.
C. Sure. Leave me out.

A. 當然。算我一份。
B. 當然。看情況。
C. 當然。我不參與。

詳解 　　　　　　　　　　　　　　　　　　　　　　　　答案：A

　　從選項的 Sure 可推測題目會是疑問句。從 Would you like to join~ 可知，主要是問對方是否願意參加某活動。選項中一開始提到的 sure 表示願意的意思，選項 A 的 count 是數數和計算的意思，count me in 意指把我算在內（而 count me out 則是不要把我算在裡面，也就是我不想參與）。而 C 的 leave me out 是我不想參與的意思，不過前面說 sure（表示願意），後面不能說 leave me out，否則前後矛盾。選項 B 提到願意，後面又說 It depends.，表示沒辦法確定是否要參加，前後矛盾。

Q7

Never forget to eat breakfast.
千萬別忘了吃早餐。

A. I was.
B. I can.
C. I won't.

A. 我曾經是。
B. 我可以。
C. 我不會的。

詳解 　　　　　　　　　　　　　　　　　　　　　　　　答案：C

　　從 Never ~ 可知，主要是用祈使句跟對方說不要做什麼。選項中最適合的答案是 C，說話者用祈使句提出建議或命令時，回應時用 I will 或 I won't 回答。請見以下例句：
A: Please remember to call me. 請記得打電話給我。
B: I will. 我會（記住）的。

A: Don't forget to do it. 別忘了去做。
B: I won't. 我不會（忘記）的。

補充說明

　　用祈使句請對方做某事時，有時也會在後面加上附加問句（如 will you?）來表達，請見以下例句：
Clean up your room, will you?（整理你的房間，好嗎？）

215

Q8

The end-of-the-year sale starts today.
年終特賣會今天開始。

A. Why did it end so early?	A. 為什麼這麼早結束？
B. What are we waiting for?	B. 我們還在等什麼？
C. It starts today.	C. 它今天開始。

詳解　　　　　　　　　　　　　　　　　　　　　　答案：B

　　從 ~ sale starts today 可知，主要是陳述拍賣會今天開始的事實。因為今天才開始，很明顯 A 的回答文不對題。C 只是重複陳述這件事實，沒回應到說話者。聽到 sale 可判斷是某某特賣會，因為終於開始了，所以建議對方立即前往，用「還在等什麼呢？」來表達。

Q9

Jack is down with the flu.
Jack 得了流行性感冒。

A. He just can't sit still.	A. 他就是不能乖乖地坐著。
B. We should pick him up at the airport.	B. 我們應該到機場去接他。
C. I hope he gets well soon.	C. 我希望他早日康復。

詳解　　　　　　　　　　　　　　　　　　　　　　答案：C

　　從 Jack ~ with the flu 可推測，主要是陳述 Jack 感冒的事實。聽到某人感冒，最適合的回應就是希望對方早日康復，所以答案是 C。若有外國友人生病了，探病時可以在卡片上寫一句：Get well soon. 。

Q10

Why do you like to travel?
為什麼你喜歡旅行？

A. To experience different cultures.	A. 為了體驗不同的文化。
B. To memorize every word.	B. 為了記住每一個字。
C. To finish this school year.	C. 為了完成這一學年。

第 1 回
第 2 回
第 3 回
第 4 回
第 5 回
第 6 回

詳解

　　從選項都是「To + 動詞」（為了～）的表達可推測，會聽到與「做什麼」或「為何要做什麼」相關的問句。從 Why ~ you like ~ travel 可知，主要是問對方喜歡旅遊的理由。選項中最適合的回答是「為了體驗不同的文化」。

Q11

It's getting foggy out there.
外面起霧了。

A. You can hear the noise it makes.
B. You should clean it with soap.
C. You had better slow down and turn on the headlights.

A. 你可以聽到它發出的噪音。
B. 你應該要用肥皂清洗它。
C. 你最好減速並打開大燈。

詳解 答案：C

　　從 getting foggy ~ 可知，主要是陳述起霧的事實。但如果把 foggy（有霧的）聽成 frog（青蛙），可能會選 A。「濃霧」是 fog，foggy 是「有濃霧的」的意思，最為合理的回應是放慢速度並打開大燈。

單字片語 foggy [ˋfɑgɪ] 有霧的 / **noise** [nɔɪz] 聲響，噪音 / **soap** [sop] 肥皂 / **slow down** 慢下來 / **headlight** [ˋhɛdˏlaɪt] 大燈

Q12

Remember to dress formally for the interview.
記得面試時要穿著正式的服裝。

A. Should I wear a tie?
B. Where are my jeans?
C. Don't you think the scene is beautiful?

A. 我應該打領帶嗎？
B. 我的牛仔褲呢？
C. 你不認為風景很美嗎？

詳解 答案：A

　　從 Remember ~ dress ~ interview 可知，主要是提醒對方面試時的穿著方式。若聽不懂 formally 是什麼意思，也可以從 dress（穿著）和 interview（面試）來推斷在該場合的穿著，提到是否要打領帶的 A 是正確答案。

單字片語 formally [ˋfɔrmḷɪ] 正式地 / **interview** [ˋɪntəˏvju] 面試，訪談 / **jeans** [dʒinz] 牛仔褲 / **formal** [ˋfɔrmḷ] 正式的 / **former** [ˋfɔrmə] 前者的

I have to say that smoking is a really bad habit.
我必須說抽菸真是一個壞習慣。

A. I think something is burning.　　A. 我想有東西著火了。
B. I haven't told them about the fire.　B. 我還沒告訴他們關於那場火的
　　　　　　　　　　　　　　　　　　　事情。
C. I can't agree more.　　　　　　C. 我非常同意。

詳解　　　　　　　　　　　　　　　　　　　　　　　　　　答案：C

　　從 I ~ say that smoking ~ bad habit.可知，主要是陳述抽菸不好的想法。smoke 可當名詞或動詞，當名詞有「濃煙」的意思，而當動詞是「抽菸」的意思。因為抽菸是壞習慣，所以最合理的回應是「我同意」，即選項 C，英文字面上表示「再同意不過了」。

|單字片語| **burn** [bɜ˙n] 著火

Hey, look where you are going!
嘿，走路看路！

A. Thank you. This is just what I want.　A. 謝謝你。這正是我想要的。
B. I'm sorry. It's all my fault.　　　B. 對不起。這都是我的錯。
C. Never mind. Don't do it again.　　C. 沒關係。以後別再這樣。

詳解　　　　　　　　　　　　　　　　　　　　　　　　　　答案：B

　　從 look where you ~ going 可知，主要是用祈使句提醒對方注意看路。look where you are going 在英文字面上是「看你往哪裡走去」，意思就是走路不要不長眼睛，要看路。說話者應該是被冒失鬼撞到，才會說出這句話。選項中最合理的回應是承認自己的錯，答案是 B。

What's your excuse for being late again?
你再次遲到的藉口是什麼呢？

A. Let me introduce myself.　　　　A. 讓我自我介紹。
B. You should be proud of yourself.　B. 你應該為自己感到驕傲。
C. There was a traffic jam.　　　　C. 塞車。

詳解

　　從 What's your excuse ~ late 可知，主要是問對方遲到的藉口。選項中最合理的回應是 C 提到有塞車的狀況。我們都知道 excuse me 表示不好意思，而 excuse 當名詞時是「藉口」的意思，和 reason 不同，reason 是合理的理由。以西方文化的角度來看，塞車是藉口，而不是理由，因為我們在出發前應該預留可能會塞車的時間。

◁補充說明▷

　　在開會或和別人交談中需要暫時離開時，可以說 please excuse me for a moment.（失陪一下）。

Q16

Woman: Oops. Looks like I pressed the wrong button. The words on the screen are all gone.

糟糕，看起來我按錯按鍵了，螢幕上的字都不見了。

Man: You can always hit the "undo" button.

妳可以按「還原」鍵。

Woman: I'm afraid you have to show me how to do it.

恐怕你要教我怎麼做。

Q: **What does the woman need help with?**
這位女士有什麼事需要幫忙？

A. Computer knowledge.
B. Movie ticket information.
C. Physical exercise.

A. 電腦知識。
B. 電影票資訊。
C. 體能訓練。

詳解

答案：A

從 What ~ woman need help 可知，主要是問女子需要什麼樣的幫忙。從 button（按鍵）、words（文字）和 screen（螢幕）這些關鍵字，可推斷這位女士需要幫忙的是電腦方面的知識。

Q17

Man: I can't find my cell phone. Did you hide it somewhere?

我找不到我的手機。你把它藏到哪去了嗎？

Woman: You can only have it back after the exam.

你在考完試之後才可以拿回去。

Man: Come on, Mom. I need to use it as an alarm clock.

哎唷，媽。我需要用它來當鬧鐘。

Q: **Why does the man need his cell phone?**
為什麼這位男士需要他的手機？

A. To play online games.
B. To take an exam.
C. To wake him up.

A. 為了玩線上遊戲。
B. 為了參加考試。
C. 為了叫醒他。

第 1 回
第 2 回
第 3 回
第 4 回
第 5 回
第 6 回

詳解　　　　　　　　　　　　　　　　　　　　　　　　　答案：C

　　從選項都是「To + 動詞」（為了～）的表達可推測，會聽到與「做什麼」或「為何要做什麼」相關的問句。從 Why ~ man need ~ cell phone 可知，主要是問男子需要手機的理由。一開始男士提到找不到手機 (cell phone)，最後說需要手機當鬧鐘 (alarm clock)，表示需要手機的目的是為了叫自己起床。

|單字片語| **hide** [haɪd] 藏起來 / **exam** [ɪgˋzæm] 考試 / **alarm clock** 鬧鐘 / **take an exam** 考試 / **wake... up** 把…叫醒

Q18

Woman: Why did you lie to me? You went out with Nancy, didn't you?
　　　　你為什麼騙我？你跟 Nancy 出去，不是嗎？
Man:　　She needed help with her exam. It wasn't a date.
　　　　她的考試需要幫忙，那不是個約會。
Woman: You could have told me the truth. I'm not the jealous type.
　　　　你可以跟我說實話的，我不是那種愛吃醋的人。

Q: **What does the woman mean?**
　　這位女士的意思是什麼？

A. The man should have been honest.　　A. 男士之前應該誠實的。
B. The man should be jealous.　　　　　B. 男士應該嫉妒。
C. The man should help her with her　　 C. 男士應該為她的課業提供協
　 schoolwork.　　　　　　　　　　　　　助。

詳解　　　　　　　　　　　　　　　　　　　　　　　　　答案：A

　　從 What ~ woman mean 可知，主要是問女子在對話中所表達的意思。從女子一開始對男士說 Why did you lie to me?（你為什麼騙我），以及最後提到 You could have told me the truth（你可以跟我說實話的）可得知，女子認為男子之前應該誠實，而不應該說謊。

〈補充說明〉

　　「主詞 + could have p.p.」在口語中經常會用到，用來表示「當初可以這樣做／可能會發生，但其實沒做／沒發生」。我們可以把 could have p.p. 理解為「可以…（但沒做）」或「很有可能…（但沒發生）」。請見以下例句：
You could have said no to him. 你原來可以跟他說不的（但卻沒說不）。
He could have been killed. 他很有可能被殺死（但沒發生）。

|單字片語| **date** [det] 約會 / **tell the truth** 說實話 / **jealous** [ˋdʒɛləs] 忌妒的，吃醋的 / **honest** [ˋɑnɪst] 誠實的

Q19

Man: The air up here is really fresh.
這上面的空氣真是清新。

Woman: We might even see snow if we are lucky.
如果我們幸運的話,我們可能還會看到雪。

Man: I can't believe I am standing above the clouds.
我無法相信我正站在雲朵的上方。

Q: Where are the speakers?
說話者可能在什麼地方?

A. In the mountains.
B. By the lake.
C. At the beach.

A. 在山上。
B. 在湖邊。
C. 在海灘。

詳解

答案:A

從選項都是「介系詞 + 地方名詞」(在~)的表達可推測,會聽到與「在哪裡」、「在什麼地方」相關的問句。從 Where ~ speakers be 可知,主要是問說話者的位置。從 air up here ~ fresh(這上面的空氣清新)、see snow(看到雪),以及「站在雲朵的上方」這三個提示,可推測說話者在山上。

Q20

Woman: Mr. Covey is not in the office at the moment. Would you like to leave a message?
Covey 先生此刻不在辦公室。您想要留言嗎?

Man: Yes. This is Mr. Lee from the National Tax Department. I need him to return my call as soon as possible. He knows my number.
要,我是國稅局的李先生。我需要他盡快回我的電話。他知道我的號碼。

Woman: I got it down. Is there anything else, sir?
我寫下來了。先生,請問其他還有什麼事嗎?

Q: What is the woman's job?
這位女士的工作是什麼?

A. She is a police officer.
B. She is a principal.
C. She is a secretary.

A. 她是一名警察。
B. 她是一位校長。
C. 她是一名祕書。

第 1 回

第 2 回

第 3 回

第 4 回

第 5 回

第 6 回

詳解   答案：C

　　從選項都是「She is + 職位」的表達可推測，題目會問女士的工作。從女子提到的 Would you like to leave ~ message 可推測，最有可能記下留言的工作是祕書。

Q21

Man:　　　I got a C for math. It's the worst grade I have ever gotten.
　　　　　　我的數學拿到 C。這是我所拿過最糟糕的成績。

Woman:　I studied really hard but I still got a D.
　　　　　　我很努力念書，但我還是拿到 D。

Man:　　　Maybe we should go to a cram school just like our classmates.
　　　　　　或許我們應該要像我們同學一樣去補習班。

Q:　What is true about the conversation?
　　關於對話，何者正確？

A. The man and the woman are in a cram school.

B. The man's math grade is worse than the woman's.

C. The man and the woman did poorly on a math test.

A. 這位男士和女士都在補習班。

B. 男士的數學成績比女士的糟糕。

C. 男士和女士在數學測驗的表現都很差。

詳解   答案：C

　　從 What ~ true ~ conversation 可知，主要是問選項中與對話相符的敘述。這題有點麻煩，必須在有限的時間內利用刪去法找到答案。說話者一開始都提到對自己的成績不滿意，因為都拿到低分，還說到應該要去補習班，表示他們目前沒有在補習，所以選項 A 是錯的。男生的成績是 C，女生的成績是 D，所以選項 B 也是錯的。正確答案為：男生和女生在數學測驗的表現都很差。

Q22

Woman:　I have trouble reading the words on the whiteboard.
　　　　　　我看不太到白板上的字。

Man:　　　Mr. Chen shouldn't use green markers. The color is too light.
　　　　　　陳先生不應該用綠色的白板筆，顏色太淺了。

Woman:　You mean you have the same problem? I thought there was something wrong with my eyes.
　　　　　　你的意思是你也有同樣的問題嗎？我以為是我的眼睛有問題。

Q: **What seems to be the problem?**
　　問題似乎是什麼？

A. There is something wrong with the woman's eyes.　女士的眼睛有問題。

B. Mr. Chen should use a darker color.　B. 陳先生應該用深一點的顏色。

C. The light in the room is not working.　C. 房間裡的燈壞了。

詳解　　　　　　　　　　　　　　　　　　　　　　　　**答案：B**

　　從 What ~ the problem 可知，主要是問對話中提到的問題。女子一開始提到 trouble reading the words，表示看不到字，男子回應 Mr. ~ shouldn't use ~ markers. The color is too light.，由此可知問題是陳先生使用的顏色太淺了，也就是需要用深一點的顏色，所以答案是 B。

補充說明

　　light 可以當名詞、動詞或形容詞。名詞的 light 是「燈」的意思，當動詞時是「點亮」的意思，當形容詞有「輕的」和「淺的」之意。當動詞時，light 的過去式為 lit。而加上 ing 的 lighting 則是指室內的燈光或燈具。

Q23

Man:　I can't believe it. I put on so much weight during the summer vacation.
　　　我無法相信，我的體重在暑假增加了這麼多。

Woman:　I thought you are a regular member of the gym.
　　　我以為你是健身房的固定會員。

Man:　I am. I guess I had too much soda.
　　　我是啊。我想我喝太多汽水了。

Q: **What can be said about the man?**
　　關於這位男士提到了什麼？

A. He didn't gain any weight.　A. 他的體重沒有增加。

B. He didn't control his diet.　B. 他沒有控制他的飲食。

C. He didn't work out in the gym.　C. 他沒有在健身房運動。

詳解　　　　　　　　　　　　　　　　　　　　　　　　**答案：B**

　　從選項都是「He ~」的表達可推測，題目會問與男士相關的問題。從 What ~ said about the man 可知，主要是問對話中關於男子的正確選項。從一開始提到

的 I put on so much weight during the summer 可知，男子提到自己體重增加，所以 A 不正確。女子提到男子是固定會員，男子也承認自己是會員，表示他有在健身房運動，所以 C 也不正確。男子最後說自己喝了太多汽水，也就是沒有控制好自己的飲食，答案是 B。

|單字片語| **believe** [bɪˋliv] 相信 / **put on weight** 體重增加 / **gym** [dʒɪm] 體育館，健身房 / **member** [ˋmɛmbə] 會員 / **regular** [ˋrɛgjələ] 固定的，有規律的/ **soda** [ˋsodə] 汽水 / **control** [kənˋtrol] 控制 / **work out** 運動

Woman: Emma's birthday is next week. Do you have any bright ideas?
　　　　Emma 的生日是下個星期。你有任何好點子嗎？

Man: 　She doesn't like dolls and she doesn't like flowers, either.
　　　　她不喜歡娃娃，也不喜歡花。

Woman: Let's give her a treat instead of buying her a gift.
　　　　我們與其買禮物給她，不如請她吃飯。

Q: **What will the speakers do for Emma?**
　說話者會為 Emma 做什麼？

A. They will buy her a birthday present.　A. 他們會買生日禮物給她。
B. They will get her some roses.　　　　　B. 他們會給她一些玫瑰花。
C. They will take her to a restaurant　　　C. 他們會帶她到餐廳享用晚餐。
　 for dinner.

詳解　　　　　　　　　　　　　　　　　　　　答案：C

　　從 What ~ speakers do for Emma 可知，題目是問會為 Emma 做的事為何。一開始提到 Emma's birthday，可知正在討論 Emma 的生日。最後女子用祈使句建議為 Emma 慶生的方式，也就是請她吃東西，而非送禮。instead of + Ving 可理解為「與其做～，不如…」或「不做～，而是…」。所以答案是 C。

◀補充說明▶

　　treat 這個單字很好記，因為單字裡面有 eat，所以可以想成跟吃東西有關，也就可以聯想到「請客」的意思。其用法有：Give someone a treat. Treat someone to something. It's someone's treat.。請見以下例句：
Are you giving us a treat? 你要請我們嗎？（treat 當名詞用）
Are you treating us to dinner? 你要請我們吃晚餐嗎？（treat 當動詞用）
It's my treat. 我請客。（treat 當名詞用）

　　萬聖節會說的 treat or trick，意思就是「請吃東西（treat）或整人搗蛋（trick），二選一」。

Man:　　May I borrow some money from you?　我可以向你借一些錢嗎？

Woman:　Well, I lent you two hundred dollars last week and you haven't…, you know.
　　　　這個嘛，我上個星期借你兩百元，但你還沒…，你知道的。

Man:　　Forget it. I will ask someone else.　算了，我問別人好了。

Q: What is true about the speakers?
　　關於說話者，何者正確？

A. The man wants the woman to return him the money.　　A. 男士要女士還他錢。

B. The man wants to lend her some money.　　B. 男士要借些錢給女士。

C. The man hasn't returned the woman the money he borrowed.　　C. 男士向女士借的錢還沒還。

詳解　　　　　　　　　　　　　　　　　　　　　　　　　　答案：C

　　從選項可推測，對話內容會跟借錢或還錢相關。從 What ～ true about the speakers 可知，問題是問與對話相符的選項。遇到這類題型，要聽清楚男士、女士所提到的細部資訊，並用刪去法選出答案。一開始男士說要向女士借錢，所以 A 不正確。女士接著說之前有借錢給他，但從語氣推測男士應該還沒還錢，所以才沒有馬上答應要借男士錢，C 才是正確答案。

第四部分 / 短文聽解

Q26

For question number 26, please look at the three pictures.

Please listen to the following announcement.　請聽以下的公告廣播。

Where should the mother of the child go?
這名孩子的母親應該去哪裡？

Attention all shoppers. A young child about two to three years old was found crying in the women's restroom. The boy is wearing a yellow T-shirt with a Mickey Mouse cartoon on it. He is now at the information counter, which is at the main lobby on the first floor. Would the parent or family member of the child please come here as soon as you hear this announcement? Thank you.

各位購物者請注意。一名年約兩到三歲的孩子被發現在女廁哭泣。這名男孩身穿印有米老鼠卡通圖案的黃色 T 恤。他目前在一樓大廳的服務台。請小孩的家長或家人聽到廣播後儘快過來。謝謝。

A.　　　　　　　B.　　　　　　　C.

詳解　　　　　　　　　　　　　　　　　　　　　　**答案：C**

先注意三張圖片，從圖片不同的地點可推測，題目會問與「～在哪裡」相關的內容。從 Where should ~ mother of ~ child go 可知，題目是問母親要去的地點為何。從一開始的 shoppers，以及 He is ~ at the information counter 中的 information counter（服務台）可判斷，廣播的地點是在賣場或百貨公司，而文中提到小男孩原在廁所哭泣（young child ~ was found crying in ~ restroom），現在正在服務台（now at the information counter）所以孩子的母親應該去圖片內容為服務台的 C。

單字片語 shopper [ˈʃɑpɚ] 購物者 / **restroom** [ˈrestruːm] 化妝室，洗手間 / **cartoon** [karˈtun] 卡通 / **information counter** 服務台

227

For question number 27, please look at the three pictures.

Please listen to the following telephone message. 請聽以下的電話留言。

What will the speaker do tomorrow?
說話者原本打算先做什麼？

Mr. Cornwell, this is Mr. Lee from J.K. publishing company. When I was about to design the cover page for your book, I found that the company computer is down. It should take no more than a day to fix, but it means I can only work on the cover tomorrow morning.

Cornwell 先生，我是 J.K. 出版社的李先生。當我正要開始設計你書的封面時，我發現公司的電腦壞了。維修的時間應該不會超過一天，但這表示了我要到明天早上才能做封面。

A.   B.   C.

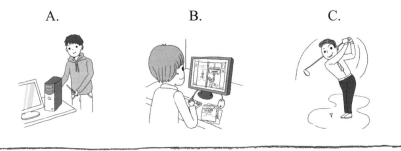

詳解　　　　　　　　　　　　　　　　　　　　　　　　　　　答案：B

從 What ~ speaker plan to do first 可知，主要是問說話者原本要先做的事情。聽到題目出現 first（首先）或是 in the morning 等等的時間副詞時，要特別注意談話中關於時間點的訊息。說話者一開始提到 When I ~ start designing the cover page ~ the company computer was down. 表示說話者原本要先設計書的封面，但電腦故障。又說 I can only work on the cover tomorrow morning.，由此可知現在沒辦法進行封面設計。所以在使用電腦設計封面的 B 是正確答案。

|單字片語| **publishing** [`pʌblɪʃɪŋ] 出版的 / **cover page** 封面 / **fix** [fɪks] 維修

Q28

For question number 28, please look at the three pictures.

Please listen to the following short talk.　請聽以下簡短談話。

Where will the speaker go on Friday?
說話者星期五時會去哪裡？

　　Today is Wednesday. We have visited the national museum and the art gallery. We will take the kids to the amusement park tomorrow, and they can enjoy themselves for the whole day. I guess I will just watch and take photos. The day after tomorrow we will be in the mountains and enjoy the famous hot spring or see some wild monkeys.

　　今天是星期三，我們已經參觀了國家博物館和畫廊。我們明天要帶孩子們去遊樂園，然後他們可以好好玩一整天。我想我只會在旁邊看並且拍照。後天我們會到山上去，並好好享受著名的溫泉，或者看一些野生的猴子。

A.

B.

C.

詳解　　　　　　　　　　　　　　　　　　　　　　　　　　　答案：B

　　從 3 張圖片是不同的地點可推測，題目會問與「～在哪裡」相關的內容。從 Where ~ speaker go ~ Friday 可知，題目是問說話者星期五要去的地方。請注意，談話的第一句就說今天是星期三這個時間，所以明天是星期四，後天（the day after tomorrow）是星期五，接著在後天時提到 in the mountains... try out the famous hot spring 以及 see some wild monkeys，所以去泡溫泉、背景有山的 B 是正確答案。

|單字片語| **visit** [ˋvɪzɪt] 參觀 / **museum** [mjuˋzɪəm] 博物館 / **gallery** [ˋgælərɪ] 畫廊 / **amusement park** 遊樂園 / **famous** [ˋfeməs] 著名的 / **hot spring** 溫泉

For question number 29, please look at the three pictures.

Please listen to the following news broadcast.　請聽以下的新聞廣播。

What seems to be the problem?
什麼東西似乎成為了問題？

　　With so many factories nearby, air pollution has become a serious problem. People here complained about thick layers of dirt on their cars and the windows in their houses. Parents are worried because children have to put on a mask even when in school. Just to show how bad the problem is, a school teacher collected some rainwater. The rainwater was so dirty that no one believed it came directly from the skies above.

　　因為附近有這麼多工廠，空氣汙染已經變成了一個嚴重的問題。這裡的人抱怨車子和自家窗戶上有厚厚的灰塵。家長們都很擔心，因為孩子們甚至在學校也都要戴上口罩。為了要讓大家知道問題有多嚴重，一名學校的老師收集了一些雨水。這些雨水很髒，髒到沒有人相信它是直接從天空下下來的。

A.　　　　　　　　B.　　　　　　　　C.

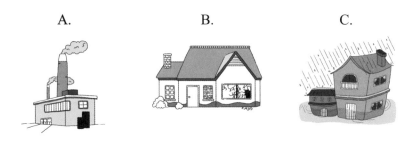

詳解　　　　　　　　　　　　　　　　　　　　　　　　　　　

　　圖片都是不同的建築物以及不同的狀況。從 What ~ be the problem 可知，題目是問廣播中提到的問題。一開始聽到關鍵字 factories、air pollution 以及 serious problem，可以推測主要的問題是空氣汙染（air pollution）。後面還提到小朋友上學必須戴口罩，而空氣污染的原因來自附近的工廠（factories）。選項中有工廠的 A 是正確答案。

|單字片語| **nearby** [ˋnɪrˏbaɪ] 在附近 / **air pollution** 空氣汙染 / **complain** [kəmˋplen] 抱怨 / **layer** [ˋleɚ] （一）層 / **dirt** [dɝt] 汙垢，泥土 / **mask** [mæsk] 口罩 / **rainwater** [ˋrenˏwɔtɚ] 雨水

Q30

For question number 30, please look at the three pictures.

Please listen to the following short talk. 請聽以下的簡短談話。

Which picture shows "Level one"?
哪一張圖顯示的是「第一層」？

Welcome to my house. What I'm going to say will sound totally confusing to those of you from the United States. We are at ground level right now but we do not call it level one. Level one is the second floor, level two is the third floor and so on. So if you need to go to the first floor, you are going to the "ground level."

歡迎來到天空夢想大樓。接下來我要說的，對你們美國人來說很容易搞混。我們目前在地面樓層，但我們不叫它第一層。第一層是二樓，第二層是三樓，以此類推。所以如果你需要去一樓，你要去的地方也就是這裡的地面樓層。

A. 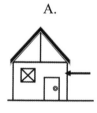　　B. 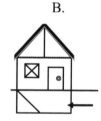　　C.

詳解　　答案：C

從 Which ~ shows "Level one" 可知，主要是問哪一張圖才是 Level one。談話中提到 Level one is the second floor（二樓），level two is the third floor，由此可知 Level one 指的是圖片中二樓的位置，也就是 C。

補充說明

在說明樓層時，英式的用法和我們的有點不同。我們的一樓，英式英文是 ground level，就字面意義上可理解為在地上（ground）的樓層（level），而 level one 則是從地面算起再上去一樓，也就是我們的二樓，以此類推。

單字片語 confusing [kən`fjuzɪŋ] 讓人混淆的 / ground [graʊnd] 地面 / call [kɔl] 叫，稱呼 / first [fɝst] 第一的 / second [`sɛkənd] 第二的 / third [θɝd] 第三的

第四回

初試 閱讀測驗 解析

第一部分 / 詞彙

Q1

My parrot copied what I said _____ repeated it word for word.

我的鸚鵡複製我說的話,而且逐字重覆。

A. while
B. because
C. and
D. if

詳解 答案:C

　　這題主要是考連接詞的用法,以及語意的理解。空格前面是一個有主詞、動詞、受詞的完整子句,而後面是一個動詞片語,選項都是連接詞,語意上來看最適合的是 C。and 是對等連接詞,可以連接兩個名詞、兩個動詞或兩個句子。A 和 D 後面要接一子句或動詞-ing,B 後面要接子句。

Q2

This place is getting _____. A lot of people are waiting to see the fireworks. Let's find some seats before it is too late.

這個地方越來越擁擠了。很多人等著要看煙火。在還沒有太遲之前,我們找個座位吧。

A. damaged 損壞的
B. interested 感興趣的
C. crowded 擁擠的
D. polluted 汙染的

詳解 答案:C

　　這題主要是考單字與語意理解。選項都是形容詞,要接在 getting 之後,以表示「越來越~」。從 a lot of people(很多人)跟 find some seats(找座位)這些關鍵字可知,地方越來越擁擠(crowded),所以答案是 C。

〈補充說明〉

　　crowd 是名詞,表示人群的意思,而 crowded 是形容詞,形容人群很多、擁擠的意思。

Q3

After the terrible accident, those with serious injuries _____ to the nearest hospital at once.

在可怕的意外後，那些傷勢嚴重的人立刻被送到最近的醫院。

A. took
B. will take
C. were taken
D. have taken

詳解　　　　　　　　　　　　　　　　　　　答案：C

　　這題主要是考動詞用法與語意的理解。選項都是與 take 相關的動詞，題目中 those ~ injuries 為主詞，表示「傷勢嚴重的那些人」，空格後面是「最近的醫院」，從語意上來理解，可以知道那些人「被」送到醫院，所以要用【被動語態】的 C。

|單字片語| **injury** [ˋɪndʒərɪ] 受傷，傷害 / **hospital** [ˋhɑspɪtəl] 醫院 / **at once** 立刻

Q4

I would like to _____ you to my birthday party next week.

下星期我想要邀請你來我的生日派對。

A. visit 拜訪；參觀
B. invite 邀請
C. celebrate 慶祝
D. report 報告；報導

詳解　　　　　　　　　　　　　　　　　　　答案：B

　　這題主要是考單字。選項中都是動詞，空格後面是受詞 you（你）和介系詞片語 to my birthday party（來我的生日派對），由此可知最適合的動詞是 B。

Q5

The music is too loud. Could you _____ it _____ a little, please?

音樂太大聲了。你可以把音量調低一點嗎？拜託。

A. turn; on 打開
B. turn; off 關掉
C. turn; down 調低
D. turn; up 調高

詳解　　　　　　　　　　　　　　　　　　　答案：C

　　這題主要是考動詞片語。選項中都是動詞 turn 與不同的副詞。題目提到音樂很大聲，而 could you...表示拜託對方做某事的句型，因此最適合的動詞是 C，將音量降低。

第 1 回
第 2 回
第 3 回
第 4 回
第 5 回
第 6 回

有些動詞片語，其動詞與介系詞／副詞可以「拆開」，也就是位置可以放在受詞之前或之後。例如 turn on the radio 可以寫成 turn the radio on。但有些動詞片語無法拆開，要如何區分其實不難，只要它的中文意思可以翻成「把…怎樣」的話，那這個動詞片語就能拆開。而不能翻成「把…怎樣」的，就不能拆開。以 turn on 和 get on 為例，turn on 是「打開（電器開關）」，我們可以說「打開收音機」，也可以說「把收音機打開」。反之，get on（上車）則無法拆開，中文翻譯無法說成「把…」的結構。請見以下例句：

Let's turn on the radio. 我們來把收音機打開。
Let's turn the radio on. 我們來把收音機打開。

Let's get on the bus. 我們上公車吧。
Let's get the bus on.（錯誤示範）

Q6

You have been living in Taiwan for many years, _____?

你住在台灣已經很多年了，不是嗎？

A. don't you
B. haven't you
C. aren't you
D. won't you

詳解　　　　　　　　　　　　　　　　　　　　　　　

這題考的是【附加問句】，【附加問句】是直述句後面再加上的問句，類似中文的「你…，不是嗎？」，這種「是嗎？」「不是嗎？」的句型就是【附加問句】。空格前面是肯定直述句，時態是現在完成式，附加問句就要用否定表達，時態也要一致的用現在完成式，所以答案是 B。若前面直述句是否定句，後面就要用肯定表達。以下利用表格來把動詞的文法搞清楚。

	肯定 + 否定附加問句	否定 + 肯定附加問句
be 動詞	He **is** a doctor, isn't he?	He **isn't** a doctor, is he?
一般動詞	She **likes** flowers, doesn't she?	She **doesn't** like flowers, does she?
助動詞	They **can** swim, can't they?	They **can't** swim, can they?
現在完成式	He **has** come home, hasn't he?	He **hasn't** come home, has he?

Q7

I left my wallet here but now it is _____. Someone must have taken it.

我之前把錢包留在這裡，但是現在不見了。一定是有人拿走了。

A. missing 不見
B. disappearing 消失
C. running 跑步
D. preparing 準備

詳解

答案：A

這題主要是考單字與語意的理解。空格前面提到錢包留在某處，空格後面提到一定是有人拿走，最合理的答案是不見了。選項中 disappearing 和 missing 都可翻譯為消失和不見蹤影，差別在於 it is disappearing 是漸漸消失，也就是還看得見，例如彩虹正在消失中，或者某種行業正在消失中，所以正確答案是 A。

Q8

Does the cell phone come _____ an extra battery?

這個手機配有額外的電池嗎？

A. from
B. with
C. out
D. in

詳解

答案：B

這題主要是考介系詞。空格前面是此句的主要動詞 come，後面是名詞片語，選項中都是介系詞，請檢視動詞 come 與各介系詞組合後的語意。come from 表示「來自於」。with 帶有附上、一起的意思，我們可把 come with 理解為附贈，也就是某個東西來的時候搭配另一個東西。come out 表示「出來」。come in 則是「以某種方式而來」，例如來的時候有三種顏色（come in three colors），或是有各種形狀和尺寸（come in various shapes and sizes）。最合理的答案是 B。

Q9

_____ who are getting on the train should give way to those who are getting off.

要上火車的乘客應該讓位給那些正在下車的乘客。

A. Passage 通過
B. Passer-by 路過的人
C. Passionate 熱情的
D. Passengers 乘客

第 1 回
第 2 回
第 3 回
第 4 回
第 5 回
第 6 回

詳解

　　這題主要是考單字。從 getting on ~ train（上火車）以及 getting off（下車），可判斷做此動作的主詞是乘客 passengers。

Q10

He has a fever. He was _____ in the rain last night.

他發燒了。他昨晚淋到雨。

A. dropped

B. caught

C. fallen

D. held

詳解

　　這題主要是考動詞與語意理解。空格前面提到某人發燒，從後面的 rain last night 可推測是原因，「被雨淋濕」可用片語 be caught in the rain 表達，所以答案是 B。

第二部分 / 段落填空

Questions 11-14

(11) One of the hardest things to do is get along with your neighbors. The key to (12) having friendly neighbors is respect. Learn to respect others before you expect them to listen to you. Greet them whenever you see them, (13) especially those who are elder. Give them a big warm smile. Share with them some gifts during special occasions such as Chinese New Year, Mid-autumn Festival or even Christmas.

It is common to have small disagreements. Understand that these little problems cannot be avoided but keep in mind that they are little problems, (14) so do not turn them into big problems. It is not worth the time and trouble getting angry over who is right and who is wrong.

　　最難做的事情之一就是跟鄰居相處。擁有和藹友善的鄰居，其關鍵在於尊重。在你要求別人聽你說話之前，先學習尊重別人。每當你看到他們就先打個招呼，尤其是對那些年長者。給他們一個溫暖的笑容。在特殊節日期間，例如農曆新年、中秋節，甚至聖誕節，跟他們分享一些禮物。

　　小小的意見不合是很常見的事。要明白這些小問題是難以避免的，但要謹記，這些都只是小問題，所以不要把它們變成大問題。為了究竟是誰對誰錯這點事生氣，是很浪費時間又製造麻煩。

Q11

A. One 一個　　　　　　　　B. Some 一些
C. Any 任何一個　　　　　　D. Both 兩者都

詳解　　　　　　　　　　　　　　　　　　　　　　　答案：A

　　這題主要是考代名詞。從空格到 of the hardest things to do 是主詞，主要動詞是 is，而從選項應該要知道題目考的文法概念是主詞動詞一致原則。從單數動詞 is 可知主詞是單數，因此答案是 One。any 用於否定句與疑問句。

Q12

A. have　　　　　　　　　　**B. having**
C. be having　　　　　　　　D. have had

詳解

　　這題主要是考動名詞。選項都是 have 的各種變化，空格接在 key to 後面，這裡的 to 是介系詞，所以動詞要以 -ing 的形態表示。一般情況下，to 後面要加原形動詞 V，to V 為不定詞。不過，如果 to 是介系詞，就要接 V-ing 或名詞，就像 go to school 中的 to 一樣，後面接名詞，而動名詞 V-ing 也屬於名詞的形態。to 當介系詞的用法並不多，可以背起來，而 to 加 V-ing 的文法是高中老師最喜歡出的題目。請見以下例句。

to + V	to + V-ing
I want **to win.**	The key **to winning** is practice.
We would like **to meet** you.	We look forward **to meeting** you.
I used **to sleep** late.	I am used **to sleeping** late.

Q13

A. instead 作為替代
B. especially 尤其是
C. than 比
D. however 然而

詳解

　　這題主要是考副詞與語意理解。空格前面是祈使句，提到「向他們打個招呼」，從上一句可知「他們」指的是鄰居，而後面是一個名詞子句 those who are elder，根據語意來判斷：向某某人打個招呼，「尤其是」那些年長的人，用副詞 especially 會比較通順。

Q14

A. so do not turn them into big problems
　　所以不要把它們變成大問題
B. but it is important to wear a smile
　　保持微笑很重要
C. in other words, it is lucky to have a friendly neighbor
　　換句話說，有一位友善的鄰居是很幸運的
D. however, to get along well with your neighbors is hard
　　然而，要跟鄰居和睦相處很難

詳解

　　從文章一開始可知是談到跟鄰居相處的主題，而此段開頭提到意見不合是很常見的，空格前面提到：意見不合只是小問題，空格後面提到去爭誰對誰錯

而搞到彼此生氣不值得，可推測空格是填入跟「建議不要把問題搞到很複雜」相關的句子。故正確答案是 A.。

Questions 15-18

I have never traveled to any foreign country. One reason is (15) that I do not want to spend so much money on air tickets. Another reason is I think Taiwan is big and beautiful (16) enough. There are many parts of Taiwan I have never set foot on.

Last month, I visited Xitou in Nantou. It was located in the mountains and the air was fresh. Despite the hot summer, it was cool and comfortable in the forest. As a matter of fact, it got a little cold in the early morning as the (17) temperature dropped below twenty degrees Celsius. I took a lot of pictures and my friends were amazed. (18) We compared these photos with those that my friends took in Switzerland and it was hard to tell the difference. Therefore, I would encourage you to visit every part of Taiwan before you decide to travel abroad.

　　我從來沒去過國外。一個原因是我不想要花這麼多錢在機票上。另一個原因是我認為台灣夠大也夠美。台灣有許多地方我從來沒有去過。

　　上個月，我去了南投的溪頭。這個地方座落於山區，且空氣很清新。儘管是炎熱的夏天，森林裡還是很涼爽、很舒服。事實上，一大早時有點冷，因為溫度降到了攝氏二十度以下。我拍了很多照片，而我的朋友們都感到很驚豔。我們拿這些照片跟朋友之前在瑞士拍的照片做比較，它們之間難以分辨有什麼不同之處。因此，我會鼓勵你們在決定出國旅遊之前，到台灣各個地方走走。

Q15

A. this
B. that
C. which
D. why

詳解　　　　　　　　　　　　　　　　　　　　　　　　　　答案：B

　　這題主要是考關係代名詞。空格前面有主詞與 be 動詞，後面則是子句，由此可知，需要一個關係代名詞 that 來連接，來讓後面的子句（I do... tickets）變成這整個句子的補語。

Q16

A. yet 卻；還沒　　　　　　B. though 雖然；儘管如此
C. still 依然；還是　　　　　D. enough 足夠

詳解　　　　　　　　　　　　　　　　　　　　　　　　答案：D

　　這題主要是考副詞。空格前面是形容詞，同時也有一個子句，而副詞可以用來修飾形容詞、動詞、一整個句子，因此現在要來看語意與擺放位置。選項中 A、B、D 可放在句尾修飾句子，但 A、B 帶有讓語氣轉折的意思，所以不正確。D 放在句尾可修飾前面的形容詞，表示「夠…」的意思，是正確答案。

Q17

A. climate 氣候　　　　　　　B. weather 天氣
C. heat 熱氣　　　　　　　　　D. temperature 溫度

詳解　　　　　　　　　　　　　　　　　　　　　　　　答案：D

　　這題主要是考名詞與語意理解。空格前面是一個子句，提到一早氣溫會有點冷。空格所在位置是主詞。後面有動詞 dropped 以及 twenty degrees（20度），由此可知，會下降到 20 度的是溫度，答案是 D。

Q18

A. We compared these photos with those that my friends took in Switzerland
　我們拿這些照片跟朋友之前在瑞士拍的照片做比較

B. My friends encouraged me to travel abroad
　我朋友鼓勵我出國旅行

C. It is highly recommended to visit Taiwan for your first travel this year
　強烈推薦各位今年的第一趟旅行就來台灣

D. We soon realized that these photos were lost
　我們很快意識到這些照片弄丟了

詳解　　　　　　　　　　　　　　　　　　　　　　　　答案：A

　　空格前面提到：我拍了很多照片，我的朋友們都感到很驚豔。可推測空格是跟照片拍得很好有關。空格後面提到難以分辨有什麼不同之處，可知空格應該是提到把照片做比較。選項 A. 比較符合句意，故選 A.。

Questions 19-21

From:	sueroberts@cghadmin.com
To:	jeffreychen11058@gmail.com
CC:	
Subject:	Results of a checkup

Dear Jeffrey Chen,

We have the results of your checkup. Everything seems fine, except your blood sugar. That is a little high. Please make another appointment with Dr. Wu. He will talk with you about the test results and also give you some advice.

Thank you very much.

Sue Roberts
Administration
County General Hospital

寄件者：	sueroberts@cghadmin.com
收件者：	jeffreychen11058@gmail.com
副本：	
主旨：	健檢報告結果

親愛的 Jeffrey Chen

我們這邊有您的健檢結果。一切看起來都不錯，除了您的血糖這個項目之外。有些偏高。請跟 Wu 醫師約下一次的診。他會跟您談談您的健檢結果，並給予一些建議。
非常感謝您。

Sue Roberts
行政人員
縣立總醫院

County General Hospital Automated Booking Service		
Patient's Name	Doctor	Date/Time
Jeffrey Chen	**Dr. Wu**	**At 9:00 AM** **Wednesday May 5th**

縣立總醫院 自動預約掛號系統		
病患姓名	醫師	日期／時間
Jeffrey Chen	Wu 醫師	早上 9 點 五月五日星期三

Q19

Why did Sue Roberts write to Jeffrey Chen?

為何 Sue Roberts 寫信給 Jeffrey Chen？

A. To tell him about a health problem.

　告知他關於健康的問題。

B. To explain what blood sugar is.

　解釋什麼是血糖。

C. To suggest a treatment on blood sugar.

　建議血糖的治療方式。

D. To introduce a new hospital to him.

　介紹一間新醫院給他。

詳解　

　　在第一篇文的信中的署名 Sue Roberts 可知，Sue Roberts 代表縣立總醫院寫信給 Jeffrey Chen。文中提到：We have the results of your checkup. Everything seems fine, except your blood sugar. That is a little high.，表示 Sue Roberts 這邊有 Jeffrey Chen 的健檢結果，且血糖這個項目有些偏高。所以此信是要告知關於血糖的健康問題，故答案選 A。

Q20

What will Jeffrey Chen do on Wednesday May 5th?

Jeffrey Chen 五月五日星期三要做什麼事？

A. Reschedule his doctor's appointment.

　重新跟他的醫師約診。

B. Get some medical treatment suggestions.

　得到一些醫療上的建議。

C. Show up at 10:00 PM in County General Hospital.

　晚上十點到縣立總醫院。

D. Meet Sue Roberts for a checkup.

　跟 Sue Roberts 見面來做檢查。

詳解　

　　在信中提到：Please make another appointment with Dr. Wu. He will talk with you about the test results and also give you some advice.，表示請 Jeffrey Chen 跟 Wu 醫師約下一次的診，在當天的看診，醫師會跟 Jeffrey Chen 談談他的健檢結果，並給予一些建議。而從第二篇文的表格可知，即信中提到的約診，表格上的時間是五月五日星期三，病患為 Jeffrey Chen，醫師為 Wu 醫師。透過這兩篇

第 1 回
第 2 回
第 3 回
第 4 回
第 5 回
第 6 回

文的對照可知，五月五日當天 Jeffrey Chen 會去看 Wu 醫師，並接受血糖問題的相關建議，故答案選 B。

Q21

Which of the following statements about Dr. Wu is correct?

有關於 Wu 醫師的敘述，下列何者為真？

A. His blood pressure is too high.
他的血壓太高。

B. He did a checkup for himself.
他為自己做了健康檢查。

C. He will see his patient on May 5th.
他將在五月五日為他的病人看診。

D. He hasn't worked in County General Hospital in a long time.
他已經沒在縣立總醫院工作，沒做很長一段時間了。

詳解 答案：C

　　根據第一篇文可知，血壓高的是 Jeffrey Chen，Wu 醫師是在為 Jeffrey Chen 做檢查，而非替自己做檢查，因此 A、B. 不正確。根據第二篇表格，表格上的時間是五月五日，病患為 Jeffrey Chen，醫師為 Wu 醫師，所以 Wu 醫師五月五日要替他的病人看診，故答案選 C.。從表格上的標題 County General Hospital 可知，Wu 醫師還在縣立總醫院工作，所以 D. 不正確。

|單字片語| result 結果 / appointment 約診，會面 / advice 建議

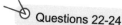 Questions 22-24

Euro dollars at all-time low
Now is the time to visit Europe

Twin package: NT$150,000 per person
Family package (at least four members): NT$135,000 per person.

10 Day Tour to Europe
All packages include air tickets, hotels, meals, transport and entrance fees to museums and amusement parks.

Tips for local guides at 20 Euros a day per person, including children.
Call Horizon Travel at 0800-330-XXX or surf our website below for more
information.

www.horizontravel.com/home

歐元歷史新低
現在正是去歐洲的好時機

雙人套裝行程：每人新台幣 150,000 元
家庭套裝行程（至少四人）：每人新台幣 135,000 元

歐洲 10 天行程
所有配套包含機票、飯店、餐點、交通以及博物館與遊樂園的門票。

當地導遊小費為一人一天 20 歐元，包含兒童。
撥打 0800-330-XXX 給 Horizon 旅遊，或瀏覽我們以下的網頁，以便獲得更多資訊。

www.horizontravel.com/home

|單字片語| all-time 空前的 / Europe [`jʊrəp] 歐洲 / package [`pækɪdʒ] 套裝行程，一組事物 / include [ɪn`klud] 包含 / meal [mil] 餐點 / transport [`træns͵pɔrt] 交通 / entrance fee 門票 / tip [tɪp] 小費 / local [`lokəl] 當地的 / guide [gaɪd] 導遊 / below [bə`lo] 在⋯以下

Q22

Who is possibly interested in this advertisement?
誰最有可能對此廣告有興趣？

A. A traveler who gets lost.
   迷路的遊客。
B. A newlywed couple who is planning a honeymoon travel.
   正在計畫蜜月旅行的新婚夫妻。
C. A graduate who is looking for a job.
   正在找工作的畢業生。
D. A mother who has difficulty with sleeping.
   有睡眠問題的媽媽。

245

從標題的 Now is the time to visit Europe（現在正是去歐洲的好時機）、內文的 Tour to Europe（歐洲行程）、Twin package（雙人套裝行程）可知，會對此廣告有興趣的會是想去旅行的人，故答案選 B.。

Q23

What is the main reason for traveling to Europe during this time?

這個時候到歐洲旅遊的主要原因是什麼？

A. It is the peak season. 現在是旺季。

B. It is less expensive. 現在比較不貴。

C. It is free of charge. 現在免費。

D. It is more convenient. 現在比較方便。

　　從 What ~ reason ~ traveling to Europe during this time 可知，主要是問這段期間去歐洲的原因。一開始從標題的 Euro dollars ~ low 與 Now is the time to visit Europe 可知，因為歐元創新低，所以現在最適合到歐洲去，也就是比較不貴的意思。

Q24

If Mr. and Mrs. Lin with their 2 sons are joining the tour, how much do they have to pay for the tips in total?

若林先生、林太太與兩位兒子正參加這個行程，他們總共要給多少小費？

A. 200 Euros 200 歐元

B. 400 Euros 400 歐元

C. 800 Euros 800 歐元

D. 1000 Euros 1,000 歐元

　　從 how much ~ they ~ pay for the tips ~ total 可知，主要是問小費總共要付多少。從文中可知，此行程為 10 天的行程（10 Days Tour），當地導遊小費為一人一天 20 歐元，包含小孩也要給小費（Tips for local guides at 20 Euros a day per person），所以小費總共是 20 歐元 x 10 天 x 4 人 = 800 歐元。

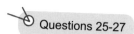

You are invited to the wedding party of John Woo and Mary Wang

Venue: The Holy Cross Church
Address: 40, Heping West Road, Taipei City.
Date: 28 Feb 2016 (Sunday)

您受邀參加 John Woo 和 Mary Wang 的婚禮

地點：神聖十字架教堂
地址：台北市和平西路 40 號
日期：2016 年 2 月 28 日（週日）

Time:
5:00 ~ 5:30 p.m. (PPT Slideshow)
5:30 ~ 6:00 p.m. (Speech by fathers from both sides)
6:00 ~ 6:30 p.m. (Wedding Ceremony)
6:30 ~ 7:30 p.m. (Dinner)
7:30 ~ 8:00 p.m. (Photo-taking with newly-wed couple)

時間：
傍晚 5:00 ~ 5:30 播放投影片
傍晚 5:30 ~ 6:00 雙方父親致詞
傍晚 6:00 ~ 6:30 結婚儀式
傍晚 6:30 ~ 7:30 享用晚餐
傍晚 7:30 ~ 8:00 和新人合照

Please kindly be seated half an hour before the slideshow presentation.
You are welcome to sign on the guest book and view the wedding pictures.
Instead of the traditional wedding dinner, we will have an all-you-can-eat buffet.
Vegetarian food will also be provided.

懇請大家在播放投影片前三十分鐘就座。

歡迎各位在貴賓留言簿上簽名，並欣賞婚紗照。

不同於傳統的結婚晚宴，我們將提供自助式吃到飽。

也將會提供素食餐飲。

|單字片語| **wedding** [ˋwɛdɪŋ] 婚禮 / **be invited to** 受邀到 / **holy** [ˋholɪ] 神聖的 / **church** [tʃɝtʃ] 教堂 / **ceremony** [ˋsɛrəˏmonɪ] 儀式 / **slideshow** 投影片 / **newly-wed** 新婚的 / **be seated** 就座 / **guest book** 留言簿 / **buffet** [buˋfe] 自助式 / **vegetarian** [vɛdʒəˋtɛrɪən] 素食的

What time are the guests expected to show up?

預計賓客幾點要出席？

    A. 4:30 p.m.

    B. 4:45 p.m.

    C. 5:00 p.m.

    D. 5:30 p.m.

> **詳解**   答案：A

    從 What time ~ guests ~ show up 可知，主要是問賓客要到場的時間。從 You are invited to the wedding party 可知，這是一張婚宴邀請函。時間表的第一行提到，5:00 開始會有 Slideshow（播放投影片），下方的說明提到 Please ~ be seated half an hour before the slideshow，表示請賓客在播放投影片前半小時就座，所以預計賓客四點三十分出席。

How many people will be invited to speak?

有多少人受邀致詞？

    A. 1

    B. 2

    C. 4

    D. 8

> **詳解**   答案：B

    從 How many people ~ speak 可知，主要是問有多少人要致詞。時間表上在 5:30 p.m. ~ 6:00 p.m. 的地方提到 Speech by fathers from both sides，表示雙方的父親會致詞，所以會有兩個人要致詞。

Q27

What is NOT true about this invitation?

關於這個邀請函，何者不正確？

A. The wedding will be held in a church. 婚禮將在教堂舉辦。

B. Vegetarian food is provided for the buffet. 有提供自助式素食餐點。

C. Friends are invited to take pictures with the couples.
  朋友們受邀和新婚夫妻拍照。

D. Those who arrive early will be seated in the first row.
  早到的人將會安排在第一排入座。

〔 詳解 〕　　　　　　　　　　　　　　　　　　　　　答案：D

　　從題目可知，主要是問文中未提到的內容。文中提到 Venue ~ Church，Vegetarian food ~ provided，以及 Photo-taking with newly-wed couple，因此可知 A、B、C 都有提到，但並沒說明早到的人將會被安排在第一排。

 Questions 28-30

　　It is no secret that more people are killed on the road than in the air. Driving around is much more dangerous than traveling on a flight. Take the recent news for example, when a tire burst, sending the passengers in the car over the bridge, six lives were lost. Only a woman survived. Family members and hospital staff are still keeping her in the dark. They fear that she will blame herself for her friends' deaths, which might make her injuries worse.

　　Most traffic accidents can be avoided. There are several important things drivers can do to ensure safety. First, have the car checked on a regular basis, especially for cars that are in service for more than 10 years. Have the mechanics check everything inside out, from the engine to the tires. Second, keep a safety distance and avoid change lanes suddenly. Make sure you check the rear and side mirrors to see if there are cars behind or beside you before you change lanes. Last but not least, keep in mind that the higher the speed, the more dangerous it becomes. Do not go beyond the speed limit. Remember, it is always better to be late than never. A little patience makes all the difference.

　　比起在空中，有更多人是在馬路上喪失性命的，而這早已不是祕密了。開車

比搭飛機更加危險。以最近的新聞為例，當時一個輪胎爆胎，造成車裡的乘客從橋上墜落，六人喪生。只有一名女性存活。家人和醫院人員依舊對她隱瞞。他們擔心她會因為朋友的死而責怪自己，而這有可能會讓傷勢更加嚴重。

　　大部分的交通事故都可以被避免。為確保安全，有幾件重要的事是駕駛可以做到的。首先，定時檢查車子，特別是使用超過十年的車子。讓技工從裡到外檢查所有的東西，從引擎到輪胎。第二，保持安全距離，並且避免突然變換車道。在變換車道前一定要看一下後照鏡和側鏡，以確認是否有車在你後面或旁邊。最後但也同樣重要的是，切記速度越快、就越危險。不要超速。記得，遲到總好過到不了。多一點的耐心就會讓結果非常不同。

┃單字片語┃ **in the air** 在空中 / **travel** [ˋtrævəl] 移動，旅行 / **recent** [ˋrisənt] 最近的 / **burst** [bɝst] 爆炸 / **tire** [taɪr] 輪胎 / **survive** [səˋvaɪv] 存活 / **fear** [fɪr] 害怕 / **blame** [blem] 責怪 / **ensure** [ɪnˋʃʊr] 確保 / **safety** [ˋseftɪ] 安全 / **in service** 使用中的 / **mechanic** [məˋkænɪk] 技工 / **engine** [ˋɛndʒən] 引擎 / **distance** [ˋdɪstəns] 距離 / **lane** [len] 車道 / **rear** [rɪr] 後面的 / **last but not least** 最後的但同樣重要的 / **keep in mind** 記住 / **beyond** [bɪˋjɑnd] （範圍）超出，越出 / **makes the difference** 有影響，有關係 / **patience** [ˋpeʃəns] 耐心

Q28

What is true about the only person who survived the car accident?

關於那位唯一在車禍中存活下來的人，何者正確？

A. She doesn't have any injury at all. 她完全沒受傷。

B. She doesn't know the other people in the car.
她不認識車上的其他人。

C. She doesn't want to believe that the accident happened.
她不想相信發生了意外。

D. She doesn't know that the other passengers have died.
她不知道其他乘客已經死亡。

┃詳解┃　　　　　　　　　　　　　　　　　　　　　　　　　答案：D

　　從題目可知，主要是問與唯一生還者相關的正確內容。從第一段的 make her injuries worse 可知，唯一的生還者也受了傷，而且死者都是她的朋友（her friends' deaths），而非不認識的人。文中並未提到這位生還者不想相信意外的發生。文中有提到 Family ~ keeping her in the dark. They fear that she will blame herself ~ might make her injuries worse，表示為避免她因責怪自己而讓傷勢更加嚴重，家人和院方人員沒有告訴她其他乘客死亡的消息，言下之意是她還不知道其他人死亡的消息。

┃單字片語┃ **keep someone in the dark** 對某人隱瞞

Q29

How can accidents be avoided?

意外可以如何避免？

A. Check the car once every ten years. 每十年檢查一次車子。

B. Follow the car in front closely. 緊跟著前方的車子。

C. Keep within the speed limit. 保持在速限內。

D. Drive faster when you are late. 遲到的時候開快一點。

詳解　　　　　　　　　　　　　　　　　　　　　　　　答案：C

　　從題目可知，主要是問避免意外的方式。從第二段一開始提到的 Most traffic accidents can be avoided 可知，接下來會提到避免的方法。文中的 have the car checked on a regular basis 可知，on a regular basis 是經常的意思，所以車子要經常做檢查。也提到 keep a safety distance 和 the higher the speed, the more dangerous ~ Do not go beyond the speed limit，可知選項 A、B 和 D 都違反了安全準則。要避免意外，開車時應該保持在速限內。

Q30

What is the writer trying to say in the last paragraph?

撰文者在最後一段想說什麼？

A. Time is precious. 時間是寶貴的。

B. All doctors are patient. 所有醫生都很有耐心。

C. Being careful and patient makes driving safer.
小心與耐心讓行駛更加安全。

D. It's better to stay in a hospital. 待在醫院裡比較好。

詳解　　　　　　　　　　　　　　　　　　　　　　　　答案：C

　　從題目可知，主要是問第二段的重點。從定時檢查車子（have the car checked on a regular basis）、保持安全距離（keep a safety distance）可知，這裡主要是講對行駛方面的小心謹慎，而從不要超速（Do not go beyond the speed limit）點出了要有耐心，所以 C 是正確答案。

全民英檢初級

第五回 初試 聽力測驗

TEST05.mp3

本測驗分四個部分，全部都是單選題，共 30 題，作答時間約 20 分鐘。作答說明為中文，印在試題冊上並經由光碟放音機播出。

第一部分　看圖辨義

共 5 題（為第 1 題至第 5 題）。每題請聽光碟放音機播出題目和三個英語句子之後，選出與所看到的圖片最相符的答案。每題只播出一遍。

例題：（看）

（聽）Look at the picture.
Which is the cheapest?
A. The computer.
B. The telephone.
C. The TV set.

正確答案為 B，請在答案紙上塗黑作答。

A:　Question 1

B:　Question 2

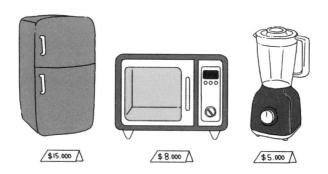

C: Question 3

Departure from Taoyuan International Airport	Rome	Paris	London
Weekdays	☑		☑
Weekends		☑	☑

D: Question 4

E: Question 5

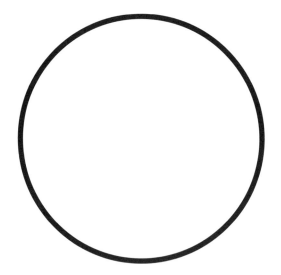

共 10 題（為第 6 題至第 15 題）。每題請聽光碟放音機播出的英語句子，再從試題冊上三個回答中，選出一個最適合的答案。每題只播出**一遍**。

例：　（聽）　Do you speak English?
　　　（看）　A.　No, I speak English quite well.
　　　　　　　B.　Yes, a little.
　　　　　　　C.　No, it's a useful language.

正確答案為 B，請在答案紙上塗黑作答。

6.　A.　Peter turned it on.
　　B.　It's Peter's turn.
　　C.　I think it belongs to Peter.

7.　A.　You had better go to bed.
　　B.　Can't we get there by train?
　　C.　Why don't we eat out?

8.　A.　Only for items with a red dot.
　　B.　You can't take a day off on the weekend.
　　C.　Yes, I remembered.

9.　A.　How long has it been?
　　B.　How often do you take a nap?
　　C.　How many times did you call me?

10.　A.　Yes, I have visited a few countries.
　　B.　Yes, I have bought it.
　　C.　Yes, I have spoken to someone.

11.　A.　You can get it anytime.
　　B.　I don't think that is convenient.
　　C.　Go down this road and take a right.

12.　A.　I don't enjoy rock music.
　　B.　I'm not an outdoor person.
　　C.　I can't eat meat.

13.　A.　How nice of you!
　　B.　What a good idea!
　　C.　That's too bad.

14. A. At least two hours before the flight takes off.
    B. The passengers will be there on time.
    C. We can buy it next month.

15. A. Fine. Everything is OK.
    B. Japan. I have been there twice.
    C. Red. I always like red beans.

第三部分　簡短對話

　　共 10 題（為第 16 題至第 25 題）。每題請聽光碟放音機播出一段對話和一個相關的問題後，再從試題冊上三個選項中，選出一個最適合的答案。每段對話和問題只播出<u>一遍</u>。

例：　(聽)　(Woman)　Could I sit here?
　　　　　　(Man)　　I'm sorry, but this seat is occupied.

　　　　　　Question: Where do you think the dialogue takes place?

　　(看)　A.　In an office
　　　　　B.　In a taxi
　　　　　C.　In a restaurant.

正確答案為 C，請在答案紙上塗黑作答。

16. A. The man bought the woman a diamond ring.
　　B. A real one of the diamond ring is expensive.
　　C. The ring is made of plastic.

17. A. In a restaurant.
　　B. In a hospital.
　　C. In a museum.

18. A. France.
　　B. Germany.
　　C. England.

19. A. Fishing.
　　B. Dancing.
　　C. Eating.

20. A. July 8th.
　　B. July 9th.
　　C. July 10th.

21. A. They share the same interest.
　　B. They are writing a book.
　　C. They are waiting for someone.

22. A. There was a special sale.
　　B. There was a live TV show.
　　C. There was an accident.

23. A. He doesn't have enough time to study.
    B. His grades are not good enough.
    C. He is not rich enough to travel around the world.

24. A. She entered the wrong restroom.
    B. She embarrassed the man.
    C. She forgot to turn off the light.

25. A. NT$1,000.
    B. NT$2,000.
    C. NT$4,000.

第四部分　短文聽解

　　共 5 題（為第 26 題至第 30 題）。每題有三個圖片選項。請聽光碟放音機播出的題目，並選出一個最適當的圖片。每題只播出**一遍**。

例：　（看）

A.　　　　　　B.　　　　　　C.

（聽）
Listen to the following short talk. What might Judy buy?

　　Judy is making a cake for her boyfriend. She checked her refrigerator and found that she had run out of sugar. But she still has lots of flour.

正確答案為 C，請在答案紙上塗黑作答。

Question 26

A.

B.

C.

Question 27

A.

B.

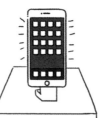

C.

Question 28

A.

B.

C.

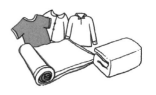

Question 29

A.

B.

C.

Question 30

A.

B.

C.

本測驗分三部分，全部都是單選題，共 30 題，作答時間 35 分鐘。

第一部分：詞彙

　　共 10 題，每個題目裡有一個空格。請從四個選項中選出一個<u>最適合</u>題意的字或詞作答。

1. Nobody will _____ you the truth if you always get angry.
   A. say
   B. tell
   C. talk
   D. speak

2. Mrs. Chen: Do we have any flour left?
   Mr. Chen: There's only _____ in the box.
   A. a little
   B. a few
   C. several
   D. a lot of

3. Have you _____ about your future? How are you going to make a living?
   A. though
   B. thought
   C. through
   D. taught

4. Margaret is feeling _____ because the boy she likes is chatting to another girl happily.
   A. jealous
   B. curious
   C. honest
   D. talkative

5. I am terribly sorry. It's all my _____. I should have listened to you.
   A. effort
   B. fault
   C. hope
   D. service

6. Since young, he has always been curious _____ science and nature.
   A. about
   B. of
   C. with
   D. by

7. Oh no! It's my turn to give a speech. I am so _____ that my knees are shaking.
   A. famous
   B. serious
   C. generous
   D. nervous

8. I am not allowed to watch TV _____ on Sundays for less than two hours.
   A. despite
   B. except
   C. although
   D. besides

9. The Internet is _____ you can get free information quickly.
   A. that
   B. what
   C. where
   D. when

10. Some fresh graduates went abroad in search of better job _____.
    A. advertisements
    B. examples
    C. opportunities
    D. manners

第二部分：段落填空

　　共 8 題，包括二個段落，每個段落各含四個空格。每格均有四個選項，請依照文意選出<u>最適合</u>的答案。

Questions 11-14

　　I was born and ___(11)___ in a single-parent family. I have no memory of my dad during my childhood. He never cared to go to any teacher-parent meeting. Once, I was surprised to hear one of my elementary classmates ___(12)___ that my dad was in school. It ___(13)___ that it was my mom. She wore her hair short and she was wearing pants. My friends thought she was a 'he'. I was too embarrassed to say anything. Since then, I told her not to go to my school unless necessary. As a result, I studied really hard ___(14)___. Until today, she still has no idea what made me study so hard. She didn't realize that her looks and dressing was the reason I got good grades in school.

11. A. brought up
　　B. called on
　　C. taken off
　　D. dressed in

12. A. say
　　B. says
　　C. said
　　D. to say

13. A. turned in
　　B. turned out
　　C. turned up
　　D. turned down

14. A. so as to make my dreams come true
　　B. so that the teachers would not ask to see her
　　C. and I went to school with one of my classmates
　　D. even if I didn't get along well with her

Questions 15-18

Is online gaming good or bad? _____(15)_____ it is true that we need a good balance between work and play, teenagers can lose themselves in the world of fantasy. There are so many interesting games to play that one can never finish playing all of _____(16)_____. The fact that online gaming is now possible with WIFI hotspots has made matters _____(17)_____. Teenagers can play online games not only in front of their computers but also on their smartphones while on the bus and in MRT stations. _____(18)_____, most of them are staring at electronic products. The days when passengers read a paperback or the newspaper were gone.

15. A. Which
    B. While
    C. Whether
    D. Whenever

16. A. it
    B. its
    C. them
    D. their

17. A. well
    B. better
    C. best
    D. worse

18. A. When the first smartphone was introduced to the world
    B. As work and play are both important
    C. Even though teenagers are crazy about online games
    D. Instead of making use of their time to read something meaningful

第三部分：閱讀理解

　　共 12 題，包括 4 個題組，每個題組含 1 至 2 篇短文，與數個相關的四選一的選擇題。請由試題冊上的選項中選出最適合的答案。

Questions 19-21

School Club List

Dance Club	meet **Mon. & Wed.**	**4:00-5:00 PM**
Chess Club	meet **Saturday**	**1:00-3:00 PM**
Art Club	meet **Tue. & Thur.**	**4:00-5:00 PM**
Movie Club	meet **Mon. & Thur.**	**4:00-5:00 PM**
Guitar Club	meet **Saturday**	**3:00-5:00 PM**

Cindy's School schedules

	Mon.	Tue.	Wed.	Thur.	Fri.	Sat.	Sun.
10:00 AM-12:00 PM	Class	Class	Class	Class	Class	Class	Free
1:00 PM-3:00 PM	Class	Class	Class	Class	Class	Free	Free
3:00 PM-5:00 PM	Class	Free	Class	Free	Class	Free	Free

Dear Cindy,

Your teacher just called, but you weren't home, so I left this note for you. Your teacher asked me to tell you that you should pick up a new club to attend for this new semester. He said you should choose one when you are free from classes. Anyway, I know you are interested in music and hope you can choose what you really like.

Love you!

Mom

19. According to Cindy's mother, which club will Cindy probably choose?
   A. Chess Club.
   B. Guitar Club.
   C. Art Club.
   D. Movie Club.

20. According to Cindy's class schedule, which of the following clubs can be chosen?
   A. Chess club, dance club and movie club.
   B. Art club, chess club and guitar club.
   C. Movie club, art club and dance club.
   D. Guitar club, chess club and movie club.

21. Which of the following statements is correct?
   A. Cindy has no class on Tuesday morning.
   B. Cindy's father left the note.
   C. Cindy didn't get her teacher's call.
   D. Movie club meets every Monday and Wednesday.

Questions 22-24

Flight No.	Departure Time	Destination	Gate	Terminal
QQ373	07:30	Tokyo	A6	T1
JJ469	07:45	Paris	A8	T1
BB725	08:00	Rome	B2	T2
KK618	08:15	London	B4	T2

Please be reminded that check-in counters will be opened two hours before departure. Also, please report to the boarding gate at least 30 minutes before takeoff.

22. Where will you most likely see the information?
    A. Bus station.
    B. Subway station.
    C. Airport.
    D. Post office.

23. What is the earliest time you can check in if you are going to Paris?
    A. 05:30
    B. 05:45
    C. 07:15
    D. 07:45

24. What time do you have to be at gate B4 at the latest?
    A. Seven o'clock.
    B. A quarter past seven.
    C. A quarter to eight.
    D. Eight o'clock.

NT$5,000 REWARD
Help us find our beloved pet, Bobby.

Last seen in Central Park on 26 January
Wearing a silver dog tag
Has a pink birthmark on its back

Bobby has been part of our family for eleven years. He is like an elderly human. We are really worried because he is not able to take care of himself. Please call us if you see him. We offer NT$5000 to anyone who finds him. Please call us at once if you have any news.

0927898XXX or 02-3580-XXXX

25. What is the purpose of this notice?
    A. To look for a missing person.
    B. To look for a missing animal.
    C. To look for a missing item.
    D. To look for a missing car.

26. What is true about Bobby?
    A. He has a pet at home.
    B. He has a birthmark on his body.
    C. He will pay the NT$5000 reward.
    D. He will answer the call at once.

27. Where can we most likely see the information?
    A. In the ocean.
    B. In a park.
    C. In a zoo.
    D. In an airport.

Questions 28-30

Taiwan experiences three to four hits by typhoons a year. Strong winds can break windows and send metal roofs flying. Heavy rain can also cause landslides and flooding. Farmers are affected the most during typhoon seasons. A day of rain can destroy crops and plants that take months to grow. People living in the mountains are also in danger because landslides can destroy buildings and roads with them. However, a typhoon may be a blessing in disguise sometimes.

A typhoon brings the island a lot of water it needs. A lack of water could affect a lot of people. In early 2015, many cities suffered from a lack of water and it almost turned into a major crisis. Families and businesses cannot function without clean water. Water supply was shut off in many cities for two days in a week, which caused much inconvenience. Typhoons are necessary as a source of water but there is no way we can control them. Therefore, we should look into the possibility of turning seawater into drinkable water, which is what Singapore has already succeeded in doing.

28. Why might strong winds be dangerous?
    A. People may get hit by falling or broken objects.
    B. People may be hurt by landslides.
    C. People may get killed by flooding.
    D. People may be blown away.

29. What is the best explanation for 'a blessing in disguise'?
    A. Something which was good at first became something bad.
    B. Something which was bad at first became something good.
    C. Something which was bad at first became something worse.
    D. Something which was good at first became something better.

30. According to the passage, what happened in early 2015?
   A. A super typhoon hit Taiwan.
   B. Many places were flooded.
   C. It did not rain for a long period of time.
   D. A lot of people drank seawater.

第五回

初試 聽力測驗 解析

Q1

For question one, please look at picture A.

What is true according to the map in the picture?

根據圖片中的地圖，何者屬實？

A. The school is across from the hospital.

B. The bank is between the park and the school.

C. The convenience store is next to the school.

A. 學校在醫院對面。

B. 銀行在公園跟學校中間。

C. 便利商店在學校旁邊。

詳解

答案：C

　　從圖中可知，左上角是公園，右上角是學校與便利商店，左下角是醫院，右下角是銀行。聽到 What is true ~ picture 可知，主要是問與圖相符的敘述。學校的對面是銀行，不是醫院，選項 A 是錯的。銀行也不是在公園跟學校中間，選項 B 也是錯的，便利商店確實在學校旁邊，C 是正確答案。請注意位置相關的介系詞，如 across from（在～對面），between（在～之間），next to（在～旁邊）。

Q2

For question two, please look at picture B.

What can you tell from the picture?

從這張圖片可得知什麼？

A. The blender is the least expensive of all.

B. The microwave oven costs less than the blender.

C. The blender is more expensive than the refrigerator.

A. 攪拌機是最便宜的。

B. 微波爐比攪拌機便宜。

C. 攪拌機比電冰箱貴。

詳解

答案：A

　　從圖中可知，有 3 個不同價位的家電商品，冰箱最貴，攪拌機最便宜。聽到 What ~ tell from the picture 可知，主要是問與圖相符的敘述。A 提到攪拌機最不貴 (the least expensive)，也可以說成最便宜 (the cheapest)，A 是正確答案。因為 cheap 也有廉價和低賤的意思，所以有些人喜歡說某個東西比較不貴 less expensive。B 提到微波爐比攪拌機便宜，但已知攪拌機是最便宜的，所以不正確。

Q3

For question three, please look at picture C.

Departure from Taoyuan International Airport 從桃園國際機場離境	Rome 羅馬	Paris 巴黎	London 倫敦
Weekdays 平日	☑		☑
Weekends 週末		☑	☑

Look at the flight schedule. Which of the following information is correct?
請看這張班機行程表。以下哪一個資訊正確？

A. There is a flight to England on Saturdays.
B. Flights depart to all three cities on weekends.
C. You can take a plane to France on Wednesdays.

A. 星期六有一班班機前往英國。
B. 週末的班機這三座城市都有飛。
C. 你在星期三可以搭機到法國。

詳解

答案：A

　　從表中可知是班機時刻表，有 3 個目的地，以及 2 個不同時間。聽到 Which ~ information ~ correct 可知，題目是問與表格內容相符的敘述。A 提到星期六前往英國，而星期六也就是週末，正好符合表格內容，是正確答案。B 提到 3 座城市與週末，但週末時班機不飛羅馬。C 提到星期三到法國，也就是平日的意思，但平日沒有到巴黎的班機。

補充說明

歐洲國家	首都
英國（England）	倫敦（London）

法國（France）	巴黎（Paris）
義大利（Italy）	羅馬（Rome）
德國（Germany）	柏林（Berlin）
西班牙（Spain）	馬德里（Madrid）
捷克（Czech）	布拉格（Prague）
俄羅斯（Russia）	莫斯科（Moscow）
荷蘭（Holland）	阿姆斯特丹（Amsterdam）
希臘（Greece）	雅典（Athens）

Q4

For question four, please look at picture D.

What's wrong with the car?
這台車子怎麼了？

A. It is running out of gas.
B. It is getting too hot.
C. It is breaking down.

A. 快沒油了。
B. 變得太熱了。
C. 正在拋錨。

詳解　　　　　　　　　　　　　　　　　　　　　答案：A

　　看圖可知是車子儀表板的油表，指針指著 Empty，表示快要沒有油。聽到 What's wrong ~ car 可知，主要是問車子的狀況。A 提到 running out of gas.，表示要沒油了的意思，是正確答案。一般車子的油量儀錶器會顯示「滿」F = Full 和「空 E = Empty，指針接近 E 表示車子快沒油了。另一個是引擎溫度儀錶器，H 代表熱 Hot，C 代表冷 Cold。

Q5

For question five, please look at picture E.

What shape do you see?
你看到什麼形狀？

A. A square.
B. A triangle.
C. A circle.

A. 正方形。
B. 三角形。
C. 圓形。

第 1 回

第 2 回

第 3 回

第 4 回

第 5 回

第 6 回

詳解

　　看圖可知是一個圓形。聽到 What shape 可知，題目是問這張圖片的形狀名稱。C 提到圓形，所以是正確答案。circle 當名詞時是圓圈和圈子的意思，當動詞時是畫圓圈的意思。angle 是角度的意思，tri-有三的意思，有三個角（angle）表示三角形，四邊形為 rectangle。

Q6

Whose turn is it to do the laundry?
輪到誰洗衣服？

A. Peter turned it on.
B. It's Peter's turn.
C. I think it belongs to Peter.

A. Peter 打開的。
B. 輪到 Peter。
C. 我想它是屬於 Peter 的。

詳解 答案：B

　　選項都提到與 Peter 相關的不同敘述。聽到 Whose turn ~ do the laundry 可知 whose 是指誰的（某人的），而 turn 是輪流的意思，題目是問換誰洗衣服，由此可知 Peter's turn 是正確答案。

 補充說明

　　turn 原本是轉動的意思，在題目中指的是輪到某某人的順位。玩桌遊時，miss a turn 表示本來論到某人，卻跳過一次的意思。

|單字片語| **laundry** [ˋlɔndrɪ] 要洗的衣服，洗好的衣服 / **turned on** 打開 / **belong to** 屬於

Q7

I'm tired of cooking every meal by myself.
我對於每一餐都自己煮感到厭倦了。

A. You had better go to bed.
B. Can't we get there by train?
C. Why don't we eat out?

A. 你最好上床睡覺了。
B. 我們不能坐火車去那裡嗎？
C. 我們何不去外面吃？

詳解 答案：C

　　選項都提到與建議對方或所有人相關的不同敘述。聽到 I'm tired of cooking ~. 可知，是一個抱怨總是要自己做菜的直述句，選項中與三餐相關的是 C，表示既然厭倦自己煮，便建議對方吃外食。be tired 指疲倦，be tired of something 表示對某個東西或事物感到厭倦。

|單字片語| **be tired of** 對⋯感到厭倦 / **cook** [kʊk] 煮 / **meal** [mil] （一）餐 / **go to bed** 上床睡覺 / **train** [tren] 火車 / **eat out** 吃外食

Q8

Do members get another five percent off?
會員還可以再多 5% 的折扣嗎？

A. Only for items with a red dot.
B. You can't take a day off on the weekend.
C. Yes, I remembered.

A. 有紅點的商品才有。
B. 你在週末不能請假。
C. 是的，我記得。

詳解　　　　　　　　　　　　　　　　　　　　　答案：A

　　選項 A 提到某種特定商品，B 提到不能請假，C 提到自己記得。聽到 Do members get ~ five percent off 可知，說話者詢問會員是否享有更多折扣，表示說話者人在商店，要回答這個問題的聽者應該就是店員。店員的合理回應為 A。

|單字片語| **member** [`mɛmbɚ] 會員 / **dot** [dɑt] 點 / **item** [`aɪtəm] 項目，商品 / **take a day off** 請一天假 / **weekend** [`wik`ɛnd] 週末

Q9

I have a bad cough and I can't sleep well.
我咳嗽咳得很嚴重，而且睡不好。

A. How long has it been?
B. How often do you take a nap?
C. How many times did you call me?

A. 這樣已經多久了？
B. 你多常睡午覺？
C. 你打給我幾次了？

詳解　　　　　　　　　　　　　　　　　　　　　答案：A

　　選項都是與 How 相關的不同問句。聽到 I have a bad cough~.可知，說話者應該是病人，聽者可能是是醫生，而醫生最有可能會回應的是回問病人咳嗽的症狀已經多久了。

|單字片語| **cough** [kɔf] 咳嗽 / **sleep** [slip] 睡覺 / **take a nap** 睡午覺

Q10

Have you ever been abroad?
你曾經去過國外嗎？

A. Yes, I have visited a few countries.
B. Yes, I have bought it.
C. Yes, I have spoken to someone.

A. 是的，我去過幾個國家。
B. 是的，我已經買了。
C. 是的，我已經跟某個人說了。

選項全都是用 Yes 表達出肯定的直述句，可猜想聽到的題目應該是疑問句。聽到 Have you ~ been abroad?可知，主要是問聽者是否有出國的經驗。選項中與 abroad（到國外）相關的敘述是 A。問別人有沒有到過某個地方，英文可以說 Have you ever been to…?。abroad（國外）和 overseas（海外）的意思一樣，而到國外留學可以說 study abroad 或 study overseas。

Q11

Could you tell me how to get to the nearest convenience store?
你可以告訴我要如何去最近的便利商店嗎？

A. You can get it anytime.
B. I don't think that is convenient.
C. Go down this road and take a right turn.

A. 你隨時都可以拿到它。
B. 我不認為那樣方便。
C. 這條路直走然後右轉。

選項 A 和 B 是與給予訊息、意見相關的直述句，而 C 用祈使句告知路線資訊。聽到 Could you tell me how ~ to ~ store? 可知，說話者是在問路，所以最合理的答覆是 C。若聽到 convenience store（便利商店）就選擇聽起來很相似的 convenient（方便的）的話，就掉到陷阱裡面了。

|單字片語| **near** [nɪr] 靠近的 / **convenience store** 便利商店 / **anytime** [ˈɛnɪˌtaɪm] 隨時，在任何時候 / **convenient** [convenient] 方便的 / **take a right turn** 右轉

Q12

Would you like to go rock climbing with us next month?
下個月你想要和我們去攀岩嗎？

A. I don't enjoy rock music.
B. I'm not an outdoor person.
C. I can't eat meat.

A. 我不喜歡搖滾樂。
B. 我不是個熱衷戶外活動的人。
C. 我不能吃肉。

選項都是表達個人意見的否定直述句，可猜想題目可能是詢問意願的疑問句。聽到 Would you like ~ rock climbing ~?可知，題目是邀約聽者一起去攀岩。若聽者要婉拒說話者對於攀岩的邀約，最合理的答案為 B。

|單字片語| **rock climbing** 攀岩 / **rock music** 搖滾樂 / **outdoor** [ˈaʊtˌdor] 戶外的

第 1 回
第 2 回
第 3 回
第 4 回
第 5 回
第 6 回

<補充說明>

表達「我不是個⋯的人」時，⋯的位置也可以放名詞，例如：

I am not a dog person.（我不是個「狗」的人），意思是 I am not a dog lover.（我不是一個愛狗人士）。

Q13

I'm afraid I can't make it to your party tonight.
今晚我恐怕不能去你的派對了。

A. How nice of you!	A. 你人真好！
B. What a good idea!	B. 真是個好主意！
C. That's too bad.	C. 真可惜。

詳解

答案：C

選項都是感嘆句表達，可猜想題目應該是一個直述句，陳述一個事件。聽到 I'm afraid I can't make it to your ~.的 I'm afraid 就可知，題目是表達無法做某事，所以聽者最合理的回應是 C。

<補充說明>

很久以前有個廣告台詞：Trust me. You can make it.（相信我。你辦得到），make it 表示「可做到、辦到、成功」的意思，can't make it 則是「辦不到、沒辦法」的意思。

Q14

When do we need to be at the airport?
我們需要什麼時候到機場？

A. At least two hours before the flight takes off.	A. 至少在班機起飛前兩小時。
B. The passengers will be there on time.	B. 乘客們會準時到那裡。
C. We can buy it next month.	C. 我們可以下個月再買。

詳解

答案：A

選項 A 和 B 的敘述與飛機和乘客相關，可推測題目可能是跟班機相關的疑問句。聽到 When ~ need to be at the airport? 可知，主要是問需要到機場的時間，最合理的答案是提到班機起飛前兩小時的特定時間的 A。

|單字片語| **airport** [`ɛr͵port] 機場 / **flight** [flaɪt] 班機 / **take off** 起飛 / **passenger** [`pæsəndʒɚ] 乘客 / **on time** 準時

Q15

Is that you, Susan? How have you been?
Susan，是妳嗎？妳最近如何？

A. Fine. Everything is OK.
B. Japan. I have been there twice.
C. Red. I always like red beans.

A. 很好。一切都還不錯。
B. 日本。我已經去過兩次了。
C. 紅的。我一直以來都喜歡紅豆。

詳解

　　聽到 ~ Susan? How have you been? 可知，聽者是 Susan，主要是問聽者的近況如何，因此最適合的回答是 A。How have you been? 相當於中文的「最近過得如何？」。

第 1 回

第 2 回

第 3 回

第 4 回

第 5 回

第 6 回

第三部分 / 簡短對話

Q16

Woman: Oh my gosh! This diamond ring is so big.
我的天啊！這個鑽戒好大。

Man: Well, it's fake. It's made of a special kind of glass.
嗯，這是假的。它是由一種特別的玻璃做成的。

Woman: A real one this size would cost at least a few million dollars.
一個這麼大的真的鑽戒至少要幾百萬。

Q: What is true about the conversation?
關於這個對話，何者屬實？

A. The man bought the woman a diamond ring.
B. A real one of the diamond ring is expensive.
C. The ring is made of plastic.

A. 這位男士買了一個鑽戒給女士。
B. 真正的這種鑽戒很貴。
C. 這個戒指是塑膠做的。

詳解 答案：B

　　從選項中都提到 diamond ring 可猜想對話可能與鑽戒有關。聽到 What is true ~ conversation? 可知，主要是問與對話內容相符的敘述。雖然女士一開始說鑽戒很大，但也沒有向男士表示道謝，無法判斷此鑽戒是否為男士買給女士的。男士提到鑽戒不是真的，是由 a special kind of glass（一種特別的玻璃）製成的，所以 C 也不正確。女子最後提到 A real one ~ cost at least a few million dollars，可知 B 是正確答案。

|單字片語| **my gosh** 我的天啊 / **diamond ring** 鑽戒 / **be made of** 由…製成 / **glass** [glæs] 玻璃 / **cost** [kɔst] 花費 / **million** [ˈmɪljən] 百萬 / **expensive** [ɪkˋspɛnsɪv] 貴的 / **plastic** [ˈplæstɪk] 塑膠

Q17

Man: I will have the spaghetti and the soup of the day.
我要義大利麵與今日指定湯。

Woman: Just a salad for me. I'm on a diet.　我只要一個沙拉。我在節食。

Man: I think that will be all.　我想這樣就好了。

Q: Where are the speakers?
說話者在什麼地方？

A. In a restaurant.
B. In a hospital.
C. In a museum.

A. 在餐廳。
B. 在醫院。
C. 在博物館。

詳解

答案：A

　　從選項可猜想題目會問對話進行的地點在哪裡。從對話中提到的 I will have the spaghetti（我要義大利麵）、soup（湯）和 salad（沙拉），可判斷說話者在餐廳。

|單字片語| **spaghetti** [spə`gɛtɪ] 義大利麵 / **soup** [sup] 湯 / **salad** [`sæləd] 沙拉 / **on a diet** 在節食，在減肥

Q18

Woman:　Have you ever been to Europe?　你去過歐洲嗎？

Man:　　Never. But I plan to visit Germany.
　　　　從來沒有。但是我計畫去德國。

Woman:　I'm visiting my aunt in Paris in France in December.
　　　　我十二月要去法國巴黎拜訪我的阿姨。

Man:　　Wow! Sounds great!　哇！真好！

Q: Which country will the woman probably go?
這位女士應該會去哪一個國家？

A. France.
B. Germany.
C. England.

A. 法國。
B. 德國。
C. 英國。

詳解

答案：A

　　從選項可猜想題目應該會問對話中提到的國家。女士一開始問男士是否去過歐洲，她還提到十二月要到巴黎拜訪她的阿姨，因此她應該會去法國巴黎。（歐洲主要國家首都請見 278 頁）。而題目也問到 Which country ~ woman ~ go，主要是問女士會去的國家，所以答案是 A。由於題目是最後才播，考生不僅要記得聽到的對話內容，還必須記得說話的男士和女士分別說了什麼。

Q19

Man: Look what I caught! It's huge!　看我捉到什麼！牠好大！

Woman: Be careful. Don't fall off the boat.　小心。別從船上掉下去。

Man: Take a picture of me and the fish, will you?
　　　　　幫我和魚拍張照，好嗎？

> **Q: What might the speakers be doing?**
> 　說話者們可能在做什麼？
>
> A. Fishing.　　　　　　　　　A. 釣魚。
> B. Dancing.　　　　　　　　　B. 跳舞。
> C. Eating.　　　　　　　　　　C. 吃東西。

詳解　　　　　　　　　　　　　　　　　　　　　　　　答案：A

　　從選項可猜想題目應該會問對話中提到在做的事情。男子一開始提到抓到某東西，女子提到 Don't fall off the boat，表示他們應該在船上，男子還提到 the fish，從關鍵字（caught、boat、fish），可知說話者可能正在釣魚。而最後聽到題目 What ~ speakers ~ doing 可知是問正在做的事，所以答案是 A。

|單字片語| **caught** 捉（**catch** 的過去式）/ **huge** [hjudʒ] 大的 / **be careful** 小心 / **fall off** 從…掉下去 / **boat** [bot] 船 / **take a picture** 拍照

Q20

Woman: Today's the eighth of July. Isn't Amy's birthday tomorrow?
　　　　　今天是七月八日。Amy 的生日不是明天嗎？

Man: Her birthday is the day after tomorrow.　她的生日是後天。

Woman: I think I'm getting old.　我想我老了。

> **Q: When is Amy's birthday?**
> 　Amy 的生日是何時？
>
> A. July 8th.　　　　　　　　　A. 七月八日。
> B. July 9th.　　　　　　　　　B. 七月九日。
> C. July 10th.　　　　　　　　C. 七月十日。

詳解　　　　　　　　　　　　　　　　　　　　　　　　答案：C

　　從選項可推測題目應該會問對話中提到的日期。女子一開始提到今天的日期，即七月八日，又提到 Amy 的生日，而男士糾正女士說 Amy 的生日是在後天，即七月十日。最後聽到題目 When ~ Amy's birthday? 可知是問 Amy 的生日日期，所以答案是 C。

|單字片語| **the day after tomorrow** 後天 / **birthday** [ˋbɝθˌde] 生日

第1回　第2回　第3回　第4回　第5回　第6回

Man: We seem to have a lot in common. I love novels written by this writer. 我們似乎有很多共通點。我喜歡這位作者寫的小說。

Woman: I find his stories touching. 我覺得他的故事很感人。

Man: I can't wait for his next book. 我迫不及待看他下一本書了。

Q: What can be said about the speakers?
關於說話者，提到了什麼？

A. They share the same interest.
B. They are writing a book.
C. They are waiting for someone.

A. 他們有共同的興趣。
B. 他們在寫一本書。
C. 他們在等人。

詳解　　　　　　　　　　　　　　　　　　　　　　　答案：A

從選項可猜想題目應該會問對話中人物的相關事項。男子一開始提到 we have ~ in common，表示男子與女子兩人有共通點，也就是說有共同的興趣，之後兩人都對於提到的作者與作品表示肯定的回應。最後聽到題目 What ~ said about ~ speakers 可知，是問與說話者兩人相關的事實，所以正確答案是 A。common 是「普遍的；常見的；共同的」的意思。

單字片語 **in common** 共同 / **novel** [ˋnɑvəl] 小說 / **writer** [ˋraɪtɚ] 作家 / **touching** [tʌtʃɪŋ] 感人的 / **can't wait for** 等不及⋯ / **interest** [ˋɪntərɪst] 興趣 / **share** [ʃɛr] 共有，分享

Woman: We need an ambulance. Two people are badly hurt. 我們需要救護車。有兩個人受了重傷。

Man: Please tell me where you are. 請告訴我你在哪裡。

Woman: Let me see. Queen Street. 我看看。皇后街。

Q: What might have happened?
可能發生了什麼事？

A. There was a special sale.
B. There was a live TV show.
C. There was an accident.

A. 有一個特賣會。
B. 有一個現場直播的電視節目。
C. 有一場事故。

詳解　　　　　　　　　　　　　　　　　　　　　　　答案：C

一開始聽到 We need an ambulance，還提到 Two people ~ hurt，表示有人受傷，所以需要救護車。從男子所問的內容可推斷，男子不在現場，所以女子應

該是撥打 119 通知男子需要救護車，並提到有兩人受重傷，也提到路名，可推測是發生了一場事故。

|單字片語| **ambulance** [ˈæmbjələns] 救護車 / **hurt** [hɝt] 受傷 / **Let me see.** 我看看。 / **sale** [sel] 拍賣會 / **live** [laɪv] 現場直播的 / **accident** [ˈæksədənt] 事故

第 1 回
第 2 回
第 3 回
第 4 回
第 5 回
第 6 回

Q23

Man:　　I have a feeling I won't be able to get into a senior high school I want.　我覺得我沒辦法進入我想念的高中。

Woman:　Look on the bright side. It's not the end of the world.
　　　　　往好的方面去想吧，這不是世界末日。

Man:　　But most of my classmates will be there. I should have studied harder.　但是我大部分的同班同學都會在那裡。當初我應該要更加用功讀書才對。

Q: What is the man's problem?
　　這位男士的問題是什麼？

A. He doesn't have enough time to study.
B. His grades are not good enough.
C. He is not rich enough to travel around the world.

A. 他沒有足夠的時間讀書。
B. 他的成績不夠好。
C. 他不夠有錢去環遊世界。

詳解　　　　　　　　　　　　　　　　　　　　　　答案：B

　　從選項中的 He 和 His 可推測，題目會問與男士相關的問題。一開始男士提到 won't be able to get into a senior high school I want，表示沒辦法進入所選的高中，最後一句又說 I should have studied harder，表示當初應該更加用功讀書，可推斷這位男士的成績不夠好，所以正確答案是 B。

|單字片語| **be able to** 能夠做… / **senior high school** 高中 / **grade** [gred] 成績 / **travel** [ˈtrævəl] 旅行

Q24

Woman:　I'm terribly sorry. I thought this was the ladies' restroom.
　　　　　非常抱歉，我以為這是女廁。

Man:　　It's all right. Sometimes it happens.　沒關係，有時候就是會這樣。

Woman:　This is so embarrassing.　真是尷尬。

Q: What's wrong with the woman?
這位女士怎麼了？

A. She entered the wrong restroom.
B. She embarrassed the man.
C. She forgot to turn off the light.

A. 她走進了錯的洗手間。
B. 她讓這位男士感到尷尬。
C. 她忘了關燈。

詳解   答案：A

　　從選項中的 She 可推測，題目會問與女士相關的問題。一開始女士提到 sorry，向男士說抱歉，又說 I thought this was the ladies' restroom.，表示以為這是女廁，言下之意這裡其實是男廁，可見她進錯了洗手間，所以正確答案是 A。女廁通常簡稱為 Ladies，男廁由紳士 Gentlemen 表示，簡稱為 Gents。

|單字片語| **terribly** [ˋtɛrəblɪ] 非常 / **restroom** [ˋrɛstruːm] 洗手間 / **embarrassing** [ɪmˋbærəsɪŋ] 使人尷尬的 / **enter** [ˋɛntɚ] 進入 / **wrong** [rɔŋ] 錯的 / **embarrassed** [ɪmˋbærəst] 感到尷尬的

Q25

Man:　　Lower the price a little and I will take two.
　　　　價格低一點，那我就買兩個。

Woman: Two thousand NT dollars each. Final offer.
　　　　一個新台幣兩千元，這是最後的價格。

Man:　　It's a deal. 成交。

Q: How much will the man pay the woman?
這位男士將付給這位女士多少錢？

A. NT$1,000.
B. NT$2,000.
C. NT$4,000.

A. 新台幣一千元
B. 新台幣兩千元
C. 新台幣四千元

詳解   答案：C

　　從選項中的金額可推測，題目會問與多少錢（How much）相關的問題。一開始男士提到 Lower the price 和 I will take two，表示希望對方降價，而且若對方降價男士會買兩個，女士則說一個要兩千元（Two thousand ~ dollars each），這裡的重點為 each，為「每一個」的意思。男士回應 It's a deal（成交），由此可知男士會花 2,000 x 2 = 4,000 元買兩個，所以正確答案是 C。

|單字片語| **lower** [ˋloɚ] 降低 / **price** [praɪs] 價格 / **thousand** [ˋθaʊzənd] 千 / **pay** [pe] 付

第 1 回
第 2 回
第 3 回
第 4 回
第 5 回
第 6 回

第四部分 短文聽解

Q26

For question number 26, please look at the three pictures.

Please listen to the following voice message. 請聽以下的語音訊息。

Where does the man want the listener to go during lunch time?
這位男士要聽者在午餐時間時去哪裡？

Honey, my car broke down on my way to work this morning. The car is in the repair shop near our apartment. I don't think it will be ready by noon time. Alice will leave school after lunch. Can you go pick her up before 12:30? Let her stay with you at the office and make sure she does her homework.

親愛的，今天早上我去工作的途中車子拋錨了。車子停在我們公寓旁的修車廠。我不認為在午餐時間前會修好。Alice 會在午餐後離開學校。你可以在 12:30 之前去接她嗎？讓她跟你一起待在辦公室，並確認她有寫功課。

A.

B.

C.

詳解

答案：B

　　從圖片的不同地點可推測，題目會問與在哪裡（Where）相關的問題。一開始提到 my car broke down ~ this morning.，又說 Alice will leave school after lunch. Can you go pick her up before 12:30?，一開始就提到了「今天早上」「午餐之後」「12 點半」這些時間點，請注意這些時間點，通常這類有關時間點、行程的題型，圖片可能會依照早上、下午和晚上的時間順序由左至右，但有時候考官會故意顛倒順序。關鍵字為午餐時間，語音留言提到請對方在 12:30 之前要到學校接孩子，所以聽者在午餐時間會到學校去。

|單字片語| **during** [ˋdjʊrɪŋ] 在…期間 / **lunch time** 午餐時間 / **break down** 停止運轉，失靈，拋錨 / **on one's way to** 在去…的途中 / **repair shop** 修車廠 / **apartment** [əˋpɑrtmənt] 公寓 / **office** [ˋɔfɪs] 辦公室

For question number 27, please look at the three pictures.

Please listen to the following short talk. 請聽以下的簡短談話。

What product is the speaker talking about?
說話者在談論什麼商品？

We are pleased to announce our latest product: the Super Mini Wear-Gear. You will find it useful. You can use its voice control function to make phone calls, read messages and even check your heartbeat as it is worn on your wrist just like a watch. What are you waiting for? Get our Super Mini Wear-Gear today!

我們很高興宣布我們的最新產品：超級迷你穿戴裝置。你會發現它非常有用。你可以利用語音控制功能來打電話、讀簡訊，甚至能檢測你的心跳，因為這個裝置就戴在你的手腕上，就跟手錶一樣。你還在等什麼？今天就購買我們的超級迷你穿戴裝置吧！

A.

B.

C.

詳解　　　　　　　　　　　　　　　　　　　　　　　　　　　　**答案：A**

從圖片是不同物品可推測，題目會問與什麼事物（What）相關的問題。一開始提到 ~ announce our latest product: the Super Mini Wear-Gear. ，可以知道將介紹一個最新產品，可預測接下來會說明此產品的特色。接著提到 You can use ~ voice control function to make phone calls~ 等功能，又說 it is worn on your wrist. ~ like a watch，從 wrist（手腕）、和 like a watch（像手錶）可知是戴在手腕上的產品。所以圖片中的智慧型手錶是正確答案。

|單字片語| **announce** [əˋnaʊns] 宣布 / **useful** [ˋjusfəl] 有用的 / **voice** [vɔɪs] 語音 / **control** [kənˋtrol] 控制 / **function** [ˋfʌŋkʃən] 功能 / **make a phone call** 打電話 / **message** [ˋmɛsɪdʒ] 簡訊 / **heartbeat** [ˋhɑrt͵bit] 心跳 / **wrist** [rɪst] 手腕

第 1 回
第 2 回
第 3 回
第 4 回
第 5 回
第 6 回

Q28

For question number 28, please look at the three pictures.

Please listen to the following news report. 請聽以下的新聞報導。

What is most needed right now?
現在最需要的是什麼？

Due to heavy rains, mud slides occurred in several mountain areas. Many houses in Ren-Ai village in Taitung were destroyed. Since our report two days ago, food and medical supplies have arrived with amazing speed. The villagers are no longer in need of such items. What they need now is winter clothes and blankets as temperatures are expected to drop further.

由於豪雨的關係，幾個山區發生了土石流。在台東仁愛村的許多房子遭到破壞。自從我們兩天前的報導，食物和醫療用品都已經以驚人的速度送到。村民不再急需這些物品了。他們現在需要的是冬天的衣服和毯子，因為溫度預期會持續降低。

A.

B.

C.

詳解

答案：C

從圖片中的不同物品可推測，題目會問與什麼事物（What）相關的問題。從一開始提到的 heavy rains、mud slides，以及 Many houses ~ were destroyed 可知，有土石流，而且已造成房屋損毀。報導接著提到 food and medical supplies have arrived ~ The villagres are no longer in need of such items.，由此可知村民不再需要食物和醫療用品。而聽到 What they need now is winter clothes and blankets，可以知道目前所需要的是衣服和毯子（clothes and blankets）。

|單字片語| **news report** 新聞報導 / **mud slide** 土石流 / **occur** [əˋkɝ] 發生 / **mountain area** 山區 / **village** [ˋvɪlɪdʒ] 村莊 / **destroy** [dɪˋstrɔɪ] 摧毀 / **medical** [ˋmɛdɪkəl] 醫療的 / **villager** [ˋvɪlɪdʒɚ] 村民 / **no longer** 不再 / **blanket** [ˋblæŋkɪt] 毯子 / **temperature** [ˋtɛmprətʃɚ] 溫度 / **drop** [drɑp] 降低

Q29

For question number 29, please look at the three pictures.

Please listen to the following short talk. 請聽以下的簡短談話。

Where does the girl want to go?
這位女孩想要去哪裡？

Mom, the yearly comic fair is here again. It will be held in Taipei from July 4th to July 15th. Dad can get his favorite novels at 30% off, so why don't we go there? I promise I will work hard next semester and get top three in class.

媽，一年一度的漫畫展又來了。七月四日到十五日將會在台北舉辦。爸爸可以用七折買到他最喜歡的小說，所以我們何不去那裡呢？我答應妳下個學期會努力念書，考到全班前三名。

A. 　　B. 　　C.

詳解　　　　　　　　　　　　　　　　　　　　　　　　　　　　　　　　答案：C

　　從圖片的不同地點可推測，題目會問與地點（Where）相關的問題。從一開始提到的 comic fair is here 以及 It ~ held in Taipei 可知會有漫畫展，地點在台北。我們從 comic（漫畫）、novel（小說）、magazine（雜誌）這些關鍵字可推測，男孩要去的地方是書展或漫畫展，圖片中比較接近的答案是 C。

補充說明

　　fair 當形容詞使用時是「公平」的意思，而當名詞時是「展覽」的意思。book fair 為「書展」的意思，travel fair 為「旅展」的意思。

|單字片語| **yearly** [ˋjɪrlɪ] 年度的 / **comic** [ˋkɑmɪk] 漫畫 / **fair** [fɛr] 展覽 / **favorite** [ˋfevərɪt] 最喜歡的 / **semester** [səˋmɛstə] 學期 / **in class** 班上

Q30

For question number 30, please look at the three pictures.

Please listen to the following short talk.　請聽以下的簡短談話。

What does the place look like right now?
這個地方現在看起來像什麼？

A hundred years ago, this place used to be a military base. where there were soldiers. Later on, a temple was built on the site as locals prayed for good luck during fishing seasons. Recently, the temple was pulled down in order to build a public library. Inside this newly-built library, old pictures which tell the history of this place can be seen along the walls.

一百年前，這個地方曾是一個軍事基地。之後有一座廟蓋在這裡，做為當地人在打魚季時祈求好運的地方。最近，這座廟被拆了來興建公共圖書館。在這個新蓋的圖書館裡，你可以在牆上看到述說著這個地方歷史的舊照片。

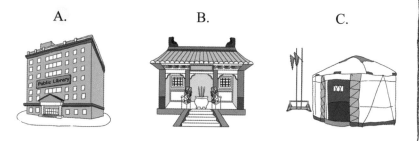

A.　　　　　　　　B.　　　　　　　　C.

詳解　　　　　　　　　　　　　　　　　　　　　　　　　答案：A

從圖片的不同地點可推測，題目會問與在哪裡、地點相關的問題。一開始提到 this place used to be a military base，點出了某一個地點，說明這個地方曾是軍事基地。接著又說 a temple ~ built on the site 以及 Recently, the temple was pulled down ~ build a public library 和 Inside this newly-built library，可以知道這個地方從軍事基地改為廟宇的變遷，而從 Inside this newly-built library 也可知現在已經是圖書館了。題目是問此地現在看起來的樣子（look like right now），問的是「現在」的狀態，描述軍事基地（military base）和廟宇（temple）時都是「過去」時態，所以公共圖書館的 A 是正確答案。

|單字片語| **hundred** [ˋhʌndrəd] 百 / **military** [ˋmɪləˌtɛrɪ] 軍事 / **base** [bes] 基地 / **soldier** [ˋsoldʒɚ] 士兵，軍人 / **later on** 之後 / **temple** [ˋtɛmpl] 寺廟 / **build** [bɪld] 建造 / **pray for** 為…祈求 / **be pulled down** 被拆下 / **library** [ˋlaɪˌbrɛrɪ] 圖書館 / **along** [əˋlɔŋ] 沿著

初試 閱讀測驗 解析

第一部分 / 詞彙

Q1

Nobody will _____ you the truth if you always get angry.

如果你總是生氣的話，沒有人會告訴你真話。

A. say 說
B. tell 告訴
C. talk 講話；聊天
D. speak 講話；演講

詳解　　　　　　　　　　　　　　　　　　　　　　　　　　　答案：B

　　這題主要是考動詞。空格後面是受詞 you 和 the truth，直接受詞是 the truth，所以要選出與 the truth 搭配使用的動詞，正確答案是 B，當要表達「說實話」時，要用 tell the truth。其他與 tell 相關的還有：講笑話（tell jokes）、說故事（tell a story）、分辨差異（tell the difference）。

|單字片語| **nobody** [ˋnobadɪ] 沒有人 / **get angry** 生氣 / **truth** [truθ] 真相

Q2

Mrs. Chen: Do we have any flour left?
Mr. Chen: There's only _____ in the box.

陳太太：我們麵粉還有剩嗎？
陳先生：盒子裡只剩一點點。

A. a little 一點（用在不可數名詞）
B. a few 一些（用在可數名詞）
C. several 幾個（用在可數名詞）
D. a lot of 很多（可用在可數與不可數名詞）

詳解　　　　　　　　　　　　　　　　　　　　　　　　　　　答案：A

　　這題主要是考量詞。一開始 Mrs. Chen 提到 any flour left（麵粉是否還有剩），而在 Mr. Chen 的回應中，從空格前面的 only 可知，麵粉的量只剩一點點，因為「只有很多」的表達不合邏輯。選項中表達「一些」、「一點」的有 A 和 B，麵粉（flour）是不可數名詞，所以只能用選項 A，答案為 A。

|單字片語| **flour** [flaʊr] 麵粉 / **have...left** …還有剩 / **box** [bɑks] 盒子

Q3

Have you _____ about your future? How are you going to make a living?

你曾經想過你的未來嗎？你要如何維持生計？

A. though 雖然

B. thought 想；思考

C. through 透過；藉由

D. taught 教

詳解

答案：B

　　這題主要是考動詞。選項都是拼字相似的單字，但空格內要填入動詞（現在分詞），只有 B 和 D 是動詞，就語意上來看，think about your future 比 teach about your future 合理，所以答案是 B。這題的動詞以現在完成式 have + p.p.呈現，thought 是 think 的過去式、過去分詞形態。

|單字片語| **future** [ˈfjutʃə] 未來 / **make a living** 維持生計

Q4

Margaret is feeling _____ because the boy she likes is chatting to another girl happily.

Margaret 感到嫉妒，因為她喜歡的男孩正開心地跟另一個女生聊天。

A. jealous 嫉妒的

B. curious 好奇的

C. honest 誠實的

D. talkative 健談的

詳解

答案：A

　　這題主要是考形容詞與語意理解。空格在 is feeling（感到）後面，就語意來看，因為 Margaret 喜歡的男孩正跟另一個女生聊天，所以她感到「嫉妒」，因此答案是 A。

|單字片語| **admire** 欽佩 / **envy** 羨慕 / **jealous** 嫉妒的

Q5

I am terribly sorry. It's all my _____. I should have listened to you.

我非常抱歉。都是我的錯。我當初應該聽你的。

A. effort 努力

B. fault 錯

C. hope 希望

D. service 服務

第 1 回
第 2 回
第 3 回
第 4 回
第 5 回
第 6 回

詳解

答案：B

　　這題主要是考名詞與語意理解。空格在所有格形容詞後面。就語意來看，題目先提到「我非常抱歉」，後面提到「我當初應該聽你的」，由此可知，中間這一句會提到「都是我的錯」。

〈補充說明〉

　　fault 和 mistake 都可以表達「錯誤」，但用法不同，所搭配的動詞也不同，請見以下例句：
It's all my fault. 都是我的錯。（be 動詞 + 所有格形容詞 + fault）
I made a mistake. 我犯了錯。（動詞 make + 不定代名詞 a + mistake）

Q6

Since young, he has always been curious _____ science and nature.

從小，他一直都對科學和大自然感到好奇。

A. about   B. of
C. with   D. by

詳解

答案：A

　　這題主要是考介系詞。空格在形容詞 curious 後面，就語意來看主要是要表達「對…好奇」的意思，與 curious 搭配的介系詞是 about，所以答案是 A。其他形容詞與介系詞的搭配還有： scared of（對…感到害怕）、bored with（對…感到無聊）、surprised by（對…感到驚訝）。

|單字片語| **young** [jʌŋ] 年輕 / **curious** [ˋkjʊrɪəs] 好奇的 / **science** [ˋsaɪəns] 科學 / **nature** [ˋnetʃɚ] 自然

Q7

Oh no! It's my turn to give a speech. I am so _____ that my knees are shaking.

不會吧！輪到我要演講了。我太緊張了，以至於我的膝蓋在發抖。

A. famous 出名的   B. serious 認真的；嚴重的
C. generous 大方的；慷慨的   **D. nervous 緊張的**

詳解

答案：D

　　這題主要是考形容詞與語意理解。選項都是形容詞，就語意來看，一開始提到自己要演講了，後面又說到膝蓋在發抖，最合理的形容詞是「感到緊張」，所以答案是 D。

I單字片語I **give a speech** 演講 / **knee** [ni] 膝蓋 / **shake** [ʃek] 發抖

I am not allowed to watch TV _____ on Sundays for less than two hours.

我不被准許看電視，除了在星期天能看不到兩個小時之外。

A. despite 儘管

B. except 除了…之外

C. although 雖然

D. besides 除了…還有

詳解　　　　　　　　　　　　　　　　　　　　答案：B

　　這題主要是考介系詞與語意理解。就語意來看，一開始提到自己不被准許看電視，後面又說在星期天看不到兩個小時，「我不被准許看電視，除了在每個星期天能看不到兩個小時」比「雖然／儘管每個星期天看不到兩個小時，我不准看電視」來得通順。except 和 besides 在翻譯上都是「除了…之外」，這容易造成混淆。請把 except 理解為「除了…之外不是」、把 besides 理解為「除了…還有」，就能區分兩者的用法和意思。

I work every day except on weekends. 除了週末（不用）之外，我每天都工作。
I work on weekdays besides weekends. 除了週末（要工作），我平日也要工作。

The Internet is _____ you can get free information quickly.

網路是你可以快速得到免費資訊的地方。

A. that

B. what

C. where

D. when

詳解　　　　　　　　　　　　　　　　　　　　答案：C

　　這題主要是考關係副詞。先就語意來看，一開始提到網路，後面說到你可以快速得到資訊，由此可知我們可以把「網路」理解為「得到資訊的地點、來源」，所以答案要選有地點意義的 where。請見以下關係詞懶人包的四大規則：

　　1. 前面是人，關係代名詞用 who
　　2. 前面是物，關係代名詞用 which
　　3. 前面是地點、來源，關係副詞用 where
　　4. 前面是時間，關係副詞用 when

Some fresh graduates went abroad in search of better job _____.

有些剛從大學畢業的人到海外尋求更好的工作機會。

A. advertisements 廣告   B. examples 例子
C. opportunities 機會   D. manners 禮貌

詳解　　　　　　　　　　　　　　　　　　　　　　　答案：C

　　這題主要是考單字。選項都是名詞，就語意來看，一開始提到主詞「大學畢業生」，後面說到動詞 went abroad（出國）以及 in search of better job（尋找更好的工作），能夠與 job 組成合乎語意的名詞片語的選項，最適合的答案是「工作機會」。

〈補充說明〉

　　chance 和 opportunity 都有「機會」的意思，不過 opportunity 是比較正式的用法，而 chance 有運氣成份。請見以下例句：
better job opportunity 更好的工作機會
a better chance of getting a job 更有機會找到工作

‖單字片語‖ **graduate** [ˋgrædʒʊ͵et] 畢業生 / **go abroad** 出國，到海外 / **in search of** 尋求…
/ **job** [dʒɑb] 工作

第 1 回
第 2 回
第 3 回
第 4 回
第 5 回
第 6 回

第二部分 / 段落填空

Questions 11-14

I was born and (11) brought up in a single-parent family. I have no memory of my dad during my childhood. He never cared to go to any teacher-parent meeting. Once, I was surprised to hear one of my elementary classmates (12) say that my dad was in school. It (13) turned out that it was my mom. She wore her hair short and she was wearing pants. My friends thought she was a 'he'. I was too embarrassed to say anything. Since then, I told her not to go to my school unless necessary. As a result, I studied really hard (14) so that the teachers would not ask to see her. Until today, she still has no idea what made me study so hard. She didn't realize that her looks and dressing was the reason I got good grades in school.

　　我出生成長於一個單親家庭。在我的童年之中，我對於父親沒有什麼記憶。他從不在乎要參加任何親師懇談會。有一次，我驚訝地聽到我的其中一位國小同學說我爸爸在學校。結果原來是我媽。她留著短髮，而且穿著長褲。我朋友都以為她是男的。我尷尬到說不出話來。在那之後，我告訴她除非有必要，不然不要到學校來。因此，我很努力讀書，這樣老師才不會要求要見她。直到今天，她還不知道是什麼讓我這麼用功讀書的。她沒有想到她的樣貌和穿著就是我在學校得到好成績的原因。

Q11

A. brought up 帶大　　　　　B. called on 拜訪
C. taken off 脫掉　　　　　D. dressed in 穿著

詳解　　　　　　　　　　　　　答案：A

　　選項都是動詞過去分詞，就語意上來看，空格前面是 was born（出生），後面是 in ~ family，選項中最合理的是 bring... up（扶養）的過去分詞（be）brought up，答案是 A。表達「扶養長大」，英文可用 bring... up 或 raise... up。教養的英文為 upbringing。

A. say   B. says

C. said   D. to say

詳解   答案：A

　　選項都是與 say 相關的動詞變化，就句子結構來看，空格前面是主詞與主要動詞 I was surprised to hear（我當時很驚訝聽到），請注意 hear 是感官動詞，像是 see、hear、feel、notice 等感官動詞後面的動詞都要用原形或動名詞 V-ing 形態，所以 A 是正確答案。請見以下例句：

We saw the man take your money. 我們看到那個男人拿你的錢。

We felt the house shaking. 我們感覺到房子在搖晃。

A. turned in 繳交   B. turned out 結果

C. turned up 出現   D. turned down 拒絕

詳解   答案：B

　　選項都是 turn 與不同副詞／介系詞組合的動詞片語，就句子結構來看，空格前面是主詞 it，後面是子句 it was my mom（是我媽），就語意來看，從上下文來判斷 it 是虛主詞。前面提到「我聽到我同學說我爸爸在學校」，這裡提到「是我媽」，所以最通順的 It turned out that（結果是），來表示語意上的對比，是正確答案。

A. so as to make my dreams come true
　　為了讓我的夢想成真

B. so that the teachers would not ask to see her
　　這樣老師才不會要求要見她

C. and I went to school with one of my classmates
　　然後我和我一位同學一起去上學

D. even if I didn't get along well with her
　　即使我和她相處得不太好

詳解   答案：B

　　空格前面提到：告訴媽媽說除非有必要，不然不要到學校來，所以就很用功讀念書。後面提到：媽媽沒有想到她的樣貌和穿著，是自己在學校得到好成

績的原因，可知空格的重點要放在不希望媽媽來學校，不管是什麼樣的原因。從選項中來看，選項 B. 跟筆者很用功念書有關，且跟前後文的文意也通順。故答案選 B.。

Questions 15-18

Is online gaming good or bad? (15) While it is true that we need a good balance between work and play, teenagers can lose themselves in the world of fantasy. There are so many interesting games to play that one can never finish playing all of (16) them. The fact that online gaming is now possible with WIFI hotspots has made matters (17) worse. Teenagers can play online games not only in front of their computers but also on their smartphones while on the bus and in MRT stations. (18) Instead of making use of their time to read something meaningful, most of them are staring at electronic products. The days when passengers read a paperback or the newspaper were gone.

　　打線上遊戲到底是好還是壞？雖然我們在工作與玩樂之間確實需要良好的平衡，但青少年可能會在幻想世界中迷失自己。可以玩的有趣遊戲是這麼多，以至於這些遊戲永遠也玩不完。線上遊戲現在在有 WIFI 熱點的地方也能玩的這個事實，讓事情變得更糟。青少年除了能在電腦前面玩線上遊戲，就連在公車上或捷運上也能用智慧型手機玩。他們現在大部分都是盯著電子產品，而非善用時間讀點有意義的東西。乘客閱讀書或報紙拿著的那一段日子已經回不去了。

Q15

A. Which 哪一個　　　　　B. While 雖然；而；當
C. Whether 無論；是否　　D. Whenever 每當；無論何時

詳解　　　　　　　　　　　　　　　　　　　　　　答案：B

　　選項都是連接詞。前面先用問句質疑線上遊戲到底是好還是壞，空格後面是兩個子句，第一個子句提到工作與玩樂之間需要平衡，暗指確實需要玩樂，後一個子句卻暗指線上遊戲的虛擬世界對青少年是不好的，可以知道此兩句有「雖然…，但是…」的意思，所以答案要選 B。while 有「當…時」、「而…」、「雖然」的意思，要依上下文來判斷所表示的意思，請見以下例句：
You can read the magazines **while** you are waiting. 當你在等待的時候，你可以看這些雜誌。
Some people like dogs, **while** others like cats. 有些人喜歡狗，而其他人則喜歡貓。

While it is true that houses are expensive, people are still buying them. 雖然房子很貴這件事是真的，但還是有人買。

Q16

A. it

B. its

C. them

D. their

詳解

答案：C

選項都是代名詞，這時先判斷語意，找出這個代名詞是要代替哪個名詞。空格和前面 all of 的組合是 playing 的受詞，從 playing（玩）可知，受詞應該就是文章所談論的線上遊戲，也就是代替前面的 so many interesting games，因為是複數，因此代名詞用 them。

Q17

A. well 好地

B. better 更好的

C. best 最好的

D. worse 更糟的

詳解

答案：D

從選項可推測，答案要選形容詞或副詞。空格前面是這句的主要動詞 has made 和受詞 matters，意指「讓事情...」。就語意來看，前面的內容提到線上遊戲會讓青少年在幻想世界中迷失自己，點出它不好的地方，而空格後面又提到現在無論是在電腦前還是在公車上、捷運上都在玩線上遊戲，而非善用時間讀點東西，暗指情況變得更糟，所以 D 的 worse 是正確答案。

Q18

A. When the first smartphone was introduced to the world
當第一部智慧型手機問世時

B. As work and play are both important
工作和玩樂兩者都很重要

C. Even though teenagers are crazy about online games
即使青少年對線上遊戲很瘋狂

D. Instead of making use of their time to read something meaningful
不善用時間讀點有意義的東西

詳解　　　　　　　　　　　　　　　　　　　

　　空格前面提到：青少年會在電腦前面玩線上遊戲，在公車上或捷運上也會用智慧型手機玩，表示不管什麼時候都是在用 3C 產品。而後面提到：大部分的青少年現在都是盯著電子產品，看書或看報紙的日子已經回不去了，可推測空格是跟閱讀書籍有關的內容。從選項來看，只有選項 D. 跟閱讀有關，且跟前後文的文意也通順。故答案選 D.。請注意到，以 Instead of 連接兩個子句時，這兩個子句的意義會是相反的。

補充說明

　　在形容詞的字尾中，-ful 帶有「有」的意思，而 -less 帶有「沒有」的意思。

-ful	-less
meaningful 有意義的	meaningless 沒意義的
useful 有用的	useless 沒用的
helpful 有幫助的	helpless 無助的
harmful 有害的	harmless 無害的

School Club List

Dance Club	meet **Mon. & Wed.**	**4:00-5:00 PM**
Chess Club	meet **Saturday**	**1:00-3:00 PM**
Art Club	meet **Tue. & Thur.**	**4:00-5:00 PM**
Movie Club	meet **Mon. & Thur.**	**4:00-5:00 PM**
Guitar Club	meet **Saturday**	**3:00-5:00 PM**

學校社團清單

舞蹈社	聚會時間：週一與週三	下午 4 點到 5 點
棋藝社	聚會時間：週六	下午 1 點到 3 點
美術社	聚會時間：週二與週四	下午 4 點到 5 點
電影社	聚會時間：週一與週四	下午 4 點到 5 點
吉他社	聚會時間：週六	下午 3 點到 5 點

Cindy's School schedules

	Mon.	Tue.	Wed.	Thur.	Fri.	Sat.	Sun.
10:00 AM-12:00 PM	Class	Class	Class	Class	Class	Class	Free
1:00 PM-3:00 PM	Class	Class	Class	Class	Class	Free	Free
3:00 PM-5:00 PM	Class	Free	Class	Free	Class	Free	Free

Cindy 的學校課表

	週一	週二	週三	週四	週五	週六	週日
早上 10 點到 12 點	上課	上課	上課	上課	上課	上課	休息
下午 1 點到 3 點	上課	上課	上課	上課	上課	休息	休息
下午 3 點到 5 點	上課	休息	上課	休息	上課	休息	休息

Dear Cindy,

Your teacher just called, but you weren't home, so I left this note for you. Your teacher asked me to tell you that you should pick up a new club to attend for this new semester. He said you should choose one when you are free from classes. Anyway, I know you are interested in music and hope you can choose what you really like.

Love you!

Mom

親愛的 Cindy

你的老師剛才來電,但是你不在家,所以我留了這張紙條給你。你的老師要我告訴你,你在這個新的學期應該要選個新的社團來參加。他說你要在你沒課的時段選個社團。總之,我知道你對音樂有興趣,也希望你可以選到你真正喜歡的社團。

愛你的媽媽

第1回
第2回
第3回
第4回
第5回
第6回

According to Cindy's mother, which club will Cindy probably choose?

根據 Cindy 的母親，Cindy 可能會選哪個社團？

- A. Chess Club.
  棋藝社。
- B. Guitar Club.
  吉他社。
- C. Art Club.
  美術社。
- D. Movie Club.
  電影社。

詳解　　　　　　　　　　　　　　　　　　　　　　　　　**答案：B**

　　在第三篇文的信件中的署名 Mom 可知，這封信是媽媽寫給 Cindy，信件最後一句提到：Anyway, I know you are interested in music and hope you can choose what you really like.，提到媽媽知道 Cindy 對音樂有興趣，也希望她可以選到真正喜歡的社團。言下之意，Cindy 應該會選擇跟音樂相關的社團，而從第一個表格可知，跟音樂有關的社團只有 Guitar Club（吉他社）。故答案選 B。

Q20

According to Cindy's class schedule, which of the following clubs can be chosen?

根據 Cindy 的課表，以下哪些社團是可以選擇的？

- A. Chess club, dance club and movie club.
  棋藝社、舞蹈社與電影社。
- B. Art club, chess club and guitar club.
  美術社、棋藝社與吉他社。
- C. Movie club, art club and dance club.
  電影社、美術社與舞蹈社。
- D. Guitar club, chess club and movie club.
  吉他社、棋藝社與電影社。

詳解　　　　　　　　　　　　　　　　　　　　　　　　　**答案：B**

　　根據第二篇的課程表可知，Cindy 的沒課時間為: 週二、四的下午 3 點到 5

點、週六下午 1 點到 5 點，以及週日全天。配合第一篇的社團清單得知，美術社、棋藝社與吉他社是可以選擇的。故答案選 B。

Q21

Which of the following statements is correct?

以下敘述何者正確？

A. Cindy has no class on Tuesday morning.
   Cindy 週二早上沒有課。

B. Cindy's father left the note.
   Cindy 的父親留了紙條。

C. Cindy didn't get her teacher's call.
   Cindy 沒接到老師的來電。

D. Movie club meets every Monday and Wednesday.
   電影社每週一、三進行。

詳解

答案：C

　　在第三篇的信中提到：Dear Cindy, Your teacher just called, but you weren't home, so I left this note for you.，可知 Cindy 的老師來電，但她不在家，所以她媽媽留了紙條給 Cindy。所以答案要選 C。從信件的署名可知留紙條的是媽媽，而非爸爸，所以 B. 不正確。從 Cindy 的課表可知 Cindy 週二早上有課，從社團清單也可知，電影社（Movie Club）每週一、四進行（meet Mon. & Thurs.），所以 A、D 不正確。

單字片語 attend 參與，參加 / semester 學期 / choose 選擇

Questions 22-24

Flight No. 班機號碼	Departure Time 出發時間	Destination 目的地	Gate 登機門	Terminal 航廈
QQ373	07:30	Tokyo 東京	A6	T1
JJ469	07:45	Paris 巴黎	A8	T1
BB725	08:00	Rome 羅馬	B2	T2
KK618	08:15	London 倫敦	B4	T2

Please be reminded that check-in counters will be opened two hours before departure. Also, please report to the boarding gate at least 30 minutes before takeoff.

請注意登機櫃台將在出發兩小時前開放。此外，請在起飛前至少三十分鐘到登機門報到。

|單字片語| **remind** [rɪ`maɪnd] 提醒 / **check-in** 登機 / **counter** [`kaʊntə] 櫃台 / **departure** [dɪ`partʃə] 出發 / **report to** 報到 / **boarding gate** 登機門 / **takeoff** [`tek,ɔf] 起飛 / **at least** 至少

Q22

Where will you most likely see the information?
你最有可能在哪裡看到此資訊？

    A. Bus station.
       公車站。
    B. Subway station.
       地鐵站。
    C. Airport.
       機場。
    D. Post office.
       郵局。

詳解　　　　　　　　　　　　　　　　　　　　　　答案：C

    從表格上的關鍵字 Flight No.（班機號碼）、Departure Time（出發時間）、Gate（登機門）以及目的地該欄的各國外城市名，可推測這是在機場可以看到的資訊，所以答案要選 C。

Q23

What is the earliest time you can check in if you are going to Paris?
如果你要去巴黎，可以辦理登機手續的最早時間是幾點？

    A. 05:30
    B. 05:45
    C. 07:15
    D. 07:45

第 1 回
第 2 回
第 3 回
第 4 回
第 5 回
第 6 回

詳解 答案：B

　　從表格可知，到巴黎的航班為 JJ469 班機，從 Departure Time 可知此班機的出發時間是 07:45，而文中又提到 check-in counters ~ opened two hours before departure，表示在出發的兩個小時前會開放辦理登機手續，言下之意就是最早可在 05:45 去辦理。

Q24

What time do you have to be at gate B4 at the latest?

最遲幾點必須到 B4 登機門？

A. Seven o'clock. 七點。

B. A quarter past seven. 七點十五分。

C. A quarter to eight. 七點四十五分。

D. Eight o'clock. 八點。

詳解 答案：C

　　從 What time ~ be at gate B4 at the latest 可知，主要是問最晚必須到 B4 登機門的時間。從表格中可知，B4 登機門是前往倫敦的 KK618 班機，此班機起飛的時間為 08:15，而文中提到 report to the boarding gate at least 30 minutes before takeoff，表示在起飛前半小時必須抵達登機門，也就是最晚要在 07:45 到。

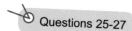 Questions 25-27

NT$5,000 REWARD
Help us find our beloved pet, Bobby.

Last seen in Central Park on 26 January
Wearing a silver dog tag
Has a pink birthmark on its back

Bobby has been part of our family for eleven years. He is like an elderly human. We are really worried because he is not able to take care of himself. Please call us if you see him. We offer NT$5000 to anyone who finds him. Please call us at once if you have any news.

0927898XXX or 02-3580-XXXX

懸賞新台幣五千元
請幫我們找到我們心愛的寵物 Bobby。

最後一次看到牠是在中央公園，時間是在一月二十六日
戴著銀色狗牌
背上有粉紅色胎記

Bobby 十一年來一直都是我們家的一份子。牠就像是一個老人。我們很擔心，因為牠無法照顧自己。如果你看到牠的話，請撥電話給我們。我們提供五千元給任何一個找到牠的人。如果有任何消息請立刻與我們聯絡。

|單字片語| **reward** [rɪ`wɔrd] 懸賞 / **tag** [tæg] 標籤 / **pink** [pɪŋk] 粉紅色 / **birthmark** [`bɝθˌmɑrk] 胎記 / **elderly** [`ɛldɚlɪ] 年長的 / **take care of** 照顧 / **at once** 立刻

What is the purpose of this notice?
這張公告的目的是什麼？

    A. To look for a missing person. 尋找失蹤的人。
    B. To look for a missing animal. 尋找失蹤的動物。
    C. To look for a missing item. 尋找不見的物品。
    D. To look for a missing car. 尋找不見的車子。

詳解

      從 What ~ purpose ~ notice 可知，主要是問這篇文章的目的。從一開始的 Help us find our beloved pet（幫我們找到我們心愛的寵物）中的 pet 可知，這張公告的目的是為了尋找失蹤的動物。

What is true about Bobby?
關於 Bobby，何者正確？

    A. He has a pet at home. 他家裡有寵物。
    B. He has a birthmark on his body. 他身上有胎記。
    C. He will pay the NT$5000 reward. 他將會付五千元的獎賞。
    D. He will answer the call at once. 他將立刻接聽電話。

第 1 回
第 2 回
第 3 回
第 4 回
第 5 回
第 6 回

詳解

答案：B

從一開始的 our beloved pet, Bobby 可知，Bobby 是走失的寵物的名字，而在後面又提到 Has a pink birthmark on its back（背上有粉紅色胎記），選項中只有 B 是正確答案。

Q27

Where can we most likely see the information?

我們最有可能可以在哪裡看到此資訊？

A. In the ocean.
   在海邊。

B. In a park.
   在公園裡。

C. In a zoo.
   在動物園裡。

D. In an airport.
   在機場。

詳解

答案：B

從一開始的 NT$5,000 REWARD（懸賞新台幣五千元）、Help us find our beloved pet（幫我們找到我們心愛的寵物）可知是協尋寵物的公告。公告內文第一行提到 Last seen in Central Park on 26 January，提到這隻寵物最後一次的身影是在公園，可推測寵物主人會在這公園附近貼公告。因此最有可能在公園看到此公告，所以答案要選 B。

Questions 28-30

Taiwan experiences three to four hits by typhoons a year. Strong winds can break windows and send metal roofs flying. Heavy rain can also cause landslides and flooding. Farmers are affected the most during typhoon seasons. A day of rain can destroy crops and plants that take months to grow. People living in the mountains are also in danger because landslides can destroy buildings and roads with them. However, a typhoon may be a blessing in disguise sometimes.

A typhoon brings the island a lot of water it needs. A lack of water could affect a lot of people. In early 2015, many cities suffered from a lack of water and it almost turned into a major crisis. Families and businesses cannot function without clean water. Water supply was shut off in many cities for two days in a week, which caused much inconvenience. Typhoons are necessary as a source of water but there is no way we can control them. Therefore, we should look into the possibility of turning seawater into drinkable water, which is what Singapore has already succeeded in doing.

　　台灣一年平均經歷三至四個直撲而來的颱風。強風會破壞窗戶，並使鐵皮屋頂掀飛。豪雨也會造成土石流和淹水。在颱風季節期間，農夫受的影響最為嚴重。一天所降的雨會摧毀需要花好幾個月才長成的農作物與植物。住在山區的人也身處危險之中，因為土石流會沖走建築物和道路。儘管造成這些災難，颱風有時候卻可能讓我們因禍得福。

　　颱風會為台灣帶來所需的寶貴水源，缺乏水資源的話，會讓很多人受影響。在 2015 年初，許多城市慘遭缺水之苦，幾乎成為重大危機。家庭和商家若沒有乾淨的水難以運轉。許多城鎮一週停水兩天，造成許多不便。颱風是必要的水源之一，但我們沒辦法控制颱風。因此，或許我們應該研究淡化海水的可能性，而這在新加坡已成功辦到了。

[單字片語] **typhoon** [taɪˋfun] 颱風 / **roof** [ruf] 屋頂 / **landslide** [ˋlændˏslaɪd] 土石流 / **flooding** [ˋflʌdɪŋ] 洪水 / **farmer** [ˋfɑrmɚ] 農夫 / **affect** [əˋfɛkt] 影響 / **crop** [krɑp] 農作物 / **plant** [plænt] 植物 / **grow** [gro] 種植，成熟 / **in danger** 有危險 / **blessing** [ˋblɛsɪŋ] 好運 / **in disguise** 偽裝的 / **suffer** [ˋsʌfɚ] 遭受 / **lack** [læk] 缺乏 / **crisis** [ˋkraɪsɪs] 危機 / **shut off** 關掉，切斷 / **inconvenience** [ˏɪnkənˋvinjəns] 不便 / **necessary** [ˋnɛsəˏsɛrɪ] 必要的 / **source** [sors] 資源 / **drinkable** [ˋdrɪŋkəbl̩] 可飲用的 / **succeed** [səkˋsid] 成功

Why might strong winds be dangerous?
為什麼強風可能會造成危險？

A. People may get hit by falling or broken objects.
　　人們可能會被掉落的或破裂的東西擊中。

B. People may be hurt by landslides. 人們可能因土石流而受傷。

C. People may get killed by flooding. 人們可能因淹水而死。

D. People may be blown away. 人們可能被吹走。

詳解　　　　　　　　　　　　　　　　　　　　　　　答案：A

　　從 Why ~ strong winds ~ dangerous 可知，主要是問強風造成危險的原因。

文中第一段第二行提到 Strong winds can break windows ~ send metal roofs flying，表示強風會破壞窗戶，並將屋頂掀起來，言下之意是有人可能會被掉落物或被破壞了的物體擊中，所以正確答案是 A。

第 1 回
第 2 回
第 3 回
第 4 回
第 5 回
第 6 回

Q29

What is the best explanation for 'a blessing in disguise'?
a blessing in disguise 最好的解釋是什麼？

- A. Something which was good at first became something bad.
  原本是好事，後來變成不好的事。
- B. Something which was bad at first became something good.
  原本是不好的事，後來變成好事。
- C. Something which was bad at first became something worse.
  原本是不好的事，後來變得更糟。
- D. Something which was good at first became something better.
  原本是好事，後來變得更好。

詳解

答案：B

　　a blessing in disguise 出現在第一段最後一行。若不認識這些單字，可從上下文推敲。第一段整段都是提到颱風造成的不良影響，如造成破壞與產生危險，而第二段卻又提到颱風正面的地方，也就是提供豐富的水資源。由此推測，Despite all these 在這裡是表達「縱使有這些不好的影響」的意思，接著說的 typhoon may be a blessing in disguise 是為第二段所鋪設的轉折句，表達「颱風也有好的地方」，選項中最接近的答案是 B。

補充說明

　　表達上帝保佑（God bless you.）時，「祝福」和「保佑」都用 bless，而 blessing 是它的名詞形態。disguise 當動詞時是假扮、偽裝的意思，disguise as 是「偽裝成…」的意思；disguise 當名詞時也是偽裝的意思，常用於 something/someone in disguise（偽裝的某人或某物）。

Q30

According to the passage, what happened in early 2015?
根據此文章，2015 年初發生了什麼事？

- A. A super typhoon hit Taiwan. 一個超級颱風襲擊台灣。
- B. Many places were flooded. 很多地方淹水。
- C. It did not rain for a long period of time. 很長一段時間沒下雨。
- D. A lot of people drank seawater. 很多人喝海水。

從 what happened in early 2015 可知，主要是問 2015 年初所發生的事。文中第二段提到 In early 2015, many cities suffered from a lack of water，由此可知 2015 年初發生缺水問題，也就是很長一段時間沒下雨的意思。

全民英檢初級

第六回 初試 聽力測驗

TEST06.mp3

本測驗分四個部分，全部都是單選題，共 30 題，作答時間約 20 分鐘。作答說明為中文，印在試題冊上並經由光碟放音機播出。

第一部分　看圖辨義

　　共 5 題（為第 1 題至第 5 題）。每題請聽光碟放音機播出題目和三個英語句子之後，選出與所看到的圖畫最相符的答案。每題只播出**一遍**。

例題：（看）

（聽）Look at the picture.
　　　Which is the cheapest?
　　　A.　The computer.
　　　B.　The telephone.
　　　C.　The TV set.

正確答案為 B，請在答案紙上塗黑作答。

A: Question 1

Class 103's favorite animals.

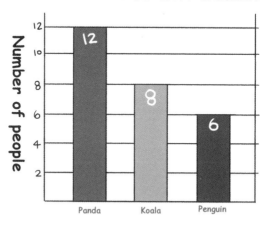

B: Question 2

C: Question 3

D: Question 4

E: <u>Question 5</u>

第二部分　問答

　　共 10 題（為第 6 題至第 15 題）。每題請聽光碟放音機播出的英語句子，再從試題冊上三個回答中，選出一個最適合的答案。每題只播出一遍。

例：　（聽）　Do you speak English?
　　　（看）　A.　No, I speak English quite well.
　　　　　　　B.　Yes, a little.
　　　　　　　C.　No, it's a useful language.

正確答案為 B，請在答案紙上塗黑作答。

6. A. Do you want some coins?
   B. How long will it take?
   C. Who knows?

7. A. Let me explain everything.
   B. It tastes really bad.
   C. I like the color.

8. A. Here it is.
   B. I'll see you next time.
   C. You can't take it back.

9. A. My pleasure.
   B. Why not?
   C. Chocolate ice cream.

10. A. Give me a big hand.
    B. Push here to open.
    C. I'm sorry.

11. A. She hurt herself while she was cooking.
    B. Don't tell me she is getting married.
    C. Let's put the poster on the wall.

12. A. I can't sleep without air conditioning.
    B. You should make a police report.
    C. It's getting colder and colder.

13. A. I left it at home.
    B. I'll do it now.
    C. Perhaps we can work it out together.

14. A. What makes you think so?
    B. Why is he standing on the stage?
    C. How can we make ourselves more comfortable?

15. A. Take the stairs, not the elevator.
    B. I think you should see a doctor.
    C. I didn't see a fire.

第三部分　簡短對話

　　共 10 題（為第 16 題至第 25 題）。每題請聽光碟放音機播出一段對話和一個相關的問題後，再從試題冊上三個選項中，選出一個最適合的答案。每段對話和問題只播出**一遍**。

例：　（聽）　（Woman）　Could I sit here?
　　　　　　（Man）　　I'm sorry, but this seat is occupied.

　　　　　　Question: Where do you think the dialogue takes place?

　　（看）　A.　In an office
　　　　　　B.　In a taxi
　　　　　　C.　In a restaurant.

正確答案為 C，請在答案紙上塗黑作答。

16. A. The man should eat breakfast.
　　B. The man should not read books.
　　C. The man should not give her money.

17. A. The man is teaching the woman how to cook.
　　B. The man cares a lot about his health.
　　C. The man will see a doctor.

18. A. In a forest.
　　B. In a desert.
　　C. In a museum.

19. A. To pray for good health for himself.
　　B. To pray for more money for his son.
　　C. To pray for good grades for his son.

20. A. Go and buy some food.
　　B. Study for his math test.
　　C. Clean up the room.

21. A. Quit the school team.
　　B. Work hard to be on the school team.
　　C. Become the coach of the school team.

22. A. A florist.
    B. An actress.
    C. A boss.

23. A. Doctor and patient.
    B. Coach and dancer.
    C. Customer and clerk.

24. A. Give a speech on stage.
    B. Do the housework at home.
    C. Turn on the radio in her room.

25. A. The woman thought there was an earthquake.
    B. The man thinks that the woman is too heavy.
    C. The woman thinks that the man should lose some weight.

第四部分　短文聽解

共 5 題（為第 26 題至第 30 題）。每題有三個圖片選項。請聽光碟放音機播出的題目，並選出一個最適當的圖片。每題只播出一遍。

例：　(看)

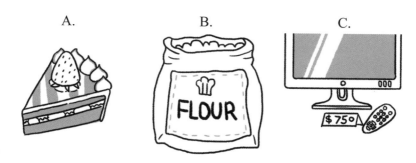

(聽)

Listen to the following short talk. What might Judy buy?

Judy is making a cake for her boyfriend. She checked her refrigerator and found that she had run out of sugar. But she still has lots of flour.

正確答案為 C，請在答案紙上塗黑作答。

Question 26

A.

B.

C.

Question 27

A.

B.

C.

Question 28

A.

B.

C.

Question 29

A.

B.

C.

Question 30

A.

B.

C.

第六回 初試 閱讀測驗

本測驗分三部分，全部都是單選題，共 30 題，作答時間 35 分鐘。

第一部分：詞彙
　　共 10 題，每個題目裡有一個空格。請從四個選項中選出一個<u>最適合</u>題意的字或詞作答。

1. I'm feeling a little sick. I think I need to _____ the doctor a visit.
   A. pay   B. give
   C. see   D. join

2. These two insects look _____ but they are actually different.
   A. special   B. familiar
   C. similar   D. particular

3. You should learn to _____ and forget. You will feel better when you can do that.
   A. forgive   B. focus
   C. damage   D. delay

4. Medicines should be kept out of children's _____.
   A. touch   B. reach
   C. take   D. swallow

5. The yearly meeting will _____ in a five-star hotel.
   A. be taken place   B. be held
   C. be occurred   D. be happened

6. My husband has a good sense of _____. He always makes me laugh.
   A. biology   B. knowledge
   C. reason   D. humor

7. It has been several years _____ I last saw my elementary school principal.
   A. from
   B. for
   C. since
   D. about

8. The manager knows what the old man will order because he is a _____ customer.
   A. foreign
   B. regular
   C. dangerous
   D. terrible

9. A new type of scooter with two doors will be _____ next month.
   A. introduced
   B. affected
   C. happened
   D. treated

10. We have to arrive at the airport at least two hours before the flight _____.
    A. flies away
    B. takes off
    C. puts on
    D. stops by

第二部分：段落填空

　　共 8 題，包括二個段落，每個段落各含四個空格。每格均有四個
選項，請依照文意選出<u>最適合</u>的答案。

Questions 11-14

　　Mei-lin is a first year senior high school student. She did very
___(11)___ on the exams last year. She studied hard to get into this senior
high school and she is ___(12)___ to wear the school uniform. However,
she finds it hard to get the same grades she ___(13)___ get in junior high
school. Take English for example, she used to score at least 95 for every
test, but now she struggles just to pass. She is as hardworking as before, but
she is not getting the excellent grades she wants. Mei-lin has never attended
any cram schools. She doesn't like to repeat what she already knows and
learns in school. Her mom keeps telling her that ___(14)___. Mei-lin
decided to give herself one more semester. If things do not go well this
semester, she will have to look for a cram school during the summer
vacation.

11. A. good
　　B. hard
　　C. well
　　D. badly

12. A. necessary
　　B. loud
　　C. proud
　　D. dishonest

13. A. used to
　　B. is using to
　　C. was used to
　　D. has used to

14. A. she needs to wake up early
　　B. going to a cram school may
　　　 be helpful in improving her
　　　 grades
　　C. she is not good at English
　　　 and Math
　　D. they plan to go abroad
　　　 during this summer
　　　 vacation

328

Questions 15-18

Singapore is an island nation. It is so small that most people have trouble ___(15)___ it on the world map. Even Taiwan, which is fifty times the size of Singapore, appears small compared to China and Japan. ___(16)___.

___(17)___, such a small country with no natural resources at all is one of the richest nations in Asia. Singapore's airport and seaport are ___(18)___ the very best globally. The government is well-known for managing the nation like a company. Everything is about goals and improvement. Government workers who fail to live up to expectations can be fired just like employees in a private company. Singapore is also known for its strict laws. The first announcement one hear on the plane before arrival is the death sentence for carrying drugs.

15. A. find
    B. to find
    C. finding
    D. found

16. A. Many of my friends often take a trip to Singapore.
    B. Some say that there are five continents in the world.
    C. That explains why Singapore is smaller than a tiny dot.
    D. Singapore is famous for "Gardens by the Bay"

17. A. Surprise
    B. Surprising
    C. Surprisingly
    D. To surprise

18. A. among
    B. away
    C. against
    D. along

第三部分：閱讀理解

　　共 12 題，包括 4 個題組，每個題組含 1 至 2 篇短文，與數個相關的四選一的選擇題。請由試題冊上的選項中選出最適合的答案。

Questions 19-21

THSR Train Schedule

Stops/Train No.	536	621	747	859
Leaving at	09:00	09:20	09:40	10:00
Taipei	O	O	O	O
Banqiao	O	O	X	X
Taoyuan	O	O	X	O
Xinzhu	O	O	X	X
Taichung	O	O	O	O
Jiayi	O	O	X	X
Tainan	O	O	X	O
Zuoying	O	O	O	O

O = Stops
X = Non-stops

Taipei to Zuoying: NT$1800
Enjoy early-bird discount of up to 35% if you book in advance.
Note: Number of early-bird seats limited.
Students with valid student ID card can purchase tickets at half price.

19. Where can we most likely see the information?
    A. In an airport.
    B. In a post office.
    C. In a train station.
    D. At school.

20. Which train stops at the fewest of all the stations from Taipei to
    Zuoying?
    A. Train 536.
    B. Train 621.
    C. Train 747.
    D. Train 859.

21. Mr. Chen got a 20% early-bird discount. How much does he need to
    pay from Taipei to Zuoying?
    A. NT$1800
    B. NT$1440
    C. NT$1350
    D. NT$1200

4.5.2020

Dear Neighbors,

A new bookstore is coming, just near where you live. **On Monday April 20th**, doors are opening for you. We have a large selection of books around for your purchases. We also have a nice coffee shop, so you can enjoy some coffee while looking through books. Because you are our neighbors, enclosed please find a coupon we offered, of course, **only** for you!

If you have any questions or suggestions, please contact me directly. (Please see my name card for contact information). Your feedback is always welcome!

Regards,

Mike Lin
Marketing Manager
International Village Books

★ Coupon ★

This coupon is good for one hot drink in International Village Coffee Shop, and you can also get 10% off on any books you buy in the bookstore.

Valid until April 30th.

International Village Group

Mike Lin

Marketing Manager

Mobile: 0936-099-675
Email: mike_lin@intervillage.com
Fax: (02)2356-9856

22. When will the new bookstore open?
    A. April 5th.
    B. April 20th.
    C. April 30th.
    D. April 10th.

23. What can you get with the coupon?
    A. Hot drinks and a free book.
    B. 10% off the regular prices on any books.
    C. Free magazines and a cold drink.
    D. Buy one book and get another free.

24. What is Not true about Mike Lin?
    A. He is a manager in International Village Books.
    B. He can be reached at 0936099675.
    C. He is the owner of the coffee shop.
    D. He welcomes customers' feedback.

Peter's Pizza House

Dear customers,

To celebrate our first successful year in business, we will offer unbelievable discounts on April 11 2016.

(5)   To reward our regular customers, purchase any pizza and get another one free.

     Simply show us your personal membership card and your ID to enjoy this offer.

First-time customers will receive 20% on all pizzas on that day.

P/S: Free pizza has to be of the same price of the one bought, or

(10)   lower. Offer is only valid on April 11 2016.

25. What is the purpose of this poster?
    A. To encourage customers to purchase something.
    B. To invite guests to a movie premiere.
    C. To ask customers to fill out a form to get a membership card.
    D. To explain how to subscribe to a magazine.

26. Who might have written this poster?
    A. A restaurant owner.
    B. A regular customer.
    C. A club member.
    D. A first-grader.

27. What is true about the poster?
    A. Members can lend their membership card to their friends.
    B. Members can get a free pizza which costs more.
    C. First-time customers do not enjoy the buy-one-get-one free offer.
    D. First-time customers can enjoy a 20 percent discount for the whole
        month of April.

Questions 28-30

Mrs. Wang is worried about her father. His memory is failing and he keeps forgetting things. Last month, he left the house with the gas stove still on. As a result, the kitchen was on fire. Luckily, she managed to put the fire out. Once, the police called her and told her to pick up her dad at the police station. One of the police officers said that they found him in another person's house. Mrs. Wang explained that the house used to belong to them but they sold it to the present owner ten years ago. The owner made a police report. Her father seemed to think that it is still their house. Mrs. Wang has spoken to a doctor about her father's problem, but her father refused to receive treatment. Old people like him are so afraid of hospitals that they think doctors are evil. The biggest problem with him is that he doesn't believe he has one because he can't remember it. Mrs. Wang read in an article that playing card games can help to improve memory. She is trying her best to 'trick' her father into playing card games with the grandchildren. She hopes that things will get better.

28. Why was the kitchen on fire?
    A. Mrs. Wang didn't use the microwave properly.
    B. Mrs. Wang's father smoked in the kitchen.
    C. Mrs. Wang's father forgot to turn off the gas stove.
    D. Mrs. Wang forgot to turn off the heater.

29. How come Mrs. Wang's father was in the police station?
    A. He thought that was his house.
    B. He didn't have a place to live in.
    C. He didn't want to stay in the hospital.
    D. He went into someone else's house.

30. What is NOT true about the passage?
    A. The old house they used to live in was burned down.
    B. Mrs. Wang's father seems to remember where they used to live.
    C. Mrs. Wang's father believes that doctors will harm him.
    D. Playing card games might help Mrs. Wang's father.

第六回

初試 聽力測驗 解析

第一部分 / 看圖辨義

Q1

For question one, please look at picture A.

What is true according to the chart?
根據這張圖表，何者屬實？

A. Most students like the koala.
B. The same number of students likes the panda and the penguin.
C. The panda is the most popular animal.

A. 多數學生喜歡無尾熊。
B. 喜歡熊貓和企鵝的人數一樣。
C. 熊貓是最受歡迎的動物。

詳解　　　　　　　　　　　　　　　　　　　　　　　　　　　**答案：C**

　　從圖片可知是一張長條圖，從上面的文字、數字可知，是統計喜歡特定動物的人數。題目主要是問圖表所要表達的內容。喜歡熊貓的人數為 12 人，比其他動物的愛好者人數多，因此熊貓是最受歡迎的動物。

Q2

For question two, please look at picture B.

Which bin should you put your plastic bottle in?
你應該把寶特瓶放入哪一個桶子？

A. Bin A.
B. Bin B.
C. Bin C.

A. 桶子 A
B. 桶子 B
C. 桶子 C

詳解　　　　　　　　　　　　　　　　　　　　　　　　　　　**答案：B**

　　從圖片以及上面的文字可知，是三個裝不同物品的垃圾桶。從 Which bin ~ plastic bottle in 可知，題目是問寶特瓶要放進哪個桶子裡。寶特瓶（plastic bottle）由塑膠製成，應該放在桶子 B。

Q3

For question three, please look at picture C.

What does the woman do for a living?
這位女士以做什麼為生？（她的職業是什麼？）

A. She is an actress.
B. She is a director.
C. She is a photographer.

A. 她是一名演員。
B. 她是一名導演。
C. 她是一名攝影師。

詳解

答案：A

　　從圖中可判斷是拍片現場，導演和攝影師都是男士，女士是一名演員。從 What ~ woman do ~ living 可知是問女士的工作，聽到 actress 是知道是正確答案。

Q4

For question four, please look at picture D.

What might be this special day?
今天可能是什麼特別的日子？

A. Christmas.
B. Dragon Boat Festival.
C. Valentine's Day.

A. 聖誕節。
B. 端午節。
C. 情人節。

詳解

答案：B

　　從圖片可推測是和節日相關的問題。從題目 What ~ day 可知是問圖片是什麼日子。從炎炎夏日和粽子可知是端午節。

Q5

For question five, please look at picture E.

What's the matter with the boy?
這個男孩怎麼了？

A. He has a bad cough.
B. He hurt his shoulder.
C. He is running a fever.

A. 他咳嗽咳得很嚴重。
B. 他弄傷了他的肩膀。
C. 他在發高燒。

詳解

答案：C

　　從圖片可知一小孩臥病在床的樣子。從題目的 What's ~ matter ~ boy 可知是問小男孩遇到的問題為何。溫度計顯示 38.9 度，可知這個男孩在發高燒，running a fever 的 C 是答案。

Q6

What made her change her mind so suddenly?
是什麼讓她如此突然地改變心意？

A. Do you want some coins?
B. How long will it take?
C. Who knows?

A. 你要一些硬幣嗎？
B. 需要多久？
C. 誰知道？

詳解　　　　　　　　　　　　　　　　　　　　　　　答案：C

　　選項都是問句。從問句的 What made ~ change ~ mind 可知，是問改變某人心意的原因。mind 當名詞為「頭腦；心智」的意思。是什麼讓某人如此突然地改變心意，最為合理的答覆是「誰知道？誰曉得？」

補充說明

　　mind 當名詞時，有以下用法：make up one's mind（拿定主意），keep in mind（牢記在心），out of one's mind（瘋了）。mind 也可以當動詞使用，意思是「介意；注意」。
　　Do you mind opening the door for me? 你介意幫我開門嗎？
　　Please mind the platform gap. 請注意月臺縫隙。

|單字片語| **mind** [maɪnd] 心智；頭腦 / **coin** [kɔɪn] 硬幣 / **suddenly** [ˋsʌdənlɪ] 突然地

Q7

Your grades are terrible. What do you have to say?
你的成績真糟糕。你有什麼要說的？

A. Let me explain everything.
B. It tastes really bad.
C. I like the color.

A. 讓我解釋這一切。
B. 嚐起來真的不好吃。
C. 我喜歡這個顏色。

詳解　　　　　　　　　　　　　　　　　　　　　　　答案：A

　　從口氣和說話內容 Your grades ~ terrible 可知，說話者應該是家長，對象是孩子，提到對方成績不理想，選項中最適合的是需要好好解釋。

|單字片語| **grade** [gred] 成績 / **terrible** [ˋtɛrəbl] 糟糕的 / **explain** [ɪkˋsplen] 解釋 / **taste** [test] 品嚐 / **color** [ˋkʌlɚ] 顏色

Q8

Can I have another plastic bag?
我可以要另一個塑膠袋嗎？

A. Here it is.
B. I'll see you next time.
C. You can't take it back.

A. 這裡，給你。
B. 下次見。
C. 你不能拿回去。

詳解

從 Can I have ~ bag 可知說話者要求多拿一個塑膠袋，選項中最適合的回應應該會說「這裡，給你」。

補充說明

here 是副詞，表示「在這裡」的意思，一般放在句尾，但常以倒裝句方式作以強調，請見以下例句：
Here you are. 你要的東西在這裡。
Here comes the bus. 公車來了。

Q9

What would you like to have for dessert?
甜點你想要吃什麼？

A. My pleasure
B. Why not?
C. Chocolate ice cream.

A. 我的榮幸。
B. 為什麼不？
C. 巧克力冰淇淋。

詳解

答案：C

從 What ~ you like ~ dessert 可知，主要是問想吃什麼甜點。選項中最適合的回應是 C 的巧克力冰淇淋。

|單字片語| **dessert** 甜點 / **desert** 沙漠

Q10

Excuse me, sir. Please be quiet in the library.
先生，不好意思。在圖書館內請保持安靜。

A. Give me a big hand.
B. Push here to open.
C. I'm sorry.

A. 請幫我一個忙。
B. 推這裡打開。
C. 抱歉。

第 1 回

第 2 回

第 3 回

第 4 回

第 5 回

第 6 回

詳解　答案：C

　　從祈使句 please be quiet ~ library 可知，主要是提醒對方要保持安靜，言下之意就是對方太大聲了，選項中最適合的回應是提到抱歉。

|單字片語| **library** [ˋlaɪˏbrɛrɪ] 圖書館

Q11

Did you notice the ring on Jessica's finger?
你有注意到 Jessica 手指上的戒指嗎？

A. She hurt herself while she was cooking.
B. Don't tell me she is getting married.
C. Let's put the poster on the wall.

A. 她在煮飯時弄傷了自己。
B. 別告訴我她要結婚了。
C. 我們把海報貼在牆壁上吧。

詳解　答案：B

　　從疑問句 Did you notice ~ ring on ~ finger 可知，主要問對方是否有注意到某人戴的戒指。選項中最適合的回應是懷疑戒指主人是否要結婚。

|單字片語| **notice** [ˋnotɪs] 注意到 / **finger** [ˋfɪŋgɚ] 手指 / **get married** 結婚 / **poster** [ˋpostɚ] 海報

Q12

This summer heat is killing me.
這夏天的熱氣真是要命。

A. I can't sleep without air conditioning.
B. You should make a police report.
C. It's getting colder and colder.

A. 沒有空調我無法入睡。
B. 你應該報警。
C. 越來越冷了。

詳解　答案：A

　　從題目的 summer（夏天）和 Killing me 可得知，主要是表達天氣越來越熱，最合理的回覆是提到需要冷氣的 A。

|單字片語| **heat** [hit] 熱氣 / **air conditioning** 空調 / **make a police report** 報警

補充說明

　　這裡的 it's killing me，並非真的「殺死」，而是像中文常用的「熱死了；痛死了」。此外，kill time 是「打發時間」的意思，不是殺死時間。

Q13

You didn't write your address on the envelope.
你沒有在信封上寫你的地址。

A. I left it at home.
B. I'll do it now.
C. Perhaps they can work it out together.

A. 我把它放在家了。
B. 我現在寫。
C. 或許他們可以一起解決。

詳解 答案：B

　　從 You didn't write ~ address 可知，主要是提醒對方在信封上寫地址。最合理的回應是 B。

|單字片語| **address** [ə`drɛs] 地址 / **envelope** [`ɛnvə‚lop] 信封

Q14

I think my girlfriend is lying to me.
我認為我的女朋友在欺騙我。

A. What makes you think so?
B. Why is he standing on the stage?
C. How can we make ourselves more comfortable?

A. 你為什麼會這麼認為？
B. 他為什麼站在舞台上？
C. 我們要如何讓自己更舒服呢？

詳解 答案：A

　　選項都是疑問句。從 I think ~ girlfriend ~ lying 可知說話者認為女朋友在欺騙他，選項中最合理的回應是問說話者為什麼會這麼認為。

　　lie 有兩個意思：「說謊；躺下」，動名詞都是去 ie 加 ing 變成 lying。而另外一個容易搞混的動詞 lay 則是「下蛋」之意。

原形動詞	過去式	過去分詞	動名詞
lie 說謊	lied	lied	lying
lie 躺下	lay	lain	lying
lay 下蛋	laid	laid	laying

第 1 回

第 2 回

第 3 回

第 4 回

第 5 回

第 6 回

Q15

What should you do if there is a fire?
如果發生大火你應該做什麼？

A. Take the stairs, not the elevator.
B. I think you should see a doctor.
C. I didn't see a fire.

A. 走樓梯，不能搭電梯。
B. 我認為你應該去看醫生。
C. 我沒有看到火災。

詳解

答案：A

　　題目是說如果發生大火（there is a fire）該是怎麼辦。這裡的 fire 是指火災，不是指「開除」，B 是故意混淆考生的選項，正確答案為 A，發生火災時走樓梯，不能搭電梯。

Q16

Woman: You didn't eat breakfast again? How come the hundred dollars I gave you this morning is still in your wallet? 你又沒吃早餐了嗎？為什麼我今天早上給你的一百元還在你的錢包裡？

Man: Mom, I wasn't hungry at all. 媽，我一點都不餓。

Woman: You are saving up money to buy your favorite comics, aren't you? 你在存錢買你最喜歡的漫畫，對吧？

Q: What does the woman mean?
這位女士的意思是什麼？

A. The man should eat breakfast.   A. 這位男士應該吃早餐。
B. The man should not read books.   B. 這位男士不應該看書。
C. The man should not give her money.   C. 這位男士不應該給她錢。

詳解   答案：A

從選項可推斷題目是問與男士相關的內容。從對話內容可知說話的女士是媽媽，媽媽叫兒子別為了買漫畫而不吃早餐。

|單字片語| **how come** 為什麼 / **wallet** [ˋwɑlɪt] 皮夾 / **save up** 存錢 / **comics** [ˋkɑmɪks] 漫畫

Q17

Man: Make sure you use less oil and salt.
一定要用少一點油和鹽。

Woman: I will. I can't believe you are eating vegetables.
我會的。我無法相信你都在吃蔬菜。

Man: I am on a diet. 我在減肥。

Q: What is true about the conversation?
關於這段對話，何者屬實？

A. The man is teaching the woman how to cook.   A. 這位男士在教女士如何烹飪。
B. The man cares a lot about his health.   B. 這位男士很在乎他的健康。
C. The man will see a doctor.   C. 這位男士將去看醫生。

詳解

答案：B

　　從選項都是 the man 可知，要特別注意男士的對話內容。男士一開始要求用少一點油和鹽，而且也在吃蔬菜以及減肥，可見他非常重視自己的健康。

|單字片語| **make sure** 務必要 / **oil** [ɔɪl] 油 / **salt** [sɔlt] 鹽巴 / **on a diet** 節食，控制飲食

Q18

Woman:　I have never seen trees as tall as these.
　　　　我從來沒看過像這些這麼高的樹。

Man:　　Look! There are squirrels and birds in the tree.
　　　　你看，樹上有松鼠和小鳥。

Woman:　It's really good for us to get to nature sometimes.
　　　　有的時候接近大自然對我們來說是好的。

Q:　**Where might the speakers probably be?**
　　說話者可能在什麼地方？

A. In a forest.
B. In a desert.
C. In a museum.

A. 在森林裡。
B. 在沙漠。
C. 在博物館。

詳解

答案：A

　　從選項中都是 in + 名詞可推測，題目是問與「在哪裡」相關的問題。女士一開始提到有樹，男士則說有松鼠與鳥，最後又提到大自然（nature），可知最接近的答案是森林。

|單字片語| **squirrel** [ˋskwɝəl] 松鼠 / **nature** [ˋnetʃə] 大自然

Q19

Man:　　I have to go to the temple now.　我現在要去廟那邊了。

Woman:　Are you going there to ask for good luck for your son?
　　　　你是要去為你的兒子祈求好運嗎？

Man:　　Yes, the national exams are only two weeks away.
　　　　是的，離會考只有兩個星期。

Q: Why is the man going to the temple?
這位男士為什麼要去廟裡？

A. To pray for good health for himself.   A. 為自己祈求健康。
B. To pray for more money for his son.   B. 為兒子祈求更多錢。
C. To pray for good grades for his son.   C. 為兒子祈求好成績。

詳解   **答案：C**

　　從選項中都是「To + 動詞」可推測，題目會問與「做什麼的目的為何」相關的問題。從這位男士的回應：「離考試只有兩個星期」，可知他要為兒子祈求好成績。

|單字片語| **temple** [ˋtɛmpl] 廟 / **pray** [pre] 祈禱

Q20

Woman: Jerry, look at your room. It's a mess.
　　　　Jerry，看看你的房間。真是一團亂。

Man: 　Relax. I know where everything is.
　　　　放心。我知道所有東西所在的位置。

Woman: Why are there food wrappers under the desk?
　　　　為什麼書桌下有食物包裝紙？

Q: What does the woman want the man to do?
這位女士要男士做什麼？

A. Go and buy some food.   A. 去買一些食物。
B. Study for his math test.   B. 去為數學測驗準備。
C. Clean up the room.   C. 打掃房間。

詳解   **答案：C**

　　從選項都是祈使句可推測題目會問與「做～」相關的問題。女士說男子的房間亂成一團，書桌下還有食物包裝紙，言外之意是要男子打掃房間。

|單字片語| **math** [mæθ] 數學 / **clean up** 打掃

Q21

Man: 　I am afraid that I am not able to get into the school baseball
　　　　team. I feel like giving up.
　　　　我沒有進入學校棒球隊的本事。我想要放棄。

第 1 回
第 2 回
第 3 回
第 4 回
第 5 回
第 6 回

Woman: You can't give up now. The coach hasn't made up his mind yet.

現在你不能放棄。教練還沒拿定主意。

Man: All right. I will try my best. 好吧。我盡力而為。

Q: What will the man do?
這位男士將會做什麼？

A. Quit the school team.   A. 離開學校。
B. Work hard to be on the school team.   B. 努力進入校隊。
C. Become the coach of the school team.   C. 成為校隊的教練。

詳解　　　　　　　　　　　　　　　　　　　　**答案：B**

　　從選項都是祈使句可推測，題目會問與「做什麼」相關的問題。男子一開始說 I ~ am not able to get into ~ baseball team，又說 feel like giving up，可知這位男士對自己缺乏信心，不過在這位女士的鼓勵下，他會努力進入球隊。

|單字片語| **be able to** 能夠 / **baseball team** 棒球隊 / **give up** 放棄 / **coach** [kotʃ] 教練 / **make up one's mind** 決定 / **try one's best** 盡力

Q22

Woman: Orange roses are excellent for your boss.
橘色的玫瑰送老闆再好不過了。

Man: Really? I don't want her to get the wrong idea.
真的？我不希望她會錯意了。

Woman: She won't unless you send her pink or red roses.
她不會的，除非你送她粉色或紅色的玫瑰。

Q: What is the woman?
這位女士是做什麼的？

A. A florist.   A. 花商。
B. An actress.   B. 演員。
C. A boss.   C. 老闆。

詳解　　　　　　　　　　　　　　　　　　　　**答案：A**

　　從選項可推測題目會問與職業相關的問題。說話者的談話內容一直圍繞著玫瑰花（rose），以及應該送什麼顏色比較好。這位女士提出了一些建議，她應該是花商。

|單字片語| **orange** [ˈɔrɪndʒ] 橘色的 / **rose** [roz] 玫瑰 / **excellent** [ˈɛksləmt] 優異的 / **unless** [ʌnˈlɛs] 除非 / **pink** [pɪŋk] 粉紅色 / **red** [rɛd] 紅色的

347

Q23

Man: Move your hands and your shoulders like this. Look at yourself in the mirror. Ready?
像這樣移動你的雙手和肩膀。看著鏡子的你。好了嗎？

Woman: That's too fast. I can't keep up with the music.
太快了。我跟不上音樂。

Man: You will get used to it soon. 很快你就會習慣的。

Q: What is the relationship between the two speakers?
兩位說話者之間的關係是什麼？

A. Doctor and patient.
B. Coach and dancer.
C. Customer and clerk.

A. 醫生和病患。
B. 教練和舞者。
C. 顧客和店員。

詳解

答案：B

從選項都是職業類別可推測，題目會問與身分相關的問題。從移動雙手（move ~ hands）、看鏡子（look ~ in the mirror）和跟上音樂（Keep up with the music）這些關鍵字，可判斷說話者之間的關係是教練和舞者。

|單字片語| **mirror** [`mɪrə] 鏡子 / **keep up with** 跟上 / **get used to** 習慣

Q24

Woman: I am so nervous that I am shaking all over.
我緊張到我全身發抖。

Man: Take a deep breath. Look at me when you go on stage. Give me a big smile. Come on.
深呼吸。上台後看著我。給我一個大大的微笑。來吧。

Woman: Oh no! It's my turn to speak now. 糟了！輪到我要演講了。

Q: What will the woman probably do next?
這位女士接下來應該會做什麼？

A. Give a speech on stage.
B. Do the housework at home.
C. Turn on the radio in her room.

A. 上台演講。
B. 在家做家事。
C. 在房間裡打開收音機。

第 1 回
第 2 回
第 3 回
第 4 回
第 5 回
第 6 回

詳解

　　從選項都是祈使句可推測，題目會問與「做什麼」相關的問題。這位女士一開始提到很緊張（I ~ nervous），從男士提到的 go on stage 和女士提到的 my turn to speak，合理推斷她應該是要上台演講。

|單字片語| **nervous** [ˋnɝvəs] 緊張的 / **shake** [ʃek] 抖動 / **all over** 到處，全身 / **stage** [stedʒ] 舞台 / **turn** [tɝn]（依次輪流時各自的）一次機會

Q25

Man: Did you feel it? Was that an earthquake?
　　你有感覺到嗎？那是地震嗎？

Woman: I sat down on the sofa. That's all.
　　我坐在沙發上，就只是這樣而已。

Man: To be honest, you do need to lose some weight.
　　老實說，你的確需要減重。

Q: What is true about the conversation?
　　關於這段對話，何者屬實？

A. The woman thought there was an earthquake.

B. The man thinks that the woman is too heavy.

C. The woman thinks that the man should lose some weight.

A. 這位女士以為有地震。

B. 這位男士認為女士太重了。

C. 這位女士認為男士應該減重。

詳解

　　男士一開始問是不是有地震，女士解釋她只是坐下來而已，可見這位女士非常有「分量」，可知他的意思是女士太重了，需要減肥。

|單字片語| **earthquake** [ˋɝθˏkwek] 地震 / **to be honest** 老實說 / **lose weight** 減肥

Q26

For question number 26, please look at the three pictures.

Please listen to the following short talk.　請聽以下的簡短談話。

What might the game look like?
這個遊戲看起來可能是什麼樣子？

　　This is not the kind of game where you become a hero and shoot people. It's about knowledge. There are many areas to choose from. For example, you can touch the flag button here and you will be asked questions about your favorite country. You can also download pictures with beautiful scenery into your cell phone.

　　這不是那種讓你成為英雄然後開始射人的遊戲。這是關於知識的遊戲。有很多區域可以選擇。例如，你可以觸碰這裡的國旗按鈕，然後你會你被問到關於你最喜歡的國家的問題。你也可以下載有美麗風景的照片到你的手機裡。

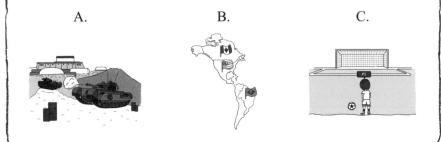

A.　　　　　　　　　B.　　　　　　　　　C.

詳解　　　　　　　　　　　　　　　　　　　　　　　　　　　**答案：B**

　　此三張圖分別是坦克、北美與南美的疆域與國旗、足球，可開始聯想題目內容可能與戰爭、國家或與足球遊戲有關。音檔一開始提到 What ~ game ~like 可知，以下內容與遊戲相關。談話中提到，這個遊戲不是那種射擊遊戲，選項 A 是錯的，也沒提到是運動類型的遊戲，所以 C 不正確。這個遊戲是有關不同國家的知識問題（ ~ about knowledge ~ touch the flag button ~ questions about your favorite country），應該會長的像圖 B。

|單字片語| **game** [gem] 遊戲，比賽 / **hero** [ˋhɪro] 英雄 / **shoot** [ʃut] 射擊 / **knowledge** [ˋnɑlɪdʒ] 知識 / **area** [ˋɛrɪə] 區域，領域 / **choose** [tʃuz] 選擇 / **flag** [flæg] 國旗 / **button** [ˋbʌtn] 按鈕 / **download** [ˋdaʊn.lod]] 下載 /**scenery** [ˋsinərɪ] 風景

第 1 回
第 2 回
第 3 回
第 4 回
第 5 回
第 6 回

Q27

For question number 27, please look at the three pictures.

Please listen to the following short talk. 請聽以下的簡短談話。

Who might the speaker be?
說話者可能是誰？

Dear visitors. Welcome to Woodlinton National Park. Please feel free to take pictures and walk along the paths. Many of these trees are over a hundred years old. The forest is home to birds and animals. Look! There's a squirrel under that tree. Please follow me for a 10-minute walk or go back to the bus if you are too tired.

親愛的訪客。歡迎來到武林頓國家公園。請隨意沿著小徑散步和拍照。這些樹很多都超過一百歲了。這座森林是鳥類和動物的棲息地。你看！那棵樹下有隻松鼠。請跟著我的步伐來走這 10 分鐘的路程，如果您累了的話也可以回到巴士上。

A.

B.

C.

詳解

答案：B

此三張圖都是不同身分的人物，而且題目問句也問到 Who ~ speaker，可知要注意聽題目內容才能判斷說話者是誰。從一開始的 Dear visitors（親愛的訪客）、Welcome to ~ National Park.（歡迎來到~國家公園）可知說話者在為訪客介紹國家公園，中間又說到 feel free to take pictures and walk along the paths，表示請訪客自由拍照，最後提到如果累的話可以回到巴士，可知他應該是一名導遊。

|單字片語| **visitor** [ˋvɪzɪtə] 觀光者，參觀者，訪客 / **take pictures** 拍照 / **path** [pæθ] 小徑 / **forest** [ˋfɔrɪst] 森林 / **home to** 是～的棲息地/ **species** [ˋspiʃiz] 種類 / **deer** [dɪr] 鹿 / **squirrel** [ˋskwɝəl] 松鼠

351

Q28

For question number 28, please look at the three pictures.

Please listen to the following telephone message. 　請聽以下的電話留言。

What seems to be the problem?
似乎出了什麼問題？

　　Hi there, Mr. Smith. This is your neighbor, Mr. Clinton. I can't help but notice that you left the garbage on the driveway without taking it away. The smell is just horrible. Could you please do something about it? Thank you.

　　Smith 先生你好。我是你的鄰居，Clinton 先生。我沒辦法不注意到你放在車道上的垃圾，卻沒有拿去倒。味道真得很難聞。你可以採取行動解決這個問題嗎？謝謝。

A. 　　　　　　　　　B. 　　　　　　　　　C.

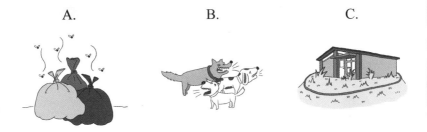

詳解　　　　　　　　　　　　　　　　　　　　　 答案：A

　　三張圖片分別是垃圾、野狗亂吠、雜草，可先聯想題目與某問題有關。一開始的提示訊息提到 Please listen ~ telephone message，可知這是一則給某人的電話留言，接著聽到 What ~ problem 可知語音內容是關於某某問題。一開始表明自己的身分是隔壁鄰居（neighbor），接著說 notice ~ you left the garbage ~ without taking it away，可知困擾說話者的問題是垃圾問題，所以答案的 A。

|單字片語| **neighbor** [`nebə] 鄰居 / **can't help but** 不得不 / **notice** [`notɪs] 注意到 / **garbage** [`gɑrbɪdʒ] 垃圾 / **driveway** [`draɪˌwe] 車道 / **smell** [smɛl] 味道 / **horrible** [`hɔrəbl] 可怕的，糟透的

第 1 回
第 2 回
第 3 回
第 4 回
第 5 回
第 6 回

Q29

For question number 29, please look at the three pictures.

Please listen to the following news report. 請聽以下的新聞報導。

What might the weather be like these few days?
這幾天的天氣可能會如何？

With the strange weather conditions we are experiencing, many areas in Taiwan are facing a shortage of water. The rainy season that usually comes in May turned out to be the driest month in history. On such cloudless days, the temperature can rise as high as 38 degrees Celsius. To deal with the water shortage problem, people are advised to take short showers instead of long baths.

由於我們正經歷到的怪異天氣狀況，台灣許多地區都面臨缺水問題。通常是雨季到來的五月成為史上最為乾旱的月份。在晴朗無雲的這段日子，溫度可上升至攝氏三十八度。為了應付缺水問題，建議人們應該縮短淋浴時間而不要長時間泡澡。

A.

B.

C.

詳解

答案：A

　　三張圖片都與天氣狀況相關，可先聯想題目是關於天氣。從一開始提示訊息提到的 Please listen ~ news report，以及接著聽到的 What ~ weather ~ like these few days，可知這是一則氣象預報。一開始提到 strange weather conditions，可知是怪異的天氣，接著說到 ~ shortage of water以及 ~ May turned out to be the driest month 可知原本是雨季的五月成為乾旱的月份，表示今年五月並沒有下雨。報導提到溫度（temperatune）可上升到高達攝氏三十八度 38 degree Celsius，可見天氣非常炎熱，答案為 A。

|單字片語| **weather conditions** 天氣狀況 / **shortage** [ˋʃɔrtɪdʒ] 短缺 / **rainy season** 雨季 / **turn out** 結果成為 / **dry** [draɪ] 乾燥的 / **cloudless** [ˋklaʊdlɪs] 晴朗無雲的 / **temperature** [ˋtɛmprətʃə] 溫度 / **Celsius** [ˋsɛlsɪəs] 攝氏 / **advise** [ədˋvaɪz] 建議 / **shower** [ˋʃaʊ⋅] 淋浴 / **bath** [bæθ] 泡澡

For question number 30, please look at the three pictures.

Please listen to the following announcement. 請聽以下的公告廣播。

What is the usual time the school library closes?
學校圖書館通常什麼時間關閉？

Attention all students. Because of the coming monthly exams, the library will be opened for another two hours until 10 o'clock at night. You will be asked to pack your bags and prepare to leave at a quarter to ten. Please be reminded that no eating or drinking is allowed in the library.

各位學生請注意。因為即將來臨的月考，圖書館會多開放兩小時直到晚上十點。在 9 點 45 分的時候，你會被要求收拾書包並準備離開。再次提醒，圖書館裡不准吃東西或喝飲料。

A.   B.   C.

詳解

　　三張圖片分別指出不同時間，可先聯想題目與時間相關。從一開始提示訊息提到的 Please ~ announcement 可知是一則公告廣播，從接著聽到的 What ~ the usual time ~ library closes? 可知是問圖書館平常閉館的時間。

　　一開始提到 Because of ~ monthly exams ~ library ~ opened for another two hours until 10 o'clock at night，從 exams、opened for another two hours 和 until 10 o'clock 可知，因為有考試而多開放兩個小時，直到晚上10點才閉館，言下之意平常的閉館時間是兩小時之前，也就是晚上八點，所以答案是 A.。

|單字片語| **monthly** [`mʌnθlɪ] 每月的 / **exam** [ɪg`zæm] 考試 / **library** [`laɪˌbrɛrɪ] 圖書館 **another** [ə`nʌðə] 另一個 / **until** [ən`tɪl] 直到 / **pack** [pæk] 打包 / **a quarter to ten** 9 點 45 分 / **remind** [rɪ`maɪnd] 提醒 / **allow** [ə`laʊ] 允許

第六回

初試 閱讀測驗 解析

第一部分 / 詞彙

Q1

I'm feeling a little sick. I think I need to _____ the doctor a visit.

我覺得有點不舒服。我認為我需要去看個醫生。

A. pay 支付；進行（拜訪）　　B. give 給
C. see 看到　　D. join 加入

詳解

答案：A

　　選項都是動詞，這時要注意空格後面有兩個受詞 the doctor 和 a visit，片語「pay 某人 a visit」指拜訪某人，是比較客氣的說法，通常對象為醫生或年長者，所以答案是 A。

|單字片語| **pay ~ a visit** 拜訪

Q2

These two insects look _____ but they are actually different.

這兩隻昆蟲看起來很相似，但他們其實是不同的。

A. special 特別的　　B. familiar 熟悉的
C. similar 相似的　　D. particular 特別的

詳解

答案：C

　　選項都是形容詞，請注意此句子是由 but 連接的兩個子句。乍看之下，可能會認為選 special 很合理，但後半句提到「其實他們是不同的」，所以比較洽當的表達為：看起來很相似，但其實是不同的。

|單字片語| **insect** [ˈɪnsɛkt] 昆蟲 / **actually** [ˈæktʃʊəlɪ] 其實 / **different** [ˈdɪfərənt] 不同的

Q3

You should learn to _____ and forget. You will feel better when you can do that.

你應該學習去原諒和淡忘。當你這麼做時，你會覺得比較舒服。

  A. forgive 原諒   B. focus 專注
  C. damage 破壞   D. delay 耽誤

詳解   答案：A

     這題主要是考語意，選項都是動詞。試著從選項中的動詞一一填入 learn to ~ and forget ~ will feel better 可知，最適合的語意是「學習原諒和淡忘…會覺得比較舒坦」，所以答案是 A。forgive and forget 是英文的慣用語，主要是勸導我們不要記仇。

Q4

Medicines should be kept out of children's _____.

藥物應該放在孩子們拿不到的地方。

  A. touch 觸碰   B. reach 拿到；達到
  C. take 拿   D. swallow 吞

詳解   答案：B

     本題主要是考語意理解。請注意空格是在 children's 後面，主詞是 medicine（藥物），動詞是 should be kept（應放在），就語意上來看：藥物應放在孩子們拿不到的地方，片語 out of somebody's reach 是正確答案。片語 within one's reach 指「伸手可及」，out of one's reach 剛好相反，表示「拿不到」。reach 的另外一個意思「到達」跟 arrive 雷同，可用於 I'll call you when I reach/arrive home.（我會到家打電話給你）。

Q5

The yearly meeting will _____ in a five-star hotel.

年度會議將在五星級飯店舉辦。

  A. be taken place   B. be held
  C. be occurred   D. be happened

詳解   答案：B

     本題主要是考動詞。主詞是 meeting（會議），就選項來看主要是想表達「會議被舉行」，要表達「舉行」，英文可用 hold 或 take place 來表示。請注意，當主詞是人時（某人舉辦 hold 某個會議），hold 用主動語態。若把會議當

主詞，必須用被動語態（會議將會被舉辦 will be held）。take place 則用於主動語態，主詞不用人物，而是事物，the meeting will take place at...（會議在某地方進行）。occur（發生）通常用在自然現象，例如地震（earthquake）或海嘯（tsunami）。happen（發生）則用在意外（accident）或突發事件（something unexpected）因此答案是 B。

|單字片語| **yearly** [ˋjɪrlɪ] 年度的 / **meeting** [ˋmitɪŋ] 會議 / **five-star** 五星級的 / **hotel** [hoˋtɛl] 飯店

Q6

My husband has a good sense of _____. He always makes me laugh.

我的丈夫有幽默感。他總是讓我笑。

A. biology 生物
B. knowledge 知識
C. reason 原因
D. humor 幽默

詳解　　　　　　　　　　　　　　　　　　　　　　　　　　　答案：D

　　本題主要是考語意理解。空格前面是 a good sense of，表示「有～感」，後面提到 always makes me laugh（總是讓我笑），由此可知主要是要表達「有幽默感」，所以答案是 D。sense 是「感官」的意思，five senses 指五種感官，即 sense of sight（視覺）、sense of hearing（聽覺）、sense of smell（嗅覺）、sense of taste（味覺）和 sense of touch（觸覺）。而 sixth sense 是第六感。a sense of...表示「…感」，例如幽默感（a sense of humor）、方向感（a sense of direction）和 a sense of security（安全感）。

Q7

It has been several years _____ I last saw my elementary school principal.

自從我上次看到國小校長到現在已經過好幾年了。

A. from
B. for
C. since
D. about

詳解　　　　　　　　　　　　　　　　　　　　　　　　　　　答案：C

　　現在完成式 have + p.p. 經常搭配 for 或 since 一起使用。表示「自從…已經…」時會用 have + p.p... since，表示「已經…了多久」用 have + p.p... for。
　　本題主要是考介系詞。空格前面有 has been several years，用現在完成式提到一段時間，後面是過去式的 ~ saw my ~ principal.。

|單字片語| **several** [ˋsɛvərəl] 好幾個 / **last** [læst] 上一次 / **elementary school** 國小 / **principal** [ˋprɪnsəpl] 校長

Q8

The manager knows what the old man will order because he is a _____ customer.

經理知道這位老人家會點什麼，因為他是一位常客。

A. foreign 國外的
B. regular 固定的
C. dangerous 危險的
D. terrible 糟糕的

詳解

　　本題主要是考形容詞。題目由 because 連接兩個子句，所以前後兩子句有因果關係。前面提到經理知道這位老人家會點什麼，從選項中可推斷後一子句要表達的是因為他是常客。常客的英文是 regular customer，答案是 B。

|單字片語| **manager** [ˋmænɪdʒɚ] 經理 / **order** [ˋɔrdɚ] 點餐，下訂單 / **customer** [ˋkʌstəmɚ] 顧客

Q9

A new type of scooter with two doors will be _____ next month.

一種有兩個門的新款機車將會在下個月推出。

A. introduced 介紹；推出
B. affected 影響
C. happened 發生
D. treated 對待；治療

詳解

　　本題主要是考動詞與語意理解。空格和前面的 will be 是本句的主要動詞，主詞是 A new type of scooter，而空格後面是 next month，從選項來推斷語意可知主要是要表達下個月有新款機車要推出，正確答案是 A。

|單字片語| **type** [taɪp] 種類，款式 / **scooter** [skutɚ] 機車

Q10

We have to arrive at the airport at least two hours before the flight _____.

我們必須在班機起飛前至少兩小時抵達機場。

A. flies away 飛走
B. takes off 起飛；脫掉
C. puts on 穿上
D. stops by 路過

詳解

　　本題主要是考動詞片語與語意理解。本題句子是由兩子句組成，由 before 連接。從 arrive at the airport（抵達機場）和 flight（班機）可知，最恰當的動詞時 takes off（起飛）

Questions 11-14

Mei-lin is a first year senior high school student. She did very (11) well on the exams last year. She studied hard to get into this senior high school and she is (12) proud to wear the school uniform. However, she finds it hard to get the same grades she (13) used to get in junior high school. Take English for example, she used to score at least 95 for every test, but now she struggles just to pass. She is as hardworking as before, but she is not getting the excellent grades she wants. Mei-lin has never attended any cram schools. She doesn't like to repeat what she already knows and learns in school. Her mom keeps telling her that (14) going to a cram school may be helpful in improving her grades. Mei-lin decided to give herself one more semester. If things do not go well this semester, she will have to look for a cram school during the summer vacation.

美琳是高中一年級的學生。她去年在考試中表現得很好。她努力讀書才進入這所高中的，她為穿上制服而感到自豪。然而，她發現要得到跟過去念國中時一樣的成績很困難。以英文為例，她以前每次測驗都考至少 95 分，但是現在要及格都很辛苦。她跟以前一樣努力，但還是得不到她想要的優越成績。美琳從來沒有上過任何補習班。她不喜歡重覆念已經知道而且在學校所學的東西。她的媽媽一直告訴她，去補習班應該會有助於改善成績。美琳決定給自己多一個學期。如果這學期狀況沒有好轉，她在暑假期間就會去找補習班了。

Q11

A. good 好的   B. hard 努力地
C. well 好地   D. badly 糟地

詳解   答案：C

空格在 did very 後面，由於 did 是動詞，副詞修飾動詞，形容詞修飾名詞，因此「在考試中表現得很好的」中的「很好」用 well，即 do well on the exam。

|單字片語| **arrive** [əˈraɪv] 抵達 / **airport** [ˈɛrˌport] 機場 / **flight** [flaɪt] 班機

第 1 回
第 2 回
第 3 回
第 4 回
第 5 回
第 6 回

Q12

A. necessary 有必要的
B. loud 大聲的
C. proud 自豪的
D. dishonest 不誠實的

詳解

答案：C

選項都是形容詞，空格在 she is 和 to wear 之間，就語意上來看，is proud to wear ... uniform（很自豪地穿制服）比其他選項來得通順，是正確答案。

│單字片語│ **proud** 自豪；驕傲的 / **pride** 光榮；自尊

Q13

A. used to
B. is using to
C. was used to
D. has used to

詳解

答案：A

選項都是與 used 相關的用法，空格在主詞 she 和動詞 get 之間，就這整句語意上來看，先把此句拆成一段一段來理解：she finds it hard/to get the same grades/she ~ to get/in junior high school.（她發現很難／取得一樣的成績／她～取得／在國中時），言下之意就是，她現在不太能獲得她過去在國中時獲得的成績，選項中能表示「過去習慣」的是 A. 的 used to。請見以下例句：
I am used to walking to the office. 我習慣走路去上班。（現在經常做的事）
I used to smoke. 我以前常抽菸。（現在沒有了）
She used to live here. 她以前住這裡。（現在沒有了）

Q14

A. she needs to wake up early
   她需要早點起床

B. going to a cram school may be helpful in improving her grades
   去補習班應該會有助於改善成績

C. she is not good at English and Math
   她的英文和數學不太好

D. they plan to go abroad during this summer vacation
   他們計畫今年暑假去國外

詳解

答案：B

空格前面主要提到美琳的成績變得沒以前好，且從來沒上過補習班，以及她沒去上補習班的理由。空格後面則提到如果狀況沒有好轉，她就會去找補習

361

班。可推測空格的內容應該是跟補習班有關。選項中與上補習班有關的是 B.，接續在「她的媽媽一直告訴她」後面，表示美琳的媽媽建議她要去上補習班，這樣成績才會進步。故答案選 B.。

Questions 15-18

Singapore is an island nation. It is so small that most people have trouble (15) finding it on the world map. Even Taiwan, which is fifty times the size of Singapore, appears small compared to China and Japan. (16) That explains why Singapore is smaller than a tiny dot. (17) Surprisingly, such a small country with no natural resources at all is one of the richest nations in Asia. Singapore's airport and seaport are (18) among the very best globally. The government is well-known for managing the nation like a company. Everything is about goals and improvement. Government workers who fail to live up to expectations can be fired just like employees in a private company. Singapore is also known for its strict laws. The first announcement one hear on the plane before arrival is the death sentence for carrying drugs.

新加坡是個島國。它是如此地小，以至於大部份的人很難在世界地圖上找到它。即便是比新加坡面積大五十倍的台灣，相較於中國和日本看起來還是很小。這說明了為什麼新加坡比一個小點還要小。

令人驚訝的是，這個毫無天然資源的小國卻是亞洲其中一個最富裕的國家。新加坡的機場和海港屬於全世界最好的之一。政府以管理公司的方式治理國家而聞名。一切都是關於目標和進步。沒有達到期望的公務員可能就像私人公司那樣被解雇。新加坡也以嚴厲的法律而知名。在入境新加坡之前，在飛機上聽到的第一個廣播是攜帶毒品將面臨死刑。

Q15

A. find
C. finding

B. to find
D. found

詳解　　　　　　　　　　　　　　　　　　　　　　　答案：C

選項都與 find 相關，空格在 have trouble 和受詞 it 之間，這時要知道以下重點 have trouble V-ing, have difficulty V-ing, have a hard time V-ing，接在 trouble 等名詞後的動詞都要用 ing 的形態。

Q16

A. Many of my friends often take a trip to Singapore.
我的許多朋友經常去新加坡旅行。

B. Some say that there are five continents in the world.
有些人說世界上有五大洲。

C. That explains why Singapore is smaller than a tiny dot.
這說明了為什麼新加坡比一個小點還要小。

D. Singapore is famous for "Gardens by the Bay".
新加坡以濱海灣花園而聞名。

詳解　　　　　　　　　　　　　　　　　　　　　　　答案：C

　　空格前面主要提到新加坡的面積很小，提到比它大 50 倍的台灣也是看起來很小，因此可推測空格的內容應該也是跟面積很小有關。選項中與面積大小有關的是 C.。故答案選 C.。

Q17

A. Surprise
B. Surprising
C. Surprisingly
D. To surprise

詳解　　　　　　　　　　　　　　　　　　　　　　　答案：C

　　選項都與 Surprise 相關，空格放在句首，逗號前面，是屬於修飾整個句子的副詞位置。選項中有副詞意義的是 C.。另外一個可以放在句首的還有 To one's surprise（讓某人驚訝的是）只有副詞可以獨立出現在句首，後面接逗點。例如昨天（yesterday）是時間副詞，可以放在句首或句尾，放在句首必須加逗點。同樣的，Surprisingly 是副詞，所以可以放在句首。

I went to Kenting **yesterday**. 昨天我去墾丁。
Yesterday, I went to Kenting. 昨天我去墾丁。
It rained **suddenly**. 突然下雨了。
Suddenly, it rained. 突然下雨。

Q18

A. among 在⋯之中
B. away 在⋯以外
C. against 依靠著⋯
D. along 沿著⋯

詳解　　　　　　　　　　　　　　　　　　　　　　　答案：A

　　選項中有介系詞、副詞，空格放在 be 動詞和名詞 the very best 之間，可知

空格要填介系詞，才能接名詞。就前後文來看，前一句開始提到 Singapore 的優點，像是「是亞洲其中一個最富裕的國家」，可以得知空格要填入 among，來表示「在最好的名單之中」。請了解 between 是「兩者之間」的意思，而 among 是「眾多…之中」的意思。

Among all my friends, he is the only one I can trust.
在我眾多朋友之中，他是我唯一可以信任的。

第 1 回
第 2 回
第 3 回
第 4 回
第 5 回
第 6 回

Questions 19-21

THSR Train Schedule

高鐵火車行程

Stops/Train No. 停靠站/車號	536	621	747	859
Leaving at 於～點發車	09:00	09:20	09:40	10:00
Taipei 台北	O	O	O	O
Banqiao 板橋	O	O	X	X
Taoyuan 桃園	O	O	X	O
Xinzhu 新竹	O	O	X	X
Taichung 台中	O	O	O	O
Jiayi 嘉義	O	O	X	X
Tainan 台南	O	O	X	O
Zuoying 左營	O	O	O	O

O = Stops 停靠
X = Non-stops 不停靠

Taipei to Zuoying: NT$1800
Enjoy early-bird discount of up to 35% if you book in advance.
Note: Number of early-bird seats limited.
Students with valid student ID card can purchase tickets at half price.

台北到左營：新台幣 1800 元
如果提早訂票可享有高達 65 折的早鳥優惠。
注意：早鳥優惠座位有限
學生可憑有效的學生證以半價購票。

|單字片語| discount [ˋdɪskaʊnt] 折扣 / book [bʊk] 預訂 / in advance 提早 / limited [ˋlɪmɪtɪd] 有限的 / valid [ˋvælɪd] 有效的 / purchase [ˋpɝtʃəs] 購買 / ticket [ˋtɪkɪt] 票券

Q19

Where can we most likely see the information?

我們最有可能在哪裡看到這資訊？

    A. In an airport. 在機場。

    B. In a post office. 在郵局。

    C. In a train station. 在火車站。

    D. At school. 在學校。

詳解　　　　　　　　　　　　　　　　　　　　　　　　　　答案：C

    從一開始的標題 Train Schedule，可知最有可能在火車站看到此資訊。故答案選 C。

Q20

Which train stops at the fewest of all the stations from Taipei to Zuoying?

從台北到左營，那一趟列車停靠的站最少？

    A. Train 536.

    B. Train 621.

    C. Train 747.

    D. Train 859.

詳解　　　　　　　　　　　　　　　　　　　　　　　　　　答案：C

    題目問的是從台北到左營，哪一班列車停靠最少站。列車 747 號只在台北、台中、左營停靠，停靠三站，而列車 859 號停靠五站，答案為 C。

Q21

Mr. Chen got a 20% early-bird discount. How much does he need to pay from Taipei to Zuoying?

陳先生得到了八折的早鳥優惠。他從台北到左營需要付多少錢？

    A. NT$1800

    B. NT$1440

    C. NT$1350

    D. NT$1200

詳解

答案：B

從台北到左營的全票是 NT$1800。陳先生有八折 20%的早鳥票，NT$1800 X 0.8 = NT$1440。

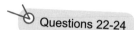

Questions 22-24

4.5. 2020

Dear Neighbors,

A new bookstore is coming, just near where you live. On Monday April 20th, doors are opening for you. We have a large selection of books around for your purchases. We also have a nice coffee shop, so you can enjoy some coffee while looking through books. Because you are our neighbors, enclosed please find a coupon we offered, of course, only for you!

If you have any questions or suggestions, please contact me directly. (Please see my name card for contact information). Your feedback is always welcome!

Regards,

Mike Lin
Marketing Manager
International Village Books

第 1 回

第 2 回

第 3 回

第 4 回

第 5 回

第 6 回

國際村書局

親愛的鄰居們，

　　一間新的書店要來了，就在你住的地方附近。4 月 20 日星期一，大門為你而開。我們有大量的各類書籍供您購買。我們也有一間很棒的咖啡廳，所以你可以在翻閱書籍時，享用一些咖啡。因為你是我們的鄰居，我們附上了一張折價券。當然，這是你獨享的喔！

　　假如你有任何問題或建議，請直接跟我聯繫（聯絡資訊請見我的名片）。我們永遠歡迎您的意見回饋！

誠摯的祝福，

Mike Lin
行銷經理
國際村書店

★ Coupon ★

This coupon is good for one hot drink in International Village Coffee Shop, and you can also get 10% off on any books you buy in the bookstore.

Valid until April 30th.

$$折價券$$

這張折價券可於國際村咖啡館兌換一杯熱飲，並可在本書店所購的任何書籍上享九折折扣。

有效期間到 4 月 30 為止。

International Village Group
Mike Lin
Marketing Manager

Mobile: 0936-099-675
Email: mike_lin@intervillage.com
Fax: (02)2356-9856

國際村集團
Mike Lin
行銷經理

手機號碼：0936-099-675
電子郵件信箱：mike_lin@intervillage.com
傳真號碼：(02)2356-9856

Q22

When will the new bookstore open?

新書店何時開幕？

A. April 5th. 4 月 5 日。
B. April 20th. 4 月 20 日。
C. April 30th. 4 月 30 日。
D. April 10th. 4 月 10 日。

在第一篇文的信中提到: A new bookstore... On Monday April 20th, doors are opening for you. ，可知新書店將在 4 月 20 日開幕。故答案選 B。

Q23

What can you get with the coupon?

用這張折價券可以獲得什麼？

    A. Hot drinks and a free book.
       熱飲與一本免費的書。

    B. 10% off the regular prices on any books.
       任何書籍可享原價九折。

    C. Free magazines and a cold drink.
       免費的雜誌與一杯冷飲。

    D. Buy one book and get another free.
       買書可享買一送一優惠。

在第二篇文的折價券提到: This coupon is good for one hot drink... also get 10% off on any books you buy in the bookstore. ，表示這張折價券可兌換一杯熱飲，並可在任何書籍上享九折折扣。故答案選 B。

Q24

What is Not true about Mike Lin?

關於 Mike Lin 哪一項不為真？

    A. He is a manager in International Village Books.
       他是國際村書店的經理。

    B. He can be reached at 0936099675.
       可以用 0936099675 的電話聯繫到他。

    C. He is the owner of the coffee shop.
       他是咖啡廳的擁有者。

    D. He welcomes customers' feedback.
       他歡迎顧客的回應。

詳解

　　從第一篇信件的署名、第三篇的名片上的 Marketing Manager、Mobile: 0936-099-675 可知 A、B是正確的敘述。而在信中的最後一句：Your feedback is always welcome 也可知 D 正確。文中並未提到 Mike Lin 是咖啡廳的擁有者，故答案選 C。

|單字片語| **purchase** 購買物　**suggestion** 建議　**feedback** 回應回饋　**marketing manager** 行銷經理

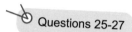

Questions 25-27

Peter's Pizza House

Dear customers,

To celebrate our first successful year in business, we will offer unbelievable discounts on April 11 2016.

To reward our regular customers, purchase any pizza and get another one free.
Simply show us your personal membership card and your ID to enjoy this offer.

First-time customers will receive 20% on all pizzas on that day.

P/S: Free pizza has to be of the same price of the one bought, or lower. Offer is only valid on April 11 2016.

Peter 的比薩屋

親愛的顧客：

為了慶祝我們成功經營的第一年，我們將在 2016 年 4 月 11 日提供不可思議的折扣。

為了獎勵我們的常客，披薩買一送一。
只要給我們看你的個人會員卡和個人證件就能享有這項優惠。

新顧客當天可享有所有比薩八折優惠。

請看：免費贈送的比薩必須跟所購買的比薩同價，或更低價。優惠只有在 2016 年 4 月 11 日當天有效。

|單字片語| **pizza** [ˋpitsə] 比薩 / **customer** [ˋkʌstəmə] 顧客 / **celebrate** [ˋsɛlə‚bret] 慶祝 / **successful** [səkˋsɛsfəl] 成功的 / **unbelievable** [ʌnbɪˋlivəbl] 難以置信的 / **discount** [ˋdɪskaʊnt] 折扣 / **reward** [rɪˋwɔrd] 獎勵 / **regular** [ˋrɛgjələ] 固定的 / **purchase** [ˋpɝtʃəs] 購買 / **membership** [ˋmɛmbə‚ʃɪp] 會員 / **offer** [ˋɔfə] 優惠的提供 / **receive** [rɪˋsiv] 收到 / **price** [praɪs] 價格 / **valid** [ˋvælɪd] 有效的

Q25

What is the purpose of this poster?
海報的目的是什麼？

A. To encourage customers to purchase something.
   鼓勵顧客購買東西。

B. To invite guests to a movie premiere.
   邀請貴賓參加電影首映禮。

C. To ask customers to fill out a form to get a membership card.
   要求客戶填寫表格以獲取會員卡。

D. To explain how to subscribe to a magazine.
   解釋如何訂閱雜誌。

詳解

　　從文章中的 we will offer unbelievable discounts、purchase any pizza and get another one free.、First-time customers will receive 20% on all pizzas on that day.都在提到折扣，可知此海報目的是透過折扣的宣傳，來吸引顧客來此店消費，所以答案是 A。

Q26

Who might have written this poster?
誰有可能寫這張海報？

A. A restaurant owner. 餐廳業者。

B. A regular customer. 常客。

C. A club member. 社團會員。

D. A first-grader. 一年級生。

詳解　　　　　　　　　　　　　　　　　　　答案：A

　　從 Who ~ written this poster? 可知，主要是問寫這張海報的人是誰。從標題的 Pizza House（比薩屋）、customer（顧客）、discounts（折扣）、purchase any pizza and get another one free（比薩買一送一）可知這是餐廳的宣傳海報，最有可能寫這張海報的應該是餐廳業者。

Q27

What is true about the poster?

關於這張海報，何者正確？

A. Members can lend their membership card to their friends.
   會員可以把會員卡借給朋友。
B. Members can get a free pizza which costs more.
   會員可以得到一個價值更高的比薩。
C. First-time customers do not enjoy the buy-one-get-one free offer.
   第一次購買的顧客不能享有買一送一的優惠。
D. First-time customers can enjoy a 20 percent discount for the whole
   month of April. 第一次購買的顧客在整個四月份可享有八折。

詳解　　　　　　　　　　　　　　　　　　　答案：C

　　從 What ~ true ~ poster? 可知，主要是問與文中相符的選項。文中並未提到會員卡可借給他人，還提到會員必須出示證件，A. 不正確。免費贈送的比薩必須跟所購買的比薩同價，或更低，所以不能超過所購買的比薩價格。新顧客只有 4 月 11 日當天可獲得 8 折優惠，不是整個四月，選項 A、B 和 D 都是錯誤的。新顧客在週年活動當天可享有八折，而買一送一的活動只限老顧客。

 Questions 28-30

　　Mrs. Wang is worried about her father. His memory is failing and he keeps forgetting things. Last month, he left the house with the gas stove still on. As a result, the kitchen was on fire. Luckily, she managed to put the fire out. Once, the police called her and told her to pick up her dad at the police station. One of the police officers said that they found him in another person's house. Mrs. Wang explained that the house used to belong to them but they sold it to the present owner ten years ago. The owner made a police report. Her father seemed to think that it is still their house. Mrs. Wang has spoken to a doctor about her father's problem, but her father refused to receive treatment. Old people like him are so afraid of hospitals that they think doctors are evil. The biggest problem with him is that he doesn't believe he has one because he can't remember it. Mrs. Wang read in an article that playing card games can help to improve memory. She is trying her best to 'trick' her father into playing card games with the grandchildren. She hopes that things will get better.

王太太很擔心他的父親。他的記憶在衰退中，所以他一直忘記事情。上個月，他瓦斯爐沒關就離開家裡。結果廚房著火。幸好，她把火勢撲滅。有一次，警方打電話給她，叫她到警察局接她的父親。其中一個警官說，他們發現他在另一個人的房子裡。王太太解釋說這個房子之前是他們的，但是他們在十年前把房子賣給現在的屋主。因此，此屋主報了警。她的父親似乎認為那還是他們的房子。王太太已經跟醫生談過她父親的問題，但是父親拒絕接受治療。像他這樣的老人家是如此害怕醫院，以至於他們認為醫生是邪惡的。最大的問題是，他不相信自己有問題，因為他根本不記得那個問題。王太太在一篇文章讀到，玩紙牌遊戲可以幫助改善記憶。她正在努力「騙」她父親跟孫子們玩紙牌遊戲。她希望事情會好轉。

|單字片語| **memory** [`mɛmərɪ] 記憶 / **fail** [fel] 衰弱 / **forget** [fɚ`gɛt] 遺忘 / **gas stove** 瓦斯爐 / **put out** 撲滅 / **pick up** 接送 / **police station** 警察局 / **explain** [ɪk`splen] 解釋 / **used to** 過去習慣於 / **belong** [bə`lɔŋ] 屬於 / **owner** [`onɚ] 主人 / **refuse** [rɪ`fjuz] 拒絕 / **treatment** [`tritmənt] 治療 / **evil** [`ivl] 邪惡的 / **remember** [rɪ`mɛmbɚ] 記得 / **article** [`ɑrtɪkl] 文章 / **improve** [ɪm`pruv] 改善 / **trick** [trɪk] 哄騙

Why was the kitchen on fire?
為什麼廚房起火？

A. Mrs. Wang didn't use the microwave properly.
王太太沒有妥善地使用微波爐。

B. Mrs. Wang's father smoked in the kitchen.
王太太的父親在廚房抽菸。

C. Mrs. Wang's father forgot to turn off the gas stove.
王太太的父親忘記把瓦斯爐關掉。

D. Mrs. Wang forgot to turn off the heater.
王太太忘記把暖爐關掉。

詳解

從 Why ~ kitchen on fire? 可知，主要是問廚房失火的原因。文中一開始就提到 Mrs. Wang is worried about her father ~ he keeps forgetting things，可知王太太的父親時常忘東忘西，接著說 he left the house with the gas stove still on. 以及 she found the kitchen on fire，由此可知是因為王太太的父親忘記把瓦斯爐關掉，以至於廚房失火，正確答案是 C。

第1回
第2回
第3回
第4回
第5回
第6回

Q29

How come Mrs. Wang's father was in the police station?
為何王太太的父親會在警察局？

A. He thought that was his house. 他以為那是他的房子。
B. He didn't have a place to live in. 他沒有地方住。
C. He didn't want to stay in the hospital. 他不想待在醫院。
D. He went into someone else's house. 他進入別人的家。

詳解　　　　　　　　　　　　　　　　　　　　　　　答案：D

　　從 How come Mrs. Wang's father ~ in the police station 可知，主要是問王太太父親在警察局的原因。文中並未提到王太太的父親把警局當成自己家，也沒提到沒有地方住和不想住院才跑到警局去。選項 A、B 和 C 都是錯誤的。王太太之前的房子已經賣給別人，可是王太太的父親卻把這件事忘了，跑到別人家裡，所以對方屋主只好報警。

Q30

What is NOT true about the passage?
關於這篇短文，什麼不是正確的？

A. The old house they used to live in was burned down.
他們之前住的舊房子被燒毀了。
B. Mrs. Wang's father seems to remember where they used to live.
王太太的父親似乎還記得他們以前住在哪裡。
C. Mrs. Wang's father believes that doctors will harm him.
王太太的父親相信醫生會害他。
D. Playing card games might help Mrs. Wang's father.
玩紙牌遊戲或許可以幫助王太太的父親。

詳解　　　　　　　　　　　　　　　　　　　　　　　答案：A

　　從 What ~ NOT true ~ passage? 可知，主要是問不正確的內容為何者。只要找出文中正確的線索，就能挑出不正確的選項。雖然王太太的父親記憶開始退

化，卻還記得他們之前住的地方，所以才會去那裡，B. 是正確的。他不相信醫生，認為醫生是邪惡的，所以不肯就醫，C 也正確。王太太在一篇文章讀到，玩紙牌遊戲可以幫助改善記憶，所以選項 B、C 和 D 都是正確的。關於他們之前住的房子，他們已經賣給別人了，不過沒提到舊房子已燒毀。

學習筆記欄

國際學村

全民英語能力分級檢定測驗 初級初試試答案紙（第一回）

聽力測驗答對題數分數對照表

答對題數	分數	答對題數	分數	答對題數	分數
30	120	20	80	10	40
29	116	19	76	9	36
28	112	18	72	8	32
27	108	17	68	7	28
26	104	16	64	6	24
25	100	15	60	5	20
24	96	14	56	4	16
23	92	13	52	3	12
22	88	12	48	2	8
21	84	11	44	1	4
				0	0

閱讀能力測驗答對題數分數對照表

答對題數	分數	答對題數	分數	答對題數	分數
30	120	20	80	10	40
29	116	19	76	9	36
28	112	18	72	8	32
27	108	17	68	7	28
26	104	16	64	6	24
25	100	15	60	5	20
24	96	14	56	4	16
23	92	13	52	3	12
22	88	12	48	2	8
21	84	11	44	1	4
				0	0

考生姓名：＿＿＿＿＿＿＿

注意事項：

1. 限用 2B 鉛筆作答，否則不予計分。
2. 劃記要粗黑、清晰，不可出格，擦拭要清潔，若劃記過輕或污損污損不清，不為機器所接受，考生自行負責。
3. 作答樣式：

　正確方式 ■

　錯誤方式 ☑ ⊠ □ ◍

聽力測驗

1. A B C
2. A B C
3. A B C
4. A B C
5. A B C
6. A B C
7. A B C
8. A B C
9. A B C
10. A B C
11. A B C
12. A B C
13. A B C
14. A B C
15. A B C
16. A B C
17. A B C
18. A B C
19. A B C
20. A B C
21. A B C
22. A B C
23. A B C
24. A B C
25. A B C
26. A B C
27. A B C
28. A B C
29. A B C
30. A B C

閱讀能力測驗

1. A B C D
2. A B C D
3. A B C D
4. A B C D
5. A B C D
6. A B C D
7. A B C D
8. A B C D
9. A B C D
10. A B C D
11. A B C D
12. A B C D
13. A B C D
14. A B C D
15. A B C D
16. A B C D
17. A B C D
18. A B C D
19. A B C D
20. A B C D
21. A B C D
22. A B C D
23. A B C D
24. A B C D
25. A B C D
26. A B C D
27. A B C D
28. A B C D
29. A B C D
30. A B C D

國際學村 全民英語能力分級檢定測驗
初級初試答案紙（第二回）

閱讀能力測驗答對題數與分數對照表

答對題數	分數	答對題數	分數	答對題數	分數
30	120	20	80	10	40
29	116	19	76	9	36
28	112	18	72	8	32
27	108	17	68	7	28
26	104	16	64	6	24
25	100	15	60	5	20
24	96	14	56	4	16
23	92	13	52	3	12
22	88	12	48	2	8
21	84	11	44	1	4
				0	0

聽力測驗答對題數與分數對照表

答對題數	分數	答對題數	分數	答對題數	分數
30	120	20	80	10	40
29	116	19	76	9	36
28	112	18	72	8	32
27	108	17	68	7	28
26	104	16	64	6	24
25	100	15	60	5	20
24	96	14	56	4	16
23	92	13	52	3	12
22	88	12	48	2	8
21	84	11	44	1	4
				0	0

考生姓名：_____

注意事項：

1. 限用 2B 鉛筆作答，否則不予計分。
2. 劃記要粗黑、清晰，不可出格，擦拭要清潔，若劃記過輕或污損不清，不為機器所接受，考生自行負責。
3. 作答樣例：
   正確方式 ■
   錯誤方式 ☒ ⊠ ▣ ◕

聽力測驗

1 A B C
2 A B C
3 A B C
4 A B C
5 A B C
6 A B C
7 A B C
8 A B C
9 A B C
10 A B C
11 A B C
12 A B C
13 A B C
14 A B C
15 A B C
16 A B C
17 A B C
18 A B C
19 A B C
20 A B C
21 A B C
22 A B C
23 A B C
24 A B C
25 A B C
26 A B C
27 A B C
28 A B C
29 A B C
30 A B C

閱讀能力測驗

1 A B C D
2 A B C D
3 A B C D
4 A B C D
5 A B C D
6 A B C D
7 A B C D
8 A B C D
9 A B C D
10 A B C D
11 A B C D
12 A B C D
13 A B C D
14 A B C D
15 A B C D
16 A B C D
17 A B C D
18 A B C D
19 A B C D
20 A B C D
21 A B C D
22 A B C D
23 A B C D
24 A B C D
25 A B C D
26 A B C D
27 A B C D
28 A B C D
29 A B C D
30 A B C D

國際學村

全民英語能力分級檢定測驗
初級初試答案紙（第三回）

閱讀能力測驗答對題數分數對照表

答對題數	分數	答對題數	分數	答對題數	分數
30	120	20	80	10	40
29	116	19	76	9	36
28	112	18	72	8	32
27	108	17	68	7	28
26	104	16	64	6	24
25	100	15	60	5	20
24	96	14	56	4	16
23	92	13	52	3	12
22	88	12	48	2	8
21	84	11	44	1	4
				0	0

聽力測驗答對題數分數對照表

答對題數	分數	答對題數	分數	答對題數	分數
30	120	20	80	10	40
29	116	19	76	9	36
28	112	18	72	8	32
27	108	17	68	7	28
26	104	16	64	6	24
25	100	15	60	5	20
24	96	14	56	4	16
23	92	13	52	3	12
22	88	12	48	2	8
21	84	11	44	1	4
				0	0

考生姓名：＿＿＿＿＿＿＿

注意事項：

1. 限用 2B 鉛筆作答，否則不予計分。
2. 劃記要粗黑、清晰、不可出格，擦試要清潔，若劃記過輕或污損不清，不為機器所接受，考生自行負責。
3. 作答範例：
   正確方式　▮
   錯誤方式　☑ ☒ ▢ ●

聽力測驗

	A	B	C			A	B	C
1	A	B	C		26	A	B	C
2	A	B	C		27	A	B	C
3	A	B	C		28	A	B	C
4	A	B	C		29	A	B	C
5	A	B	C		30	A	B	C
6	A	B	C					
7	A	B	C					
8	A	B	C					
9	A	B	C					
10	A	B	C					
11	A	B	C					
12	A	B	C					
13	A	B	C					
14	A	B	C					
15	A	B	C					
16	A	B	C					
17	A	B	C					
18	A	B	C					
19	A	B	C					
20	A	B	C					
21	A	B	C					
22	A	B	C					
23	A	B	C					
24	A	B	C					
25	A	B	C					

閱讀能力測驗

	A	B	C	D			A	B	C	D
1	A	B	C	D		26	A	B	C	D
2	A	B	C	D		27	A	B	C	D
3	A	B	C	D		28	A	B	C	D
4	A	B	C	D		29	A	B	C	D
5	A	B	C	D		30	A	B	C	D
6	A	B	C	D						
7	A	B	C	D						
8	A	B	C	D						
9	A	B	C	D						
10	A	B	C	D						
11	A	B	C	D						
12	A	B	C	D						
13	A	B	C	D						
14	A	B	C	D						
15	A	B	C	D						
16	A	B	C	D						
17	A	B	C	D						
18	A	B	C	D						
19	A	B	C	D						
20	A	B	C	D						
21	A	B	C	D						
22	A	B	C	D						
23	A	B	C	D						
24	A	B	C	D						
25	A	B	C	D						

國際學村

全民英語能力分級檢定測驗 初級初試答案紙（第四回）

閱讀能力測驗答案選填及分數對照表

答對題數	分數	答對題數	分數	答對題數	分數
30	120	20	80	10	40
29	116	19	76	9	36
28	112	18	72	8	32
27	108	17	68	7	28
26	104	16	64	6	24
25	100	15	60	5	20
24	96	14	56	4	16
23	92	13	52	3	12
22	88	12	48	2	8
21	84	11	44	1	4
				0	0

聽力測驗答案選填及分數對照表

答對題數	分數	答對題數	分數	答對題數	分數
30	120	20	80	10	40
29	116	19	76	9	36
28	112	18	72	8	32
27	108	17	68	7	28
26	104	16	64	6	24
25	100	15	60	5	20
24	96	14	56	4	16
23	92	13	52	3	12
22	88	12	48	2	8
21	84	11	44	1	4
				0	0

考生姓名：_____

注意事項：

1. 限用 2B 鉛筆作答，否則不予計分。
2. 劃記要粗黑、清晰、不可出格，擦拭要清潔，若劃記過輕或塗污損不清，不為機器所接受，考生自行負責。
3. 作答樣例：
   正確方式 ■
   錯誤方式 ☑ ⊠ □ ◑

聽力測驗

題號	A	B	C		題號	A	B	C
1	A	B	C		26	A	B	C
2	A	B	C		27	A	B	C
3	A	B	C		28	A	B	C
4	A	B	C		29	A	B	C
5	A	B	C		30	A	B	C
6	A	B	C					
7	A	B	C					
8	A	B	C					
9	A	B	C					
10	A	B	C					
11	A	B	C					
12	A	B	C					
13	A	B	C					
14	A	B	C					
15	A	B	C					
16	A	B	C					
17	A	B	C					
18	A	B	C					
19	A	B	C					
20	A	B	C					
21	A	B	C					
22	A	B	C					
23	A	B	C					
24	A	B	C					
25	A	B	C					

閱讀能力測驗

題號	A	B	C	D		題號	A	B	C	D
1	A	B	C	D		26	A	B	C	D
2	A	B	C	D		27	A	B	C	D
3	A	B	C	D		28	A	B	C	D
4	A	B	C	D		29	A	B	C	D
5	A	B	C	D		30	A	B	C	D
6	A	B	C	D						
7	A	B	C	D						
8	A	B	C	D						
9	A	B	C	D						
10	A	B	C	D						
11	A	B	C	D						
12	A	B	C	D						
13	A	B	C	D						
14	A	B	C	D						
15	A	B	C	D						
16	A	B	C	D						
17	A	B	C	D						
18	A	B	C	D						
19	A	B	C	D						
20	A	B	C	D						
21	A	B	C	D						
22	A	B	C	D						
23	A	B	C	D						
24	A	B	C	D						
25	A	B	C	D						

國際學村

全民英語能力分級檢定測驗
初級初試試答案紙（第五回）

聽力測驗答對題數換算分數對照表

答對題數	分數	答對題數	分數	答對題數	分數
30	120	20	80	10	40
29	116	19	76	9	36
28	112	18	72	8	32
27	108	17	68	7	28
26	104	16	64	6	24
25	100	15	60	5	20
24	96	14	56	4	16
23	92	13	52	3	12
22	88	12	48	2	8
21	84	11	44	1	4
				0	0

閱讀能力測驗答對題數換算分數對照表

答對題數	分數	答對題數	分數	答對題數	分數
30	120	20	80	10	40
29	116	19	76	9	36
28	112	18	72	8	32
27	108	17	68	7	28
26	104	16	64	6	24
25	100	15	60	5	20
24	96	14	56	4	16
23	92	13	52	3	12
22	88	12	48	2	8
21	84	11	44	1	4
				0	0

考生姓名：＿＿＿＿＿＿＿＿

注意事項：

1. 限用 2B 鉛筆作答，否則不予計分。
2. 劃記要粗黑、清晰、不可出格，擦拭要清潔，若劃記過
   輕或塗污損不清，不為機器所接受，考生自行負責。
3. 作答樣例：

正確方式　■

錯誤方式　☑　⊠　◨　●

聽力測驗

	A	B	C
1	A	B	C
2	A	B	C
3	A	B	C
4	A	B	C
5	A	B	C
6	A	B	C
7	A	B	C
8	A	B	C
9	A	B	C
10	A	B	C
11	A	B	C
12	A	B	C
13	A	B	C
14	A	B	C
15	A	B	C
16	A	B	C
17	A	B	C
18	A	B	C
19	A	B	C
20	A	B	C
21	A	B	C
22	A	B	C
23	A	B	C
24	A	B	C
25	A	B	C
26	A	B	C
27	A	B	C
28	A	B	C
29	A	B	C
30	A	B	C

閱讀能力測驗

	A	B	C	D
1	A	B	C	D
2	A	B	C	D
3	A	B	C	D
4	A	B	C	D
5	A	B	C	D
6	A	B	C	D
7	A	B	C	D
8	A	B	C	D
9	A	B	C	D
10	A	B	C	D
11	A	B	C	D
12	A	B	C	D
13	A	B	C	D
14	A	B	C	D
15	A	B	C	D
16	A	B	C	D
17	A	B	C	D
18	A	B	C	D
19	A	B	C	D
20	A	B	C	D
21	A	B	C	D
22	A	B	C	D
23	A	B	C	D
24	A	B	C	D
25	A	B	C	D
26	A	B	C	D
27	A	B	C	D
28	A	B	C	D
29	A	B	C	D
30	A	B	C	D

國際學村　全民英語能力分級檢定測驗
初級初試答案紙（第六回）

聽力測驗答對題數與其分數對照表

答對題數	分數	答對題數	分數	答對題數	分數
30	120	20	80	10	40
29	116	19	76	9	36
28	112	18	72	8	32
27	108	17	68	7	28
26	104	16	64	6	24
25	100	15	60	5	20
24	96	14	56	4	16
23	92	13	52	3	12
22	88	12	48	2	8
21	84	11	44	1	4
				0	0

閱讀能力測驗答對題數與其分數對照表

答對題數	分數	答對題數	分數	答對題數	分數
30	120	20	80	10	40
29	116	19	76	9	36
28	112	18	72	8	32
27	108	17	68	7	28
26	104	16	64	6	24
25	100	15	60	5	20
24	96	14	56	4	16
23	92	13	52	3	12
22	88	12	48	2	8
21	84	11	44	1	4
				0	0

考生姓名：＿＿＿＿＿＿＿

注意事項：

1. 限用 2B 鉛筆作答，否則不予計分。
2. 劃記要粗黑、清晰、不可出格，擦拭要清潔，若劃記過輕或污損不清，不為機器所接受，考生自行負責。
3. 作答樣例：

正確方式　■

錯誤方式　☑　☒　□　◑

聽力測驗

1. A B C
2. A B C
3. A B C
4. A B C
5. A B C
6. A B C
7. A B C
8. A B C
9. A B C
10. A B C
11. A B C
12. A B C
13. A B C
14. A B C
15. A B C
16. A B C
17. A B C
18. A B C
19. A B C
20. A B C
21. A B C
22. A B C
23. A B C
24. A B C
25. A B C
26. A B C
27. A B C
28. A B C
29. A B C
30. A B C

閱讀能力測驗

1. A B C D
2. A B C D
3. A B C D
4. A B C D
5. A B C D
6. A B C D
7. A B C D
8. A B C D
9. A B C D
10. A B C D
11. A B C D
12. A B C D
13. A B C D
14. A B C D
15. A B C D
16. A B C D
17. A B C D
18. A B C D
19. A B C D
20. A B C D
21. A B C D
22. A B C D
23. A B C D
24. A B C D
25. A B C D
26. A B C D
27. A B C D
28. A B C D
29. A B C D
30. A B C D

（自己的姓名）＿＿＿＿＿＿＿＿＿ 這次英檢初級初試一定會過！

填表日期：＿＿＿＿＿年＿＿＿＿＿月＿＿＿＿＿日

達成日期：＿＿＿＿＿年＿＿＿＿＿月＿＿＿＿＿日

滿分！

過關了！

| 120 |
| 110 |
| 100 |
| 90 |
| 80 |
| 70 |
| 60 |
| 50 |
| 40 |
30	● 閱讀
20	● 聽力
10	我一定要過英檢！
0

示範　第一回　第二回　第三回　第四回　第五回　第六回

完成每次測驗後，請將所得到的成績用黑點●標示在表格上，就能感受到自己分數的進步。

台灣廣廈 國際出版集團
Taiwan Mansion International Group

國家圖書館出版品預行編目（CIP）資料

全新！NEW GEPT全民英檢初級聽力&閱讀題庫解析【新制修訂版】/
國際語言中心委員會、郭文興著. -- 初版. -- 新北市：國際學村, 2021.03
　面；　公分
ISBN 978-986-454-152-2（平裝）
1. 英語 2. 讀本

805.1892   110002623

 國際學村

全新！NEW GEPT全民英檢
初級聽力&閱讀題庫解析【新制修訂版】

作　　　者／國際語言中心委員會、 郭文興	**編輯中心編輯長**／伍峻宏・**編輯**／古竣元 **封面設計**／何偉凱・**內頁排版**／菩薩蠻數位文化有限公司 **製版・印刷・裝訂**／東豪・弼聖・紘億・秉成

行企研發中心總監／陳冠蒨　　　**媒體公關組**／陳柔衣
　　　　　　　　　　　　　　　　綜合業務組／何欣穎

發　行　人／江媛珍
法律顧問／第一國際法律事務所 余淑杏律師・北辰著作權事務所 蕭雄淋律師
出　　版／國際學村
發　　行／台灣廣廈有聲圖書有限公司
　　　　　　地址：新北市235中和區中山路二段359巷7號2樓
　　　　　　電話：（886）2-2225-5777・傳真：（886）2-2225-8052
讀者服務信箱／cs@booknews.com.tw

代理印務・全球總經銷／知遠文化事業有限公司
　　　　　　地址：新北市222深坑區北深路三段155巷25號5樓
　　　　　　電話：（886）2-2664-8800・傳真：（886）2-2664-8801
郵政劃撥／劃撥帳號：18836722
　　　　　　劃撥戶名：知遠文化事業有限公司（※單次購書金額未滿1000元需另付郵資70元。）

■出版日期：2021年3月　　　　ISBN：978-986-454-152-2
　　　　　　2024年7月9刷　　　版權所有，未經同意不得重製、轉載、翻印。